Over the Limit

Brand of Justice
Book 4

Lisa Phillips

TWO DOGS PUBLISHING, LLC.

Copyright © 2023 by Lisa Phillips

All rights reserved.

No part of this book may be reproduced in any form or by any electronic or mechanical means, including information storage and retrieval systems, without written permission from the author, except for the use of brief quotations in a book review.

eBook ISBN: 979-8-88552-164-2

Paperback ISBN: 979-8-88552-165-9

Large Print Hardback ISBN: 979-8-88552-166-6

Published by: Two Dogs Publishing, LLC. Idaho, USA

Cover Design by: Sasha Almazan and Gene Mollica, GS Cover Design Studio, LLC

Edited by: Christine Callahan, Professional Publishing Services

Chapter One

11:34 pm
Western Colorado

"So this is what you do?"

Private Investigator Kenna Banbury glanced at the young man lying in the dirt beside her. She'd met him the day before at a diner in the next town. "Usually there's no talking."

"She's down there." Luca started to get up. "We need to go."

Kenna grabbed his sleeve and pulled him back down. "*I* say when we go."

"It's been too long. She's down there." Luca hissed the words, worry permeating his whisper.

She shifted, prone on the dirt and grass at the top of the ridge. In front of her, moonlight glinted across the surface of the pond. Beyond the house, shed, and barns, mountains reached up to the stars. "You won't be doing her any favors charging in there without knowing what you're walking into."

She needed him past the fear and strategizing instead. "Tell me what all these buildings are."

Luca had given her a rundown of this ranch when he'd explained who he was, and how multiple families were kept as captives here. Migrant workers with no one to file a missing person's report. Two years ago, the coyote Luca paid to get him across the border and into the US handed him over to the man who ran this ranch. Luca's girlfriend, Camila, had been brought in weeks later. They'd been together since.

"That's the house." Luca pointed. "The middle one is the barn, where he has five horses. Three of them are in bad shape. And a couple of ATVs. The next building is the bunkhouse. That's just what they call it, but we don't have rooms—just the cellar underground where we're supposed to sleep."

He'd already told her about the living conditions. The backed-up toilet, just a sink to wash up in, and bare mattresses on the floor to sleep on. His clothes were decently made but worn. Jeans and old boots. A tattered shirt. She'd had him wash up in the bathroom of her motel room, but the grime on his hands and face seemed to have soaked into his skin. As though the life he lived permeated beneath the surface.

Kenna didn't want to think if the same thing had happened to her. If the things she'd been through had...seeped into her. She wasn't one of those people who projected a façade. But for the last few months, she'd had to contend with the silence.

Cabot, the mutt she'd adopted, had undergone surgery and now lived with Kenna's former boss...or business associate —she didn't know what Stairns was to her.

The loneliness of the past few months traveling alone had saturated everything. She had spent weeks looking for Maizie. Waiting for something to show up on the website where someone, who she assumed was the teen girl she was looking for, had previously left her information.

Nothing.

Cue, staying under the radar. Waiting for the FBI to come up with a new lead when she had no movement on the case to identify a deadly organization that held entire towns in their grip and destroyed lives.

Her friend Jax, an FBI agent, had his own life.

Javier and Valentina Ryson had theirs.

Kenna wasn't willing for whoever had tracked her and tried to destroy everything to decide they were going to target the people around her that she cared about. The Rysons had a baby. Jax had a career. At least Stairns, formerly a Special Agent in Charge, had quit the FBI before he started helping her.

Also, Stairns didn't care if or how a deadly organization decided to come at him. He relished the idea of it.

Kenna and Stairns had met up so she could see Cabot after the surgery. They'd exchanged numbers to brand-new burner phones and gone back to work. And all the radio silence of no new leads had started to grate on Kenna. When Luca came along, she'd jumped on the chance to work a case.

She'd thought she was doing the right thing keeping everyone at arm's length. For years she had embraced the loneliness, but now there were people in her life who cared about her, it was harder to shut them out and be content.

"Are you even paying attention?"

She glanced over at Luca, who had said he was twenty-three, but looked closer to seventeen. "Where will the owner be?"

"Drinking. Probably sitting in his recliner. That's why we have to go now."

It was almost midnight, so if the homeowner normally

drank himself to sleep, he had likely already passed out. But they needed to be certain. She glanced at the corners of the buildings. "What about any surveillance?"

"Like cameras?"

She nodded.

"They put trackers on each of us, but I cut mine off." He tugged up his sleeve to reveal a grimy bandage on his wrist.

Kenna wasn't going to repay the favor by pulling back the long sleeve of her army green Henley. The scars she had on her forearms from a run in with serial killer a few years ago didn't play a part in this. She neither required sympathy, nor intended to elicit a reaction out of this young man. Luca only wanted to find Camila tonight.

Kenna was here to rescue all of them from the man holding them captive.

Then she would get back on the road. Looking for leads on this organization—looking for Maizie.

"Let's go." Kenna stood and brushed dirt from her jeans. She unsnapped the holster on her hip but didn't draw the weapon. She knew Luca had a knife. He didn't know how many other weapons she had on her person—lethal or nonlethal.

As they descended the hill at the edge of the ranch, Kenna asked questions to focus Luca on providing answers rather than rushing into this. "Tell me again what his name is."

The first time, he told her it didn't matter. She had looked at the landowner online. Now, Luca said, "Brian Preston."

This area of Colorado, just outside the town of Montrose, was owned by several members of the Preston family. Brian had two brothers who each resided on neighboring ranches. The father had died years ago, and Kenna had no idea what happened to the mother. Their uncle, Elliott Preston, was the local county sheriff and the reason why she hadn't simply called in law enforcement about a group of people being held captive.

The reports Stairns had been able to dig up from the state patrol indicated the sheriff was more likely to side with his family than with innocent victims—or a private investigator with a famous father, far too many news articles about her, and a tendency to rub law enforcement the wrong way. The Colorado investigator's license notwithstanding.

"And he lives alone?" She asked, now seeing focus amid the anger on Luca's face.

"He had a woman for a while, but I think she figured out how he treated his workers."

"She never came back?"

"Most of them never come back. No one has ever tried to help us out. Probably all scared of the sheriff, or the clearing."

"The clearing?" Kenna tried to keep her voice neutral, just a little curious. Not like she was dragging out the conversation to keep them talking.

"It's where he takes those of us who don't want to listen to orders."

"What happens in the clearing, Luca?"

He glanced at her. Side by side, crossing the long grass of Brian Preston's grazing field. "There's a stump. The tree came down during a bad storm, and he carved up the rest. Turned it into a platform, and you get tied down to it. Whipped until there's blood and tears. He leaves you out there all night, sometimes for a couple of days, before he shows up and drags you behind his horse back to the ranch."

Kenna's jaw hurt she clenched so hard on her molars. The temptation to palm her pistol and visit Brian Preston in his house nearly overrode everything else. "We need to look in the window and make sure he's asleep."

If either of them went inside, Brian Preston might not make it through the night.

"If he's sleeping, we go in the bunkhouse and get them all out. Okay?" She asked the question more for herself than for him. "Together."

Being with someone else working a case felt different enough from the last few months. All she had was herself in a way that hadn't been good for her. Maybe she actually needed this connection with someone.

They crept down the side of the house.

Luca stopped by the window. "We should be able to see the living room from here."

Kenna nodded. At least one of them would get their people back in their life tonight.

She lifted up and peered inside. The TV flickered and a man sat in a recliner, chin to his chest and several cans of beer on the table next to him. "Does he have a dog?"

"He used to. I think he shot it after it bit him."

"Okay, let's head for the bunkhouse."

The padlock on the door took some doing to get open, but they managed. Luca tossed the thing aside, and Kenna went first. The ranch smelled of cow deposits from the herd on the eastern hill, but the scent inside the bunkhouse was a mixture of mold and dirt—and desolation. The concentrated version of the cloud that showed up with Luca.

She'd had that stench in her life before. In a way it still lingered in her memories, coating the past.

Luca could wash it off. The young man could take his girlfriend and leave this place. They'd be able to start a new life somewhere else, where they made new memories and discovered a hope for the future. Something Kenna wasn't sure if she would ever have for herself.

Luca led her to a spot in the middle of the barn floor. A trapdoor that was also padlocked.

The first thing Luca had told her was of the day after he'd arrived. He'd seen a man who had crossed the border with him struck by Brian Preston's horse when it reared up on its hind legs. All because the landowner decided he didn't like something the man did.

Brian Preston had ordered the rest of the people he held captive to drag the man into the bunkhouse and throw him through the trapdoor.

Where he'd died from his injuries days later.

When the trapdoor opened, and all she saw beneath was the black of darkness, for a second Kenna was back in the past. The whole scene was far too similar to what she—and her FBI agent partner at the time—had endured at the hands of a serial killer.

She shuddered off the sensation of falling. "Everyone come out of there. Now, quickly."

Luca spoke in Spanish. He lowered a wooden ladder into the dark, leaning against the opening. He spoke again. Kenna understood enough of the words to know he told them much the same as she had.

The first person to ascend was an older man, weathered by the sun and long years of life. Luca clasped his hand. She helped some, and they both hauled the older man out onto the floor of the bunkhouse. Two more men and a woman came next. Then a couple of children, barely teenagers.

The final person was another man, moving stiffly. Favoring his left leg where his jeans were stained with blood.

"Where is Camila?" Luca glanced around. He shifted, as though about to descend the ladder himself.

The final man shook his head.

"Pedro, where is she?" Luca got in the man's face.

Kenna shifted, just in case she had to break up a fight. One of the children started to cry, and the woman pulled the kid close. Kenna realized it was a little girl under all the dirt and matted hair.

"Not here." Pedro shoved Luca back. "And in a moment, I won't be here either."

Two guys were already at the door. Pedro strode after them. Luca turned to the woman and the children. "Where is Camila?"

The mother shook her head.

Kenna stood in front of her and held out her hands. "May I look at the tracker?" When the woman lifted her wrist, Kenna cradled it in one hand and tugged her knife from the back of her belt.

One of the children gasped.

"Let's get this off. Then no one will be able to find you when you leave." Kenna cut the tight plastic zip ties. "You and your children will be safe."

The woman shook her head. "They...not my children."

Kenna's stomach clenched. "Will you make sure they get somewhere safe? Take them somewhere you trust, and make sure whoever receives them will take good care of them." Given the local sheriff was related to the landowner here, they weren't going to get a fair shake with him. She didn't know how to advise her instead of just making sure they got to safety herself. "Actually, I'll drive you to the city and we'll find a church. That's where we'll ask for help."

The woman nodded, but before she could say anything, shouting erupted from outside the bunkhouse.

Kenna jogged through the door. Luca had Pedro up against the siding, holding his throat while the older man batted his arms and chest. "Where is she?"

Someone yelled from the house.

The window smashed. Brian Preston landed on the dirt among shards of glass, still yelling when he hit the ground. The landowner blinked and looked around. "All of you get back in the bunkhouse."

Pedro shoved Luca back and launched himself at Brian Preston, kicking and punching the man when he tried to get up. The vicious slams of his boot impacted Brian Preston's abdomen over and over again. Then Brian's face and head.

Kenna and Luca both pulled him off. "Enough," she said. "We're not going to kill him."

"No." Pedro glared at her. "Because *I* am. Alone."

"Not before you tell me where she is," Luca said. "What did he do with Camila?"

The woman Kenna had thought was a mother moved into view beside them. "She sick. He took her away."

Brian Preston lay in the dark, covered in blood. His nose broken. One eye already swelling up.

"Where would he take her?" Kenna didn't want to think about the clearing Luca had told her about. They needed to know for sure before they started a hike across the ranch.

One of the kids whimpered.

The woman said, "He said he could no afford for any of the rest of us to get sick."

Luca turned to face her.

"I don't think he knew she is pregnant."

Chapter Two

Kenna spun around, trying to ascertain if that was news to Luca. From the look on the young man's face, he'd already known his girlfriend was carrying a baby. "Where did Brian take her?"

"I don't know." The woman's voice shook.

The door to the house opened and two men walked out, carrying rifles. Kenna stiffened, but they didn't lift the weapons to point at any of the gathered crowd standing around Brian Preston.

The ranch owner lay still, each inhale rattling. He seemed to be at least partially conscious but didn't make any attempt to get up or even sit up. One of the men moved to stand over Brian, where he aimed the gun at the man's head.

Kenna held one hand out. "We need to know where Camila is."

"Then you kill him after." His tone held an edge of something dark. "Don't leave him alive when you're done."

Behind him, the second man who held a weapon said, "We will go kill the brothers. And then the sheriff."

Kenna twisted around. "You can't—"

Pedro shoved Kenna back before she could finish. The two men broke off and started to walk away toward the trees. Running after them to try to convince them that this wasn't the right course of action would take time she didn't have. Time Camila might not have left.

"Don't touch me." She glanced at Pedro.

His eyes lit with a whole lot of shadows. "I will kill this man."

"Not until we find Camila." In a show of good faith, she let him use her knife to cut the tracker from his wrist. "Now hand the knife back to me."

He almost smiled.

By the time they found the young woman Luca had brought her here to rescue, Kenna planned to have a way to convince Pedro not to kill this man, even though he wanted to.

She lifted her chin. "Revenge might make you feel better for five minutes. But then that empty feeling of frustration and anger you're living with now comes back, and you realize you don't feel any better than you did before you got your revenge."

He leaned toward her. "I want my five minutes."

One of the children whimpered.

Luca got between them. "I won't let you kill him before I find her."

Pedro folded his arms across his chest.

The easiest place to look first was the house. Kenna jogged to the back door and went inside. The soles of her boots made almost no noise on the cheap wood floor. The door didn't close behind her but slammed against the wall and Luca barreled in, moving after her as Kenna went room by room looking for Camila.

She searched the front rooms, then glanced at the young man. "Do you think he might have taken her to the clearing?"

Luca frowned. "I don't want to go all the way out there if she's still here. We have to check here first."

"You think he's got her in his house, or in one of the other buildings?"

A look crossed Luca's face.

"Let's find her." Kenna would rather look around than talk about Brian about what he might do to a young woman, anyway. If something had already happened, then it was too late to change it. What they could do, however, was ensure it never happened to Camila again.

The bedroom was empty. Kenna pulled open the closet while Luca checked the bathroom. He came out, shaking his head. When they had exhausted every space, she said, "Let's look in the other buildings next."

On the way down the hall back to the door, she pulled open a linen closet and grabbed some blankets. On the kitchen counter, amid papers and wrappers from frozen dinners, she found his wallet.

Kenna relieved Brian Preston of his cash and took the keys to his truck. She brought it all outside and gave blankets to the two kids and the woman. Then she handed over the rest.

"Take his vehicle and get yourselves out of here. You won't be able to drive it for long before you run the risk of getting pulled over driving a stolen truck. Find a place to dump it and get to a church or someplace else safe where you can ask for help."

The woman nodded. "Gracias."

"Be careful." She herded the children away, and they all wrapped blankets around themselves. When Kenna turned back, Pedro was studying her. Kenna fixed him with a stare. "We need to find Camila."

"She means nothing to me."

Kenna didn't doubt it. "So what does mean something?"

"I will kill him for you."

She shook her head. "You're going to kill him for *you*." While she was going to find a hurt and possibly pregnant young woman who had been abandoned. "Find out what he knows. Ask him where he left her. That's what I want."

Knowing a young woman was out here somewhere, alone and scared for her life, solidified Kenna's resolve in a way nothing else did. Just a few years ago she'd been that woman. Alone. Facing the end of everything, not to mention pregnant. That same night Kenna lost her FBI Special Agent partner—and the father of her nascent baby—and started a chain of events that put her life on a completely new path.

One that brought her to this evening and allowed her to be here to save Camila's life, or at least try.

Luca came out of the barn, shaking his head. "We need to check the clearing."

She called back, "How far is it?"

She might have old injuries to her forearms, but there was nothing wrong with her legs.

The only thing wrong? Usually her dog Cabot did these walks with her, searching for missing victims. After they'd been in a vehicle crash Kenna had a vet check her out. The dog was diagnosed with cancer and had undergone surgery. Months later she was living with Stairs at his house, where she could get daily care and regular checkups—in one place and not on the road with Kenna. A different veterinarian every time.

"About three kilometers." Luca motioned to the corral. "I will saddle horses."

Kenna turned back to Pedro, still standing over Brian Preston. She knelt beside the rancher's shoulder and took ahold of his collar. She then lifted Brian's head off the ground so his face was close to hers. "Where is Camila?"

His lips spread in a kind of smile, his teeth covered with blood. "That was a sweet girl." The way he said it gave Kenna several impressions, none of them good. All of them things that would make Luca and Pedro both want to kill this man.

Part of her closed off, her conscience unable to object if that was what they wanted to do Brian Preston. But the piece of her that remained determined to follow the law even when no one was looking grated against the rest.

In a county like this, where these people would see no justice, a country that would simply send them back to their homes regardless of what the situation there would be like—or the way they'd been treated here—it might even be considered "right" to end this man's life. A way for these people to take his future into their hands the way he had done with them.

Except that each of them had to live with it. Even Kenna. She would have to walk away knowing she'd allowed a murder, even in the name of justice.

The only kind of justice these people might find was what they took for themselves. Kenna had built a brand of justice that was hers, and hers alone. Pedro and Luca—and the others—had to do the same. Like everyone, they had to make the choice. But after choices had been taken from them it would be a hard decision.

The question was whether they would be able to live with themselves after.

She dropped Brian Preston back to the ground. He groaned and shifted. She straightened. "Is Camila at the clearing?"

Brian gave her no answer.

"She was delirious with fever," Pedro said. "He probably hoped she would die, and he could bury her like he buried the others."

Luca walked over with two horses, both saddled.

In the distance, a gunshot rang out. The horses sidestepped and one shook its head.

The other two men had found what they were looking for. But just in case, she prayed for Camila. A quick plea that the young woman would have a life after this night the way Kenna had been able to continue.

Regardless as to how things turned out, she was who she wanted to be. Even if it was a lonely life. It belonged to her.

Kenna stepped into the stirrup with one foot and grabbed the lip of the pommel. She used mostly leg strength to lever herself up and throw her leg over the horse. Her arms could do more than they used to, but they would never be able to hold her body weight.

Luca handed her the reins. "You know how to ride?"

Kenna watched him climb on. "I know enough. Lead the way."

She looked back at Pedro over her shoulder as they rode away. The dark-featured man curled his arm around Brian Preston's neck. With one hard jerk, he snapped it. The man who had kept these people captive flopped back to the ground, his head lolling to one side.

Pedro turned and walked away.

Luca led her down a path the horses knew. When the trees thinned out, he picked up speed, moving them to a fast trot. Kenna shifted the reins to one hand and slid out her phone from her back pocket. No signal.

She tucked it away again to watch the shadows of the night between the trees for predators of all kinds. Luca pressed his horse on, up the trail to where the trees broke away. Then he galloped across the grass. Kenna's horse did the same, following him.

Luca pulled on the reins. "Whoa."

Kenna got her horse to stop and slid off. She patted the

horse's neck. "Thank you." Though, her gratitude was more about the fact she hadn't been bucked off.

Luca dropped his reins to the ground in front of the horse, so Kenna copied him. He jogged toward what had been a tree at one time, dead center in the middle of the clearing. He cried out Camila's name as he ran, then fell to his knees in front of a stump.

Camila lay curled up on the dirt in front of the stump, her hands bound with rope tied to a stake that had been shoved deep in the ground. She wore a thin shirt, jeans, and a pair of ragged sneakers.

Kenna pressed two fingers to the cold skin of her neck while Luca patted her cheeks. When she felt a faint pulse, she let out a relieved breath. "She's alive. We need to get her to a hospital."

Luca shook his head. "We can't go to a doctor, or the sheriff will find us."

"We can ride to my car." The second time she had made that invitation tonight. "We'll find a doctor nowhere near here and get her checked out." The girl could have hypothermia at best, being out here in this temperature for hours. Already ill, or with morning sickness.

Luca ran back to the horse. He tugged something off the neck of his animal and brought it back over. A blanket. He wrapped it around Camila.

Kenna couldn't let go of what Brian had said. "Luca, is Camila's baby yours?"

"It doesn't matter." He smoothed hair away from Camila's forehead. "If she'll have me, they'll both be mine." He stood and lifted the young woman in his arms. "I'll carry her in front of me."

She watched him go, respect for him warming her. This

young man would do whatever he could to keep his family. "Okay, let's go."

Kenna took the reins and helped keep the horse steady while he set Camila up on the saddle and climbed up behind her. "You good?"

Luca took the reins. "Come on."

She agreed with his sense of urgency. There were so close, finding Camila alive while it wasn't too late and having the means to get her to a doctor. They took the same trail back toward the ranch. As they closed in, she spotted the headlights of a vehicle turning onto the lane.

"Car." Kenna shifted her hold on the reins in case they had to make a run for it. "Someone's coming."

She didn't want to get into a gunfight or answer questions that would only land all three of them in a jail cell. Regardless of right or wrong about what had been happening on this ranch, they were still trespassing. Breaking and entering. Brian Preston had been murdered. Even though it wasn't either of them that had done the deed, they might have to answer for it anyway.

Luca tugged his reins. "Go west."

They crossed open country, the horses moving quickly, and headed toward where they had left her car just off the road. Whoever had shown up wouldn't have seen her beat-up compact Ford. But they would have noticed two people leaving on horses.

A shot rang out across the night. Cows let out their low moan in response. One moved in front of Luca's path, so he had to turn the horse and swerve out of the way. "Come on."

Kenna looked back instead, her pistol already in her hand. Too far to get off a clean shot. Firing a warning would only be a waste of bullets.

Light flashed, and another rifle shot cracked off.

She hissed out a breath and pressed the horse on. They made it to the edge of the field, up the hill, and tore between the collection of trees, ignoring the path Luca and Kenna had walked down to get to the ranch house.

They ditched the horses close to where she had parked the car. Kenna ran for the driver's side, jumped in, and turned the engine on. She got back out and held the rear door open for Luca to climb in carrying Camila.

It wouldn't take long for whoever had been shooting at them to catch up.

One of the horses bolted.

Kenna slammed the rear door. She did same the driver's door, which creaked against the silence of night. She winced and shoved it in drive. Hit the gas and peeled out of the gravel onto the blacktop away from the ranch—the place Luca and Camila had been held captive.

Each one of the victims had scattered. It would be up to them what happened next, whether they survived. What kind of lives they chose to lead. The same way she had taken each step the last few years, deciding for herself what her life would be after she was cut loose from the FBI.

Moving on.

Trusting Stairns even though he was a big part of the reason she had lost her career. Forgiving Taylor and working to repair their relationship as much as Kenna's life allowed. Letting Jax in as a friend. Taking on the cases she wanted.

Finding the lost—the way she would do with Maizie.

Disbanding an organization that terrorized people and entire towns with their sadistic actions.

She squeezed the wheel and pushed the gas pedal down harder. Her phone buzzed in her pocket for a second, but she ignored it.

. . .

Two counties over, she pulled into an all-night urgent care. Luca carried Camila out of the car. He paused before he walked away. "Thank you, Kenna."

She squeezed his shoulder. "Take good care of them."

Kenna watched them walk through the automatic doors and then pulled out her phone. She read the screen and frowned.

> File too large to download.

Chapter Three

Two days later

Desert stretched out on either side of the highway. The afternoon sun beat down, shimmering on the asphalt ahead of her.

Kenna gripped the wheel, wondering if everything was all right with the two young people and the baby Camila was carrying. But unless she saw them again, she likely wouldn't be privy to that personal information.

After she'd dropped them at the urgent care, Kenna had driven on. She'd found another place to stay, paid cash with no ID, and crashed while her laptop downloaded the file because her phone couldn't handle it.

The next day she hadn't wasted any time putting as many miles as possible between her and that county. She'd driven all day, checked into another place for the night, and paid for overnight shipping for a printed-out copy.

Her phone, mounted above her steering wheel to the left, illuminated. She swept her finger across the screen and put the call on speaker. "Hey."

"You didn't sleep for long," Stairns said. "I can hear the sound of the road. Where are you?"

"No point in lying in bed in a crappy motel staring at the ceiling," she replied, dodging his question.

She gripped the wheel tighter, her attention focused on the road through her sunglasses. Strategically ignoring both the ache in her forearms from the recent exertion and the low grind that shouldn't be coming from her engine.

"Is that really what you were doing?"

Kenna wasn't about to admit that instead of being an insomniac she had been scrolling through the packet of information. "Fine. I was reading on my laptop since when I tried to print the file all that came out were pages and pages of junk code that means nothing. Like the printer translated the packet into another language, or something?"

Even though she should've been sleeping, she'd only dozed between reading pages of the file packet that had been sent. Scrolling. Reading. Scrolling.

"Huh," Stairns said. "Maybe some kind of failsafe to keep it from being a hard copy, or something else?"

"Maybe." Kenna needed the rest of the updates first. "Tell me what's new."

"Luca and Camila were both seen by the doctor, and they checked out not long after an anonymous donor called in to pay their bill in its entirety."

Kenna smiled to herself. "That was nice."

"I called again this morning about the trailer that belonged to your father," Stairns continued. "The person who listed it for sale is still giving me the runaround about their name, let alone the name of the person who purchased it. Still, I managed to track down their information from some of their other social media posts and had a friend of mine at the NSA give me their personal information."

"So you're becoming a professional stalker now?"

"You want that trailer, don't you?"

Kenna glanced at the speedometer, lifting her foot a fraction, as she approached eighty five miles per hour. "When the last post on the Utah True Crime blog was a link to the sale of my father's trailer, I figured it had to do with this case."

"And now you don't?"

The draft posts were never published. Someone had been entering information—case files, links, and images. Effectively, leaving her messages in a way that couldn't be traced. Since the owner of the Utah True Crime blog had died in a fire, Kenna had taken it over. Two bodies had been recovered from that house, and she agreed with the ME's ruling that it'd been the occupant and his friend.

Whoever left the messages had been hacking in every time.

Each piece of information was relevant to the case. The hunt for an organization who victimized people. And when the police tried to investigate, they'd destroyed sheriff's department property and killed whoever was inside. Same with a church full of federal agents and other law enforcement from California.

Kenna had figured it was the runaway Maizie. Though she couldn't be sure that young woman even existed—or whether that was in fact her name.

They had age regressed the only photo of Maizie. It matched a child who had been reported as having disappeared years ago.

Long enough no one even remembered her.

Kenna had been determined not to forget, no matter how long it took.

Now it had been months of nothing. Just a link to a trailer

for sale, and then Maizie was gone. If she'd ever been there in the first place.

The note Kenna figured was Maizie's inclusion to the packet?

Not good.

"What about Cabot?" she asked. Even with cancer and the surgery, talking about her dog was the happiest part of Kenna's life. Or, at least, the part with the lowest amount of potential threat.

"The three-legged mutt is doing fine," Stairns said. "Elizabeth even took her for a little walk yesterday. They strode to the back fence together and watched the deer across the stream. I'll send you a couple of photos she took."

"Thanks."

Kenna had rescued the dog from being abandoned, tied up outside a diner in Salt Lake City. They'd been through an intense case together. More than one case really, but Kenna considered it all one since there were so many pieces to this puzzle she hadn't managed to solve yet.

They'd been in more than one car crash, Cabot had befriended a guy who turned out to be a dangerous serial killer, and then the dog had wound up nearly being taken out by cancer after all that.

"Ryson sent me an email," Stairns said. "Baby Luci is crawling, pulling herself up on the furniture to standing. I'll forward you the pictures he sent."

"Thanks." Again. "You read through the case file?"

"A cold case murder of a Russian diplomat from fifteen years ago?" He paused. "I'm more interested in the fact that it says 'If you have this, then I'm dead.'"

Kenna swallowed against the lump in her throat. *Maizie.*

"I did some digging. I think I know who sent it to you."

After all this time, she hadn't been able to find Maizie. "Someone dead now?" It was too late.

"I dug around for everyone who's ever been involved with this case, then widened that to associates of those people."

Kenna's foot slipped off the gas pedal. "You found her?"

"*Her?* The person who died in the last two days, right around the time you received that with the ominous note attached, is Thomas. The lab technician from the Salt Lake City FBI office."

"Thomas is dead?" She been certain it was Maizie he was about to tell her had died.

"Who were you thinking it was?" Stairns asked.

"It doesn't matter." Kenna shook her head. "What happened to him?"

"It was a car accident."

"Anything suspicious?"

"Nope."

She frowned. "But you think it's related?"

"The timing fits. Thomas is killed, even if it was genuinely an accident, and then you get that file with a note that says, *If you have this, then I'm dead*. But it's circumstantial at best, even if it's a decent theory."

"We need to see if there's any connection between him and the Utah True Crime blog."

"You think it was him adding those drafts full of information or your missing girl?"

Kenna shook her head. "I have no idea."

"I can call Jax, but..." His voice trailed off.

"But what?" she finished. Given everything that happened, she wouldn't have been surprised to hear that he was in a coma. Or newly married, and off on his honeymoon—even though the thought brought with it a jab of pain.

Jax was perfectly at liberty to live his own life, and to

make his decisions without her input. Sure, they were friends. To an extent and wrapped in the fact they hadn't spoken to each other in months. It was safer that way, especially if Thomas's death wasn't an accident. Sure, there was attraction between them. At least on her part, anyway.

That didn't mean she had room in her life for a relationship.

"He's currently out of the office on a special assignment," Stairns said.

Kenna frowned. "Another undercover operation?"

Even as the Special Agent in Charge at the Salt Lake City field office, he'd still been working the case she was on. Something that wouldn't go down well when his boss found out. He'd been trying to figure out who had buried the truth of how a church full of law enforcement died. Not the natural gas explosion that had been reported.

They'd met up accidentally in New Mexico a few months ago. She didn't know how he was managing to be the SAIC in Salt Lake *and* work her case. He'd better not get in trouble with the FBI because of her.

"Actually..." Stairns hesitated. "Jax is in Las Vegas."

"What?" The skyline of that exact city appeared ahead of her. "Vegas?"

"Seems like a popular place right now," he said. "Considering the FBI director is in town as well. I think he's heading up the special assignment. But he's also there with the former Utah governor Pacer and former president Masonridge."

Kenna gripped the steering wheel even tighter. "Please tell me something is going on that has nothing to do with me, or anything I might be looking into in the next couple of weeks."

"You're in Vegas?"

"I will be." Her stomach clenched. "In about an hour."

Silence filled the line.

"What are Pacer, Masonridge, and the FBI director doing?"

Stairns stayed quiet for a few seconds. "In a few days, there's an event at the University of Nevada, Las Vegas. The dedication of the new law department building, Bradley Pacer Hall."

Kenna said nothing.

"UNLV is his alma mater."

"I know that." Kenna kept her focus on the road. The steering wheel under her fingers. The tension in her hips from driving for hours on end. The smell of popcorn from the empty bag she'd finished a couple of hours ago.

"Maybe they'd like you to respond to the invitation for—"

She cut him off. "That's not going to happen."

"After all the hubbub dies down and everyone goes home, you might consider paying a visit to the hall and seeing it for yourself."

It was by sheer force of will that she managed to not cut him off again.

Kenna pushed out a long breath. "I'll be busy working a cold case. Trying to figure out why whoever sent me this packet thinks the death of a Russian diplomat fifteen years ago is connected to this organization I've been hunting. The one that has meant I had to push everyone I care about out of my life, leave everything I have behind—because most of it was destroyed by them—and go completely under the radar. When *that* case is solved, then I'll consider what I'm going to do next."

"Understood," Stairns said.

If she were honest with herself, she would be willing to admit that Stairns' presence in her life was the only reason she hadn't lost her marbles completely. After all, there had been plenty of times over the last few years she could have crossed the line and become somebody she didn't want to be. She might've taken a case that consumed her to the extent she wouldn't be able to maintain the tenuous grasp on her identity that she tried to safeguard.

Over the last four months or so that had been twice as hard. She'd gone from having friends back in her life to having to push them away all over again whether she liked it or not.

For their own good.

Knowing what she was giving up had been twice as hard as walking away the first time.

Stairns grunted. "Everyone except me who has any connection to this case, taking down this organization, is currently in Las Vegas. I'm at home babysitting a dog."

"My dog. So stay there." Kenna didn't want him getting hurt—like when he'd been captured by a serial killer in Albuquerque. She winced. "Besides, Special Agent Torrow, the guy from the Albuquerque office who was there in Hatchet, taking down the prosecutor—"

"Bodie Torrow's name is on the list of agents with this special assignment," Stairns interrupted. "And that agent we met at the hotel, Dean? All of you will be in the same place at the same time."

Kenna flinched. "The last time that happened, a bomb went off and everyone except us was killed."

"Because you were smart enough to realize what was happening." Stairns cleared his throat. "That's the only reason we walked out of that church seconds before it blew."

"No one else believed me that they were in danger. That it was by design everyone working the case and all the evidence was in the same place." She rolled her shoulders, trying to get rid of some of the concrete tension in her muscles. "I need to get out of the car."

"And do what?"

"How about you call the hotel where the special assignment agents are staying and tell them they need to sweep for bombs?" Kenna had enough people in her life who had believed she was crazy enough to threaten lives. She didn't need to be the one who made that call.

"I can do that, if you think it's necessary." On his end of the call, papers rustled. "They're staying at the Bergamot Hotel. It used to be the Ace of Spades Resort and Casino, but it was rebranded a few years ago."

"Okay." She still wasn't staying there.

"Are you going to get a room at the Bergamot? I can call ahead and make a reservation."

She could barely believe Stairns had wanted to do research for her, or be a sounding board. The fact he was actually volunteering to make travel arrangements like he was her assistant? She needed to take another nap before she passed out.

"It could help if you get a room at the Bergamot," he added. "Considering that's where the special assignment for the FBI is meeting. Plus, that's where the murder happened."

"No, that's where they found him." Kenna shook her head, even though he couldn't see her. "He was killed somewhere else."

"You already figured that out?"

Kenna took the first exit, heading for North Las Vegas so she could avoid even looking at the hotel she had no intention of stepping foot in. She pulled into a gas station, zipped into a parking space, and shoved the car in park. The grinding noise ceased. Then she shut the engine off, leaned her head back on the seat, and closed her eyes. *Too much. This is too much.*

"Find a place to stay and get some sleep, Kenna. I'll keep working on this case file and seeing if I can find anything related that might be useful to you." Stairns sighed. "You'll call the FBI and connect with them about this whole thing, and our cold case?"

"And distract them all from whatever 'special assignment' they have going on?" Kenna wanted to pretend the two were likely not one and the same, but she'd never done well at playing dumb. "How about you just warn them that their lives could be in danger, and we'll leave it at that?"

"Maybe I should fly over there and give you a hand working on this case."

"You need to stay and help Elizabeth with Cabot," s said.

"She doesn't need—"

"I thought you working for me was about staying home. What did Elizabeth say the last time you joined in?" Kenna didn't normally push it, but he was going to put his life in danger. The same way he had going up against the serial killer, Peter Conklin.

A priest had died, and Stairns nearly ended up the same way.

"Stay where you are and feed me whatever information you can," she pressed. "I've got a cold case to solve."

Kenna ended the call.

Chapter Four

The automatic doors swished open. Kenna walked into the Bergamot Hotel dressed in her bodyguard outfit—black pants suit and white collared shirt.

Now the hotel was for sure explosives-free, thanks to a sweep from security with specialized sensing equipment none of the guests would recognize, she wanted a look at that room. She glanced up at the surveillance camera in the corner, hidden of course, and gave them a good shot of her face. Las Vegas hotels were some of the most heavily surveilled spots in the US.

After she'd checked into a motel, Stairns had made her a reservation for room 444 here—the exact room where the Russian diplomat had been found dead—just so she could take a look. Her phone buzzed with an email. She'd created a generic account no one could trace to her, connected only to this burner phone.

She headed through the crowd and got in line for the automatic check-in booths. Cigarette smoke permeated the air, along with music and the rhythmic chime of slot machines. She joined the line behind a deeply tanned woman with wrinkles on her seventy-ish face wearing white pants and a salmon blouse, gold strappy sandals, and a huge white hat. The lady dragged a leopard print suitcase behind her. From this vantage point Kenna could see two restaurants, and the walkway that connected this hotel underground to the neighboring one. An entire world below street level.

Kenna glanced at the attendants behind the row of front desks.

The placement of it, and the expanse of the room, seemed familiar. She'd been in Vegas before years ago, but why think about what had happened during that visit? It wasn't like she'd have to deal with that while she was here.

This was about solving a murder—but only if it put her one step closer to Maizie.

There was nothing that would keep her from finding the young woman. If she was out there to find.

Maizie could be nothing but an online persona. Or someone else entirely had been loading up information on the Utah True Crime blog, in drafts. Passing Kenna intel. Until the link for her father's trailer—and then everything just stopped.

Kenna didn't want to be irritated. Nor did she want to give in to the fear.

This was about focus. The way she'd told Luca he needed to be if he wanted to find Camila. One hundred percent on task. Everything pointed to the goal, no distractions. No emotion to cloud her judgment and get her off track, reacting for the sake of vengeance.

She'd lost plenty in her life. She knew how to handle it.

She'd never met Maizie.

The truth was, if it turned out the girl wasn't real, she would probably mourn at least for a few moments. Longer if the girl was real—and dead.

Or lost.

Kenna didn't want to get hung up on this task and lose all her perspective.

Work the problem.

She checked into the hotel, and the kiosk spat out a key card. She didn't expect to find anything in the room—not when it had been fifteen years since the Russian diplomat was found dead on the bed. However, like her dad had taught her, she was going to start at the beginning and treat this case like any other.

By the elevators, tucked away from the casino floor, Kenna tugged out the burner phone and let Stairns know she was headed up to the room.

Then she scrolled through the pictures he'd sent of Cabot lying on a blanket on the grass. Sunshine. Another one, she had her head in the lap of Stairns' wife, Elizabeth, petting the dog's side where the hair had grown out around the scar she'd sustained in that car accident in Bishopsville.

Months later they'd been in another accident.

Not really an *accident*, considering they'd been attacked. The FBI armored vehicle had flipped, everyone inside thrown around. Special Agent Bodie Torrow had reacted immediately, grabbing Cabot and holding her while the vehicle rolled. Safeguarding Kenna's dog in a way that told her everything she needed to know about that agent.

One of the elevators dinged.

She looked up as the doors slid open and a man in Marine Corps dress blues stepped off, holding his hand out for a woman in a white dress. Both of them couldn't be more than twenty-five. The woman beamed, her blond hair cascading over her shoulders in curls and waves. The Marine looked at her with adoration in his eyes as the two of them headed out.

Kenna stared overlong, her neck craned to see them until they were out of sight.

The ever-present ache in her chest had nothing to do with being shot a few months ago. It was about the life she'd lost, and the future she and Bradley would've had if he hadn't died. The baby she would've given birth to if that hadn't been lost to her along with the rest of it.

Truth was, she found it easier these days to consider and then set aside the pain of the past. Not just because of her determination to focus on the case at hand. The long, lonely days of the last few months enabled her to do some serious consideration. To read a few books about grief and moving on after loss.

Her phone rang just as she touched the keycard to the lock of room 444.

Kenna had only given the number to one person, so it wasn't like she had to check who was calling. "Yep?"

"I want your first impressions," Stairns said. "For the case file."

"Give me a sec." She set the phone on the desk beside the TV, on speaker.

"Settling in?"

"I booked a room at a different hotel across town. I'm not staying here, even if it's been years since there was a dead man in the room," Kenna said. "I checked in there and dropped my stuff already."

"Did you eat?"

Her stomach wanted to rumble, but she ignored it. "I'm fine."

Stairns chuckle crackled through the phone speakers. "Cabot doesn't seem that concerned about food either. Two peas in a pod."

Kenna faced the made bed but turned her head to the phone. "She needs to eat."

"So do you."

"I'll get something on my way back to the hotel. I just wanted to get a first impression." Kenna folded her arms and stared at the room. She'd seen the crime scene photos and the autopsy report in the file packet. "Run it down for me, Stairs."

The way he'd told her to do so many times when she'd worked for him at the FBI.

"Right." He chuckled. "Caucasian male, fifty-eight years old. Russian diplomat ID'd as Dmitri Alekhin. Wife was deceased. He had a daughter and one son. The son went back to Moscow. He's thirty-nine and has a family. Works for the Russian government. The daughter dropped off the radar. I'm trying to locate her, but there isn't much after she came of age. Both of them were born in the US. Dmitri was the Russian attaché in San Francisco for decades until he was killed. There were rumors he was about to retire, but he was given full honors at his funeral."

"And the murder?"

"Autopsy complete. The ME ruled it as poison. I'm not seeing any red flags." Stairs paused, gave a tiny grunt. "But I'm also not seeing a report from the Russians as to the conclusion of their investigation. The naming of the suspect they believe killed their diplomat."

"And the police in Las Vegas?"

"They weren't given much. The Russians took all the evidence."

Kenna walked to the heavy curtains and pulled them back so she could see the view. This wasn't a room someone might covet. It wasn't a suite. There was no view. Everything about it was standard. "So he was poisoned, then someone took the trouble to bring him up here. Or move him to this room. They laid him out on the bed and disturbed nothing else."

"How do you know he didn't die there?"

Kenna thought back to the crime scene photos. "He was sweaty. Clothing rumpled. Sick on his chin. But neatly positioned on the bed in a clean room with no personal belongings around him. No mess. The bed perfectly made under him, nothing touched. Nothing in the bathroom that wasn't put there by housekeeping. Wherever he died, it wasn't here." She turned in a circle. "Who was the room registered to?"

"Uh..." Stairs' typed as he found the information. "Anthony Santino."

No.

"Why do I know that name?"

She froze.

"Kenna?"

"N-no." She managed to choke that one word out. "No, no way. Did they bring him in?"

"He was cleared of suspicion. Didn't have anything to do with a guy in his room."

"It wasn't his room."

"What do you mean?" Stairs said.

"What was the Bergamot Hotel called before it was changed to what it is now? Didn't you tell me?" Kenna sank into the hard chair and squeezed the bridge of her nose. "Who owned it?"

"Huh." Stairs paused. She could hear the faint clacking of a keyboard as he typed. "The Ace of Spades was owned by Santino Holdings."

"And who owns it now?"

"Some corporation. I'm looking into them, but it's unlikely they're connected to anything," he said. "But if Anthony Santino owned the hotel, that means any rooms in his name are comps. Or spots for his friends. Associates. People he was trying to schmooze."

"In this room? Probably his worst enemy," Kenna said. "Or his mother-in-law."

Stairns snorted. "Nah, you put your mother-in-law up in the presidential suite so she's got nothing to complain about."

"Is that true?"

"Only if the hotel manager owes me a favor from a case I was working. Otherwise there's no way I can afford it."

Kenna pushed out a breath, trying to think this through rather than get caught up on sticky ethical issues.

"You could go ask him. Santino still lives—"

"That's not going to happen."

"Why? You know him?"

Kenna swallowed. "We've met."

"Oh."

"I'm not talking to him." She squared her shoulders, but only so she sounded more sure when she said, "We don't need him to solve this case."

"Copy that."

"He isn't the person who will know the significance of Dmitri being left here. He probably has no idea who stayed in the rooms of his hotel, even ones technically registered to him." The Anthony Santino she'd met was far more concerned with being charming...until he hadn't. Meanwhile her father...

Kenna pushed aside those thoughts.

"There is another avenue," Stairns said.

She was about to ask what when she heard a knock at the door. "Someone's here."

"Took him long enough."

"Stairns, who's at my door?" She used the tone of a parent asking a wayward child what was going on.

"Answer it."

The phone line went dead.

He knocked again—whoever it was. The list of options was limited. But considering the FBI special assignment agents were staying in this hotel—and that couldn't be a coincidence because she didn't believe in them—she knew who it was.

"Who is it?!" Kenna headed for the door.

"It's me. Jax."

Instead of looking, she leaned her forehead on the door. That wouldn't save anyone's life, though. She pulled the door open. "Did the bomb squad find a device?"

Jax flinched. "No...what?" Mr. Special Agent in Charge—or "acting SAIC" or whatever his position was now—seemed to have no clue what she was talking about. Considering the fact he was here on special assignment, he had to be aware there was a threat.

"Different case?" Kenna had assumed the special assignment was about the church bombing and taking down the organization she'd been trying to uncover for months. She tried not to stare at his face, or she'd have to contemplate words like *chiseled* and she hadn't been thirteen for a long time. "Did you get a haircut?"

"Hang on," he said. "What was that about a bomb?"

"Everyone who knows anything about this case is currently in one place." She held the door open still. "Though, at least this time it isn't with all the evidence as well."

"Are you talking about the church?"

"Yes. The church that was *bombed*."

"I know." He frowned. "I found the guy who did that, remember?"

She started to speak, but the words got stuck in her throat.

Clearly she was just tired and this case had been a lot from start to finish. It wasn't about him being here, or the chance to work together. That wasn't what was happening.

Denial wasn't a good place to be, and she tried to avoid it. More like having a strong mind and making her own decisions about what to think or do.

His expression softened. "You're here."

"I'm on a case."

"Of course you are. The same one as me, though?" Before she could answer, he said, "How's Cabot?"

"She's doing fine."

"But you miss her."

"Can we not do that?" Kenna said.

"How about dinner, instead?"

She stepped out of the room, let the door click shut behind her, and decided being in public—in the hallway, rather than behind closed doors of the room if they'd stepped that way—would help her keep her composure. "I could eat."

He just stood there, that slightly cocky smile curling up his lips.

"Now is not the time for that." The last thing she needed was him being charming.

Jax chuckled. "It's been a minute. It's good to see you." He enveloped her in a hug before she could object, which was probably his entire plan.

She found her face smashed against the shoulder of his suit jacket as his arms wrapped around her. Holding her steady. She let out a long breath and wrapped her arms around his back.

"There you are."

Kenna didn't know what that was supposed to mean. Only, when was the last time she got a hug from anyone?

She didn't want to let go.

"Are you ready to stop ignoring me now?" He spoke low, his mouth close to her ear.

She pressed her lips together to keep from saying something she would regret.

"Do you really think there's a bomb in the hotel?"

"Stop talking." Kenna held on. "You're ruining it."

His chest rumbled under her cheek. Jax rubbed his hand up and down her back, in a way she shouldn't like as much as she did. What was the point in relying on human contact? That wasn't her life. She liked her friends and enjoyed spending time with them. But again, not her life when the case always came first, and going after the truth put people she cared about in danger.

What she wanted took a back seat to finding the innocent that was lost and returning them home.

Her phone started to vibrate in her pocket.

Probably Stairs, completely unrepentant over the fact he'd contacted Jax to tell him she was in the hotel. But the number on the screen wasn't one she knew. She slid her thumb across the screen and tried to ignore the heat in her cheeks.

She'd practically burst into tears over the fact Jax was here.

"Banbury."

"Kenna?" the woman asked. "It's Justine Greene. Your associate said you were in Vegas, and I need your help. Austin is missing."

Kenna gripped the phone to her ear and looked at Jax. "Raincheck on dinner. I have to go." She skirted around him and headed for the elevator. "Tell me what happened."

Chapter Five

Kenna had already been seated by the time Justine showed up. She pushed back the chair and stood, in the middle of the café tables that made up patio seating. The other woman picked her way through the tables and headed for Kenna.

This was good. Much better than sticking with Jax and distracting each other. It wasn't like they were working the same case—unless something happened that made it clear to Kenna otherwise. Seeing him just now? Stairns must have thought she needed it. But she would never admit to him maybe she had. That wasn't the point.

"Hey." Kenna wasn't sure if she and Justine were the kind of acquaintances who shook hands or hugged. Kenna had spent more time with Austin, Justine's teenage son, than with the woman herself.

"Thanks for meeting me." Justine flushed, out of breath from racing here quickly. "I couldn't believe it when your colleague told me you were in Las Vegas. What are the odds?"

"I'm sure there's someone in this town who could tell

you." She waved Justine to a seat and took her own again. "But regardless, it seems to be going around right now. There are a lot of people in this town who aren't normally."

And it had her worried about the organization she was trying to uncover.

Maybe they were the ones behind the packet she had received on her phone. Maybe it wasn't Maizie's doing at all, but an elaborate trap meant to capture Kenna right where they wanted her. And the FBI, here as well.

Did Justine have a hand in any of it?

The woman across the table frowned. Her hair and makeup had been done with a skilled hand. Justine was a similar age to Kenna, but life had given her more wear so she appeared older. She wore straight cut jeans that hid her figure and a jacket over her white shirt.

Justine said, "You think there's some kind of coincidence going on?"

The last time they had spoken, Kenna had seen the letter C in Old English font on the inside of Justine's forearm.

She had at one point in her life been a part of the organization Kenna was hunting. Even if only because she'd been caught, and used, by them. That meant she knew more about them than Kenna did. Yet, Kenna had never had the opportunity to ask the other woman about it.

She might do that now. If only to ensure that what was happening right now wasn't connected to Justine needing her help.

"You told me on the phone that Austin is missing," Kenna took a sip of her coffee while Justine ignored the carafe and the empty mug on the table in front of her. "Tell me everything you can think of that might help me find him."

Justine's face flushed with relief. "Thank you." She

reached over and squeezed Kenna's hand. "It was a long shot filling out that form on your website, and you being near enough to help."

Kenna nodded.

"The police won't file a report. They figure it's just that we had a fight. Like he's acting out—or living his own life."

"You don't think so?"

"You know what we've been through. Living in Hatchet, under their thumb even though we thought we were out." Justine shook her head. "After they sent Conklin to kill me, what was I supposed to do but run? Austin and I have been a duo his whole life. All we have is each other, so there's no way he just took off without checking in. Even when we're both busy. If I have to work long hours, or he has things to do on top of work and school, we still check in. We text."

"Can you locate his phone with yours?"

"It led me to an alley. I didn't find Austin's phone."

"Okay." Kenna set her cup down. "I'd like to see the place. Plus, if it's okay with you, I'd love access to his texts and emails. If your service provider does that."

"Of course."

Some families even shared photos with each other automatically. It had come in handy on more than one occasion, finding a missing person because of pictures they'd taken after they disappeared. Images that gave enough information Kenna could get a location.

"Thanks." Kenna hoped his disappearance wasn't part of a confluence of events that signaled a deadly plan at work. That was the last thing she needed when her life had been altered by other people's choices far too many times. "If it becomes clear his disappearance is connected to Hatchet, will you tell me what you know about that organization?"

Justine shifted in her chair. "Why would you think it's connected?"

"It might not be." That was the most diplomatic response she could give this woman. Justine would have her sole focus on finding her son. Kenna could do the same thing, setting the cold case and the search for Maizie aside long enough to locate Austin. However, if these things were connected, then she would cross that bridge.

Lately, everything seemed to be tied together. Whether she wanted to acknowledge it or not.

But underneath it all, her mission to find the lost and bring innocents home overrode everything. She didn't want to go after Austin just on the off chance he led her to Maizie.

Kenna's phone buzzed in her pocket. She pulled it out and looked at the text from Jax.

> We're still having dinner.

She didn't react, even though she wanted to grin over the fact Jax had apparently processed and set aside his frustration over her leaving him standing there. She'd seen it on his face. Not that he'd said anything or objected to her walking away. But now he was ordering her around.

She sent him back a message.

> I might not have time. I think I've got another case.

His reply came quickly.

> Dinner. We can exchange notes and help each other out.

Kenna locked her phone and put it facedown on the table. "What was Austin up to yesterday when he didn't check in?"

"He said he was just out. Maybe with friends?" Justine's gaze drifted. "I don't know who he was planning on hanging out with. Just that he should have told me what his plan was for dinner—I had a shift at the restaurant. I'm the hostess. He never texted me, and I couldn't get away from work early. As soon as my boss let me go I headed for the spot where his phone said he was."

"What time was that?"

"Just before three this morning."

"What else has he been up to?"

"As soon as school got out for summer he started summer school classes. He also started working with a friend of his. The dad has a company that works with concrete, pouring patios and driveways. Things like that. Working for people doing renovations rather than moving into new subdivisions." Justine made a face. "He was glad he had a job for the summer that works around school so he could make some money before senior year starts and he has to buckle down for graduation."

"Why Vegas?" Kenna asked. The last time they'd spoken, Justine had told her that Vegas was the last place she saw Maizie. "Did you come here because I asked about that girl?"

Justine shifted in her seat again. Long enough she gave her time to figure out what she was going to say?

Kenna studied the other woman.

"I moved here after high school," Justine said. "We came on vacation when I was a kid, and I wanted to be where life seemed glamorous. But it didn't work out."

"And coming back now?"

"It has nothing to do with Maizie." And yet, despite Justine's words, Kenna couldn't help thinking that might not be true.

"Who is she...really?" Kenna asked. After all, she knew

next to nothing about Maizie Smith—if that was even her real name.

"I know I said I saw her." Justine fiddled with the napkin below her silverware. "But I just knew she was here. We didn't actually meet up."

"But you know who she is?"

"It's been a long time." Justine sniffed. "Things change. Austin is my focus now, and there's nothing I can do but accept how it all turned out. It's not like I can go back and do it again."

So Justine had history with this girl?

Kenna said, "I've been looking for Maizie."

"You won't find her if they don't want you to." Justine shook her head. "But you can find Austin if you try. I know what you do. I know you're the only one that cares enough to bother looking for a kid like him."

Kenna didn't like the idea that she would abandon the search for Maizie to find Austin. She would rather they were connected, but wishful thinking didn't make it so. Even if his disappearance was related to everything else, finding one didn't necessarily mean she would find the other.

Kenna took a moment to study the people around them. Ordinary folks, in Vegas on business or for pleasure. Some of them were here to touch—if only from a distance—the darker side of society. Others came with the sole purpose of diving in headfirst to the seedy life that ran like a river in Vegas and swept people up. And then they would leave, going back to their normal lives.

Kenna said, "I'm not going to let Austin drown."

Justine swiped a tear from under her eye. The wicker chair creaked under her. "I'm just so thankful. I can't believe you're actually near enough to help. I have no idea how to find him on my own."

"I need the most current picture of him that you have. And a list of places he hangs out, people he spends time with. Anyone I can talk to or visit. Show his picture around and see if anyone knows what happened to him."

Justine shifted her giant gold purse onto her lap and pulled out a photo. "I had one printed up this morning, so I could give it to the police."

Kenna took a picture with her phone so Justine could keep the photo printout. "Does he have a computer at home?"

Justine nodded. "It's for school, but I know he also uses it for gaming. It's not a new device. Just what I could afford after I paid first and last month's rent on the townhouse we're living in now."

"I may come by later and take a look."

Justine poured herself a cup of coffee then.

Kenna gave her a second. "So Austin got a job for the summer, and he was excited about school?"

"I think he just wants to be done with it." Justine flushed. "I couldn't wait to get out of school either, so it's not surprising. But I know he's ready to get out there in the world and figure out his purpose. What he wants to do."

"I did the same thing. Though, it took me longer than I thought. And the journey wasn't quite as straightforward as I had imagined at eighteen." She'd struggled long enough with whether to follow in her father's footsteps.

Being back in Vegas made it worse.

This place had made him become something...

Justine lowered her mug and swallowed. "I just tried to have no plan, so I wouldn't be disappointed at what happened. It seems like nothing in my life turned out right. Austin was my one hope of doing something just for me, and now he's gone." She lowered the mug to the table, her hand shaking. "What if something happened to him? What if he's laying somewhere...?"

Dead.

Kenna didn't say the word out loud. Still, both of them were thinking it. "I'll do everything I can to find out where he is, and what happened."

"Thank you."

"But I'm going to need answers about the organization you worked for if I'm going to rule out their involvement."

Kenna wasn't sure if using the word *work* quite covered what happened to Justine. Given what she knew about them, it was more likely Justine had been trafficked. Then as she got older, held under duress, and forced to work for them in one capacity or another.

Some of the young women targeted had been used and then discarded—left alive with all the wounds, and the knowledge they'd been recorded on video. As though someone derived a sick sense of satisfaction knowing they were forever changed by the trauma.

Others Kenna met had been caught up in false legal charges.

The town of Hatchet had been one giant scam, not to mention the serial killer they'd tried to control while they let him run rampant in a hotel with entire floors dedicated to his sick games. Lives had been lost. Justine had nearly been killed, but she'd managed to survive.

The last thing Kenna wanted was for Austin to be hurt, or worse, but this was about more than just one teen boy with his future ahead of him. As precious as that might be.

"Justine, I need you to tell me names. Addresses. Physical locations, businesses, and things you were forced to do. Honestly, I need a rundown of everything they involved you in."

Justine's throat bobbed, and her face paled. "Austin isn't part of that. He can't be."

"How are you so sure?" Unless this mother had made an agreement with whoever was behind the organization and safeguarded her child the way others hadn't been, how did she know? "Do you know for certain that they haven't taken him?"

"I got out. They've left us alone until now. They wouldn't…" Justine gasped. "They can't have… Not again."

"I'm going to find out either way." Kenna thought for a second. "When you left, or during any time you were a part of what they were doing, did you gather any intel? Anything at all aside from your statement that can be used as evidence?"

If Justine believed they would leave her alone, then maybe she had the leverage to make them stay away. This was the kind of woman who put things in place to take care of herself and didn't worry much about saving people if it landed her in danger in the process. And that was her choice to make.

Kenna didn't begrudge her for needing to hold herself together. Keep her son safe and live her life. Not everyone had it in them to put everything on the line for someone else. To risk losing it all on the off chance they would save someone who couldn't save themselves.

Justine winced. "I didn't think I needed it."

"But there's something?"

"It isn't going to help you save Austin. All it will do is show you the truth about me, and the things I've done."

Kenna could understand she didn't want that side of her past coming out. "I get not wanting to expose yourself, but I'm not going to turn you over to the police. You don't need to worry about getting in trouble."

"I'm not worried about anything but Austin."

Kenna studied Justine's face. "Okay."

As she wrapped up with the other woman and got everything she needed to start finding the teen, she couldn't help wondering who worried about people like Maizie when they got lost. Even Kenna had friends like Jax. Like the Rysons. Or like Stairns, who called more than she needed him to—sometimes just to check in and see if she was all right.

Who worried about people who had no one?

Chapter Six

Seventeen years ago

Kenna squeezed the brake on her handlebar and skidded to a stop beside the marble fountain trickling with water. She hopped off and leaned her bike against it. Sweat ran down her back, no breeze on the night air. She adjusted her backpack straps and headed for the front door, where she lifted her fist and pounded.

The door opened. An old guy with dark hair, like those New York mobsters, looked down at her. He smirked. "Selling Girl Scout cookies?"

"At midnight?" Kenna paused. "I'm looking for my dad."

He started to chuckle.

Someone said something behind him, but she didn't hear what it was.

"Yeah, Nico." He stepped back and held the door open. "Guess it's your lucky day."

"I've never had one of those." She crossed the threshold. "So I wouldn't know."

He laughed, shutting the door behind her.

Kenna buried the nerves that came with a closed door. This guy, the other one or any of at least two she couldn't see, didn't need to know she was about to faint. They could do anything to her now. No one knew she'd come here. No one would miss her.

She squared her shoulders and lifted her chin, like she wasn't five four and "light as a feather" as her dad said. "So where is he?"

"Come with me." He set off down a hall, shoes clipping on the stone floor.

Her sneakers squeaked as she followed him.

Kenna bit her lip and pretended like it wasn't happening. She hadn't seen her dad's car outside. He wasn't answering the cell phone he carried.

Maybe he wasn't here at all.

These people and their boss—a man she did not want to meet—could've killed her dad, and now that she'd shown up, they may plan to do the same with her.

He stepped into an open living room with the square sectional couch sunk into the floor, so it was lower than everything else. "Sir?" He moved to the side, and then she saw him.

Stretched out on the couch, his feet on the coffee table and one arm across the back. Anthony Santino sipped from a squat glass and stared at her.

"I know who you are." Kenna locked her knees, so she didn't collapse. "I looked you up at the library. According to the internet, you're a criminal. A bad guy." She shifted the backpack from her shoulders. "Give me my father back and I won't make trouble for you."

"You think you can make trouble for a man like me?"

"I can be creative."

He burst out laughing and set the glass on the coffee table. "He said you were a good kid. I can see what he meant."

"You've seen Max Banbury." Kenna lifted her chin. "So where is he?" Sure, it was a tenuous plan. Most people would believe a kid when she cried wolf about bad guys. Kenna just needed to figure out how to explain why, as a thirteen-year-old, she was in this house in the first place.

"We were just about to have dinner."

So he's here. She didn't know how to just ask without it sounding like she was a little kid, scared over her dad. Exhausted with worry. Hungry. No food in the trailer, no money in the tin where he kept spare change. What else was she supposed to do? It had been two days. He should've checked in by now.

"You should join us."

"I need to see my dad first," Kenna said. Everything was a bargain—her dad had told her that. *Don't answer a question directly. Don't show your cards.* One day she should write down all the things he'd taught her. She didn't have enough going on in her life to write even a whole page per day right now, while he kept journals of cases he said he was going to turn into books and movies one day. As if she believed that could actually happen.

The boss rounded the couch to stand in front of her, but not close enough to touch her. "How did you get here?"

The guy by the door said, "Bike."

Anthony Santino stared at her.

So she'd ridden her bike all the way here from the RV park, so what? She'd waited until after dark, so it wasn't that hot, but it didn't help much. Summer in Las Vegas was brutal. She much preferred June and July on the coast in Oregon or Washington.

"Let's get you a drink of water."

"Aren't you going to just tell me where he is? If you do that, then I can leave."

"He's here." Santino motioned to a different door. "Come on. You must be thirsty." He poured water from the refrigerator and set the glass on a gleaming counter. "Here."

Kenna downed the entire thing and had to wipe the back of her hand on her mouth. She was too embarrassed to ask for a refill, her head swimming with exhaustion and the fact she hadn't eaten since yesterday. She should have just gone to the women's shelter for food, but the last time she did that, her dad had to pick her up from child services. "Just give him to me."

"You think he's a captive?"

She stared at the mob guy. "You're a bad guy. I don't want my dad here."

He didn't laugh at her, so that was good. "You're protective of him. That's good. Men like your father and I need good women to protect us. To look out for us."

"I want to know where he is."

"We don't always get what we want."

"You think I don't know that by now?" Kenna tried not to get mad. "He's all I have."

Santino leaned against the counter. "He's been helping me with a problem. He's not a captive. He's in no danger here."

Then why didn't he call? Surely if he was fine, he'd have checked in and made sure she had food. Kenna had missed movie night at the library for this, and it was nothing?

She looked away, or else she'd say something she shouldn't. Her dad had told her so many times that no one should know what you were feeling—or thinking. It was weak to let people know your emotions. Like giving them a piece of you, it made them feel like they had power over you.

She didn't all the way understand, but it sounded right. Giving someone your thoughts or feelings was a personal thing, and she'd met enough people who took what they wanted from others. She would rather wait until someone earned it. Respect and trust went two ways.

Love was a gift people gave away for way too cheap.

"Santino, he's talking now." Her dad stopped in the doorway, the dark of night behind him. "Kenna?"

"I'll give you two a moment." Santino pushed off the counter. "Go talk to our...friend."

"Thank you for the water." She called the words after him.

He only waved a hand.

"What was that about?" Her dad wiped his hands on a towel he'd been carrying when he came in.

"I rode my bike here. He gave me a drink." She shrugged. "Are you done, or will it be another two days and I hear nothing?"

He tugged his phone from his front jeans pocket. "Dead." He sighed. "Figures."

"There's no food in the trailer, and I have no money."

Her dad winced. "I'm sorry, kiddo. I need to get paid from this job, and then we can go shopping. Grab some stuff from the pantry before you leave, okay?"

He thought she would steal from a mob boss?

"It's fine, Kenna. I'll let Santino know."

"Why are you working for him? He's a bad guy."

"We don't always get to pick and choose. Life isn't that simple." He came closer and squeezed her hand. "Go home, okay? I'll be back as soon as I can. You have things to do, don't you?"

Kenna shrugged.

"Go for swim in the pool at the RV park."

"I can't. I'm not fourteen, so I'm supposed to have an adult with me."

He touched her cheek, threaded his fingers in her hair, and squeezed the side of her neck. "I'll be done soon."

"Sure." *Whatever.* Kenna stepped away from her dad, so he had to drop her hand. She had to ride all the way back to the RV park now when she'd been lightheaded on the way here.

"Come on." He waved at the kitchen. "I'll—"

A man crashed through the door from outside, covered in blood. Screaming while he ran at her father, holding a knife above his head.

Her dad spun and grabbed something from on top of the fridge. A gun. He leveled it at the man and pulled the trigger. Kenna heard the sound past the hands she'd cupped over her ears.

The man collapsed to the floor, knocked back two feet. He left a blood smear on the white tile.

Kenna lowered her hands, her ears ringing anyway.

Her dad slid his arm around her and hurried her to the front door. "Go, Kenna. Ride home. *Now.*" He practically shoved her out, then slammed the door behind her.

Chapter Seven

Present day

The gas station attendant glanced from the register screen to her. "That guy?"

Kenna nodded. "It would've been Monday afternoon. About three?"

She'd already walked the back alley where Austin's phone provider indicated his cell had transmitted—back when Justine checked. Now the phone probably had a dead battery. The location provided was good within a few hundred feet. She'd checked around, and looked thoroughly, but didn't find the phone.

The gas station attendant's name badge said SHANDRAY. She made a face at the photo of Austin on Kenna's phone. "Sure. Maybe...actually, yeah."

"You remember him?"

"Looking for his girlfriend. That's what he said."

"Like I am, asking you if you've seen her?"

Andrea shook her head. "Nah, just got some jerky and a soda. Told me he was looking for someone." She shrugged one shoulder. "Seemed kind of sad, you know? Like he lost her a while ago."

Kenna shoved her card in the reader. Had Austin met a girl since he and his mom moved to Las Vegas? If he had, the girl would have friends and family of her own. They might know where she could find the boy. His disappearance might have nothing to do with this organization.

He might be caught up in someone else's business.

Or they'd run off together, chasing a dream.

"Receipt?" Shandray asked.

The cold brew coffee could arguably be a tax-deductible business expense, depending, but Kenna said, "No, thanks."

She twisted off the lid as she passed between the automatic doors, going from the chill of air-conditioning to the heat of the summer sun outside. Probably better she hadn't brought Cabot with her, considering the dog wouldn't be able to stay in the car while Kenna went inside.

A few months back, the camper van she'd been living in had been set on fire by the men chasing her—and Jax, and Ward Gaulding, the person who'd blown up that church and killed all those people. Ward had been under duress when he did that. Forced into it by whoever was behind this organization. He'd died before he could give her more information.

Now she had a beater car registered to a fake ID Stairs had paid a guy to create, and neither of them had asked questions about where it came from. Sure, it wasn't strictly legal, but as soon as she took down this organization, she would get her life back—and buy a new home.

Staying in motels all the time was getting old.

Kenna turned on the car engine, expecting her dog to shift in the back seat and stand on the fabric to lick her ear. But Cabot didn't do that because she was at Stairs' house in Colorado.

She unlocked her phone and scrolled again through the photos he'd sent.

Until an odd awareness crept in, but Kenna didn't look up. She tried to assess the sensation and figure out what she was feeling.

She backed up to the text thread and sent Stairs a message.

> I'm being watched.

She stowed the phone in the cup holder and pulled out onto the street, driving around in no particular direction. Kenna spotted a hole-in-the-wall bowling alley that probably should've been torn down thirty years ago.

She got caught in traffic and wound up turning the radio loud and humming along. Giving her mind time to work on the problem while she did something else often helped her have ideas. This time, it just let her focus on the cars around her.

The silver Hyundai changed lanes behind her, weaving in and out of traffic. The question was whether it was trying to make headway or if the driver wanted to catch up to her.

Kenna took a random side street.

The car followed.

She whipped into a parking garage and got up two levels as fast as she could before she backed into a space, then waited. The Hyundai passed slowly a few minutes later, and she realized who had been following her. She flipped the glove box open and stowed the pistol.

He parked in the lane between the rows of parked cars, blocking everything, then got out and came over to her car.

She rolled down the window. "Hey, how's it going?"

He wasn't fooled by her nonchalance. "We should exchange numbers."

"That would probably be easier than you stalking me."

"I wouldn't have to if you hadn't run off earlier." He leaned closer.

"I figured you were busy working on some FBI business."

"I'm off now. So we can go have that dinner."

She narrowed her eyes. "Where?"

"Follow me this time." He strode back to his car, the line of his shoulders tense. She didn't relish making him mad. Not just for the sake of frustrating him. That had never been her thing. But keeping him at arm's length? Given how her feelings wanted to latch onto him like that hug—as friends, of course—she had to fight herself when she spent time with him.

As Kenna drove, she thought about that sermon she'd listened to on the radio a few weeks back, somewhere in Nebraska. The location didn't factor, but she remembered where she was.

The pastor had been talking about the book of Romans. About the war between the flesh and the spirit. That there were things the flesh wanted to do, but which led to eventual spiritual death. The spirit had been renewed by God and wanted to do what was right. The dissonance created a sort of war inside everyone trying to follow God.

Kenna could feel that tension now, and though she wouldn't say she was a believer, she was open to the idea. Or, at least, she was exploring in a way she didn't rule it out.

Except the priest she had met had been murdered.

She needed to reconcile with a God who allowed that to happen. But that would only be after she figured out how she seemed to have all the war of being a Christian but with none of the benefits. Maybe it was that her head—logic—wanted to debate with her heart, and her emotions.

She could acknowledge that she wanted to spend time with the people she cared about. The warmth of friendship. Family. Being surrounded by people who cared about her. All that was good—and she'd enjoyed it while she had it, even being on the road.

Meanwhile the risk of having people in her life, the loss of her father and Bradley, and then people like Sheriff Joe Don Hunter and Thomas at the FBI, reminded her that she didn't like the tragedy of grief. She didn't want to feel the deep abyss of loss. Kenna descended into a dark place when that was the only thing she had to hold on to.

The priest had told her to let the light shine into her life.

But how could she do that and put the people she cared about at risk?

How could she be happy and at peace when innocents like Maizie didn't get to feel the same way?

Jax pulled into the parking lot of a neighborhood Mexican restaurant. The kind of place that didn't look like much on the outside, the paint colors bleached by the sun to a dull example of what they had been, but the food blew you away.

She inserted a key into the door handle, because that was the only way to lock her car, then joined him by the door.

He all but tapped his foot, waiting for her.

"Have you ever thought about being a school principal?" She smirked. "You'd be good at keeping all those wayward kids in line."

He held the door open. "And have hundreds of teens driving me crazy? I have my hands full enough with just you."

Kenna strode to the hostess. "Two, please."

The young woman led them to a booth, and Kenna slid in. Jax eyed the seat.

"You're not sitting next to me," she announced.

He slid in opposite. "I don't like my back to the door."

"Neither do I." If they were destined to argue about what side of the table they wanted to sit on, how were they ever going to agree on anything?

Sure, they agreed about the need for justice. Freedom came from being a citizen who abided by the law and showed kindness to others. They went into the dark places and recovered people who had been lost—it was just that his way had far more paperwork than hers.

The rest of it? The day to day? She wasn't sure they'd agree on much. Jax was granola, yoga, and getting out into nature on his days off. He'd sent her plenty of photos from the top of mountains in Utah before she ditched her phone for the burner.

Kenna only communed with nature when she was finding a body—or a live victim.

She preferred fluffy socks on her days off. Her dad's quilt, and one of the books he loved to read.

"And a side of guacamole."

Kenna realized he'd been giving the server his order. She asked for chicken fajitas. "And queso dip. Extra chips."

"Got it." The young man strode away.

Kenna studied him. "You're guacamole. I'm queso."

Jax sipped his water. "What does that mean? Both of those are great."

"On their own, sure," Kenna said. "It's never going to work."

Sure, she was more convincing herself of the fact than trying to convince him. It wasn't like they'd even talked about a relationship. She was attracted to him, he was a good guy, and there would forever be a tween girl inside Kenna who overthought everything and dreamed about having a boyfriend.

She grinned, trying to play it off. "We're incompatible. It's a good thing we're all about work, and solving cases separately because that's the nature of our jobs. Otherwise we'd realize this will never work."

He stared at her. "Why don't you just tell me what's going on?"

Two missing teens. A cold case. Jax stalking her. "You first. What's this special assignment thing you're doing at that hotel?"

He frowned. "You don't like that hotel?"

"I'm indifferent toward it. These days." Years ago she'd have said yes, she hated it. "New owner. Now tell me about the special assignment."

He leaned back in his seat, blowing out a breath in a way that indicated he didn't relax much. At least not off his mat. "The FBI director gathered us together. Just a handful of agents, including Dean from that hotel in Albuquerque, and Torrow who was in the vehicle with us when it flipped."

"Right. Love that guy." She dipped a chip in some salsa. "Torrow arrested the prosecutor in Hatchet, but I haven't heard from him after that."

"He's been quietly investigating, the same way I did that got me in Mexico on that undercover op."

Jax had brought Ward Gaulding back so he could testify against the organization. On the way he'd run into Kenna and wound up losing his lead when Ward was killed.

Their food arrived, and Jax said, "All of us have been working on it. Trying to figure out who took Ward's family and ordered him to bomb that church and kill all those agents and cops."

"And destroy all the evidence." She took an assessing bite

of the queso on a chip and decided this place wasn't half bad. "So whose idea was it to get everyone together there?"

"He was killed in the bombing."

So the trail had been planted. "Whoever is in this organization, they have access to the FBI. They have power."

He nodded. "The issue of Carl Southampton's death came up. I gave a statement, and there was talk about bringing you in for questioning, but no one could find you."

She shrugged, but the death of that lawyer wasn't something she'd ever brush off. "I'm tough to track down. It's a gift."

"I'm glad for it, as much as I dislike it at times." Before she could respond, he continued, "The director called us all together because he believes he knows who is behind the organization. He has no evidence to prove it, so the assignment is to find it—if it's there to find."

"No one floated entrapment as an idea?"

"The guy is untouchable."

Kenna didn't figure that was much of a challenge. "Just hack his computer."

Jax pulled out his phone and tapped the screen. He turned it to face her.

She almost said the man's name out loud but caught herself. There was a reason he hadn't just said it aloud. The reason stared her in the face. *Michael Rushman.* The Hammerton Dickerson CEO.

Kenna winced. "Government contracts. Access to the highest levels of encryption, and the creator of most of the cutting-edge security software available."

"Untouchable."

"There's an in. We—*you*," she corrected herself, "just have to figure out what it is."

"I get it."

She paused, mid stab on a piece of chicken. "Get what?"

"Why you stayed away. Even though I didn't like it. You knew this was the threat level."

"Not who. But what they've been capable of so far?" Kenna shrugged. "It's nice to put a face and a name to the threat. Makes him tangible, and human. Not some incorporeal thing hanging in the edge of my awareness ready to strike."

"You dumped your phone, and all your personal belongings, and you went under the radar. Until now."

"I don't care about taking him down more than I care about finding Maizie."

Jax shook his head. "Who is Maizie?"

She returned the favor and showed him the photo on her phone. "In Bishopsville, when we were figuring out it had to do with the high school, a new student popped up. I found her info on the principal's computer. An incoming transfer. I think she was trying to bait the line. With herself."

"That's all?" When she nodded, he said, "Could be a generic stock photo."

"We found a missing person. A kid who matches the age-regressed image we came up with." Kenna set her phone facedown on the table. "She's out there, and I'm going to find her."

"Seems thin."

Before he could tell her she'd be better off putting her energy toward taking down Michael Rushman, Kenna said, "I don't want to do anything else." She pushed back the swell of emotion in her chest. "Even with Austin missing, I still need to work on finding her."

He studied her. "If I come across anything, I'll pass it to you."

The rest of dinner was mostly small talk. She needed the balance after all the pressure and emotion of her open cases.

Out in the parking lot, Jax walked slightly ahead of her across the concrete and potholes. Taking up a defensive stance, no doubt.

Two cars accelerated toward them. Something that had happened to them before, but she'd nearly been hit that night in Salt Lake City.

Jax shifted. "Watch out—"

The cars screeched to a halt, one behind the other. Both she and Jax reached for their weapons, but being off duty, he'd apparently left his in his car as well.

Doors flung open. Several men climbed out. One pulled a gun and pointed it at Jax. "Don't."

Another man headed for her. "Come with us."

Jax objected immediately. "Now hold on—"

The guy in front of her glanced at him. "This doesn't concern you."

"I could drop you right now and barely break a sweat." Kenna kept her voice low. "Is that what you want to happen?"

He turned to her. "But then my men would kill your friend."

"What is this?" Like they'd admit if this was about killing her. But Kenna had to ask.

He leveled her with a steady gaze. "Mr. Santino would like to speak with you."

Jax flinched. "She's not going *anywhere* with—"

Kenna glanced over. "It's fine."

The man grabbed her elbow and dragged her to the car.

"I can walk on my own."

"Where would the fun be in that?" He shoved her against the side of the car and patted her down, divesting her of most of her weapons but not all of them. He pocketed her phone. "Let's go."

Chapter Eight

The town car came to a stop, but Kenna didn't move to get out, waiting instead for one of Santino's guys to open the door.

The house didn't look much different except for the passage of time. She stared at the dry marble with a line of calcification where the pool had previously been filled. No water ran through the fountain now. The landscaping could use some tending, and a new coat of paint would probably restore the mansion to its former glory.

The single-story structure she hadn't been to in years stretched out on either side of the double front door. A garage, disconnected from the main house, sat to the right across the driveway that went down the side of the house.

"Come on." The guy who had manhandled her in front of Jax motioned but didn't touch her. "He's waiting."

She bit back a sarcastic retort. Another one of those want to, but shouldn't, that always seemed to war within her. Focus on the ultimate goal—finding Maizie, and Austin—kept her from doing or saying things she wanted to say or do. After all, the only result would be that she wound up further from her goal.

She looked over her shoulder but didn't see Jax's car. Maybe she was wrong and he hadn't followed from the restaurant, assuming she could take care of herself. Which was, of course, correct. However, she didn't want to rule out the fact he cared about her.

Would he knock on the door like she had done looking for her father?

What a waste that had been, considering how it turned out.

A little dry heaving on the side of the road here. Some blood on asphalt where she had fallen off her bike there. Eventually she had made it back to the trailer. Dirty, bloody, and still starving. One of the neighbors had given her a can of soup and a loaf of bread. Three days later her dad had shown back up with a bundle of cash.

They left Las Vegas that same day.

Before they even reached the front door, it opened. Anthony Santino answered it himself this time. Not leaving it to one of his minions to bring her to him through the house. No, this time they picked her up at gunpoint.

Kenna stopped on the front step. "Kidnapping? Really?"

Behind her, one of his guys made a noise in his throat. Apparently, it just wasn't done to question the boss.

Kenna ignored it.

Santino looked her up and down. "Won't you come in, Ms. Banbury."

"I'm guessing that wasn't a question," Kenna said. "Because I don't have a choice."

He stepped back, holding the door wide. Then let go of it and turned his back to her so he could walk down the hallway.

Dismissing her, as well as leaving it up to her whether she followed him or not.

Kenna found him on the couch much like the first time they met. Just without the alcohol, or her father.

"Blah-blah." He waved a hand. "You dislike being dragged here. You don't like me still, even though I personally have never done anything to offend you. It's good to see you, Kenna."

She stared at him.

"It's been a long time."

"It would have been forever." Only, he had ruined that plan. "I had a nice dinner with a friend. Now he's going to think you kidnapped me."

"Another private investigator?"

"You assume he's a colleague."

Santino's brows rose. She realized then he wore no jewelry, just a simple gold watch. "It was a romantic dinner?"

"It's complicated." And why was she telling him this? "I'm going to need my phone back."

He nodded. "In a minute."

She looked around because that was better than looking at him and getting more irritated. On one wall, behind the dining table, he had a huge picture framed on the wall. The movie poster of *Over the Limit*. Based on the novel with the same name by acclaimed crime investigator Max Banbury.

"You like it? I went to the premier in LA and got the stars to come by my hotel the next day and sign my poster."

"For a bunch of fiction, it's not half bad," Kenna said. It just hadn't been based on reality whatsoever. "I was planning on avoiding you completely. Things are complicated enough."

"And if I simply wanted to ask how you are?"

"You probably would have offered me a drink already."

"All I have is milk or water."

Kenna blinked.

"Tell me about your complication."

He really wanted to know. "Fine. Fifteen years ago a Russian diplomat was murdered in a room registered to you in a hotel you owned at the time. I'm going to solve it."

Santino shrugged. "Your dad couldn't solve it. Nor could the police, though that's hardly surprising given the detective at the time was as much of an alcoholic as I was."

"We weren't here after that murder. We were here a couple of years before then." Why did he think her father had worked her cold case?

Santino shrugged. "I sent him everything I could gather about what happened. After all, we agreed it was better if he stayed away."

Except that they'd been at odds, not in agreement, when Santino and her father parted ways. "Is it because of the guy he murdered in your kitchen?"

"Sit, Kenna. Please?" He motioned to the chair across from him. "Apparently there's a lot he didn't tell you."

It turned out the chair was better cushioned than she expected for something that appeared so dainty. The same chair that had been here years ago if she remembered correctly. Or the older model had been switched out for a new version that looked identical—the way some people did with relationships.

"Nothing good will emerge from opening the can of worms that is a Russian diplomat's death." He swallowed. "Though I am certain that if anyone can solve it, it's you. But even you won't like what you might find. Certain things are best left in the past."

Which was exactly why she never had any intention of coming here.

Kenna lifted her chin. "You're telling me to leave it alone because you believe I can actually figure out the answer?"

He squared his gaze on her. "Yes. It's what your father wanted. It goes for you, too."

And he expected that to convince her? Kenna wasn't someone who overlooked the consequences, or the potential risk. Every situation she walked into she did with full knowledge that things may not turn out the way she wanted them to. She couldn't control other people or the truth she hadn't learned yet. What was the point in having expectations one way or another if they were more likely to end up being nothing like what actually happened?

Hard to be cautious when she was also making assumptions.

Santino stared at her. "You aren't going to ask me if I murdered this man?"

"Whether you did or not is a matter of a court of law being able to prove it," Kenna said.

Her job was to find enough evidence she could hand over to the District Attorney's Office. After that, they may not even decide to file charges. Politics often got in the way of justice, though not usually, thankfully.

She continued, "What I would like to know is whether you have any information I can go on as I look into it."

"Even though I told you not to."

"You warned me." She shrugged one shoulder. "I listened to your warning, and I will proceed with caution."

"Why? What does it matter to you if this mystery is solved or not?"

There, he had touched the heart of the matter.

She studied him. "I have my reasons."

Two teenagers could end up dead if she didn't figure out why the cold case was related to Maizie. It still may not link to

Austin, but as with Thomas's death there was more here than met the eye. She wasn't going to let the two of them end up like the FBI lab tech.

"There is a local group. Hobbyist mystery solvers, true crime. That kind of thing." Santino shifted on the couch and crossed one leg over the other. Considerably thinner than before. "They go by the name Intellectus. Every few months they come around asking about the murder. I believe they had the police department give them copies of the entire case file."

"I thought the Russians took everything." That was what Stairs had told her.

"The copies were what remained of the LVPD investigation."

"Did you tell these crime solvers anything, or give them an interview?"

"So I can see them on the local news a week later, dead from some accident or other?" He scoffed. "No, thank you."

"Did you know Dmitri Alekhin?"

"I decline to answer." Before she could ask why, he said, "I have my reasons."

"The room was registered to you."

"As you yourself pointed out." Santino leaned back. "At the time, I owned the entire hotel complex. Of course I had a block of rooms at the Ace of Spades under my name. For personal guests, or family."

She'd known he was married before, and that he had a child. "How is your family?"

"They are gone." He looked away and back at her, his eyes red. "Much like yours, I believe."

She wanted to argue they were nothing alike, but seeing an expression like that, she couldn't bring herself to say the words.

Kenna looked around again and spotted a couple of his

men in the corners of the room. "Where's that guy who used to work for you? What was his name? Dylan, Declan? Something like that."

She didn't turn far enough to see the doorway to the kitchen where that man had fallen, felled by the bullet from her dad's gun. Shot right in front of her.

She still had no idea who he was, and her dad had refused to tell her anything about it. What would be the reason other than guilt? Her dad had done some work for Anthony Santino at a time when they didn't have much money.

Probably, he'd done things he didn't want to admit to her.

Or done things *in front of her* that he didn't want to explain.

"Deacon." Santino nodded. "We parted ways a number of years ago. One on a long list of things that have changed." He motioned at the wall, where an ornate cross hung. "I found faith several years ago as part of my journey."

He left off that statement as though inviting her to speak.

Kenna said nothing. Not just because the last person she'd discussed faith with had wound up murdered.

Watching him sitting here, she couldn't help thinking that he seemed alone. Even in a room with other people. In a house he shared with those who worked for him—even if the men in his employ didn't stay here, they only worked here. When she'd knocked on the door all those years ago, it was more like facing down an opposing force. Her against the world.

There was none of that now.

He seemed more like her. Someone who had a life that consisted mainly of solitude. If anyone asked, she would say what she always did. That she liked her life the way it was. But being forced to keep her friends at a distance the past few months, she was starting to wonder if that was even true.

There seemed to be some part of her that was discontent with being alone. Maybe an inner dissonance Santino also felt, considering his life had been full when they had met before.

Kenna wasn't about to dredge up all of that history. It had nothing to do with the cold case she was working, which meant it also had nothing to do with Austin and Maizie's cases.

"Can I show you something on my phone?" she asked Santino.

He motioned with a wave to one of his guys, who handed him Kenna's burner. "Four missed calls."

"He's a good man," she said. And if Santino thought he was going to do anything to Jax, he would discover how deep her loyalty ran. Even to a man she had only known a few months, and most of that over the phone.

"But he's not a private investigator?"

Kenna shook her head. "FBI." Then watched for the fallout of her dropping that bomb.

Santino clicked his fingers.

One of the guys in the corner of the room turned and left.

Santino handed over her phone.

She sent Jax a quick text to tell him she was okay. She pulled up the photos and showed them to the man in front of her. First Austin's, asking, "Have you ever seen this young man?"

He shook his head.

"Does the name Austin Green mean anything to you?"

Another shake.

She swiped to the picture of Maizie. "How about this young woman?" she asked, carefully studying the skin around his eyes.

Not even a visible flex. "Who is she?"

"The only name I have that I believe may be real is Maizie." She lowered the phone. "Though, to be candid, I don't even know for sure if she's a real person. She might have been helping me. She might also have been helping the FBI."

Hopefully he wasn't close enough to this that sharing the information with him wasn't also putting Maizie at further risk.

She continued, "I don't know for sure if she's even safe right now. I haven't heard from her for long enough I'm starting to get worried something might have happened."

"And you have no idea where she is?"

"I don't even know where to start looking," Kenna said. "Except by solving the murder of that Russian diplomat."

Which meant her next stop would be this local mystery solving group, Intellectus. Though, only to get them to give her everything they had.

"I need to ask you another question."

Santino lifted both hands, then let them fall back to his sides. "Why stop there?"

She ignored the irritated tone. "Because I'm only interested in my cases, not turning your life into an embellished work of fiction."

The skin around his eyes crinkled then. "I would love to tell you what your father and I were working on together. But that is not the question you asked."

"You're right, I didn't." Because she had asked it enough, and she'd expected her father to tell her the truth. When he didn't, she realized for the first time in her life that there were things he intentionally kept from her. Maybe she knew before then, but when he withheld the truth and then eventually started to tell lies about it, she understood completely.

He'd turned the painful parts of his life into fiction in order to keep running from them.

Santino lifted his browns. "So ask the question you wish to know the answer to."

"Have you ever met Michael Rushman? He's a local guy. The CEO at—"

"I know who he is."

"Could he be connected at all to Dmitri, or his death?" Kenna asked.

"You wish to know if I believe Rushman killed Dmitri fifteen years ago?"

"Is it possible?" She would love everything she was working on to be tied together with the same neat bow. The fact life never worked out that way was beside the point.

"Given the police never had any idea who might have killed him, I suppose we have to surmise it is possible *anyone* could have done it. Until evidence suggests otherwise that puts Michael Rushman on the suspect list."

She frowned. "Did my father teach you that?"

"We taught each other many things. That is what happens when two people from different walks of life become friends."

Kenna wasn't sure what to make of that. "Why don't you like Michael Rushman?"

"Who says I don't like him?"

The pounding on the front door sounded like more than one person. Whoever they were, they resorted to ringing the bell, which chimed down the hallway.

"I suspect your friend is here."

"That means it's probably time for me to go." Kenna shrugged, as though the way they'd brought her here was no big deal. "I should get back to work."

Santino went to the front door first, though one of his men opened the door while he stood back.

Kenna ended up at the rear, peering around everyone to

see Jax on the front step with a thunderous expression on his face.

"FBI." He shoved his badge in the face of the man who'd opened the door. "Where is Kenna Banbury?"

Instead of answering, Santino turned to her. He held both of her shoulders and pressed a kiss on each cheek in turn. "It was good to see you again, dear. Good luck with your cases."

Chapter Nine

Kenna held herself together all the way outside. She climbed in the passenger seat of Jax's car, and her entire body shuddered.

"Friend of yours?" Jax said.

She shook off the oily sensation of being in there. How was it that she could walk into all kinds of situations and be fine? Caves where young women had been tied up. Basements where little kids had been held captive. The worst things a person could do to an innocent. She had seen it all. Walked in, walked out, and moved on with her life.

But her own past? Her memories? Something in her didn't want to go back there.

"Kenna?"

She managed to get out two words. "Just drive."

Head against the seat, she stared out the window and watched the world go by. The way she used to do when her dad drove the truck, pulling that Airstream behind them while she stared at home in the side mirror.

They'd spent hours, side by side, completely silent. Both of them deep in their thoughts like they needed to be. Then sometimes he'd have her write up case notes while he talked. Her dad rarely listened to music, but he'd bought her first iPod and a pair of wired earbuds she'd used to download music.

Kenna squeezed her eyes shut and saw her dad in her mind. The flash of the gun and that loud blast. "You'd think I'd have seen him kill someone earlier than that."

"Santino?"

"No, my father." She shifted in the seat. "He killed a guy in Santino's kitchen. I was thirteen. You'd think, with the way I was raised, I'd have seen something like that before."

And then she'd flinched.

Run.

She could hear his voice in her head.

Go, Kenna.

"It surprises you that you saw someone get killed when you were a kid?"

"I'm surprised I was a teen before it happened." She shrugged. "Sometimes I think about stuff like that. He managed to shelter me in some ways, and at the same time I was reading autopsy files before I turned ten. I had to go to the library to look up what mechanical asphyxia was. The librarian gave me a funny look, let me tell you." She started to chuckle.

"I'm not sure that's amusing."

"Sure it is."

Jax pulled up at a red light in a line of traffic. He unlocked his phone and handed it over, the maps app open. "Type in your hotel."

Kenna pulled it up and started the directions. "When was your first?"

He twisted around. "I'm sorry?"

"Dead body," she said. "When did you see your first one?"

"Quantico."

"Huh." She frowned. "That doesn't make him a bad dad."

"I didn't say he was." But he was probably thinking about it.

Kenna glanced over. "Plenty of people have terrible parents. Worse than mine."

"So you've decided he did the best he could?"

"I think it was more that he knew who he was supposed to be and wasn't going to apologize for it." She'd thought about her history a lot, on the road alone. "He knew what he was supposed to be doing. I didn't want to be away from him because I'd end up in foster care or some horrible situation. So I went with him."

"Homeschool?"

"He bought all the books every year. I started making my own schedule. Trying different things and figuring out how to do it." She winced. "The year I did one subject at a time, and I left all my math for the last two months, and I was doing three lessons a day? Not so fun."

"What about prom? Or sports?"

She shrugged. "You miss out on the good, but you also miss out on the bad. It's a trade-off."

"You saw a lot of places."

"Same thing, good and bad. There's a couple of spots I want to go back to, and more that I have no idea where we were."

"Vegas is a pretty memorable place. There's nowhere like it."

"Not for normal reasons, but yes." Kenna pushed out a breath.

"Anthony Santino is bad news." He glanced over. "Why is he acting like a friendly uncle around you?"

"Maybe he doesn't have anyone else."

"And you collect people with no one else, so it stands to reason you'd have him in your life."

Kenna shifted in her chair. "I haven't seen him in years!" She barely knew what to object to first. Santino being in her life when he distinctly was not, or Jax's tone when talking about the man. "You're gonna judge the guy based on law enforcement reports when you don't even know him?"

"You're going to defend him?"

"He's not *in my life*," she said.

"Didn't look that way to me."

"Are we going to argue about this?"

"Why not?" he said. "You like to argue about everything. You're the most contrary person I've ever met."

"*Excuse me.*"

"Case in point." He huffed and made the turn. "This is where you're staying?"

"It's not the Ritz Carlton, but the Wi-Fi is good."

"More like you're paying cash, and this isn't the kind of place that asks questions."

"It's not as bad as you think it is." She waved. "Number eight."

Jax pulled into a space outside the room. "One bed or two?"

"Two." She twisted around in the chair. "Why?" She dragged the word out, long enough to work out the answer to her own question. "I don't need a babysitter."

"You just got kidnapped by one of the deadliest mobsters in Nevada. You're telling me you couldn't use backup?"

"Because you need something to do during your off hours?" She studied him. "Did you get assigned to me?"

Jax looked at the ceiling, the keys in his hand.

"I love being lied to." Kenna pushed open the car door and went into her motel room. She left the door open because what was the point in closing it? He would probably flash his badge at the front desk lady and get a key. Let himself in.

The room had two queen beds. She'd put her suitcase on one and left it open. On the shelf in the closet, she'd put her own lockbox—the one with fingerprint entry. Sure, with her life she should probably be armed 24/7. But the fact was, she didn't always want a gun close by. Sometimes she wanted to drop the vigilance and relax.

She didn't need a gun to defend herself.

Which was good, considering it was in her car back at the restaurant.

Kenna kicked her shoes away and unstrapped the knife at her ankle. She shrugged off her jacket and the rest of the stuff she'd been carrying. A deep inhale strained the shirt she wore.

Jax dumped a backpack at the end of the other bed. He put his suit jacket on the back of the chair, over her other shirt that she'd been meaning to iron. He untied his shoes and lay down on the comforter in his shirt, pants, and socks.

He closed his eyes.

Two seconds later, he shifted, pulled the holstered pistol from his belt, and set it on the end table. He didn't even open his eyes.

She stared at him. "Please, make yourself at home."

His breathing evened out.

Kenna grabbed her laptop and the headphones that connected to her phone. She called Stairs and sat on the far side of her bed, away from Jax. She'd have to keep her voice as low as possible but wondered if anything would wake him up.

He'd fallen asleep almost immediately.

"Stairs." He must have answered the phone without looking at the screen.

"Just me." Kenna leaned against the headboard and

logged her laptop on. "Anything about the FBI special assignment that has to do with me, as far as you know?"

"I haven't heard anything. I called the FBI director and spoke to his assistant, but he didn't call back yet." Something in his tone gave her the impression he hesitated.

"What?"

"You got a reminder for that invitation in your email," Stairns said. "The dedication at UNLV's new law building. The Bradley C. Pacer Hall."

Kenna stared at the print of a painting on the wall until her eyes burned.

"It's a formality."

"I get that he's not trying to rub it in my face." She stretched out her hands and looked at her forearms. "I get that Governor Pacer isn't trying to make this as difficult as possible for me. But why does he think I want to go?"

"Maybe it's a politician thing," Stairns said. "He can say he remains on good terms with the woman who meant the most to his son."

"Maybe you should ask him."

Stairns was silent for a second. He didn't need to apologize to her, and she didn't want him to. They'd settled on not discussing the past. All it did was dredge up things they'd agreed to move on from. Instead, they could work together, and he could help her out. Their motivations for doing that needn't come into play.

She sighed. "Sorry."

"You don't need to say that to me. Ever."

Kenna cleared her throat. "I need a favor."

"Or just a function of my regular duties on your behalf?"

She rolled her eyes. "Fine. It's case related. Kind of."

"Hit me."

"Tell me how Cabot is first."

"She likes raw cabbage," Stairns said, amusement in his voice. "Big chunks of it. Green and purple, doesn't matter. Maybe it's the crunch."

"Cabbage?"

"Yep," Stairns said. "I'll send the video Elizabeth took. Cabot was picking it up in her mouth and tossing it, then pouncing on it and eating it."

Kenna shook her head.

"What's going on where you are?"

She glanced over at the FBI agent asleep on the other bed. Never mind that the Bureau might've yet again decided she needed to be watched, or protected, probably they wanted to see if she'd implicate herself in a crime. More likely it was that they thought she was their avenue to whoever they wanted to bring down. With the slight chance they genuinely didn't want something to happen to her—which would be all Jax.

Kenna told him about Santino taking her from outside the restaurant to his house. "Kind of like he just wanted to talk." She paused. "How he knew I'm in town, I have no idea. Maybe one of his guys spotted me."

"And he knew your father?"

She told him about the night she'd shown up at his house because her father hadn't come home in two days, and everything that happened. "I want to know who that man was," she added.

"You think it's connected to what's going on right now?"

"I doubt it," she said. "But I want to know who my dad shot in that kitchen."

"Okay." Just like that. No more explanation needed. "Description?"

"Dirty blond hair. I was thirteen, so my perception of his age and height are going to be off. He was shot, but he had other injuries. There was blood all down his face. I'll write down everything I remember and send it in an email."

"Focus on the case. Let me worry about this," Stairns said. "I'll find out who he was."

Kenna let out a long breath.

"Find anything today?"

"A gas station attendant told me Austin was looking for a girl, but I don't know who. Justine didn't mention a girlfriend."

"Maybe there's something on his computer. Social media, messaging. That kind of stuff."

"I'll pay her a visit tomorrow." Kenna rolled her shoulders. "There's definitely something she's not telling me."

"I'll call if I get anything."

"Thanks." Kenna hung up.

She glanced over at Jax, whose hands had relaxed by his sides. Even if he'd been pretending to sleep earlier, just to get her to let her defenses down, he was asleep for real now. She wasn't sure about his tendency to invade her life—and her personal space. Almost like he wanted to desensitize her to his presence. It was a tactic, but not one she normally employed.

She closed the lid of her computer, grabbed sweats and a T-shirt, and changed in the bathroom.

He knew who he was, and what he wanted. To be that sure of herself? She didn't know what it would feel like. Usually she just pushed off those worries for the sake of the case. Focusing on saving people was much better than dealing with her own issues. Though, that seemed to happen along the way.

Which, of course, didn't make her want to change anything.

Like moving back to Salt Lake City just to be near him. As if that wouldn't be the biggest mistake she'd ever made, jumping in after a relationship that was based on attraction. He'd never said he wanted any of that from her.

No way. Bad idea. Like making the first move, she'd be stepping off a cliff when she knew exactly what it felt like to hit the bottom.

Kenna got under the covers and lay there. She turned so she could see him in the light from the bathroom.

Jax was the kind of guy who didn't ask for much, while at the same time it seemed like he asked for everything he could get from her. Like whatever she gave him, he wanted her to give more. Trust. Openness. Partnership and the free exchange of information. She'd never had a friendship like that, on shared terms rather than just what she decided it was going to be. He wanted them to be equals, and it was disorienting.

The fact her heart was now getting involved didn't help. She had enough going on, and finding herself attracted to him was a distraction she didn't need. She had a case to work—and planned for that to be her reason forever. Okay, fine, it was an excuse.

What she needed was to find Maizie.

Kenna had to do *something*. The alternative was to be hamstrung by someone who thought they had power over her. She certainly wasn't going to get into a relationship beyond the professional. Or a solid friendship. More? Even the best relationships meant you gave part of yourself to the other person. That meant they had power over you, even if it was all in good ways, no matter what.

It was how relationships worked. You didn't come out unchanged, or without giving at least part of yourself away. Any woman who thought she could be an individual still, without sacrificing something, was kidding herself.

Things with Bradley hadn't been perfect, but they had

been good. It didn't factor into how things would be with Jax. Not when it was never going to happen. Kenna wasn't about relationships. She knew how it felt to lose *everything*.

For the first time in a long time, she fell asleep and didn't dream, comforted by the presence of someone she trusted and respected.

Her friend.

And that was all he would ever be.

Chapter Ten

Kenna waited until a couple of minutes after seven in the morning before essentially barging into the FBI special assignments morning meeting. "Sorry I'm late." She closed the hotel conference room door. "I wasn't invited, so I didn't know where to be."

Each of the men in the room turned to look at her. Jax kept his face completely impassive but didn't manage to hide the lack of surprise, which said more about what he thought than the shock from the rest of them.

Kenna stood by the door, surveying the room. All six FBI agents were clean-shaven, with short haircuts. Their clothing ranged from dark or gray suits to khakis and what her dad would have called a "Sunday" shirt. The room had little personality, except for the coffee station in the corner. But the tray of pastries and muffins was worth checking out.

"Kenna Banbury." The oldest man in the room was the FBI director, a guy she had never met before but whose pictures she had seen plenty of times. He rounded the back of Special Agent Torrow's chair.

Kenna winked at the Albuquerque agent.

"I'm Kenneth Billings." The FBI director held out his hand. His bald head barely came up to her nose. "Ken is fine."

Behind him, Jax lifted his brows for a second.

She shook his hand. "Nice to meet you, sir."

"I served with your father in the army. Good man."

She had no idea what to do with that information.

Thankfully, he turned and headed back to his chair, calling over his shoulder, "Have a seat, Ms. Banbury."

Kenna filled a mug of coffee and grabbed a muffin since she hadn't had breakfast. She'd come awake, aware there was someone in the shower in her motel room. After her mind caught up to who that would be, she'd fallen back asleep and woke up later to find Jax had already left. Given it was barely six in the morning at that point, she gathered he had a morning briefing meeting and set out to figure out when and where it would be.

One ride share to fetch her car and she'd headed here.

She needed to know if the FBI intended to protect her, or just keep an eye on her. Given the history between her and the Bureau, she wasn't going to be able to relax until she knew for sure which one it was.

The whole way here she'd been looking for a tail.

Whoever had been following her this morning? They were good enough she hadn't spotted them. Just an awareness of being observed.

She took a seat across from Jax, who was flanked by two agents she didn't know. "Elton, from the Denver office." He turned to his right. "And Nelson from Miami."

She smiled. "Nice to meet you both."

Special Agent Dean—the one she had met at a hotel in Albuquerque where he had helped her take down a deadly serial killer—sat closest to the director.

Between her and Dean sat Special Agent Torrow. He glanced over. "Good to see you."

"You, too." Last time that had been at the Hatchet prosecutor's office in New Mexico, where he had arrested the current prosecutor and the man's assistant. "Did you get anything from Burnam?"

Torrow shook his head. "Clammed up pretty fast. Took a plea deal to keep his mouth shut. What he should have done was testified in exchange for witness protection. He lasted a week in lockup before someone slit his throat."

Kenna winced. "So what's the deal here?" She glanced around at each of them. A chin lift to the two men she didn't know. "What is this special assignment about?"

Billings tipped his head to the side. "Special Agent Jaxton didn't read you in?"

"I believe I would need to be a consultant in order for an agent to disclose information about the case." She didn't look at Jax, but out of the corner of her eye, she was aware he didn't react. Whether he had told her about that CEO they were after or not didn't matter. What mattered was that the FBI's agenda was with her, and the organization she was trying to expose.

She didn't care if no one was convinced Jax had told her nothing.

"This special assignment falls under the guise of various different things, depending on who's asking. For the sake of clarity," Billings said, "our purpose is to take down the man we believe is the one who hired Ward Gaulding to bomb that church, kill all those people, and destroy all the evidence against him. Michael Rushman is the focus of this taskforce."

"What makes you believe he's the one behind it?"

"Six weeks ago I received a digital file via my personal email address. A recording, audio only, of Michael Rushman, the Hammerton Dickerson CEO, talking with another man regarding the fact he ordered the destruction of that church."

Having devoured her muffin, Kenna folded the paper wrapper in half, and then in half again, scoring the fold with her thumbnail.

"You see our dilemma."

"We need evidence we can substantiate," Jax said. "Which means we need to get into this guy's life and figure out his involvement."

"Any indication he wasn't working alone?" she said.

Elton from the Denver office and Nelson from Miami looked at each other.

Special Agent Dean said, "No one else is mentioned. Why do you think this is more than one person?"

She shifted in her chair to look at him. "Do you think that setup in Albuquerque, and the whole town of Hatchet, everyone involved in Bishopsville, and all the players between, have been commanded by one person? Seems to me it's more likely a group of powerful players that has been operating unchecked for some time."

Too bad her impression wasn't going to provide conclusive answers any more than their assumption it was one man.

Just like the FBI, she needed evidence in order to draw a conclusion. The question was, why the entire team wasn't laser focused on Michael Rushman. "Who is the weak link in Hammerton Dickerson that's your way into his life and his business?"

Billings almost smiled. "I'm so glad you asked that."

Kenna glanced at Jax. The corners of his mouth curled up just a fraction, but he pushed the amusement aside. The director had likely leaned on him to be the one to broach the subject with Kenna. Jax would make the request as colleagues who had worked together, although she hadn't been in the FBI at the time.

Would he really have leveraged their friendship in order to get her to work for the FBI on this case? She wouldn't have thought so, but then maybe she was wrong about him. Or the pressure he was under was too much.

Except he hadn't asked her.

He'd come after her when he thought she was kidnapped, attempted a rescue, and then stuck around all night, giving her the most restful sleep she'd had in several years.

Not that she was going to ask him to stay over in the other bed again.

Kenna intended to figure out her own life. Not to get sucked into a crutch. Just like having her friends back in her life, or having a dog again, she would only miss the companionship all the more when it was gone. Far better to never know what it would feel to have him stick around long term.

"Special Agent Torrow?" The director waved a hand.

She wondered at the choice. After Jax, Bodie Torrow was probably the only other agent in the room she would accept the sensitive request from. Did they know that in the heat of that crash, when the vehicle flipped, his gut reaction had been to grab Cabot to keep her from getting hurt? Had he been forced to explain why Kenna might be more amenable to a request from him than from anyone else other than Jax?

Jax leaned in front of Special Agent Dean. "In the course of our investigation, we have uncovered a proven connection between Michael Pushman and Anthony Santino." This time he lifted both hands, as though he could sit at this table and claim to have nothing to do with it.

"You know him?" The director paused. "We're only aware of a connection between him and your father."

"I saw him last night," Kenna replied, not wanting to

admit that she knew nothing about that particular relationship.

Billings' eyebrows rose. He glanced at Jax, chastisement in his expression.

Kenna didn't need questions. "The contents of the conversation are my business, and mine alone." Regardless of what the FBI wanted Jax to get from Kenna.

Torrow said, "We know that Santino was the owner of this specific hotel, as well as a few others in the chain. The guy is deeply mob connected, and there was nothing clean about the business."

She nodded, not surprised at all.

"Then, four years ago, Santino sells everything to a company that's a subsidiary of a sister company to Hammerton Dickerson."

Kenna flinched. "Rushman owns this hotel now?"

The director answered, "We think he strong-armed Santino into selling. We can't be sure, but that's where you come in. If he's at all disgruntled by the outcome, then it's possible he might—out of revenge—tell us what Michael Rushman is involved in. Santino could be the key to proving Rushman is the one behind the bombing."

"Why not just have voice analysis prove it's him on the recording?"

Jax shook his head. "It's not possible. Too much background noise and distortion."

There had been nothing about Michael Rushman in the packet Kenna had received from the dead lab technician, which she guessed originated from Maizie. If the FBI had received a similar packet—or one recording—had that come from her as well? And why not simply hand one person all the information? Most likely, someone had parsed out pieces of the case to different people.

Kenna did not like her choices, or her freedom, being taken from her. Not even to this extent. Although she understood it was a means to an end, she was being steered in a certain direction. By Maizie. Or someone else. The FBI, and even Stairns.

Someone occupied the spot behind the curtain. And if she didn't know who it was, then she couldn't be sure she trusted that person.

She sat back, holding the coffee mug in her hands. "You want me to flip Santino."

It wasn't a question because she already knew the answer.

A deadly organization, or one deeply connected CEO, might only be able to be taken down by getting someone to turn on him.

Like Santino.

Jax was the one who spoke. "Your prior relationship makes him already predisposed to listen to you." His face remained impassive, but she heard a faint tone in his voice. He'd seen Santino say goodbye to her the night before.

Despite the way Santino had brought her to his house, the conversation had been amicable. He'd even displayed a polite sort of care for her. Perhaps a desire for some kind of connection to his past.

She had no idea. But apparently, she was supposed to leverage it to get Santino to talk.

Torrow leaned in front of Dean again. "Do you think you can do it?"

"Oh, I can do it," Kenna said.

The question was whether she should. Or whether she wanted to.

One of those usually didn't factor, given her drive to solve cases. She wouldn't be working something if she didn't want to. The course of justice and being the kind of person who went after it was the "should." Which held more weight when she was the one who had to look at herself in the mirror every day.

If she didn't have integrity, then she didn't have anything.

Kenna shifted far enough to slide the cell phone from the clip on her belt at the small of her back. She thumbed through to the picture of Maizie and turned the screen around so the director could see. "You find her. I'll flip Santino."

He would be a means to an end. Despite the fact Kenna had no interest in spending more time with that man, she would do it for the sake of finding Maizie.

Billings frowned as he stared at her phone. He was about to speak when the door opened. Kenna had to twist all the way around but wasn't quick enough to see. Not before two Secret Service agents entered the room.

One lifted his wrist. "Clear." He kept a hand close to his holstered weapon as a suited man strode into the room on shiny shoes, an American flag pin on the lapel of his jacket.

The agents stood. Someone grunted, like a manly gasp, and Kenna set her phone facedown beside the neatly folded muffin wrapper and pushed her chair back, easing to her feet.

"Gentlemen. Director Billings." His gaze came to her. Former president Masonridge held out his hand. "Ms. Banbury."

Kenna shook with him. "Mr. President. How is Avery?"

"Alive, thanks to you." His face flushed with a smile of a father whose daughter had a mind of her own, though the smile didn't reach his eyes. "And well, thank you."

Kenna had heard that Avery Masonridge, the wild child first daughter, had decided to run for Florida's Senate seat. Given her drive to grab all of life with both hands and get as much out of it as possible, there was no doubt that even if she didn't win, she would give her opponent a run for their money. Kenna was all for a shakeup in the old guard of Washington bureaucracy.

She didn't plan on telling that to a former president now in his seventies.

Masonridge turned to Billings. "Are we still on for breakfast?"

"Right." The FBI director stood, smoothing down his tie. "Kenna, thank you for joining us. The rest of you? I'll await the report Special Agent Jaxton will send once you wrap up this meeting."

Jax nodded. "Yes, sir."

"Oliver Jaxton?" The former president strode around the table and stuck his hand out again. "Good to see you again, Son."

"You too, sir."

When he came back around the table, Masonridge stopped beside Kenna. "I trust you'll be at the ceremony the day after tomorrow?" He knew about the dedication?

"Right." She nodded. "That's coming up soon." Being forgetful was better than telling him she had no intention of being there. Unfortunately, she may have to quickly think of a reason she was in Las Vegas that had nothing to do with a case or the dedication of the new UNLV law building.

Masonridge patted her shoulder. "I'd like a minute of your time after the ceremony. So if your schedule allows, I'll have my assistant pencil you in."

"I'm sure I can make that work."

The former president and FBI director headed out, flanked by Secret Service agents, and the door clicked shut.

Kenna grabbed her mug and went for more coffee.

This entire trip to Vegas was getting more complicated by the minute.

Chapter Eleven

All the coffee in the world wouldn't solve her open cases. But Kenna was going to dream anyway because if she had no hope left inside her, she might as well give up. And that was far too similar to what Bradley had done the day she lost him.

Jax moved to stand close beside her.

Special Agent Dean said, "I'm guessing it usually happens that way with you in the room."

Kenna turned around. The other four FBI special agents were all staring at her, not talking. She looked at Dean. "Didn't you meet President Masonridge in Albuquerque also?"

"I'm not the one who saved his daughter's life." Dean shrugged. "I'm just the guy who arrested an old man and wrote a report about how his son was a serial killer."

"But it got you noticed. After all, the director pulled you in for this taskforce."

Special Agent Dean made a face. She got the impression that getting noticed and pulled in might not be something he considered career advancement. Maybe they all thought that.

Did every single one of these agents who had been drawn into this case feel as though they had no choice?

They'd each just stumbled upon something related—or stumbled upon her—and that meant there was less to explain if they were brought on this special assignment.

She glanced at Jax, figuring she knew the answer but needing to ask anyway, "Who's in charge while the director is at breakfast?"

Jax shrugged. "We all have to do things in public that give the impression we're here for a different reason than a case."

"And yours is stalking me into having dinner with you?"

Torrow snorted. "That would be better than having to watch people play golf." He shuddered. "So boring."

Elton, the agent from Denver, said, "So you all saved the former president's daughter's life? But what did I do to deserve being pulled away from my family and my open investigations?"

"Vegas not your thing?" Jax said.

"I was in the middle of a case, about to wrap up the entire thing. I had to hand it all off to a couple of guys in my office, and we had a bet going over who would solve their case first."

Considering her theory about everyone being connected to this, she wasn't sure what to make of his comment. There were people in this room she trusted, no question. Others, she trusted what she knew of them and no more. Elton and the other guy, Nelson from Miami, were the two unknowns.

Jax told Kenna, "Why don't you show me that picture you have of her?"

Elton made a face. "Yeah, Special Agent *Not-in-Charge* Jaxton. You go ahead and take charge."

"Cut it out." Dean lifted his chin. "We won't be here long, and then we can return to our real jobs."

Elton just shook his head.

Kenna handed her phone to Jax. "Type in your email address." She pointed to the screen. "It will send her photo to you." But it wasn't just one young person she was trying to find—it was two. "And the other teen I'm trying to find."

When he was done, he lifted his head. A disgruntled look on his face.

Recently he'd been dating a police detective in Salt Lake City that she'd met a few times. The relationship might have fizzled out, or never gone anywhere in the first place, but she didn't exactly want to drag it back up. Then Jax had gone on an undercover mission and found the man coerced into bombing that church. When they met up, he'd been on the run, and she got swept up in the wake of it all.

Now she had no camper van and no car—just the beater she was currently driving—and she'd had to go under the radar. No contact.

She glanced at each of them. "Too many people have died already. I've been trying to root out the problem quietly without making enough waves that mean we end up on the highway being hit by a projectile." The day she met Torrow and took down that serial killer with Special Agent Dean. "Again."

The day a priest had been murdered. Stairns had almost died.

"Now I walk in here, and there's an entire taskforce of you." She glanced around at each of them. "Looking into this got Thomas from the Salt Lake City office killed."

When someone started to ask, Jax said, "Our lab technician."

"He gave his life for this case, whether he intended to or not." She set her coffee down without finishing it. "If it was the work of Michael Rushman, then fine. He's going to answer for what he's done. If it's more than that, and the FBI director is just kidding himself that this is an-open-and-shut case. And it's important to figure out which it is."

Jax glanced at her. He said nothing, but she got the impression he agreed with her. If he spoke the agreement aloud, it put him on her side against whichever special agent in here wanted to disagree. And would pit him against his boss, the guy who could torpedo Jax's entire career.

If he sided with her, he could lose everything.

The realization hit her like a freight train. All at once, in a way that made her remember why she disliked having feelings. Why she had insisted with Bradley that they be friends for so long before they became a couple. Not just because they were FBI agent partners.

Kenna had learned the hard way what connection could do when it was torn away.

She blew out a breath. "I need to get back to working on my open cases. If that means getting Santino to flip on Rushman out of revenge for costing him his businesses, then fine. But I've got to figure out a way in, and that's going to take time."

Her phone rang before she could finish her "I'm leaving now" speech.

The number on the screen belonged to Justine. Kenna answered. "What's up?"

"Have you found out anything about Austin yet? I'm just freaking out." Justine sucked in a couple of audible breaths. "I can't stop thinking about what might be happening to him."

"I get it." Kenna wanted to walk out and take this call in private, but she also needed to ensure the FBI would look for Maizie—and hopefully Austin as well—once she went to work on the Santino side of their case. "I know it's hard, but you just have to give it time. I already found an attendant at a gas station who said he saw Austin after you lost track of him. He was looking for someone. A girl?"

"They said that?"

"Yes," Kenna said. "And I met up with some people I trust. They're going to help us find Austin, okay?"

"I thought it was going to be just you. Isn't that what you do, working alone all the time?"

When they'd first met, that was exactly what Kenna had been doing. And planned to do forever. However, even her father had paired up with other people—or whole departments—when necessary. He either worked for them as a consultant or joined the team. Like the time they had done search and rescue in Wisconsin for a summer. Tracking down a guy who had been taking children from their bedrooms in the middle of the night.

"Having help is a good thing, Justine."

"I'm not sure. I'm just so worried I can't think straight." Her voice was breathy.

"I need you to try and remember anything else about what he was doing or where he might've been going."

Justine whimpered. "I don't know anything. I don't even know what you're asking me."

"Okay, then I have a hard question for you." One that Kenna needed the answer to, preferably sooner rather than later. "Who is Austin's father?"

"Why would that be relevant?"

"Even though you may not want it, that might be helpful information for me to have." As Kenna spoke, Jax moved to his computer. She watched him pull up the photos she had sent of Maizie, and the one of Austin, and drag them into the FBI's facial recognition database.

He ran a search on Maizie first.

The other special agents did similar things, getting on

their devices or talking to each other. Kenna was just glad they weren't only standing there staring at her, listening to everything she said. Not that they would be able to tune it out completely.

When Justine said nothing, Kenna asked again, "Who is Austin's father?"

"Okay, fine. His father lives in Vegas, which is the only reason I'm telling you. Because you can rule it out quickly, and you'll know he had nothing to do with this. His name is Deacon Frost."

Kenna blinked. "Deacon Frost."

Jax turned to face her and straightened.

Kenna waved him aside from the computer and typed in the name of Austin's father. Immediately an arrest photo from years back popped up. She scanned the information and put together the puzzle pieces in her mind till it all clicked together.

"The same Deacon Frost who used to work for Anthony Santino?" Kenna had remembered Deacon from her dream enough to ask Santino about him. He didn't work for the boss anymore, but she recalled that he'd let her in the house.

"I-I guess," Justine said. "He never really told me much about what he did. We weren't together long, and we didn't really keep in touch after." She gasped. "I don't see why it's relevant."

"Is there anything that makes you willing to consider that Deacon contacted Austin? Or maybe Austin sought out his father?" Kenna had to rule it out—just like Justine had said. The question was whether the other FBI agents who were going to work her missing persons cases would write Austin off as a wayward teen who just hadn't called his mom in a few days. Hopefully they would actually follow through.

"Austin doesn't even know Deacon. He doesn't remember

him, and he wouldn't know how to start asking how to find him." Justine let out a breath. "Austin is the one who told me not to bother even thinking about his dad. He said it didn't matter who he was, or where he was, because he'd never cared about us, so we shouldn't waste a second caring about him."

"Okay." Kenna ran a hand through her hair.

If Deacon had nothing to do with Austin's disappearance, that was one thing. But the collision of the pieces of everything she was investigating right now couldn't be ignored. There were connections cropping up where statistically that was highly unlikely. Even having multiple cases, Kenna wouldn't normally suspect each open investigation to connect to all the others she was currently working.

And yet, that seemed exactly like what was happening.

Because of pure chance...or by design?

Justine sniffed. "I just want my baby back. I don't care where he is, or what happened to him. I just need to know he's all right."

"Do you have any idea who he was looking for?"

Justine was quiet for a few seconds.

"Did he have a girlfriend? Anyone he cared about enough to try and seek her out?"

"He was looking for someone. I don't even know where he was looking." Justine started to cry, loud enough that Kenna wasn't able to ask her another question.

"Please talk to me," Kenna pressed. "I need all the information you have if I'm going to be able to find him." She then strode away from the table, trying to pace out her frustration over all the unanswered questions. "Why don't you tell me where you are. I'll come to you, and we can talk about this face-to-face. That's better than being on the phone, isn't it?"

"I'm staying in the Bergamot Hotel." Justine gave her a room number.

Of course she is.

Kenna wrote down the information on a notepad Jax handed to her. As soon as she was done, he tore the top page off and handed it to Special Agent Dean. "Take Elton with you. Go." To Justine, she said, "I'm going to do everything I can to find him. It's going to take help, but it's okay to let people help you when you need it."

Jax shot her a look, probably because he'd tried to convince her of something similar not long after they met.

Justine sniffed. "You don't understand. There are things... I can't..."

The line went dead.

Kenna lowered the phone and looked at it. "She hung up on me."

Jax squeezed her shoulder. "You did good talking to her. Elton and Dean will be up there soon." He paused for a split second. "She's really staying at this hotel?"

"At this point I'm not sure anything is capable of surprising me."

"Found this Maizie person. But you aren't going to like it." Bodie Torrow motioned with his hand for her to come over. She moved to stand behind him worse she could see over his shoulder. "Is this your girl?" He pointed at the screen.

"Is that what I think it is?" Jax voiced the question, looking over her shoulder as she looked over Torrow's.

"She's on a list," Torrow said. "The lost ones, the ones law enforcement wishes they could find but probably never will. She pops up all over porn sites. Child exploitation, coming up in collections of material that's been seized. Images we will probably never identify in a way that means we can locate these children who were victimized."

Kenna said, "What do you mean 'the lost ones'?"

Jax shifted beside her. "It's not that we aren't looking for them. It's that there is little hope we'll ever be able to find them. They're the ones we say a prayer for."

"That's not good enough." If she got on this mission, Kenna would end up devoting her entire life to bringing home missing children. She would drown in cases like these. "And Maizie isn't one of them."

The girl she was looking for had reached out to her. She'd made contact.

She wasn't going to be lost forever.

Jax said, "Sometimes prayer is the most power you can have because you leave it in God's hands. But in order to do that, you have to let go of it."

She stared at him, her lips pressed into a fine line to keep her from saying something that might be the truth of how she felt but which she would regret later. It was just the heat of the moment, a gut reaction to the fear. The full knowledge of exactly what kids like that went through and how it felt to be alone and powerless.

If God was going to move, then He needed to do it now. But when did He ever listen to what she thought was best?

Special Agent Torrow said, "I'm not sure we're even going to be able to figure out what her name is or where she came from."

"We found a missing person's report from years ago but couldn't trace the parents. It was just an age-regressed photo, so we don't even know for sure if it was her."

"So she could be anyone."

"She's Maizie." Before they could try and convince her she needed to embrace reality, Kenna said, "What about Austin? Did you run him or his dad?"

"We'll find out if they've had contact," Jax said. "Or if Deacon Frost has anything to do with Austin's disappearance."

Special Agent Nelson, who'd been quiet since Elton and Dean left the room, leaned back in his chair. "You said the mom's name was Justine?" When Kenna nodded, he said, "Austin comes up as Austin Greene, and the mother is listed as his next of kin. That's who I have here on his Nevada driver's license. But here's where it gets weird."

Kenna waited. Jax moved around to look at Nelson's screen, his expression hard in a way she thought might be on her behalf. Along with the part of him torn over care for her and loyalty to the FBI. She didn't want him to feel that. Kenna needed a moment to tell him he didn't need to worry about her.

"I ran the mom's name, and she doesn't show up anywhere under the name Justine Greene." Nelson shrugged. "It has to be a fake ID. But I found a social media account, and I pulled her photo. Ran that through facial recognition. It gave me a couple of shadow social media accounts that aren't connected to anything else. One of them is a Russian site."

Kenna couldn't even absorb everything. It was all changing so fast. "Explain what that means."

Jax looked up at her. "The dead Russian diplomat, the one whose cold case you're trying to solve?"

"We're talking about two missing teens and a mom with a shady background. How does my cold case tie in?" Kenna sighed. "I need to get to work."

A connection to Maizie was flimsy at best. She had been reeling since she got to Vegas, one hit after the other. At least she didn't have to think about her father anymore. There was enough going on in the present to deal with, and Stairns was looking into who the man might've been that her father shot in Santino's kitchen that night.

The last thing she wanted to do was actually ask Santino. Though, if that helped solidify a rapport, allowing her to broach the subject of him flipping on Rushman, she would do it.

Jax replied, "Justine is the connection between the organization and Dmitri Alekhin."

Kenna stumbled to a chair and sank into it. "What on earth is happening?"

She'd been brought here by someone powerful enough to pull them all together. *Cerberus*. Kenna's actions had been directed for months now, and she had to wonder if it wasn't all so she would end up here.

Now.

Nelson said, "She was hired out to the Russian."

"She's not that much older than me. She'd have been—"

Nelson cut her off. "Barely legal." He showed her a photo of a much younger Justine in a shiny gown.

A phone rang.

Jax put it to his ear. "Jaxton." He frowned. "Thanks." Hung up. "She isn't there. Justine is gone."

Chapter Twelve

Kenna slammed her car door shut. "Still following me?"

"Seems to me like you're the one following me." Jax motioned to the white building she'd parked in front of, a newer condo complex where Deacon Frost lived. "Aren't you supposed to be working on Santino?"

Kenna had debated that exact thing on the way over here. She'd copied down the address for Austin's father, the guy who used to work for Santino years ago. The one who had answered the door when she showed up at the house looking for her father.

Why not stop by and see if he'd had a visit from Austin, or knew what had happened to him?

Kenna shrugged. "If I show back up at Santino's too soon, he'll just see through it. I'll have to work twice as hard to figure out how to get him to roll over on Bushman."

"Or, you're just avoiding it, and as soon as you ask him, Santino will jump on the chance to screw the guy over."

She glanced at the apartment complex from behind her sunglasses.

"What's the hesitation? I know you want to find those two

teens, but that's why I've got all four FBI agents back at the hotel working on finding leads. This special assignment has now become a hunt for Austin and your friend Maizie."

Kenna didn't want to explain that they'd actually never met, or even spoken.

Maizie was a photo in a high school database. An image—one of innocence. Not like what Torrow had found online, a showcase of all the ways Maizie had been victimized. Kenna had no idea what kind of life this girl had lived, whether she was in dire need of rescue now. Or if she simply wanted out, like Justine had.

Jax said, "We are going to find them."

"I hope that's true."

"What do you normally fall back on when things get bad?"

Kenna leaned against the side of her car. "When all I have are questions or worry, I fall back on what I know to be true." She wondered if Austin was inside the apartment with his father—and if he was, what state he was in. But she couldn't live her life in a panic when she had no reason to believe he was in imminent danger. "Austin is missing, but there is no reason to believe in an active threat to his life. Not from what I've found so far. That would only be fear driving me to rush in when it might be better for me to be cautious."

Jax shifted and leaned against the car beside her shoulder.

"I know what I can do. I know what I know, and what I'm capable of finding out. So it's just a case of putting one foot in front of the other." She pushed off the car and turned to him. "Like not standing around here when we could be asking Deacon if he knows where his son is."

She set off for the main doors, assuming Jax would be right behind her. She didn't want to unpack the reality that he had chosen to do the same thing as her. It just meant that their investigative tactics were born out of the same training.

One day she would hit the point where she'd been a private investigator for longer than she was ever an FBI agent.

Where she would have to realize that it had been longer since she'd had Bradley in her life than the period they were together—or the length of time they'd known each other. Where she wouldn't have to contemplate the fact that she'd had a promising career, a guy in her life that she loved and who loved her, and a baby on the way. Sure, they'd done things a little out of order, but it would have worked out in the end. Bradley had even been talking to her about the two of them running down to this city and getting married.

She remembered when he'd told her, walking out of a witness interview, that he'd made a reservation at a wedding chapel.

How had she forgotten that?

Kenna paused at the door and glanced over in the direction of the Strip. If he'd lived, they would have come down here and got married.

But why mourn the life she should have had and forget to live?

Why wish for a father who would never have done what hers did, rather than being grateful for the kind of man who kept her safe from so much?

"You okay?" Jax grabbed the door above her head and held it open.

Kenna stepped into the terra cotta tile entryway. A bank of elevators and a set of stairs filled the small lobby, flanked by rows of mailboxes. Someone had cranked up the air-conditioning. Shivering, she tugged her suit jacket tighter around her and crossed her arms.

She shook her head. "I don't know what it is about this town, but it's spinning me out."

"Stairs?"

She nodded. "He's on the second floor."

But Jax didn't let her go on without having the conversation. He followed close behind her as they headed up the stairs. "You have a lot going on. Two missing people you're worried about, and this whole business with Santino. All of it to take down the organization."

If Austin's disappearance was even connected.

"I just don't get how the FBI director is so sure it's Michael Rushman." She grabbed the rail on the first landing, but it was sticky. "Unless it was Maizie who sent him the recording. That's literally the only way I would believe it's for real."

"A teenager you've never met, who may not even be that person. It could just be someone else using that photo."

"I understand how online scams work." She sighed. "Maybe it's Rushman, or someone in his employ, stringing me along. Not everything I've received so far has put me one step closer to uncovering the organization and who's behind it."

The idea it was a single person and not a collective wasn't something that convinced Kenna of its veracity. She'd need proof beyond a confession that a single entity orchestrated all of this.

She rounded the first-floor landing. "Maybe he did order the bombing of that church, but that only makes him complicit. It doesn't make him the beginning and end of this entire case."

"I can understand the FBI director wanting it to be tied up neatly in a bow."

"But when has any case ever turned out like that? Something always throws a wrench in the works."

"Or a bear."

She paused on the next step and turned to him. "You had a case get complicated because of a bear?"

He nodded. "I'll tell you about it another time. Maybe over dinner."

"You know, if you didn't do so much exercise then you wouldn't require so much food."

"What fantastic advice." He drawled the words out. "You've just destroyed two entire industries."

"Speaking of scams..."

Probably they should unpack the whole thread of conversation they'd just had and reach an amenable conclusion, but unfortunately they were at the door. There was no time.

Kenna lifted her fist and knocked on the door. Jax stood out of the way to one side, tugging out his badge. It didn't bother her that she no longer had one. That wasn't part of her identity anymore, just part of a painful past. She could have pulled out her private investigators license, but once again she was one signature away from being an FBI consultant.

"I better be getting paid VIP consulting fees," she said.

He shot her a look. "Take that up with the director."

The door swung open.

On the other side stood a tall man, though not as tall as she remembered. He wore boxer shorts, a white tank top, tube socks, and black slides. His hair was disheveled, and he had a full chin of gray stubble.

"Special Agent Oliver Jaxton." Jax held up his badge. "We have a couple of questions for you if that's okay."

Deacon Frost looked at her.

"I'm with him." Kenna thumbed over her shoulder. "But I don't have a badge."

"So you guys can play good cop, bad cop, and I can't do

anything about it because you're not a fed." The guy shifted his weight, about to close the door.

"Do you know a teen boy named Austin Green?" she asked. "His mother is Justine."

At Kenna's question, hardness crossed Deacon's face. "What about him?"

"Do you have much contact with your son?"

"How about none at all. And that's exactly the way it's going to be, though it doesn't stop her from demanding child support every month."

"So you haven't seen him lately?"

"I just said no. Why would I?" He had to be in his fifties now. The lines on his face indicated he'd spent time in the sun, which hadn't been so much the case when he worked for Santino.

Justine must have been young when she had Austin. Which made Kenna wonder how she'd gone from an escort to diplomats to the girlfriend of a low-level guy in Santino's employ. Austin was born a couple of years before Kenna had met Santino.

Then again, the pictures of Dmitri and Justine might've been after Austin had been born.

It was Jax who said, "Has Justine been in contact with you at all? Maybe about where Austin might be, or how he might've gone missing?"

Deacon shifted. "He's missing?"

So the guy wasn't entirely without at least some care for his son. In her experience that wasn't unexpected. Even the most hardened criminal had a weakness somewhere—someone they cared for. Otherwise, they were no different than the sociopaths who killed for pleasure, or to feel something at all.

The businessmen and criminals she had met who thought

nothing of betraying a rival, or taking out someone who had wronged them, all seemed to possess some kind of loyalty. Even if it was only their will, their way. Most of the ones she had met had families that cared for them, at least to the extent they were able to feel love for someone else.

Deacon blew out a breath. "She was having an affair before she even gave birth to Austin, and she split a few months later." He shrugged. "I have no idea who the guy was, before you ask me that."

Kenna wondered if he knew about Justine's occupation, or the C tattoo on her forearm and what it meant. "You used to work for Anthony Santino, didn't you?"

"So?" Deacon eyed her. "Is that why you look familiar?"

She may as well explain. She didn't need him looking into her life or digging anything up. Asking Stairs to do it was one thing—and a whole lot less risky if he found something that didn't need to become public. "Max Banbury."

Deacon frowned, as though thinking it through. Then he said, "Kenna?" When she nodded, he barked a laugh. "Ha. No way." He looked her up and down. "You turned out pretty good."

Kenna shifted her weight from one foot to the other. "To your knowledge, what was the relationship between Anthony Santino and Michael Rushman?"

"Huh. That might've been after my time." He scratched his jaw. "I'm not sure I know they ever had any dealings with each other."

Kenna didn't believe it. And what else was he lying about? "How long has it been since you worked for Santino?" After all, it had been four years since Santino sold the hotel to Rushman's corporation.

"Almost a decade." Deacon made a face. "After Santino tried to recruit your dad ahead of all of us, there wasn't much reason to stick around. A guy should just hire from within, ya know? Rather than trying to turn your dad into some kind of right-hand man."

Kenna wanted to argue about that, but the truth was, she didn't know for sure. She remembered events back then through the eyes of a thirteen-year-old. Not a bystander, or a participant. Just a teen trying to figure out what she needed or wanted.

Jax asked, "Do you ever have any contact with Santino these days?"

Deacon snorted. "We hardly run in the same circles now."

The phone started ringing from inside the apartment.

Deacon shifted. "We're done here." Before either Kenna or Jax could argue, he slammed the door in their faces.

"Okay, then." Kenna turned to Jax.

"More to unpack," he said. "Things to go over and discuss."

She frowned. "Didn't you do that the first day we met? I recall you tried to get us all to have burgers by the police precinct."

He closed his mouth and headed for the stairs.

"Well, I know you don't like coffee, so that's out," she said, following him.

"I like coffee. I just don't drink it that much."

Kenna glanced over as they descended. "And you think we can be friends? Or is this about slowly getting me to better myself or something?"

"Because I have nothing else to do with my time but create a personal mission that gets you in a healthy place?"

"I *am* in a healthy place." She pressed her hand to the buttons of her shirt, strategically ignoring the gunshot scars from months ago. Too bad she could barely choke out the words, "I'm fine."

"You have no home, no dog, and no way to solve this case."

"It's *cases*. You misspoke." And did he have to rub it in that Cabot wasn't here? Just because he wasn't a dog person.

"That's why I'm here."

She stared at him while he stared back. "Like you want me to have you, since I have nothing else?"

Standing at the bottom of the stairs with him one step down made them eye level. Anything either of them said or did right now would put them one step closer or move them away from each other.

His phone rang.

He answered it, taking a step back so she would come with him and they could head to the door. "Special Agent Jaxton." He pushed the door open but paused. "We'll be right there."

When he hung up, she said, "What is it?"

"Austin's cell phone records were sent over from his phone provider. We use that to get info for the person he talks to most—a girl he was in high school with before they broke for summer."

"Okay." So why did he look so concerned?

"When we ran her home address, it popped. The police department had a call about a disturbance last night. The girl got attacked."

Chapter Thirteen

"You know, it would be more environmentally friendly if we carpooled."

Kenna glanced over at the spot where Jax leaned against the wall. As if she needed to be near all that for extended periods? It was bad enough just in this elevator. Carpooling sounded like a terrible idea.

The doors slid open, and she stepped out onto the fifth floor of the hospital into an ocean of activity. Medical staff walking around in all directions. Nurses in scrubs, doctors in white coats over their street clothes. Civilians going in and out of the waiting area.

The receptionist downstairs had already told Jax what room Olivia Sanderson was in. Jax went ahead of her, and Kenna got a brief reprieve from his attention as they headed for the room. He knocked politely, and when someone called out, "Coming," he stepped inside with Kenna right behind him. He introduced them both to the teen and her mom.

The young girl in the bed seemed far too much like the victims in Bishopsville, but Kenna didn't know for sure that was what happened to this one. Blond hair hung forward, covering both sides of her face. The color of her irises was only visible in the left eye, the other swollen completely shut. The whole right side of her face was mostly purple with bruising. Olivia had bandages on both hands.

Her mom sat in the chair beside the bed, though she got up to shake Jax's hand.

Kenna tuned them out and moved to the side of the bed. "Hey."

The young girl turned her head, using her good eye to look at Kenna. "I already talked to the cops."

"That's good. Talking to the police is really important. It can help them find the person who did this to you." Kenna leaned against the side of the bed. "That's not the reason we're here. We're working on a different case, but can I ask? Did you see who did this to you?"

Moisture collected in Olivia's good eye. "I fell asleep doing my homework, and when I woke up, he was in my room." She glanced at her mom and shared a look Kenna couldn't decipher.

Kenna needed a way to jog her back out of the memory. "Homework? In the summer?"

The girl nodded. "Summer school. I'm taking a college class so I can get my associates when I graduate high school."

"Wow. That's pretty impressive. You must work really hard." Justine had said Austin was doing the same thing. The only reason to take summer classes was failing or boredom—so which was it?

The mom moved to the other side of the bed, blushing. "She does work hard." Then laid a hand on the girl's shoulder. "She works extremely hard."

"Can I ask you about something else?" Kenna waited for a second. The mom let Olivia answer with a nod, so Kenna continued. "Do you know Austin Greene?"

Olivia nodded, though only slightly, as though it still hurt. "We're lab partners in chemistry. He's actually supposed to be taking biology in summer school so he can graduate next year, but my friend Sherrie, who's in that class, said he never showed up."

Mom got a plastic cup of water from the bedside table, and Olivia took a sip.

"When was the last time you saw Austin?" Kenna asked.

"Like a week ago. Maybe longer than that." Olivia paused. "Why? Did something happen to him as well?"

"I met Austin in New Mexico before he moved here. His mom asked me to try and find him because she hasn't seen him in a couple of days."

Olivia sniffed. "If something happened to him, it was probably because of his mom. I bet she did something to him."

"What makes you say that?" Kenna leaned closer.

"She's crazy. He told me some of the things she does, but like it was normal. I had to tell him there's nothing about her that's normal." Olivia glanced at her mom, then back at Kenna. "I don't know what's wrong with her, though."

They should table that part of the discussion, as all the information was only hearsay and speculation. Not that she knew Justine better than what Austin said to a friend about her. She needed more information rather than a discussion about what may or may not be the case with Justine. Still, the fact that Deacon had a similar opinion of her was beginning to color Kenna's view.

"Olivia, do you have any idea what Austin was doing recently?" Kenna paused. "Or where he might have gone?"

"Is he actually missing?" The girl's eyebrows rose.

Kenna nodded.

"He told me he was looking for someone, but it seemed to me like it's one of those stories his mom tells that aren't true.

She wrapped him up in her drama so they're both codependent. You know?"

Kenna wanted to say, *do you?*

"He couldn't do anything without her permission. He didn't even want to go out with me because he knew she would make him bring me over to the house so she can meet me. And he said it wasn't a good idea because she would tell him he couldn't hang out with me."

The mom bristled.

"Do you know why?" Kenna asked.

"Probably because she doesn't want him hanging out with anyone except her. She's like, super obsessive about him and her being just the two of them against the world, you know?"

"Okay." Kenna sighed. "Do you know who he might've been looking for?"

"It didn't make any sense. He said he was looking for his sister, but then he also told me he was an only child." Olivia shook her head. "He said he doesn't know her name right now. He's never met her, but he said she was older than him. How is he going to find her?"

"Have you ever seen a picture of the sister?"

"We were just texting. He didn't send it to me or anything." A tear ran from her eye. "Is he really missing?"

Kenna nodded. "I'm sorry."

"Maybe his sister doesn't want to be found. But his mom has got him all twisted around like he has to do this or he's not really her son. She's a total witch." Olivia glanced at her mom, who just patted her on the shoulder. "He was texting me, and he said someone was following him. I tried to help, but he told me to leave it alone."

When she trailed off, Kenna nodded. "Thank you for telling me all that." She paused a second. "Last night, did that man say anything to you?"

The mom stiffened. "We were out. He just hurt her and left. Thank God."

Kenna guessed that meant he only beat her and didn't rape her. "He was trying to scare you. It's okay if it worked." Kenna gave Olivia a second to process what she was saying. "It's okay to be scared, but don't let the fear swallow you up. Then they've won."

Olivia nodded.

Kenna glanced at the mom, then back at her. "It gets easier, but you've gotta be patient with it."

Before it got deeper than she wanted it to, Kenna headed out with Jax in her wake.

He stepped beside her at the elevator and hit the button to go down, even though she'd already pressed it. Apparently, the light didn't work. "You do a really good job in situations like that, with kids and victims."

"You would think I'd be able to see through someone like Justine." Kenna didn't even want to contemplate being so wrong about someone she'd considered just as much of a victim as any of the others. Except that Justine had survived —and she had been used the way many of the missing young women in Bishopsville had before they were released.

"You think they're right, and she's been lying to you?"

"It's not impossible. No one in the world is immune to being duped." The elevator doors opened, and Kenna stepped inside, glad two people were heading down as well. "But if she thinks she can get away with not telling the truth...?"

Jax nodded.

The elevator descended.

Kenna had honestly spent more time with Austin than with Justine. Were the two of them really enmeshed in a toxic relationship Justine had forged? It could only be Olivia's interpretation. And who knew what life experiences skewed her perception of other people's situations or her own?

Olivia could have a completely warped frame of reference. The way a lot of people who had suffered childhood trauma did.

Go, Kenna. Run.

She let out a long sigh, not liking that Justine had been manipulating or lying to her this entire time. If Justine's intention for calling Kenna to help find Austin was nothing but a cover for what she had done—a way to throw off the police and make them believe she might not have hurt him—then Justine didn't think Kenna was likely to find him.

Maybe because she knew exactly where he was. Or, Justine didn't think Kenna would ever figure out what happened to him.

They stepped off the elevator.

Jax said, "Whatever Justine is up to, it doesn't bode well for Austin."

The automatic doors opened, and they headed outside into the heat of the day. Kenna didn't mind warmth, but wearing black pants and a black suit jacket made her warm up. Even if it was a good way to conceal her weapons.

Kenna glanced at him. "Don't you have an office to run in Salt Lake City, Mr. Special Agent in Charge?" She'd heard he got that promotion, but it was before she saw him in New Mexico. As far as she knew, he had taken over Stairs' job at the FBI office there.

"Your ability to deflect knows no bounds."

"Kind of like your ability to ignore the need to fill me in on things I should know."

"Like my job status?"

Oh, there *was* something there. "Spill."

He sighed and came to a stop beside her car. "I gave up

the Special Agent in Charge position. It was a lateral move, but I had to choose when I went undercover. I could either stick around and run the department in Salt Lake City or solve this case. Considering the FBI director got involved, and he was able to sign off on it, I was on the special assignment roster even before I went to Mexico looking for Ward Gaulding."

"A lateral move." She paused. "Where you are no longer the Special Agent in Charge, you're back to being a regular Supervisory Special Agent?"

"I don't want to be the boss," he said. "I want to be out on the street solving cases. I'm not ready to get stuck behind a desk constantly pushing papers."

"You applied for the job. You got the job."

"Closing this case is more important." Jax rolled his shoulders, probably forcing himself not to fold his arms, which would look defensive. "I handed the position back, and they gave it to their next choice, Special Agent Miller, who is now running the office."

"You know how much I love that guy." Kenna might have told the people she'd worked with at the Salt Lake City FBI office what had happened the night Bradley died. But that didn't mean she would be friends with them, even if she returned to Utah and stayed there.

"He's not a bad boss. And I haven't been there much, anyway."

"You're citing my business—my case—as the reason you're tanking your career."

"That's not what this is. I'm not ready for that position."

"You'd rather be undercover, on your own with no backup?" That was how she'd run into him in New Mexico. She'd saved his butt, and they both knew it.

"We aren't going to agree on this issue. I'm here to do my

job on this special assignment. I'm here to solve cases, just like you."

"Just as long as I'm not one of them."

Jax lifted both hands but said nothing. All but admitting they were at an impasse.

Kenna took a step back. "I'll see you later."

Thankfully he didn't stop her. She pulled out of her space and drove away while he stood there, hands on his hips, watching her leave. Kenna wanted to slam her hand on the steering wheel and let out some of this frustration. Given the injury to her arms, that would be more painful than it was worth.

She didn't need a guy walking into her room and dumping his bag on the floor. Insinuating himself into her life.

Instead of stewing over it, going around and around, she called Stairs. As soon as he picked up, she said, "Who is Austin Greene's sister?"

"Is everything okay?"

She didn't know what to do next, and all she had was a bunch of frustration. "Just tell me what you know that I don't so I can figure out something to do."

"Didn't Maizie send you a whole packet that included a cold case for you to solve?"

Kenna frowned. "That's an excellent point." Who cared about Michael Rushman and whether or not he was behind all of this? The only person who had given her solid information so far had pointed her toward the death of the Russian diplomat. "Why don't you give me the information for that mystery solving group people keep talking about? What was it called? Intellection?"

"Intellectus. I'll text you the address."

"Thanks." She didn't want to visit Santino, not in the mood she was in. There was nothing about her manner right now that was going to inspire the man to cooperate. Even if he wanted to, he'd probably object on principle when she rolled in with her frustration flashing like a neon sign.

Kenna followed her phone GPS to an older end of Las Vegas, and an aging church building. Huge rough bricks and colored glass. Some of it had been boarded up, though maybe only because the glass had been broken. It seemed to have been a coffee shop at one point but now had a sign outside with the name of the mystery group in big letters, with a local phone number underneath.

She headed up the walkway to the front door, which proved to be unlocked.

Inside was a front desk, a bar-height counter with no one sitting behind it. Community posters had been pinned up on one wall, and a row of uncomfortable-looking chairs ran underneath. Like the lobby of a doctor's office in a rough neighborhood.

She looked around. As she was doing that, an inside door opened. Several people emerged. One tripped and someone else caught her. An old man grunted and all of them blinked.

The woman whispered, her eyes wide behind orange rimmed glasses, "You're Kenna Banbury."

Chapter Fourteen

The older man turned and disappeared back into the hall. That left Kenna with the woman wearing an oversized T-shirt and leggings and those orange glasses. She could've been a librarian except her outfit might be more suited to cheering a middle school track competition. The T-shirt logo caught Kenna's attention. *Utah True Crime.*

The man beside her looked like a rougher version of one of those TV doctors—and he knew it. Tight T-shirt that clung to his biceps. Canvas shoes and bare ankles below the hem of his khakis. "Kenna Banbury. Really?" He strode to her.

"I really am."

"Ben Landers." He squeezed her hand. Hard. "I've been part of this group for two years, helped solve a couple of crimes so far."

Kenna smiled. "That's great." But he needed to let go of her hand. She jerked it back, fast as she could. Pain roiled through her forearm. She stuck her fingertips in the pockets of her pants because that was all that fit.

The woman squealed in delight. She enveloped Kenna in a squishy hug that smelled like vanilla. "I'm Elaine Reardon.

I'm the librarian here, and at a few of the smaller middle schools in the district." She stepped back.

"You have a library?"

Elaine beamed. "Come and see."

Ben headed out first, striding like a renowned surgeon down the hall. Elaine padded a little slower on her white tennis shoes.

The walls were lined with movie posters, most of them Max Banbury books turned into films. They passed an office and bathrooms. At the end, Kenna pulled up short. "I haven't seen this one."

"Comes out next month. It's the series where he works with that private security team." Elaine tapped the frame, a lone man shadowed in smoke and darkness. Beside him, the silhouette of a woman.

In the context of her father solving crime, Kenna didn't want to think about a femme fatale *ever*. Especially not what they got up to between the sheets while the investigator character tried to put together whether or not she was telling the truth.

"And if I were to tell you it doesn't resemble what really happened in any way?" Kenna had tried—for all of two weeks, years ago—to convince people online that the books were embellished. The movies were worse than the books. It hadn't worked to argue over it. Even with her father's last name.

"Oh, I know that, dear." Elaine worried the bright-purple lipstick she wore onto her front teeth. "We have a few of his journals, ones we could buy at estate sales. And some lost editions of his earlier books."

"You do?"

Elaine nodded, a pained look on her face. "We could... uh...give them to you if you want them back."

"I'd love to see them." Kenna tried to smile. Even if she

did collect memorabilia from her own father's life, right now she had nowhere to put it.

They emerged through an inside door into an expansive room. The door Kenna had entered had to have been a side entry, not the church's original front doors.

"As you can see, the hooligans who bought this church from the archdiocese almost destroyed all the character it had." Elaine sighed and waved at the rafters, where spray paint swirled across the ceiling and the HVAC ducts. Scaffolding lined the right wall, tarps over the rails. Paint buckets and a ladder, all sat unused.

The church could have seated five hundred people at one point. Now it held mismatched bookshelves, just like a library. The whole place smelled like books. Air purifiers flanked the door they'd come through.

Elaine led her down the center aisle to the middle, where the shelves parted and tables and chairs had been set up. Those little table lamps with the pull chords. Extension cords where someone was charging their phone.

A circle of armchairs at the far end was occupied by a lone man, a beanie pulled down over his forehead. His chin touched his chest, bushy gray-and-white beard almost to his belt. Kenna could only see a flannel shirt rise and fall with steady breaths.

"That's Stan Tilley," Elaine whispered. "He's been a member of the group longer than me even. We all call him Sarge, though."

"Military?"

"Vietnam. But I'm pretty sure they did something to him." Elaine tapped a finger against her temple and winced. Then she spread her arms wide. "So this is it."

"There was another man who came out into the lobby with you and Ben. You have four members?"

Elaine shuddered. "Yeah, that was Larry Bourman. He was a detective with LVPD for forty years until the new brass canned him for doing the job too well. Or so he says."

Kenna nodded, able to offer a few suggestions but not more than that without knowing more. "So what does Intellectus do?"

Elaine grinned. "We're a group. We take cold cases and mysteries—plenty of those in Vegas—and see if we can solve them. Once in a while we actually hit on something, but it's mostly just for fun. So don't worry about us trying to steal your thunder or anything." She gasped. "Who told you about us? What are you working on? Is it a local legend?"

"Here." Ben appeared beside her, holding two mugs. "Coffee?"

"Thank you." Kenna accepted the warm mug.

"Kettle is boiling for tea, Elaine."

"Thanks, Benny."

Given the look on the handsome man's face, he didn't appreciate being called that.

They settled at a table, Elaine opposite Kenna. Ben occupied a chair at the head which he'd pulled back so he could set one foot on his other knee.

Kenna tugged her chair in. "I heard about you guys recently. This is a really cool space."

She glanced around, wondering where they kept her father's journals. She didn't want to take them unless they offered, but she did want to see which ones they were. She had a lot of her father's things. She went back to the storage unit periodically and spent some time reading. Searching for... she wasn't sure what.

She continued, "I'm here because of a cold case. I heard you guys have the file."

Ben set his mug on the table. "Which one?"

"A Russian diplomat. Found poisoned in his hotel room about fifteen years ago. Dmitri Alekhin?"

Ben nodded. He strode away between the shelves.

"That isn't one we've been able to figure out, I'm afraid." Elaine frowned, as though it were a personal moral failing of the group that they hadn't. "Too many unanswered questions."

"How long have you had the files?"

Elaine hesitated, swallowing. She fingered the handle of her mug.

Kenna stared at her over the lamp on the table between them. "What is it?"

Before she could answer, Ben came back over with a file box. He dumped it on the table so hard it shook. "Here's everything. I've got to go meet a buddy, but I might be back later." He turned his deep-blue eyes to her, a slight smile on his face as though they shared a secret no one else knew. "It was nice to meet you, Ms. Banbury."

"You, too." She waited until he was gone, then stood.

The guy across the seating area snorted, shifted in his chair, and then slumped deeper into sleep.

Kenna flipped the lid off the file box. "This is everything?"

"It's what Larry brought with him when he retired from the force."

"Where is he?"

"Drinking in his office—which is the break room." Elaine shrugged. "That's all he does."

An ex-cop with a drinking problem.

Elaine grimaced. "He's aware his life is a total cliché." She sighed. "A case he could never solve. Drinking too much, so his wife walked out on him and took the kids. He was living in a studio apartment until they raised the rent and he couldn't pay with the nighttime security job he does at this rundown casino on the far end of the Strip. Nothing good. I'm pretty sure he lives here now. I saw him washing up in the restroom."

Kenna leaned her palms on the edges of the box. "Did he work this case?" she asked, keeping her voice soft.

Elaine nodded. "He wanted to be able to figure it out. I think there was a lot of pressure from the higher-ups, looking for him to give them answers." She hesitated. "I also got the impression they wanted it even if it was unsubstantiated. But we don't do that. We only know what we can from the evidence we have. If we have theories or ideas, that's all they are until we can either prove or disprove them."

"I try to hold off on drawing conclusions until I have facts as well."

Elaine's expression lightened.

"Can you tell me about the case?" Kenna started removing files, papers, and photos from the box. How the ex-cop, Larry Bourman, had been entrusted with all of it was interesting in itself. Even with a cold case, the copies would have to be signed for. The PD would have a record of his possessing everything.

Or he'd stolen all of it.

"Dmitri Alekhin's death was ruled poisoning." Elaine pulled out the original crime scene report and handed it to Kenna, which she'd read from the file packet. Boxes filled out by Larry Bourman, and a written statement of how he found the hotel room and the body. "He was found in the morning by housekeeping. Who knows how long he'd been there, but the time of death was concluded as ten to twelve hours prior. Around one in the morning."

"What about the poison?"

"We had the same discussion." Elaine rooted around for the autopsy and handed it to Kenna. Again there was the basic information, but the additional pages of the report even

Kenna didn't have weren't in the papers she handed over. "But the information was never in here."

"Says here it was likely ingested." No needle marks, or other indications of the poison being administered rather than swallowed. "Stomach contents?"

Elaine nodded. "He'd eaten a meal of Chinese food. But whatever was tested to find the breakdown of the poison that killed Alekhin isn't here. If it was sent to be run by a lab, or if the report was forgotten—or intentionally left out—we have no idea. It just isn't here. When we suggested to Larry that he ask for it, he flipped out. It took two days to clean up the mess he made in here, knocking over bookshelves."

"I can ask for it." Kenna needed to know what had killed the Russian diplomat. After all, it could give them a lead as to what—and potentially who—ended his life. "Or have the FBI make the request." But it didn't solve the mystery of Larry Bourman and his connection with the entire case. "You said he's in the break room?"

Elaine twisted around, toward an exit door on the far wall.

Kenna stood up. "It would be good to find out what Larry's issue is with this case."

The other woman frowned. "You think he'll talk to you?"

"Worth a try," Kenna said. "Too much of this is tied to other things. Larry knows something. And I'm guessing it's not in this file box."

"You're going to take it, aren't you?"

"I have most of this. But there could be something I don't."

"How do you have it?"

"I was sent it by a friend of mine." Kenna sighed. "Actually, he was killed, and I believe it's because he was looking into this cold case with a mutual friend. Regardless, I'd be neglecting your safety if I didn't warn you that you might be in danger even talking to me. Or handing me this information. So try to be careful. Will you take extra security measures for a while? Just in case."

"Sure." Elaine frowned. "I can."

"Anything else you think I should know about what's in the box?" Kenna asked.

She was about to speak when a chime rang out from the aging desktop computer on the far left, beside the shelves, on a desk she'd expect for checking books out.

Elaine headed for it. "That's our website. If there's a message come in, it could be a new case to work." She trailed over there while Kenna rooted through the rest of the box.

Police had found one of Alekhin's shoes on the floor across the room, which fit with Kenna's theory he'd been hauled in there and placed on the bed after he died somewhere else. He'd also been cleaned up. The autopsy report pages said there were traces of stomach acid in his mouth—indicating the victim had thrown up before he died. Only there was no evidence of that on his clothes. Perhaps it hadn't gone farther than his lips.

Kenna packed it up and closed the lid.

She wound through the shelves, scanning the volumes looking for bound journals—the type her father used—but going more to the exit door. Another hall. A break room, with a small kitchenette. Where Larry Bourman lay stretched out, an open bottle of tequila balanced between his hip and the back of the couch.

Kenna reached out and took hold of the neck of the bottle.

Larry grabbed her wrist. "Don't."

"You're gonna want to let go of me." His grip loosened a fraction, so she said, "And sober up. 'Cause I have questions."

"So you're cut from the same cloth as your dad." He slurred the words, finally opening his eyes.

Kenna stepped back. "What does *that* mean?"

"He told me the same thing. And he shot me." Larry grunted. "He was a nasty piece of work, your dad."

Her *father* had shot him?

Kenna only knew of one person her dad shot in Vegas. Were there really more, or was Larry the former LVPD detective the guy from the kitchen with blood all over his face?

He looked nothing like that man, but it had been years.

Kenna tugged over a chair and sank into it. "That's not what I'm here to talk about. So sit up."

He turned his head only to stare at her. Shirt untucked, and a stain above the knee of his slacks. Shoes untied and discarded on the floor.

"I'm here to solve the Dmitri Alekhin case."

"No, you're not." He stared at her. "You just wanna jam me up."

"I think you mistake me for someone who cares about you."

His lips twitched. "Okay, then. I get steamrolled, all so you can solve your case. Like I said, cut from the same cloth as your dad."

All she could do was repeat what he'd said. "A guy who shot you." She wasn't sure what to make of it.

"I mean, I had a vest on under my shirt, and we staged the whole thing with dye packs, but he still did it. Hurt like you wouldn't believe, and it cracked my sternum. Took me weeks to be able to breathe deep." He frowned. "You should know. You were there, weren't you?"

Chapter Fifteen

"Maybe you're not a cliché after all." Kenna leaned back in the chair. Every move she made in Vegas seemed to have an unsettling effect—bringing yet another thing to the surface.

Larry studied her. "You're not gonna ask me about it?"

"How about I make coffee first?"

He grunted.

Kenna went to the counter and found a mediocre brand of coffee in a can and scooped enough to give the pot some flavor. It didn't take long for it to start bubbling and dripping into the carafe. She turned and leaned back against the counter, folding her arms across her chest. Her jacket splayed out so that he likely spotted the gun holstered on her belt.

Larry set the bottle on the floor and hefted his body up to sitting.

"If I thought I was going to get a straight answer, I'd ask." Kenna paused. "But since you're supposed to be solving the cold case as part of Intellectus, and yet you've got information that could probably let them do that, I have to ask…" She lifted her chin. "Did you join this group just to make sure they never solved it?" She wondered if he would bluster about her impugning his reputation. Or cave and admit his guilt.

He did neither, just lifted his chin as she had. The guy had been passed out on the couch, wearing dirty clothes and no shoes. Smelling like the open bottle. "So you've decided I lied."

"How did you lose your job?"

"I quit," he said. "And you aren't wrong. I am a cliché."

"In a lot of ways, so am I." She shrugged. "A lone investigator who lives on the road, roaming the country solving crime."

"That's not going to happen here."

Too bad for him, it was.

Larry sniffed. "And for the record? You're not like your father. You've forged your own path."

"How did you meet him?"

"If I was going to explain that, then I'd have to explain the entire case."

"Dmitri Alekhin was killed after I came to Vegas. My father wasn't here during that time."

"But Santino didn't let it go. He called your father and told him there was a chance to finish what fell apart when you saw all that in Santino's kitchen."

Kenna poured two cups and handed him one. "*All that* being when you stumbled in like you were a captive being interrogated and my father shot you in front of me?" She took a sip. "But it was a ruse?"

"If I tell the whole story, I implicate myself. I could go to jail."

Kenna looked around. "I don't see any cops here. Just you and me."

"So you don't work with the FBI?" His brows rose over the mug. "Because you met with them recently, didn't you?"

"Are you keeping tabs on me?" She'd had the feeling she was being followed.

"Santino is making sure you're safe, since that pushy guy came to his house to get you. *We* are making sure." Larry sipped his coffee. "We all owe your dad. Why wouldn't we?"

Except Kenna had literally no clue about any of this. "So it's about repaying a favor?"

The fact he didn't answer "no" confirmed she was right about her question. Kenna drank some more of the coffee and looked around the break room. "Why did Dmitri Alekhin get killed? What was he into?"

"All the usual things. The guy had diplomatic immunity, so he could do whatever he wanted. By the time he died, he was officially retired from the service, but everyone knew the Russians still had him working jobs. Passing messages back and forth. Running down people they wanted found and passing the intel back to Moscow. Spend the weekend in Vegas? Better to live there full-time. It's got to be more fun, right?" Larry shook his head. "People seem to think so."

"How did you know him?" she asked.

"Regular poker game. Santino. Dmitri. Me, and a buddy of mine from City Hall. Your dad sometimes joined when he was in town, but I don't think he ever met Dmitri."

"Do you think Santino could be the one who killed him?"

"What? No way it was him." Larry shook his head. "Those two were best friends, more like brothers."

"A made guy, a mobster who was Sicilian to the core, and a Russian?" He couldn't seriously expect her to believe that was true.

"You should've seen him when Dmitri was found." Larry blew out a breath. "Never seen Santino like that, except that was exactly what Dmitri looked like when his wife...you know."

"Presume I don't."

"She was in labor. The misses died, but the baby lived." Larry's face crumpled. "Saddest thing you've ever seen."

Dmitri had lost his wife. Then after raising a son and daughter, he'd been murdered. Kenna swallowed a sip that got stuck in her throat. She set the mug on the counter, coughing to get the liquid out of her lungs.

"You okay, girlie?"

Kenna sighed. "Elaine told me you have journals of my father's. Any of them from when he was here?"

Larry's brows shifted. "You wanna read them?"

"I'm not going to check them out and return them. Even though your setup here looks like a library, I can argue my father's property belongs to me."

"So you'd fight us with a lawsuit?"

"Did I say that?"

Larry studied her. "Yes, the ones we've got cover his time here."

"And does it tell me why he'd shoot you in a ruse?"

"Worst part was, it didn't even work."

"Why don't you just tell me," Kenna said. "That way I don't have to spend hours reading just to find out."

"Why are you so interested in this Dmitri case?"

"Someone pointed me to it as part of an ongoing investigation."

He said nothing.

"Any ideas what that might be?"

Larry clutched his mug. Stared at the contents. "We were trying to take down a bad guy. The three of us—Santino, your dad, and me."

"But it didn't work?"

He nodded. "I'm guessing that might be what you're doing. Though, I have no idea why. I don't know what you've been working on. Just that Santino clocked you when you showed up in Vegas and he hasn't taken eyes off you since."

"He had his guys drag me to his house."

"Just for a chat."

Kenna leaned closer. "You knew about that?"

"We're not all old, washed up, and not what we used to be." Larry's expression flattened. "Santino still has life in him, despite what he thinks."

Unfortunately, or fortunately, depending on how she looked at it, her father wasn't here to be in the same state. He'd been killed while she was in college. "You know, I keep meeting people who knew my dad. It doesn't make it better." She stared at him, then continued, "For years I assumed my dad cut and ran. That he didn't finish the case here because he did something bad and didn't want to face it."

"So you decided the kind of man he was?" Larry set down his coffee. "Guess there's no hope for us when you saw what you wanted. He got you out of the house before the bad guys showed up, but all you saw was a murder." He slapped a hand against his chest. "That wasn't even real."

"So I walk in years later and discover it's connected?" Kenna didn't like that at all. Not when it was entirely too coincidental.

Larry shrugged a meaty shoulder. "You don't ruffle feathers in Vegas. You let it be what it's gonna be. Except this. Why wouldn't you want to finish what he started?"

"I'm not," she said. "Because I have no idea what he left for me to pick up. This case connects to taking down a dangerous organization."

"Seems more like a chance to find out what your father was doing here."

Kenna stared at him.

Maizie had sent her that packet. Thomas had died

because of it—or so she and Stairns had concluded. But what if it didn't have anything to do with the case? What if looking into Dmitri Alekhin's murder was just a chance to resurrect her father's work, and get to know him better? She couldn't believe it...

Except for the trailer.

The last thing on the Utah True Crime blog had been a link to that trailer—for sale. She'd missed out on purchasing it, though Stairns said he was "on it." Was the packet the same? Maizie, or someone else, directing her to her father's open cases. All so she could unpack the truth and get some context to the things she'd seen.

Things she'd always believed about her dad.

Except it wasn't about Max Banbury. It was about Michael Rushman—and Cerberus.

"Why did my dad pretend to kill you?" Kenna asked.

"We worked it all out, but then you showed up," Larry replied. "Only I didn't know it. One of Rushman's men got on Santino's payroll. We needed to flush out the traitor so we could make sure he didn't realize what was actually going on. If whoever it was believed I was dead, it kept him from killing me before I could talk. He would've reported back to Rushman that I was dead."

"Michael Rushman?" The CEO of Hammerton Dickerson had been the number one topic of conversation with the FBI. That would be a clear connection to her father—but not to Dmitri's death.

Larry nodded. "The guy is whacked out. Into all kinds of sick stuff, and we were just going to keep seeing young women disappear if no one did anything."

"You said it didn't work."

Larry reached for the open bottle but drew his hand back. "You're right. I should quit. But why face the daylight when the night means I can hide? Being drunk all the time is easier."

"You wanna live in that fog?" she said.

"It's easier to deal with."

"You were after Rushman, trying to take him down?"

"After your dad left town, Santino and I had to quit, or someone would've realized what we were doing. Santino lost everything. So did I." Larry winced. "Didn't work."

"Is there a connection between your investigation into Rushman and Dmitri's death?"

The murder occurred after she and her father came to town and her dad got involved. Had the case really been going on that long?

Now the FBI had caught it. After all these years, they finally had the official go-ahead to pursue whatever case there was against Rushman. Kenna wanted to trust it would be successful. But the fact the FBI director of all people had come here meant something. She just didn't know what yet.

Larry inhaled, then pushed out the breath. Formulating an answer he could live with, or a lie she would believe. Eventually he said, "I got the feeling there was a lot about Dmitri's death that Santino didn't want public. Family pressure, and all that." He shrugged one shoulder.

"How'd you get into it with them?"

"Santino, he..." Larry seemed to deliberate, then said, "He was a confidential informant."

Kenna felt her brows rise.

"Misery acquaints a man—"

"With strange bedfellows," Kenna said. "My father used to say that. I didn't know it was about you guys."

She wondered if her dad had been thinking of Larry and Santino and what happened in Vegas when he quoted *The*

Tempest. He'd never been a straight-and-narrow guy, the kind who'd make a career out of law enforcement.

She still couldn't believe he'd cut and run.

She continued, "So you and my father started working with Santino. Trying to take down Rushman."

Larry slumped back on the couch. "Didn't matter. Rushman put a hit out on your dad. He destroyed the rest of us. Just for trying to out the man in Santino's crew that reported back to him."

"So you got too close and got your hand slapped."

He shrugged one shoulder.

"And now?"

"I'm a sorry excuse for a washed-up ex-cop."

"That's not what I mean," Kenna said. "Rushman."

Fear crept into the edge of Larry's expression. "He's gone from being a big shot to being untouchable."

"No one is above the law."

"*He* is." Larry shook his head. "There's no way. You'll get killed."

"That's it? I'll die?"

He stared at her.

"You think those odds will make me back down?"

"They should if you're smart."

"So I can join Intellectus and be ineffectual?" Kenna shook her head. They should change the name of their group to something more fitting.

His eyes narrowed. "Beats being dead."

She wasn't so sure about that. When it came down to it, Kenna remained alive because she had fight in her. If she gave up, she might as well be dead. But she never would, not while there was breath in her lungs.

She'd decided to go down swinging the day she argued for her private investigator's license. That she'd never simply walk away and accept the nothing they left her with. She would fight for the life she wanted.

Kenna tugged her phone from the clip on her belt. She thumbed through to the picture of Austin. "Have you ever seen this young man?"

Larry stared. Shook his head.

Kenna found the picture of Maizie. Showed him.

"Did Rushman get ahold of her?"

That meant he didn't know her. "Have you ever met a woman named Justine Greene?" she asked. "She was in a relationship with a guy in Santino's employ, Deacon."

"Deacon Frost was the guy we thought worked for Rushman," Larry replied. "Couldn't prove it, though. Santino kicked him anyway, a few years later. It's what Rushman does. No paperwork, just a handshake—if that. More than likely Rushman had a video or photo of Deacon doing something he wouldn't want to come to light. Held it over his head and got him to do whatever. Like inform on Santino."

"What did Rushman have on you?"

"Doesn't matter."

"There you are." Elaine strode in carrying a stack of leather-bound journals. "Thought I smelled coffee." She glanced at Kenna. "Means the coast is clear."

"So you're done painting your nails?" Larry held up his mug.

Kenna poured him some more coffee.

"These are for you, Kenna." Elaine handed over the journals.

"Thank you." Kenna took them, then turned to Larry. "I'll be back if I have any follow-up questions."

Elaine gasped. "You're leaving?"

"I have somewhere to be," Kenna told her.

Clutching her father's journals, she resisted the urge to

run for the door, as though she were stealing a prize and had to get away without being caught.

In the car she stared at the journals on the passenger seat. She laid her hand on the top one.

Drive.

She cranked the car and put it in reverse. Twisting to see behind her, she caught sight of a guy standing by the corner of a neighboring building. Watching her. It looked like the guy from Intellectus who'd left, Ben Landers.

As she pulled out, Kenna called Stairns.

"Got another name to run?"

"Actually, yes." She exhaled.

"Well, it can wait. We got a message through your website."

"From who?"

"Junk email address. Name field says *Maizie*."

Kenna gripped the steering wheel. "What does the message say?"

"Two words," Stairns said. "Help me."

Chapter Sixteen

Kenna strode through the Bergamot Hotel lobby, weaving between people and making a beeline for the conference room where the FBI had been set up.

Help me.

She sped up, almost to a jog, as she crossed from the casino area carpet, up the three steps and took a sharp right down the slender hallway.

Jax was coming from the other direction, holding a Styrofoam container. "What's going on?"

"I need an update on the search for Maizie," she said. "Have you guys found anything?"

He lifted his index finger, opened the conference room door, and set his container inside. Instead of allowing her entry, he came back out, closing the door.

"What's going on?" She shook her head.

"You tell me. The FBI director knows you haven't even approached Santino." Jax folded his arms.

"So he's watching me, making sure I keep up my end of the deal?" Kenna didn't like the sound of that at all. "Maybe I should do the same with him so I know for sure you guys are looking for Austin and Maizie."

"Or you could just ask me."

She tried to figure out from his expression what was going on. However, at times he seemed to be able to be completely inscrutable. "Just tell me if you guys have found Maizie."

"Aside from at one point being a victim, we know nothing about this girl."

Kenna pulled out her phone and showed him the screenshot that Stairns had sent her. "We know she needs help."

Jax frowned. "I know you want to find her, but all we have is an image. It's not going to be that easy."

"But you're running it through facial recognition, and you're scanning surveillance and traffic cameras in Las Vegas, right?"

"You know as well as I do that that's like trying to find a needle in a stack of needles."

"So you've just given up before you even started? What if I did that with Austin, and then he turns up dead in an alley somewhere?" She was aware she'd raised her voice but ignored it. "Justine seems to have been lying to me. I'm still supposed to find her son, and I made a promise to myself that I would find Maizie. No one else seems to be looking for her. And I'm supposed to shelve all that, and flip Santino?"

Jax took another step toward her, his expression softening. "It's okay to be scared for her. Or scared for all of them. But you already know that just because you're looking doesn't guarantee you're going to find them."

"So why bother trying? Is that it?" She shook her head.

"That's not what I'm saying, Kenna. But you need to be realistic, or you could get your heart broken." His expression turned inscrutable again.

She didn't like it. "You're assuming it's not already broken, and all I have is pieces. So what's the point worrying about that?"

Jax scratched his jaw. "You're not supposed to carry this on your own."

"And the answer is that you destroy your career?" She lifted her hands, then let them fall back to her sides. "Just so you can tell me I might not find them?"

"My career choices are my business. And not the point right now."

He only didn't want to talk about it because he wouldn't like the end of that argument. "Exactly. The point is that you guys need to find Maizie before it's too late. And find Austin." She strode away, palming her phone so she could dial Justine's number. When it went to voicemail, she left a message, "It's Kenna. Call me back when you get this."

She strode out of the hotel onto the curb, where valet drop-off and pickup hummed with people and cars. The alley-related thought she'd had about Austin stuck in her mind, and she fired off a text to Stairs, asking him to check local hospitals for John Does.

The doors behind her swished open again, and Jax strode out. "Where are you going to next?"

Kenna handed her ticket to the valet. She turned and watched the street, with all the cars moving past. Like staring at a terrarium and finding peace in the constant motion. While she remained still, life moved on around her. The way she was aware that it did while she lived in her mobile homes, camper vans, or the class C she'd had. The trailers she and her father had pulled behind his truck.

Now she had no home to closet herself away in. And all she had was a motel room that didn't feel familiar or comforting at all. The night Jax had spent in the other bed she'd had the best sleep, but it wasn't like she could ask him to do it again.

"Look," he said, "I'll make sure the special assignment group is working the Maizie thing." He touched her shoulder.

Everything in her wanted to lean toward it, but she didn't.

"As soon as we get something, I'll call you first. You can come with me."

Kenna turned just her head. "Thanks."

The valet pulled up in her car, leaving it running as he rounded the hood. She handed him a five-dollar bill. "Thanks."

"Can you at least try and talk to Santino?"

She glanced at him over the roof of the car, the driver's door open. "Find Maizie."

Kenna climbed in and headed out. At the first red light, her foot on the brake and both hands on the steering wheel, her body started to shake. She took deep breaths and tried to hold it together. Her head swam, and she had to fight the shudder with her grip on the steering wheel.

The car behind her honked.

Kenna's foot slipped off the brake, and she tapped the gas pedal.

She couldn't shake the familiar sensation of being trapped and left powerless—the way she knew Maizie was feeling right now. Even while she managed to drive with some semblance of awareness of the road, part of her was back in that basement.

With Bradley. Unable to get out.

In the end, she'd broken out.

Something almost miraculous had happened. But Kenna had, at low points, wondered why she'd survived while he didn't.

The conclusion she'd drawn was that the only reason for

still being here was to save others in the same situation. She had bargained with the FBI that they find Maizie and Austin, while she worked on Santino. Kenna couldn't help wondering if it all tied together. Or had she simply been manipulated into this situation, the way this organization had manipulated so many people and caused so many deaths?

It made her feel like she was trapped in her own life.

Even if she had the ability to go where she wanted and do what she wanted, perhaps she was only oblivious to the fact someone else pulled her strings.

Making that agreement with the FBI could've been a mistake that trapped her into a bargain she didn't want to be part of. Whether or not she got what she wanted in the end, the truth was that it could cost her the little sanity she had left. Those broken pieces of her heart that she'd told Jax were all that remained.

She didn't know what he wanted from her. Certainly nothing she had the ability to give to him.

Kenna drove to Santino's house and pulled onto the drive, right away seeing him at the hedge beside the fence. Clipping the foliage, trimming the bushes.

She checked her phone before she got out of the car, but Justine hadn't called her back. She sent Austin's mom a text that said basically what the voicemail had. Then she clicked the phone on her belt and climbed out.

Santino clipped a branch and tossed it on the pile beside his shoe. The guy wore what looked like ironed jeans and a buttoned shirt that probably cost more than Kenna's entire outfit. "That car you're driving is a travesty. I'd suggest your father might be turning over in his grave, but that could be seen as improper."

"What's wrong with my car?" Kenna glanced at it.

"I don't even know where to begin."

Kenna said, "I do." She folded her arms, even though it made her look defensive. Right now it was more about self-preservation, and holding herself together when she felt like she was spiraling apart. "You can tell me everything you know about Michael Rushman and the business you've had with him."

"And why would that be relevant?" He went back to snipping the bush. "When you are looking for two teenagers."

"I'm also helping the FBI out with something else."

He stiffened very slightly. "Rushman?"

"I'm not going to lie to you, and I'm not going to try and manipulate you." There wasn't much point in either, and she didn't want to do it anyway. "I spoke to Larry Nelson. He told me you both were working with my father to take down Rushman, but it didn't work."

"Ancient history. Hardly relevant now."

"How about you tell me everything, and I make that determination?" When he said nothing, she added, "I won't tell the FBI unless you give me permission to do that. It can be just between us."

"Out of respect for your father, I would give you that if I could."

"What has your hands tied?" Kenna glanced around, ensuring none of his staff were listening. "Does it have to do with Rushman taking your hotel?"

"He took more than that."

"Can you tell me what he did?"

"So the FBI can compel me to testify against him?" Santino scoffed.

"What do you have to lose if you do?" She needed him to come clean with her. If respect for her father garnered her that, she would take it. After all, it seemed that what she'd thought her father was up to with Santino hadn't been what she believed at all. Assuming Larry had been telling her the truth instead.

Perception and reality were funny things, especially when it came to memories.

She of all people understood that. But what she didn't get was that her father had allowed her to believe he murdered a man, and that they were leaving town quickly because he didn't want the heat of sticking around when the police were asking questions.

Except the man she thought he'd "killed" was a detective.

Kenna said, "Tell me the truth."

"I owe no one the truth. Except maybe you."

She stood there, waiting for him to talk.

Santino's expression shifted, almost like he was deliberating something. What was there to consider? According to Larry, they hadn't been able to close the case.

It was time for the next generation to pick up the baton and run with it.

The skin around Santino's eyes flexed. "I've got a better idea." He set the clippers down. "Come with me." Santino unlocked the detached garage building. Inside, he flipped a switch on the wall, and the overhead lights flickered on. "Now, *this* is a car."

"It certainly is." The sleek black Chevrolet Impala looked familiar, but she couldn't remember where she'd seen it before. Maybe on a TV show?

"It's a nineteen sixty-seven. It was for my daughter." Santino crossed the garage in front of the hood. On the other side of the room, he turned on the radio atop the workbench. When vintage rock started playing, Santino raised the volume high enough Kenna nearly set her hands over her ears. He waved her over.

She went to stand in front of him, and he leaned close.

"Rushman destroyed everything I have," Santino said.

"And yet, you allowed him to take it without hitting back at him?" A mobster like this, someone with a staff of tough guys who worked for him. She couldn't believe he had gone so long without at least attempting to get revenge. If Rushman really had taken *everything*, why would Santino allow him to continue operating? "You never wanted revenge?"

Something flashed in his eyes. Santino shifted to tug at the end of his shirt, dragging it out of his pants. Kenna saw the skin of his abdomen, then a jagged scar. She looked around the back, lifting up his shirt. She found no exit wound.

"It didn't work." Santino held her gaze with his steady one, fear at the edges of his expression. "And then when I had nothing at all, he took my hotel."

Now he thought he had to account for listening devices in his garage? That had to be his reasoning for turning up the music. Maybe Santino believed the whole house was bugged. The man who had worked for Rushman no longer worked for Santino, and still he thought there were eyes on him? That someone was watching?

Kenna said, "So now you're working on a new plan?"

The skin around his eyes flexed again. "Your father knew when to cut his losses. I should've listened."

"So he gave up?"

"Rushman had eyes on you. Your father wasn't going to put you at risk, even to take down a dangerous man."

While they had been in Vegas years ago? "I don't remember that."

"You wouldn't," Santino said. "Your dad was a good father. He let you be a kid as much as he could."

Perhaps that was what her dad had told Santino. Then again, there was that perception versus reality thing.

Santino sighed. "Rushman would have taken you—the

way he took my daughter. Just for revenge, to get us to stop." He swallowed. "She came back...broken. My wife killed herself."

And when he had sought revenge, Rushman took his business. "We can't let him get away with this."

"You can't stop him," Santino said. "That girl you're looking for? He probably already discarded her."

She pulled out her phone. Santino flinched, but she showed him the words on the screen. *Help me.*

"You think that isn't Rushman trying to draw you in?"

"I don't think it is, no." Kenna shook her head. But she couldn't prove it, could she? "But I intend to find out either way."

"I'm leaving town. I won't watch the fallout when you fail."

"And yet you stayed this whole time, knowing he would continue to get away with whatever he's doing."

"The moral high ground is an easy place to be." Santino paused while the DJ announced the next song. "Where I live, things are not quite so simple. All the..." He crossed back to the radio and lowered the volume. "...all the upholstery. It was quite the task, getting it roadworthy again. I've been taking it out for a spin once a week just so the engine doesn't seize up. But now it's yours. The gift your father would've wanted you to have."

He picked up a set of keys from a hook on the wall and came to her, holding them out.

Santino mouthed, *Take the car.*

Chapter Seventeen

Kenna's phone rang right as she pulled into the motel parking lot. Every time she spoke to anyone, pretty much since she got to Las Vegas, something had happened. She'd learned new information or been directed somewhere. What would this call give her?

She needed to search this car she'd been given. Like people just gave each other classic vehicles with a wave of the hand—except that with the way Santino had handed over this gift, it sure seemed like more.

Piecing this case together was becoming a matter of straightening up a confusing mess. Like a tangle of cords or string, all knotted together so that things that weren't supposed to connect looked as though they did. Or things that should be related were miles apart.

Kenna's head ached trying to puzzle it out.

She parked in a space close to her room and put the call on speaker. "What's up, Jax?"

"The director wants a report on what Santino just said to you."

She huffed. "I'm surprised he didn't have a way to listen in."

If Jax admitted their attempt had been hampered by a Santino turning up the volume, then she would know for sure if it was the FBI that Santino believed had bugged him or someone else.

Considering Rushman hadn't even been on her radar as someone behind the organization—whether or not she believed it was true that it was just one man doing all this—she still doubted whether or not he really was behind this. And given how much of this felt like strings being pulled, she couldn't be sure it wasn't someone else implicating him.

Maybe even the FBI director himself. Or his friend, former president Masonridge.

At this point, she only trusted Jax. And then, only outside of his role as an FBI agent. She trusted the man, not the badge he carried. Kind of like with Stairs—now that he didn't work for the FBI. Her colleague had only betrayed her because he'd been pressured into it by the governor and his wife because of what happened to Kenna's partner.

As if they were the only ones who had lost something that day.

Considering what the First Lady of Utah had done to Kenna, she had no love for that woman—before or after Jax had killed Angeline Pacer, the day she shot Kenna in her class C.

"Are you listening to me?" Jax pressed.

Kenna laid her head back on the headrest and closed her eyes. "I'm drifting. I think I'm exhausted."

"Then get some sleep. But the director wants to know how it went with Santino."

Kenna had to ask the question again, since she hadn't

heard any answer he'd given her while her mind spiraled back into the past. "Has the FBI bugged Santino?"

"No, otherwise we would know what you said to him, and what he told you." Jax paused. "We would also likely have the leverage to get him to cooperate."

"Because you think there's something in his life right now that would incriminate him?" Kenna paused. "The guy lives pretty solitary."

"Someone like that? There's no way he's squeaky-clean."

Kenna wondered if it wasn't more that Rushman, or whoever was behind the organization, had something over Santino. After all, he seemed scared enough that he was now impotent to do anything to right the wrongs or fix his life. If she explained that the FBI wanted him to testify against Rushman, would he do it? She had to believe that in the end the need for justice would outweigh the risk. Or the fact his deepest darkest secrets might be revealed.

"I'll be sure to write up a report for the director," Kenna said. "My consultant paperwork probably got lost in the mail. But you'll send a check after the case is closed, right?"

Jax's voice rumbled across the phone line. "Because you care so much about payment?"

They both knew she didn't. Though, Jax probably wasn't thinking that she made enough money off the royalties of her father's books and movies that she rarely charged anyone for working a case. Mostly, it wasn't worth having to keep everything aboveboard—given the way she had obtained the private investigator licenses she had. The last thing Kenna needed was the federal government up in her business.

Or her life.

Before she left Santino's, Kenna had shifted all her belongings to the car he insisted she take with her. She'd given him the keys to the junker and driven off with the stack of journals in the passenger seat.

Kenna said, "Intellectus gave me a few of my father's journals that they had in their library. I need to take some time and read them."

"So rest and read." Jax's tone was even, as though that was the obvious answer.

"I should be out looking for Maizie." She sighed. "And Austin. And Justine. Finding the evidence to take down Rushman, if it's even out there somewhere."

"You aren't the one that needs to solve this whole thing," Jax said. "That's why the special assignment group is here."

Kenna's eyes burned with tiredness—and something else. "What if she's hurt? I have no idea where she is, or how to find her."

"Do you think Rushman has her?"

"Do you?"

All they had was the FBI director's assertion that Rushman was guilty and they needed to bring him down. Maizie had sent her here to investigate the cold case involving Dmitri Alekhin. As far as she could see, the murder of that Russian diplomat had nothing to do with the CEO the FBI was trying to take down—aside from through Justine, which made no sense.

If there were a connection, then it would be something entirely different. But Kenna didn't know.

"I could come to you," he said. "Help you read through the journals. If that makes it easier."

"There's always a point in every case, where I hit a breakthrough. I go from having too many questions and not enough answers. Then something shakes loose, and before I know it, I'm on the last bend before the home stretch."

"So we need something to shake loose."

Kenna needed to search this car. "I have some ideas."

"Hopefully one of them is that thing where you take a nap, or a shower, and your brain is freed up to have a creative idea."

"That sounds good."

"Because I didn't suggest to you that we work out?"

Kenna grinned. "Pretty much."

"We should go for a run. There is a park on the north side of Vegas with running trails."

"You know what happened the last time I ran."

"It's time to put the past behind you and move on with your life."

Kenna snorted. "Sure, it's exactly that easy."

There was a reason why life was different now than it had been before. Why there were things she was hoping she would never have to do again, because that was easier than facing the trauma in her memories.

"I'm almost there." Jax paused. "I'm serious about giving you a hand." He continued, over someone honking their horn, "All we have is a whole lot of assumptions. Like how Austin was looking for his sister. Is it Maizie, or someone else?"

"And where is he? Maybe he got too close to finding her and was taken as well. But how is that even possible? He didn't leave any way for us to find out what he knew." And yet, Austin's friend from school had been attacked. Someone had broken into her house in the middle of the night and beaten a teenage girl, scaring her so that she stayed away from the whole thing.

All that did was convince Kenna to keep going. Because obviously there was something worth protecting—if whoever was behind this thought they would be discovered.

A car bumped into the parking lot. She twisted around and spotted Jax's rental vehicle.

Kenna hung up and climbed out of the car, leaving the driver's door open. She took off her jacket and carried the journals into the motel room before coming back out to the car.

Jax had parked and walked over to it. "Where did you get this?"

Kenna grinned. "Cool, right?"

He frowned.

Kenna moved close to him, winding her arms around him so she could give him a hug.

Jax stiffened, as though unsure what was going on.

"Just go with it," she said.

He hugged her back.

Kenna lifted up on her toes and spoke low in his ear. "Santino thought someone was listening to our conversation. He told me almost nothing, but he gave me this car."

She lowered back down, and he turned his head. This close, she could see a gray ring in his eyes.

She cleared her throat and spoke at a normal level. "Want to check it out?"

He nodded.

Kenna looked at the trunk, which turned out to be empty. She pulled up the carpet that came away from the floor and checked all the corners. Compartments. She moved to the glove box while Jax felt between the seat and the backrest in the back seat.

She did the same in the front, then checked under the floorboard mats.

"Hold up."

She turned to see he had twisted, reaching under where she sat. "What is it?"

"Give me your pocketknife."

Kenna blinked. "What knife?"

He hissed out of breath. "The one you keep in your right boot. Give it to me."

She made a face but still handed it over, then watched as Jax cut what sounded like the fabric under the seat. "What is it?"

Instead of answering, he held out his hand. A flash drive in his palm.

Kenna snatched it from him, pushed out of the car, and slammed the door shut before she headed to the room. He strode in behind her, the keys and her knife in his hands. He set both on the dresser while she pulled her laptop from the safe and booted it up.

"Whatever this is," she said, sliding it into the port, "Santino doesn't want anyone to know he gave it to me."

"Seems risky, hiding it in a car."

"Unless you keep that car under lock and key and no one knows to look there." She glanced over with a shrug. "They would check the house first."

He frowned. "Right." Which meant that the FBI had done exactly that. Considering she'd have done the same thing and started with the house, she couldn't exactly say anything about their choice.

"Let's take a look," she said. Instead of a whole packet of information she'd received about the cold case, the flash drive had a single file on it.

"Video?" Jax asked.

Kenna clicked Play on an image of a dining table, like in a high-end restaurant. Across the table, Michael Rushman faced whoever was wearing the hidden camera. "Someone recorded him. I'm guessing without his knowledge."

"Good for them," Jax said.

He stood close to her side. Near enough she could feel his warmth.

But now wasn't the time to get distracted by him, or how it had felt knowing his presence meant she slept better than she had in a long time. He wasn't the kind of person she could get used to having around.

Her dog, on the other hand? Kenna had welcomed Cabot into every part of her life.

Jax needed to have his own life. Parts of it had nothing to do with her. As opposed to what seemed to be happening right now, which was that he had given up everything else for the sake of helping her. Although he couched it in terms of a "special assignment" and a "lateral move." As if she was supposed to believe that.

It meant something to her that he had given up what he should have been working on to go undercover. But that didn't mean she had to like it. Was there really enough feeling between them that he wanted to do this for her?

Maybe it was just duty. Given how much the FBI had wronged her in the past, as an FBI agent, he should be all in to make up for that betrayal.

Maybe it was more.

But Kenna didn't have room in her life for more. Not if she wanted to keep her sanity, and those broken pieces of her heart. Because the alternative was that everything she had built obliterated, ground to dust when she got hurt again.

The priest in New Mexico had told her to let the light into the dark places of her life.

But even though the dark was the hardest place to be, sometimes that was all she knew.

Jax crouched beside her chair. He reached over and hit the button to turn up the volume.

. . .

The person wearing the camera said, "...do this to me. After everything, you're going to take my hotel as well?"

Rushman lifted the glass of wine on the table and sipped. After he had swallowed, he said, "This place?" Rushman gestured with the wine. "It's hardly worth my time. But I suppose it could come in handy."

The camera shifted. Santino had to be wearing it, and he'd moved in his seat. "I should kill you right now."

"Yes, you should." Rushman's expression didn't change. On the video feed, his eyes looked almost black. "Maybe you should have done it a long time ago."

"At least you admit the world would be a better place without you in it." The voice belonged to Santino. "But taking you out wouldn't bring my wife back. Or pull my daughter from this spiral she's in. And yet, you seem discontent with everything you've taken. You want it all."

Rushman's lips curled slightly. "At least you admit what is inevitable. I will win, and you will lose."

"Because you're pure evil."

"And you would do well to not forget."

"Don't worry," Santino said. "I never will."

The feed paused, and the video ended.

Jax stood and paced to the window and back. "At least now we have proof it's him."

"All we know is that he's the one Santino went up against." She twisted around in the chair to face him. "We have no proof he's the head of the organization."

"Then we need to get some."

"I think all we have is Santino's solid advice against pursuing this. Proof that if we do, Rushman will be there waiting. That he'll do whatever it takes to stop us from taking him down. That's why he's been operating for so long."

"He can think he's untouchable all he wants," Jax said. "But he isn't, and I'm going to make sure of it."

Kenna wasn't as convinced. "How do we know there isn't more to it than what Santino has given us? What if this is just a piece of the puzzle, and there's more scope? I never believed it was one person behind the organization that had the church bombed. Now all of a sudden it's this guy?"

"Why can't you just be satisfied with what we have?"

"I'll be satisfied when I have Maizie, and I can hear the truth from her."

Jax grasped the back of his neck. "You don't even know this girl. You think she's the only one who's going to tell you the truth?" He paused for a second. "The truth is, you don't let anyone in. You're so scared of being hurt again that you won't risk caring about anyone except a dog." He strode to the computer and pulled out the flash drive.

Kenna couldn't grab it from him. Her arms weren't strong enough to grasp anything sufficiently enough to wrestle it away from him. She followed him to the door. Before he reached for the handle, she shoved him against the wall. "You're not taking the flash drive with you."

Fire flashed in his eyes. "So this is how it's going to be?"

She worked her fingers under his and took the flash drive. "The only person going up against Rushman is *me*."

"Because you have nothing to lose?" Jax said.

He didn't want her to answer that.

Before she could formulate a response, his arms slid around her. He pulled her flush against his chest and touched his lips to hers.

Warmth and strength surrounded her. She sank into it,

drowning the way she wanted to. In comfort. And not being alone...

Until she realized what she was doing.

She wedged her hands between them and shoved him away, gasping for breath.

That was...

What had...

Jax wiped his thumb on his bottom lip. "Good thing no one cares about you." Then he walked out, leaving the door wide. "All the best with your case," he called over his shoulder.

She stood in the doorway and watched him drive away. Probably grinning, all proud of himself—like he'd gained himself a point. As if.

Battle with the FBI? Sure, that had worked so well last time.

Kenna's phone rang. Stairns' name flashed on the screen.

She swiped it and barked, "What?"

Nothing. Then, "Everything okay?"

"No, I..." She remembered the flash drive.

Jax had taken it from her.

Kenna groaned in frustration. He'd thoroughly distracted her and stolen it *back*.

"We don't have time for whatever's going on with you," Stairns said. "Your hunch paid off. I found Austin."

Chapter Eighteen

Kenna strode into the emergency room at the hospital. The waiting area was peppered with people. She needed a nap and a shower—plus about a year—to process what had just happened with Jax.

He'd kissed her.

And stolen the flash drive.

She'd decided on the way over that the two were only connected incidentally. He wasn't the kind of guy who'd kiss her to steal the evidence from her hand and take it back to the FBI. Like a traitor.

He didn't owe her much past the respect that existed between them.

Now there was something else in the air, filling the space, that made her want to run like he'd suggested. Only he was *not* coming.

She needed to work out—in a way that caught her up in the effort and discomfort. Not punish herself, just exert herself hard enough and long enough her legs shook and she could no longer stand. Try to push the thoughts from her head.

The receptionist behind the white vinyl desk didn't even look up.

Fluorescent lights washed the whole place in white, and the Plexiglass sliding doors to all the bays cut down on a lot of noise. But Kenna could still hear a baby crying.

She spotted Justine to the right, up ahead, and headed for her.

Justine slid the door to the bay closed, looking haggard. Her blond hair was stringy, and her shirt was rumpled. One sleeve was damp like she'd been wiping her nose with it.

"Hey." Kenna got near enough Justine spotted her. "How long have you been here?"

Justine just stared. "Long enough to know this"—she pointed at the closed door—"is your fault. For not finding him."

Kenna absorbed the accusation without reacting. No point calling her on it when what they should be talking about was the fact Justine had lied.

About several things.

"I thought he'd been here a few days?" Kenna said. Stairns had told her that Austin was admitted as a John Doe before Kenna even reached Vegas. Whatever had happened to him went down with no intervention from her, something she wasn't all the way comfortable with. "There's nothing I could've done."

"But you didn't find him."

"How did you?"

Justine lifted her chin. "Your friend called me. The one who works for you."

"He works *with* me."

"Whatever." Justine folded her slender arms.

Kenna turned to the clear door, looking in at Austin. The teen had been tucked in with blankets, only his arms, shoulders, and head free. Wires and tubes came in and out of him. His head had been wrapped with bandages. One whole side of his face was blue, one eye swollen.

"You did this to him."

Kenna turned. "How's that? I heard he was looking for his sister. Care to tell me about that?"

"No, I don't care." Justine sniffed.

"What's going on?" Apart from the fact Justine clearly had a few issues she hadn't mentioned. "Who could've done this to Austin when he was just looking for something?"

"I didn't know it would go like this." Justine's face crumpled, but she didn't shed tears. "How could I have? Austin and I are a team. Us against the world."

"And his sister?"

"He wanted to do this for me." Justine touched the clear Plexiglas, staring at her son.

"Who is she?" Kenna wanted to know if they'd come to Vegas for the express purpose of finding this sister.

"You know." Justine sighed, a sheen of redness in her eyes. "You asked me about her when I was the one in the hospital bed. I knew then that I needed to be here to find her."

"She works for the organization I've been trying to uncover?" Kenna paused. "And she's your daughter?"

Justine stayed silent. Finally she said, "Works for?" with a humorless laugh.

"So they took her?" Kenna thought about those photos the FBI had found. "They victimized her?"

"Austin is safe. That's all that counts. Not a fight I won't win."

"Talk to me." Kenna fought back the frustration. "I have to have the information."

Under the sleeve of her shirt, on the inside of her forearm, Justine had that scrollwork, Old English letter C tattooed on her skin. She'd been branded by this organization—by Michael Rushman, and maybe whoever else was involved. Justine had seen them. Met them. Worked for them, whether by choice or because she'd been coerced.

"They took her the same way they took you?" Kenna asked.

In New Mexico Justine had told Kenna she was targeted, nearly killed, because she wanted to get out. Kenna had believed when Austin and Justine left Hatchet and came here that they were starting over. Getting away from this whole thing.

"You brought Austin here." Kenna measured her words carefully, but she needed to say them so Justine understood. "You knew they operate here, and you brought him right to their doorstep."

The other woman turned, a hard look in her eyes. "They took her from me. I've seen her twice since."

"You told me you've seen her here."

"I can't find her." Justine's eyes filled with tears. "I can't find her anywhere."

"Neither can I." *But she keeps finding me.* "She needs our help, but I need you to talk to me, Justine. You need to tell me everything about them and what they do. Every single thing."

"Austin needs me now."

"And Maizie doesn't?" Kenna countered.

"There's nothing I can do for her."

"Where is she?"

Justine said nothing.

Kenna tugged her shoulder around. "Look at me. You have two children, and one of them is in danger."

"I have no idea where she is." Justine's gaze darted around. "I can't help her."

But Maizie thought that Kenna could help—and she

would. "Tell me where to find her."

"I can't," Justine said. "Because I *don't know*."

"There's something you're not telling me." Probably more than one thing, but Justine needed help if she was going to focus.

Kenna stared at her. "Justine, who are they?"

"You think I saw their faces?" Justine sniffed. "They did what they did. It doesn't matter. But they took her."

"And you never tried to find her?"

Justine shifted her weight from one foot to the other. "I couldn't..."

Couldn't handle what she was subjected to. Couldn't find Maizie. "Couldn't what?"

"*Everything*." Justine leaned in. "All of it."

"They tried to kill you," Kenna said. "You're protecting them if you don't tell me who is behind it."

"You can't stop them."

"I know it feels like that, but there's an FBI team in Vegas trying to take them down."

Justine flinched. "It won't work." She touched her shirt over her stomach and then the Plexiglass. "Look what happens. And I was trying to live my life."

As far as Kenna could tell, Justine represented a threat. Enough someone hurt her son as a way to force her to back off? She was a weak point someone could use to get information on whoever these people were.

"Who is Cerberus?" Kenna asked. That was what Ward Gaulding had said the C tattoo stood for.

Justine shut down. Trauma washed over her face, leaving only a blank expression behind.

"I know facing what happened is the last thing you want to do." Kenna knew, because she'd faced her own history. "It doesn't make it better, and you don't heal from reliving it all.

But you get to see the past from the perspective of who you are now. Someone who survived it."

Justine stared at Austin in the bed. "You think I...survived?"

Kenna closed her eyes for a second. Justine wasn't so different from Kenna, a broken person trying to move on with her life. Someone who could pretend with the best of them that she was "okay." Not that Kenna felt the need to pretend when she was on the road, alone and solving cases.

With the FBI she pretended.

Then Jax had begun to work his way between the cracks. He hadn't forced his way in, he'd waited for her to allow him past the surface. Something she didn't do with many people.

The way Jax disarmed her.

"Austin knows what you carry with you, and inside you," Kenna said. "You might not have told him much, or anything." Or she'd told her son all of it, and that was why he'd been so determined to find Maizie. "But he sees the brokenness. He wanted to do something about it."

"I didn't ask him to do this."

"But why would he not?" Kenna couldn't help remembering Austin's friend's comment about their codependent relationship. Family was hard without trauma involved, but when that hung in the air between two people—and one of them was a child—things got sticky fast. A person had to be seriously well-adjusted not to affect the other to at least some extent.

It didn't mean Justine created that unbalance between them on purpose.

With her father, Kenna had felt like the parent sometimes. Or at least the voice of reason. They'd depended on each other, because that was all they'd had. And letting each other down made things that much worse.

"I just want her back." Justine's words sounded hollow.

Kenna wasn't convinced, even though maybe she should've been. Maybe it was wrong to doubt Justine's sincerity, but a grown woman who had a child stolen from her? Even in the most complicated of situations, Kenna didn't see how that woman wouldn't move heaven and earth to get the child back. If it had been her, she'd have called the police, the FBI—everyone. Amber Alerts had been established for a reason.

Kenna would have screamed to the rooftops until someone listened.

Knowing Maizie for only a matter of months had her twisted up in knots, wanting to grab whoever was nearest and shake them until *someone* told her where the girl was. And she'd never even met Maizie.

"I'm going to find her."

Justine flinched.

It was on the tip of Kenna's tongue to remind Justine that Maizie had made contact. That she wanted to be helped.

"He'll destroy you."

Kenna studied the other woman, contemplating those words. "But when I'm done, he'll never destroy anyone else."

Austin let out a loud moan.

Justine pushed the door open, trying to force it to move faster than the mechanism wanted it to slide. She rushed to the bedside and grasped Austin's hand while he thrashed in the bed. Legs moving under the covers.

His free arm flailed.

Kenna moved in and caught his hand. She spotted a smudge of blood on the bed rail. On the skin of Austin's wrist, someone had inscribed a series of numbers in pen. "What is this?"

Justine frowned, not in answer to the question but at Kenna. "Who cares?"

"This is the first you've seen it?"

"He's dying!" She wailed the words.

A nurse ran in. "If you could clear the bay, both of you." He shot Justine a look. Not a fan of the mom? That was interesting given she hadn't been here long to garner a look that broke through the normal professionalism of a nurse.

Kenna read the numbers again.

"Ma'am."

"Yep." She laid Austin's arm on the blanket and strode out.

Justine wailed in the corner.

Kenna pulled out her phone and ran a search on the number. It came up as registered to a payphone across town toward the Strip. One of the few remaining public phones in existence. Maybe it had been forgotten and never dismantled.

She headed out the doors to the street, forcing herself to wait until she got in the car so there would be less background noise.

The phone rang on the other end.

Kenna gripped her cell, holding it against her ear. She didn't know what to think. If she could've gained access to security and had the authority, she'd have asked for surveillance from the ER to figure out who had written that phone number on Austin's arm in the three days since he'd been there—or if he'd shown up with it.

The call connected. "Hello?" a woman answered.

"Maizie?"

She gasped. "Kenna?" Fear laced her tone.

"I'm coming to you. I know where you are," Kenna said. "I'll be there as soon as I can be without getting pulled over, okay?"

Kenna put the call on speaker and dropped it in her lap. She backed the Impala out of the space and headed for the street. She could hear Maizie breathing deeply, as though fighting the need to cry. "It's gonna be okay. I'm coming now."

Maizie whimpered.

"You did the right thing. Now I'm gonna make sure you're safe." Kenna gripped the wheel, every muscle in her body tense. "Can you hear me, Maizie?" She frowned. "Is that even your name?"

"Yes." Maizie paused. "I think so."

"If you don't like it, or you don't want it, you can pick a new one."

"Okay." She sounded nervous, unsure.

"We'll figure it out when I get there." Which would be in about eight minutes. Kenna pressed the gas pedal to the floor, fighting the urge to honk at everyone. "Tell me how you got there. You messaged me. You wrote the phone number on Austin's arm."

"I had to wait. Then I snuck in."

Kenna held her tongue. She didn't want to cause distress when she wasn't there to gauge Maizie's reaction.

"No one said anything because I looked like I belonged in the hospital."

She remembered the smudge on the bed. "Because you're bleeding?"

"It's not bad," Maizie said. But her voice almost sounded like someone in pain.

Kenna was going to make that assessment herself.

Maizie gasped. "Someone is here. I've got to go—"

She was going to run.

Kenna blurted, "Hearst Motel. Room six."

Maizie said nothing.

"Maizie." Kenna snatched the phone from her lap. "Maizie!"

She fought the urge to throw it, since it would land out of reach. She drove the rest of the way to the payphone. A back alley, behind a row of businesses. On the corner where a rundown apartment complex had been neglected for so long the building had been condemned.

Kenna pulled up right at the pay phone. She pocketed her car keys and looked at the phone hanging down. A smudge of blood on the receiver.

She replaced the phone and looked around, wanting to call out but knowing Maizie didn't want attention drawn to her. Kenna sent Stairns a quick update text with her location and what'd happened.

Kenna didn't see any cars. She half expected black SUVs and armed men but saw nothing but a blue Ford. A compact.

She walked to the corner and glanced down the next street. The apartment complex was on the corner, a big sign on the curb. It was going to be torn down in a week.

A good place to hide.

She climbed the steps to the front doors, a smudge of blood on the handle. Kenna drew her gun, just in case the suspected kidnapper was inside.

One step into the darkened interior, and someone slammed into her.

The gun skittered across the floor.

Kenna hit the wall. Pain erupted in her shoulder.

This wasn't Maizie—it was someone much bigger. She had to plant her feet first, fix her stance so she could fight back. The smell of body odor hit her nose.

Instead of rallying, she got her head slammed against the wall.

Everything went black.

Chapter Nineteen

Kenna blinked. Her head pounded, but she was...soft. She managed to focus and realized this was a hospital bed. Everything in her surged upward.

"Easy." Jax's face swam into view. He touched both her shoulders. "Take it easy." He frowned. "I told them you'd wake up like this."

Kenna winced. She slumped back onto the pillow and whispered, "Maizie."

"What about her? Stairs told me where to find you. I guess he couldn't get ahold of you. He asked me to swing by and check. I found you knocked out in the lobby of that condemned building. Ambulance. Hospital. That's the whole story."

Kenna looked down and realized she still wore her clothes. She reached up and touched the back of her head. "Ouch."

"Yeah, don't worry about that. Someone is supposed to come and look at you in a second."

"Better idea... Let's head out."

Jax made a face, his hip leaned against the side of the bed.

"What?"

"You know what."

"Yeah, but we're still going anyway."

Jax paced around the room, which looked a lot like the one where Austin lay. Hit over the head. By the same person? Maybe when he woke up, he'd be able to tell them who'd done that to him. Not that Kenna could. She hadn't seen them.

"We need to find Maizie." She waved him over. Jax moved back to the beside. She grabbed his forearm, just below his elbow and used it to lever herself up. She hissed out a breath. "Ouchie."

He frowned. "Head or your arms?"

"Both." She stretched out her hands and rotated her wrists. "Not too bad today, but I haven't been to the range or tried to carry someone."

"It's still early." He stared at her.

Kenna's feet hung, not touching the floor. The last time they'd been this close he'd kissed her. Which would be a bad idea right now, considering she probably looked like she'd been dragged through a hedge backward. "Did the FBI get anything good from that flash drive?"

His eyes narrowed. "They're examining the file."

"So you were free to rescue me? That's nice."

A muscle in his jaw flexed. "You'd rather I left you alone, unprotected and injured?"

"Not your job." It could be, it just wasn't. Not while his priority was the FBI and his duty to the badge—the case he was on.

"The FBI director thinks it is."

"Where are my shoes?" She slid closer to the edge of the bed, not wanting to discuss the fact his assignment was likely about getting information from her. Like the task of flipping Santino.

Given her track record, she wouldn't be surprised if Anthony Santino was dead right now. As well as the former detective from Intellectus.

That was what happened to Joe Don Hunter, the last friend of her father's that she'd met. Sure, it had been because the sheriff's office in Bishopsville was burned down. He'd gone in to try to save the people trapped inside. If he hadn't been the man that he was, he would likely still be alive. But why be that when you could have honor and work to save lives?

He handed over her shoes. "You should hang on and get checked out."

She touched the back of her head. "It's just a bump. No blood."

"They took Austin to surgery to relieve the swelling in his brain. According to his mother, they're not even sure if he's going to make it."

"She told you that?"

Jax frowned. "Should I have assumed she was lying?"

That depended on whether he'd asked her to speak with the FBI in an official capacity. "Did you want to interview her, and Austin was the reason why she can't do that right now?"

Jax blinked.

"I have no idea what to make of that woman." Kenna slipped her foot into her shoes. "I don't think she's outright lying, but I'm also not sure if anything she says is actually true. Maybe partially."

"How did you get from your motel to being knocked out?"

She recounted Stairs' call that he'd found Austin. "He called Justine first, because she was here when I showed up." And after finding that phone number, Kenna had left.

"You didn't tell her about it?"

"Why? Justine wanted to stay here. If I'm going to find Maizie and give them some happy family reunion, then it's up to Maizie to tell me that's what she wants."

"What about what Justine wants?"

"We'll cross that bridge." Her head pounded from the knot on the back, radiating around her skull. "She's worrying about Austin. I'm the one finding Maizie."

"Her daughter ran off. How much does she want to be found?"

Kenna stood, mostly hiding how dizzy she was. *I'm fine.* "You're driving. We need to search that building to see if there's any indication she was taken again, or if she got away." *Please, God.* She didn't even know what words to use, or if she had the right to ask. But for Maizie's sake, she would do everything she could.

She wound up signing the form to refuse treatment, all while Jax scowled at her.

As they walked to his car, he said, "Is this how you always are, or just while I'm around?"

"You think I'm like this in order to what...play you? Or impress you?"

"You wouldn't be the first woman who fabricated the kind of person they were to convince me of something."

Kenna slumped into the passenger seat.

The first thing Jax did was go to the trunk of his car. Then he slid into the driver's seat and handed over an ice pack.

"You just keep these on hand?" she asked.

Instead of answering, he flipped open the glove box and handed over her holstered weapon as well.

She had to turn her head to him just so the sore spot didn't touch the headrest, but that left her staring at him. She held the ice pack against the bump. "I feel like there's a story there, so why don't you tell it to me while you drive back to that building." She tried not to sound like she wanted to throw up.

"She isn't there."

"How do you know? Did you check every inch after you found me?"

He started the car, frowning.

"I'm guessing that's a no." She shut her eyes.

"I should take you to your motel and then go look myself."

"But you're not going to."

"Only because I'll worry about you passing out again when there's no one there to watch out for you."

Kenna reached over and found his arm. She gently squeezed it, then laid her hand back in her lap.

"Last time I drove you somewhere after you were injured, you made me detour for...was it Greek food?" He kept his eyes on the road, a smile tugging his lips up. "Anyway, I drove all the way across Salt Lake City just because you said you wanted to stop for something to eat. Then when I'm ordering, you ditched me and headed to the house of the person who ran you over. So the two of you could hug it out."

Kenna recalled that conversation with Steven Pierce, the victim's grieving husband. A man battling anger and fear, who chose to take it out on Kenna. She'd talked to him instead of reacting the way she might've wanted to. "I don't know who hit me this time."

He sighed. "That might be worse."

"You're telling me." She let out a sigh of her own. "I just wish I could find Maizie. I was so close, talking to her on the phone. Reassuring her. Telling her to stick where she was."

"So it was a trap to lure you in."

Kenna frowned, even though it hurt. "No, she said someone was coming."

"Hmm."

It would take far too long to run DNA. Maybe that was what he was thinking. She sighed and opened her eyes. "What does that mean?"

"You're putting a lot of faith in someone you've never met."

"What if I'm the only one who ever has put faith in her?"

He took the next turn, then said, "What if this is Rushman drawing you in, and he's using this Maizie person to do it? Whether she's guilty or innocent or some gray area between. It could be about stringing you along."

"Lot of that going around."

"So you'll consider the possibility."

"Sure. Right when I look her in the eyes," Kenna said. "I wanna see her face for myself when I ask. When I sit her down and she tells me everything. From the situation in Bishopsville, to the church bombing, then Hatchet. All of it. Right up to the FBI special assignment. And whatever happens next."

"And the Russian diplomat cold case?"

She nodded. "I'll make sure Intellectus has what they need to close it." That might mean getting Santino to talk to them, but she would do it.

"I mean, don't you wonder if that wasn't a way to get you to focus on something else?"

"More like a way to get me to be distracted by my father's work here in Vegas." Like when she'd seen him shoot someone in Santino's kitchen. "But Intellectus cleared that up. More likely, if I'm under surveillance the way I think I am, then it's about finding out what Larry and Santino want these days. Keeping tabs on them to see how much of a threat they represent."

"If they were a threat, they'd have been killed a long time ago."

"And yet, no one's tried to kill me." Kenna frowned. "I'm honestly kind of insulted."

He shot her a look. Her head hurt too much to decipher what it meant. Probably that the guy who knocked her out didn't kill her—he just left her unconscious. Maybe he thought that indicated Maizie's cry for help had been nothing but a ruse.

"She wasn't lying," Kenna said. "You didn't hear her voice."

He pulled over in front of the building. "You didn't see her face."

"Oh, I will."

And when she did, she would know for sure whether Maizie was someone who needed saving…or if she was such a part of the organization Cerberus that she did whatever she was told.

Kenna pushed her door open. "Let's go."

She reached for her weapon as they approached the steps but didn't draw it. Kenna checked her pockets, even though the hospital had returned her personal belongings in a plastic bag. She had everything. She didn't have anything extra.

She pulled back both shirt sleeves, which meant unbuttoning things. In the end she just rolled them up like the stifling heat was getting to her—which wasn't untrue. "We're getting dinner after this. Something cold."

"As long as you don't throw it up."

"Let's find Maizie. Then I'll have my appetite back." She reached for the door.

"Hold up." Jax put a hand out in front of her. "I go first, okay?"

She motioned for him to proceed with an extra flourish.

Beside the stairs, he stopped to stare at the directory of

floors and the apartment numbers on each. "This is going to take forever. And I bet the elevator doesn't even work."

She glanced around, trying to see this place from the point of view of someone looking to flee captivity. Someone who may very well have fought their way free, called for help in the only way they could guarantee the right person would find it, then realized they were about to be captured again.

Kenna walked to the wall, next to the mailboxes for the first-floor apartments. About waist height, she found a smudge of blood. Just like the phone. "Maybe it won't be that hard."

Had Maizie left a trail, just like writing a phone number on Austin's hand? Kenna didn't even know where he'd been found. Justine hadn't said. Did he contact Maizie, and then get hurt? She needed Austin to wake up and tell someone what he knew.

Wake up...and...

Kenna had told Maizie her motel name and the room number. What if she was already there?

As Jax followed her down the hall, she realized she still hadn't drawn her weapon from its holster, so when she saw the same smudge leading into an open door to an apartment, Kenna stepped to the side and let him go first again.

She watched the hall to assure herself no one had tailed them. The last thing she needed was to get jumped again, but reality said whoever had been here was gone now. What about Maizie?

She understood what Jax had said about it possibly being a trap. Of course that was a possibility. It always was when she was being fed information. But something about Maizie made Kenna want to toss everything else just to find her—even if that meant forgetting about a whole organization.

Maybe it didn't make sense, but finding one person

seemed achievable. Combating a powerful group was a lot harder.

She was only one woman. What did the world want from her?

FBI agents *were* the ones who should find the person responsible for the church bombing, and the rest of it.

Kenna had her own case to work.

Jax hauled open a closet door. "Nothing. I don't see anyone."

"The window in the bedroom is open."

Jax glanced at her. "How do you know that?"

"You can't smell that? It's fresh. Doesn't smell like this room."

"It's stuffy hot in here, and there's no breeze outside."

She shrugged one shoulder.

Jax disappeared into the bedroom.

Instead of going back outside, which was what she should be doing, Kenna looked at the closet. She stepped all the way in and checked every corner. Beside the door, out of sight from anywhere but inside, the letter C had been swiped in blood.

Maybe the person behind the C on everything had been Maizie. A way for her to get Kenna to connect the dots. Then again, Kenna had seen it on tattoos. Ward Gaulding, the man coerced into bombing that church. Even Justine had the tattoo. Unless Maizie ordered it, that didn't make sense. The letter seemed like a calling card—but the places where Kenna had seen it online could still be Maizie leaving her clues.

How on earth did it relate to the death of a Russian diplomat?

Unless he'd been involved. Or the head that was cut off. Maybe Rushman got rid of Dmitri because he'd been friends with Santino, and took his place as the boss—taking over from the Russian. Had Dmitri been the head of the snake, as it were?

Kenna pointed. "She hid in here."

And now she could be in Kenna's motel room.

"One of the windows was cracked." Jax frowned. "I still think you were guessing."

Kenna shrugged. She had been, but that wasn't the point. She'd found indication someone connected to Cerberus was in here, hiding. Bleeding. "Time to go."

"I've got water in my trunk." He left and came back with an ice-cold bottle.

Kenna fished out her keys and headed for her car. "Thanks for bringing me back here."

While she walked to the Impala and drank the water, she looked for surveillance cameras. There were none, which was unsurprising since the building had been condemned. Even across the street the structures faced away, as though they didn't even want to look at this place.

The journals were still on the front seat, thankfully. She wasn't sure how she felt about driving this thing now they'd found what was hidden under the floor. As if that did any good, since a certain *FBI agent* had taken it from her, like he had more of a right to it.

She was working this case just like he was. She just happened to have her own agenda.

Maybe he knew that the second she found out anything about Maizie, her intention had been to ditch the Rushman angle altogether. That was the FBI's problem.

Maybe he'd known before she did.

Every case she worked, it was about saving the victim first. Then she would hand evidence to the police so justice could be brought against the perpetrator.

Jax followed all the way to her open car door. He

crouched, dipping his head to assess her gaze. "You need to rest."

"I'm sure I look great. I definitely don't need you to stick around and make sure I don't relapse or whatever." She grabbed the handle, about to shut the door on him if he didn't move. She needed a shower. Why was Vegas *so* hot?

"And if I argue about you being alone?" he said. "I could follow you back. Make sure you get there okay."

"I'll call Stairs if I need anything. See you tomorrow."

"Kenna—"

"I need to go."

He moved, and she shut the door. She pulled out before he got back to his car—not that he didn't know where she was going—and drove back to the motel.

Upon arrival, she practically ran to the door, hitting the card against the lock to open it.

The door swung wide.

"Maizie!" she yelled.

She needed to get her things from the car rather than leave it behind. Again. Her father's journals, and whatever else was in there—except the flash drive Jax had pilfered.

But first...

Kenna ran through the room, then checked the bathroom. "Maizie!"

The closet. Empty.

She turned and surveyed the room, breathing hard. Pain crashing through her head because she hadn't taken anything yet and the knot on her skull hurt. So close. She'd come so close to finding her, after months of wondering if Maizie was a ruse—or a figment of her imagination. She'd spoken to that girl on the phone.

"She..." Kenna couldn't even say aloud what it felt like to hear the fear and pain in Maizie's voice. To know how close she was, and yet not be able to find her. A young woman. Someone in danger. Victimized. Captive, with no way out.

She was free...and there was nothing Kenna could do to help her.

"You thought she would be here." Jax filled the doorway, far too much compassion on his face. She could barely look at him, knowing he wanted her to accept him here when all she wanted to do was rage about how all her efforts weren't working.

She had a giant tangled mess and barely anything to show for it but more questions than answers.

Kenna fought back tears. "Where is she?"

He strode to her and gathered her in his arms. "We are going to find her."

She held on tight. "What if it's too late?"

Chapter Twenty

Seventeen years ago

"But you never leave with a case unsolved," Kenna said to her father.

He pulled up to the gas pump.

They'd been on the road twenty minutes, and she hadn't yet picked up her book, which lay by her foot on the floorboard, her bookmark sticking out. Sure, it was a gas station receipt from just outside Tennessee, but it worked to keep her page marked.

"You don't understand." He sighed.

"So explain it to me." She couldn't get that image out of her head.

The moment that man ran into the kitchen, blood on his face. Her father firing that gun and then telling her to run.

He hadn't come home for two days.

During that time, she'd been *super* creeped out. Someone outside had been watching her, so she barely left the trailer except to ask the neighbor for a box of macaroni so she had something to eat. The night before, she'd heard someone right outside the front door, and through the peephole she saw a man was trying to pick the lock.

But her dad didn't care. He just yelled at her to pack up the stuff, and they pulled out so fast the trailer jerked behind them.

Now he gripped the wheel, not even getting out to start pumping gas. He just sat there. "I have another case. We need to store the trailer somewhere and buy suitcases. We're getting on a plane."

Kenna stared at him, all the teenage angst in her swirling and about to explode whether she liked it or not. "What is going on?"

He knew the signs of an impending Kenna-detonation. "Just drop it." Her dad pushed open the door. "I'll be back. I have to use the restroom."

He wasn't going to answer her questions at all, was he? Surely they had told the police what happened to that man. Probably he was a terrible bad guy, and her dad did the world a favor. That was what he did every time he solved a case—whether it ended in a death or he handed the person over to the police, with evidence or in cuffs.

The door slammed.

Her dad started the gas pumping, then strode to the store. As she reached down for her book, the cell phone he'd left on the dash started to ring.

Kenna had to unbuckle her seatbelt to reach it. She flipped it open. "Max Banbury's phone."

"You tell that—" The caller descended into a series of bad words, which she interrupted, since she knew the voice. They'd talked in his living room just a couple of days before.

"You really want me to pass on that message?"

"Tell him it didn't work, but since he *split*"—Santino spat the word—"I guess he already knows. That coward. I'll kill him."

"You'd have to catch him first." And apparently, they were getting on a plane.

Santino stayed quiet for a second. "Tell him I get it. Tell him I get that he's a slimy coward who cut and ran just because it didn't work. Just because he doesn't want to pay the price we *all* have to pay to take this guy down."

"Sure, I'll pass that along." Kenna's hormonal emotion bubble burst. She snapped the phone shut and tossed it on the dash.

Her dad came back to the vehicle, then stopped, as though he'd nearly forgotten to remove the gas nozzle.

When he got in, she told him everything Santino had said in full teenage color.

He turned the engine on and pulled out.

"Aren't you going to call him back?" She wanted to hear his explanation, and if he wouldn't give it to her, then maybe he'd give it to that mob guy.

But he said nothing.

She stared at him. *You really are a coward.*

Chapter Twenty One

Kenna didn't know how much she slept. Trying to stay awake long enough to see if Maizie showed up in the middle of the night—which meant leaving the door unlocked—didn't give her but a few snatches of stolen sleep. Those snatches came mostly when her body shut down and she had no choice but to sleep...and dream.

She needed to go see Santino. Find out exactly what that had been about.

Bottom line, they'd both reacted emotionally. But only he knew what her father had been doing here in Vegas.

Deacon had seemed to think Santino wanted her father to work for him. Then he kills someone and runs? She was being watched. Santino thought her dad gave up.

It made no sense.

First, though, Kenna rolled over and grabbed her phone off the nightstand. She pulled out the charger and looked at the screen. Stairs had messaged an hour before to tell her that he was up and nothing had come in overnight. She'd had him email back the address Maizie had given, just in case it was a functional account, and give her phone number. A long shot, but she was running out of ideas.

Kenna had a couple of new emails, both standard new case requests. Not anything that would make her wonder if it was Maizie.

Had she been recaptured?

Kenna couldn't think what she might be going through, or it would incapacitate her into inactivity. Swallowed up in the fear she knew all too well.

Two of her father's journals lay open next to her, where she'd fallen asleep while reading. Probably the reason for her dream. She'd been reading about the weeks after they left Vegas, since she hadn't found any entries that seemed to be during the time they were here.

She took a fast shower and put on clean clothes. Hair in a ponytail, even though stretching her arms up long enough to tie it hurt her forearms. She refused to surrender to the pain. Same with fear. Her injuries weren't going to stop her—even if there was a shelf life on her physical capabilities. Later didn't matter as much as what she needed to accomplish right now.

When lives depended on it.

The day she couldn't use her hands enough to even lift a hairbrush, she might retire. Or figure out a new workaround. Maybe there would be another medical option to repair the tendons Sebastian Almatter sliced with a knife the same way he cut both of Bradley's Achilles tendons. The goal had been to incapacitate them.

Every day, she lived her life while he lay cold in the ground. She worked, moved, and breathed—existing. All of it a slap in his face that what he'd tried to do to her hadn't worked.

Kenna emerged from the bathroom to her phone ringing.

Justine's name flashed on the screen.

After the last couple of days, she wasn't sure how she felt about this woman whose words and actions didn't line up. What the truth was, Kenna didn't know. What she *did* know was that she didn't like being lied to. Or manipulated.

"This is Kenna."

Justine gasped. "Austin's dad is here. At the hospital. He won't leave, he's already put his hands on me, and he won't listen to reason."

"Call for security." Getting child services involved as well might not be a bad idea. "Have them escort him out."

Justine whimpered. "I don't have legal grounds to deny him access to his son. He's got paperwork. He went to a lawyer, and now he's trying to get me kicked out."

"I'll be there soon. We'll figure it out." Kenna slid her feet into her shoes. She stuffed the journals into a backpack and took them with her to the Impala. Mostly she wanted to talk to Deacon.

Kenna found him in the emergency room.

One of the nurses gave her an odd look.

"Thanks for helping yesterday," Kenna said.

The nurse just frowned and kept on walking.

Kenna had opted for gray pants and a white shirt that morning, thinner than jeans so she wouldn't overheat outside. When this case was done, she needed a sea breeze—or some fresh mountain air with a touch of a chill in the morning. That sounded much better than this desert oven.

Hopefully it didn't last so long she wound up extra crispy.

Kenna pulled out her phone. She navigated to her texts and hit the button for speech to text. "Hey, I just had a thought. Call around the homeless shelters. See if they recognize Maizie by her description." After she corrected the bits it had messed up, she hit Send. She pocketed her phone again since these pants had pockets that actually fit her phone.

Justine stood in the waiting area at the far end of the ER, talking to a security guard.

Kenna wanted to reassure her, but she would rather just speak with Deacon. She slowed and knocked on the Plexiglass.

He glanced over, a haggard expression on his face. Classic rock black faded T-shirt, jeans, and boots. Austin lay in the bed, paler than the day before.

She eased inside but stayed closer to the door. "How is he? I heard he had surgery yesterday."

Deacon ran his hands down his face, then sat back in the chair. She spotted folded papers on the end table beside a plastic pitcher of water and a stack of cups. "I barely even know the kid. I just can't let that witch keep me away any longer. He's...hurt." His voice broke. "They say he might not even wake up. And if he does, he might not be the same kid he was." He paused. "Justine just wailed on about losing him. Like he's already dead."

"And you?"

"I get to know him. Whatever condition he's in, he's still my son." Deacon glanced at her, a ravaged expression on his face. "I've missed out on too much."

"He's a good kid." Kenna thought back to when they'd met in Hatchet a few months ago. "Austin cares about people. He doesn't want to be pushed around—not that anyone does. But he's the kind of person that stands up for people when it's needed."

"Nothing like me then. Maybe he's nothing like either of us."

Kenna wanted to ask if he really was denying Justine any access to her son at all. Austin wasn't far from being eighteen, but when the possibility of long-term care came into it, age didn't matter. What mattered was that someone who cared looked out for him.

It had been a decade since Deacon worked for Santino. When Kenna had been in Vegas, her dad, Larry, and Santino had been attempting to flush out the mole who worked for Rushman—at least according to what Larry had said.

Now she was looking at Rushman's mole.

"If it's okay, I'd like to tell you what might've happened to your son." Kenna kept her voice level.

Deacon sat back in his chair and nodded. He looked even older than he had when she and Jax interviewed him at his hotel—a function of the reality of his life hitting him in one go. Knowing he hadn't done the right thing at times. Something everyone had to come to terms with. But the determination in his eyes more than made up for it. She believed him when he'd said he wanted to do right by Austin now.

"Austin was out looking for his sister," she said. "I don't know if she's older or younger than him, but I believe at least he thinks she's his family and that he was trying to find her for Justine." She held up her phone and showed Deacon the picture of Maizie.

He didn't even react. Just waited, listening.

"When he got too close, he was attacked." Kind of like Kenna had been. "Because someone doesn't want her found."

"Who?" he asked.

"The FBI believes it's Michael Rushman," she replied. "That he's the one behind a deadly organization that targets people and victimizes them. Someone like Austin gets caught in the crossfire. I'm honestly surprised he's not dead."

"Rushman?"

Kenna nodded. "What do you know about him?" She

asked the question as though Santino and Larry hadn't both indicated he'd worked for Rushman.

Deacon's face twisted. He hung his head. "Austin should never have gone up against him." He launched from his chair. "She knew. She knew, and she let him—"

Kenna got between him and the door. "Justine?"

"She has to know it's Rushman. She probably has the same agreement I do, except I'm the one who gets screwed over in this deal. She gets to do whatever she wants."

"They victimized her, the same way they've done to other women. And they tried to kill her."

"Should've tried harder." Deacon let out an expletive. "She knew, and she let him get too close to that lion's den."

"So it is Rushman?" Kenna said. "What about the C tattoo on Justine's arm? Do you know anything about that?"

"It's a brand they give them. She worked her way out, though." Deacon shook his head. "Gotta hand it to her, she's clever. Probably got too old, so they figured what use do they have for her now. But I just know she made some deal."

"Like you did?"

"Fat lot of good it did." Deacon shrugged. "What do I have to show for it?"

"Would someone target Austin to get at you?"

"Only if they wanted me to hit back." He flashed gritted teeth.

"Who?"

"Who do you think?"

"So Rushman has everyone under his thumb?" Kenna paused. "How can he possibly keep track of all the moving pieces?"

Deacon's expression hardened. "He's a genius. Doesn't matter what, he'll have a way to get you to do what he wants."

"He's not all-powerful."

Deacon made a face, as though Rushman got people to believe that maybe he was.

"Is it just him?" she asked. "Or are there more?"

"It's him here."

So it could be others in different geographic locations—like Hatchet, or Bishopsville. The school principal had been a coordinator in Bishopsville. The FBI had arrested the county prosecutor in Hatchet. So was Rushman the head of the snake, or just the one who ran things in Vegas.

Kenna said, "Somehow I don't think it ends with him."

Deacon turned back to Austin. "I'm done talking about Rushman. I've got more important things to focus on right now."

Kenna pulled on the door, sliding it open. "I might be back if I have more questions."

"Whatever."

Justine stood tapping her foot, one hand on her hip. "Did you tell him he has to leave?"

"I'm not getting in the middle of a custody battle, Justine."

"So you'll do nothing. After you promised to help me, that you'd do *anything* to help me." Justine huffed.

"Other people need help right now," Kenna said. "Like Maizie." And yet, Justine was here—and Austin was her sole focus. "Where would she go to hide?"

"How do I know?" Justine ran a hand over her hair, making a face.

"Austin wanted to know. That's what got him hurt, right? Looking for her. For *you*."

"I didn't know this would happen!"

"You knew I'd find him, and that it would lead me to Maizie in the process." While Maizie seemed more interested in Kenna solving a cold case—until she'd called for help. "But now you don't care?"

"You think I don't care?"

"So tell me about her."

Justine pressed her lips together, breathing hard.

"You can't." Even if Justine was under duress, Kenna wasn't sure she was an innocent victim in all this. "What can you tell me?"

"Some things are best left alone."

"Not when an innocent person's safety is involved," Kenna said. "Kind of like how I showed up at your house just in time to save your life."

"Do you want a medal or something?" Justine spat. "You should've just let me die."

"I want to find Maizie."

"Get out." Justine pointed at the door. "If you're not going to get rid of Deacon, just *leave*."

Kenna glanced from her to Deacon, then headed for the exit. Out on the curb, she spotted Olivia Sanderson in a wheelchair, a staffer holding the handles, and wandered over. "Hey, they're releasing you?"

The teen nodded. "My mom is getting the car."

"Did you hear we found Austin? He was hit over the head, and he's had surgery. I'm hoping he gets better."

"That's good." Her eyes filled with tears, shimmering above the bruising on her face. Not much less swollen than it had been before, but she did seem like she felt better. Or she was just on good meds. Her blond hair had been braided back from her face, keeping it out of the way.

Kenna crouched by the wheelchair. "What is it?"

Olivia ducked her head. "The police arrested my dad."

Not what she'd expected the kid to say. "For doing this to you?"

She rubbed her nose and sniffed.

"I'm glad he's in jail then, so you can be safe."

"He stormed into the hospital. He hit my mom so the security man tackled him, and then the police were called." Olivia sniffed. "I'm glad Austin is gonna be okay. I wouldn't have been able to tell the police everything if it wasn't for him telling me..." She paused. "If I never did, it would never be over. That I had to take a stand."

Kenna wondered if that was because he believed his mother had, or because he wanted her to one day. Austin had tried to help and been hurt. She didn't believe half of what Justine had been saying to her, and not only because of Deacon's opinion of Austin's mother.

The hardest part of this case would be figuring out who was telling the truth and who had an agenda that colored what they said. Assuming people spoke truth all the time wasn't a good practice for someone with Kenna's job. She worked to find the innocent, but often the reason they were missing or targeted wasn't because their nearest and dearest were upright, God-fearing folks. More often than not, the victim hadn't been randomly targeted—it was personal.

Like Olivia.

A car pulled up.

She patted Olivia's shoulder. "I'm glad you're gonna be all right."

At least one thing in this confusing mess had been resolved.

Chapter Twenty-Two

Kenna walked into Bradley Pacer Hall at UNLV ten minutes before the ceremony was due to start. Mostly because she didn't want the chance to get waylaid into conversation—by anyone here.

The whole place had a fresh paint smell, the walls white while the carpet under her feet was new. Thankfully she had remembered to drop off her dry-cleaning the night before, because if she hadn't shown up here wearing fancy business attire, she'd have been seriously underdressed.

Kenna slipped into a seat a few rows from the back. Most of the chairs were occupied, but the hall could likely only hold maybe two hundred before the fire marshal would start squirming. Down on the stage, she recognized several people. Former president Masonridge milled about, flanked by a couple of Secret Service agents probably assigned to him full-time—which meant there would be more scattered about the room. The FBI director was down there as well, holding court with a few people. Reporters. She had to admit, he did a decent job representing the FBI.

"You look well." Someone had settled into a chair a couple of seats down from her.

The person in front of her turned, eyes widening at who it was.

Kenna knew the tenor of that voice, though not because she had spent overly much time with this man. But there was enough of Bradley in his tone that she identified him before she even glanced over.

"Do you ever tell the truth?" Kenna hadn't seen him in several years.

Since then, his wife had tried to kill her. Thankfully it was Jax who had shot Angeline Pacer, and not Kenna who was forced to do it. No, because she'd been lying on the floor in a pool of her own blood at the time.

The memory of it made her want to lift a hand and press it against her sternum that had been cracked open in order to repair the damage. That had been a lovely few months.

Instead of descending back into the mire of her memories, Kenna focused on the pattern of his tie. The fact he'd shaved for this. His fresh haircut. The way the lines on his face seemed more pronounced than they had since she'd seen him last.

Unsurprising, considering everything.

"Never mind," Kenna said. "You're a politician." When did one of those ever answer the question they were asked? She winked. "Why would *you* tell the truth?"

They'd fought their way past what life had dragged them both through, which had become remarkably easier when he finally admitted his wife had been the one who pushed him to get Kenna shoved out of the FBI with early retirement. Angeline also had a brief affair with Stairs, adding to the pressure by leveraging that.

Were it not for the fact she was dead, Kenna might

wonder if Angeline was the kind of person behind the organization Cerberus.

Pacer waved at the front of the room, where the people onstage took their seats and had final makeup brushed on their faces.

Kenna frowned. "This is being televised?"

He chuckled. "Much like that man down there"—he waved at former president Masonridge—"I am also retired from politics."

"Do you know Michael Rushman?" She had to ask the question, though considering he was up here talking to her and not down there schmoozing with some of the country's most powerful people, maybe that was enough of an answer for her on how he felt about them.

He wrinkled his nose in a way Bradley used to do. "Not exactly my taste in friends. Rushman was actually supposed to be here, but apparently he's ill." He shrugged. "His assistant sent his apologies."

"Why invite them here?"

Pacer sighed. "To be completely honest, my assistant did most of the organizing. She thought it would be good to have a big event, get Bradley's name in the news media again. What with him being a hero and all."

They both winced.

"I'm sorry. But I'm not sorry you came," he said. "I've been wondering how you are."

Kenna recalled that adage about time healing wounds. He'd let his wounds scab and then heal, while his wife encouraged a festering that turned to poison inside her.

She was about to answer when someone moved close to her left elbow. "Kenna, we have—oh, hello, sir."

It was Jax.

He reached a hand across her. "Excuse me. Oliver Jaxton, sir."

The former Utah governor shook his hand. "Pacer."

"Nice to meet you, sir."

"You, as well." Pacer stood. "Kenna."

She held out her hand, and he gave it a squeeze. Then he walked away, toward the aisle on the other side.

Jax wedged his way in front of her knees and took the empty seat beside her, closer than the former governor had sat. "Was he bothering you?"

Kenna frowned. "Bradley's father? He has more of a right to be here than I do."

"Does he?" Jax shifted in his seat, trying to see to the front.

She'd gotten some sleep the night before, but apparently not enough to energize her. Unfortunately, what gave her inspiration was solving a case. Which was what she needed to do but couldn't because she needed more creative energy.

Maybe it wasn't completely pointless coming here, using this as another way to say goodbye to Bradley. Honoring him, the way everyone else wanted to. Because he was the kind of man who had been worthy of having a law building at his alma mater named after him.

The chance to gather more intel on Rushman would not have been lost on Bradley—if the guy were here. Her former partner would have been all in for making this trip worth it.

Even better, if somehow Maizie was here and Rushman still wasn't. Kenna didn't think that would happen, but she could hope regardless.

She glanced around the room at his legacy. *Bradley.* "We were going to get married."

Jax turned to her, but when the dean of the school got on a microphone and began the ceremony, he said nothing.

Kenna swallowed. "When the case was done." The case that had killed Bradley. "He had it all booked and everything, but refused to give me a ring until he made it official." She shook her head. "One of those awful gaudy wedding chapels here in Vegas. We were going to come down and spend the weekend."

Jax smiled. "My mother would be apoplectic just hearing about that."

"Good thing you don't share her sensibilities."

"Yes, it is. Or I would still be married."

"And wouldn't that be a tragedy." Except that Kenna didn't know anything about the woman—and she refused to be a total stalker and look her up online. Even if she wanted to.

Jax smiled.

"It seems like right and wrong, good and evil, isn't so black-and-white anymore."

"Because of Maizie?"

Kenna shook her head. The person in front of her turned back and frowned, which she took to mean that they were talking too loudly. She leaned closer to Jax and whispered, "Justine is the kind of person I would have believed. And now it seems hard to reconcile. Almost like Deacon is the honorable one between the two of them."

"I'm not so sure he is on the up-and-up."

"But he's there for Austin, taking care of him."

Jax nodded, conceding the point. Kenna wondered if maybe she shouldn't simply double down on "innocent until proven guilty," and her need to see the world that way. To live as though it was black or white, with no shades between.

Up front on the stage, the FBI director glanced at Masonridge.

Kenna whispered, "What was that about, I wonder?"

Jax reached over and squeezed her knee.

She closed her mouth and kept it that way for the rest of the ceremony, while the suited men on the stage blustered about the legacy of an FBI agent cut down at the height of his career. A man with so much promise, taken from this world far too soon.

Her former partner and the man she loved hadn't been perfect, the way Kenna certainly hadn't been as well. But she wondered if one shined a light in each of these men's private lives whether they would come out smelling even half as good as Bradley.

After his death, she'd been the party who was wronged and all that. The innocent victimized by the FBI. By the family of the man she lost.

It would have been easy to stand on that moral high ground and do whatever it took to get back at them. But if she'd done that, then she would have been no better than Angeline Pacer, getting revenge for what she saw as Kenna having cost her the life of her son.

Maybe things weren't so black-and-white as the FBI wanted to believe it was.

As an agent, she'd been taught to view herself as the good guy and the criminal as the bad guy, creating a clear dividing line between right and wrong. Between the way she lived her life and those who chose to break the law. A way to maintain integrity, even when it was hard.

But life on the outside wasn't so cut-and-dried.

Except when Kenna went after missing children. Those cases made it easy to judge right from wrong. The victims couldn't save themselves, and the parents contacted Kenna for help.

Getting swept up in those cases made her wish for something simple. Which was probably why she had taken Justine up on her request to find Austin—because she wanted to believe the two of them were innocents caught up in this organization.

The truth might be something entirely different.

As soon as the ceremony wrapped up, they stood to applaud. Kenna stuck her hands in her pockets.

"I have something to show you." Jax tugged out his phone. "So don't go anywhere."

As people started to file out, she turned, blocking the way to the aisle. "What is it? Because I'm trying to figure out how to use the former governor as bait. Maybe get him to try and work his way into Rushman's organization and find out what he's up to."

"You wanna ask him to do that?" Jax frowned. "Or do you want me to?"

Kenna made a face. "No way he would believe you. Someone's been following me. They all know that you and I are…" She barely knew how to explain it.

Jax, on the other hand, thought it was highly amusing. "That we are what?"

"You think whoever knows you stayed over in my motel room the other day assumes you *weren't* in that second bed?"

He shrugged one shoulder. "You care what people think?"

"Why would I, if their opinion doesn't relate one bit to the reality of my integrity?" She was just voicing what someone might assume—if she really was being followed. Kenna would rather it was Maizie and not someone from the FBI or one of Rushman's employees watching her. Waiting to make their approach.

"Hearing you talk about integrity makes me want to kiss you again." He leaned in a little. "After all, the secret is already out."

"But why would you," Kenna said, "when I have nothing you want to steal right now?"

Jax laughed for a second, but the humor was short-lived. "You keep distracting me, and I came in here to show you this." He turned the screen of his phone so she could see. "It's surveillance video, about a mile from that abandoned apartment building."

As the surveillance rolled, nothing changed. Until a dark dressed figure crept around the corner of the building. She walked with a limp, clutching her side with one hand. Her hood obscured whatever hair she had.

"It was two days ago," Jax said. "I already searched this building where she is in the video, and the surrounding area."

"You think if she was still in there, she would come out?"

"You have reason to believe she won't?"

"As far as I know, she's a scared girl with no one to help her," Kenna said. "But since she hasn't contacted me again, I can only assume there's something she's trying to do. Other than just remaining on the run."

"Like what?"

"Better question," Kenna said, because the truth was, she had no idea. "Has anyone ever approached you and attempted to blackmail you with regard to this case?"

"You think I wouldn't have told you if they had?" Jax said.

"I didn't say you'd think about going along with it. I'm just asking if anyone's broached the subject." She didn't know what he'd been into in his past. Maybe he had skeletons in his closet. At one point he'd indicated to her that something had happened at his previous posting, before Salt Lake City. But he'd never told her what. "I don't know what's out there that I could dig up on you."

His expression darkened. "Nothing would give anyone leverage to get me to comply with something like this.

I'd be more worried about the others on the special assignment."

"Because you're so upright?"

"No," Jax said. "They know you'd never trust me otherwise."

That was true enough. She kept him at arm's length on a good day, which was decidedly easier when they weren't in the same state. Having him here and able to respond when Stairns called to say she might be in trouble definitely had its merits.

With Jax here, she didn't feel so alone.

Kenna sighed. "This entire case has been going on for decades."

"Then it ends now." Jax slipped his phone back into his pocket. "We need to put a stop to all of it."

The lecture hall had mostly cleared out. She stepped from the row into the aisle just as the door at the back flung open.

Justine strode in and glanced around, not even seeing Kenna.

And then her eyes flared.

"You!" Justine pulled the gun from her belt and pointed it at the stage, where Governor Pacer stood with former president Masonridge, along with Secret Service and reporters. "I'm gonna kill you!" Her finger shifted to the trigger.

About to fire.

Kenna stepped into the aisle in front of her and held up both hands. "No, you're not."

Chapter Twenty-Three

"Kenna, move out of the way."

The tone of Jax's voice didn't invite any other option, but Kenna had no intention of moving. Good idea, or bad idea, it didn't matter. She'd already taken the step. Now all she had to do was keep Justine from firing that gun.

Which meant she was staying put.

Especially when she was the only one standing between an armed woman and her intended target.

A handful of people scurried to the exits. Someone tripped, yelping as they hit the floor. Someone else screamed.

Kenna didn't budge, keeping all her focus on Justine. "No one is shooting anyone." She lifted her hands so Justine would see that she didn't have a weapon—at least, not within reach right now. "Justine, give me that gun."

The person she wanted to kill wasn't even here today.

"You need to pay attention to me." Or Justine would simply leave and go find him wherever he was.

After everything that had happened in the last six months, there was no way it would end like this—with Justine murdering Michael Rushman in cold blood. In front of a room full of witnesses, or at his home because he was ill. Either way, Rushman would only become a martyr, a man cut down in the prime of his sixties.

Whatever charges the US Attorney would've brought would end up buried in all the outcry about gun violence and the memorializing of the victim. In this instance? Kenna couldn't even stomach the thought of that.

She realized then that she had fallen into the same pattern of thinking as the FBI—assuming that Rushman was the sole person behind the organization. In reality, she didn't know if that was even true. Aside from the fact everyone should be considered innocent until they were proven guilty, all she had was a couple of snippets of footage and a bunch of indications Rushman targeted people, put them under duress, and got them to do what he wanted.

There was no way he was innocent. But she also didn't know how guilty he was.

Justine sniffed, her eyes glassy. She held the gun with a determined focus, in a way that indicated to Kenna that this woman knew what she was doing with a weapon. However, all the built-up emotion in her caused the gathering of sweat on her temple, and the short inhales.

"Justine, look at me." Kenna needed Justine to focus on her, not anyone else in the room. That was the first step in getting her to see reason—and the need to give up the gun and stand down.

From across the room, a rush of feet headed away from them.

Someone yelled, "Lone Wolf is on the move! He's on the move!" The Secret Service, getting Masonridge out of the room.

Kenna shifted slightly closer to Justine, using the distraction to get her within arm's reach. Almost.

Justine blanched. "I'm gonna kill him. Get out of my way, Kenna."

Kenna shifted slightly left.

Jax whispered loudly, "Kenna." Likely as a warning she'd just stepped in his line of fire.

"No one is killing anyone today. That goes for you and for anyone else here." Kenna wasn't going to let that happen. She could defuse the situation without loss of life, because that was more important than eliminating a threat. No one needed to get hurt if it was within her power to do anything about it.

Jax moved behind her.

"Justine, listen to me." Kenna studied the desperation on Justine's face. "Move your finger off the trigger. Just to start with. How about you just move your finger?"

"No. I'm going to kill him. There's nothing you can do to stop me." Justine had just given the FBI a statement of her intention.

Kenna winced. "What you don't realize is that we've already stopped you." Even though Rushman wasn't in the room, and Masonridge had been ushered out. "There's no way you're going to kill anyone right now." If the FBI had anything to do with it, that would probably extend to forever. With prison time. "It's over."

Justine blanched. "No, it's not!"

Kenna took a tiny step closer. "I'm not going to let anyone get hurt. Not even you."

"Tell that to Austin."

"I'm sorry about what happened to your family, but if you tell the FBI what you know, they can help you." Kenna motioned to the gun. "This isn't the answer to your problems. All it does is keep you from your children, because a judge is going to put you in prison."

"Who cares!" Justine motioned with the gun toward the stage. "I'll do whatever it takes!"

"That's—"

The gunshot echoed in the room.

The bullet buzzed past Kenna and slammed into Justine's shoulder, knocking her back a couple of steps. Kenna flinched hard, then grabbed Justine's wrist as she went down.

Justine slumped onto the floor, crying out.

Kenna tossed the gun aside and put her hands on Justine's shoulder, pressing down hard. The bleeding woman beneath her screamed. Kenna looked at Jax because he wasn't the one who had shot her. "Get an ambulance."

He already had his phone to his ear.

She tuned out what he was saying and looked at Justine. "You're okay. You're going to be okay." Her expression, and the fire in her eyes, bored into Kenna. As though it were her fault that Justine had been hurt. "There was no way anyone was going to let you kill someone here."

"He deserves to die painfully."

"Rushman isn't even here. But if you take him out, none of us get justice." Kenna fought back her frustration. "His life is over, and everything he's done gets buried in news coverage of the memorial, candles, and people crying. Is that what you want to see?"

"The truth will come out."

Kenna shook her head. "No, the truth will get buried, because there are people in this world who will do that, because it's in their best interest to keep it all quiet."

"He stole my baby!" Justine flailed her arms and legs while Kenna kept pressure on the gunshot wound on her shoulder. "Now I have nothing!"

"And revenge will keep you warm, and make you feel like you're loved?" Kenna asked her. "Because it doesn't."

Jax crouched. "EMTs will be here in minutes."

Justine yelled, "I don't want that!"

"Yes, you do," Kenna said. "Because if you don't fight to live, then whatever they did to you? It worked."

Jax shifted beside her. "Justine, who took your baby?" Like now was the time to interview her?

Kenna just gritted her teeth and kept the pressure on, trying to figure out how this got so out of control. She glanced over her shoulder at the armed security guard. "Did you do this?"

He swallowed. "She was going to kill someone. It's what I was trained to do."

Jax glanced at him next. "You did the right thing."

"I wasn't going to let her kill anyone." Kenna had to say that out loud. Because they needed to understand. She'd have let Justine shoot her before she let her hurt Jax, or anyone else in this room. "All that would do is jeopardize the case."

"Sure," Jax said. "That's the only reason." He shifted in his crouch. "Justine, tell me what happened with your baby."

"He took her. Where's my baby?"

Kenna's eyes filled with hot tears that burned.

"Austin is in the hospital," Jax said.

Justine's legs shifted, restless. "Where is she?"

"Maizie?" Kenna winced. "You said you saw her in Las Vegas. Tell me about that."

Justine whimpered. "She's here. Where else would she be?"

So this woman had lied to Kenna in Hatchet? And then she'd convinced her son to find the child when she had no idea where Maizie was. All of it putting Austin in the kind of danger that landed him in the hospital.

"He took my baby," Justine whimpered.

"Everyone back up. Let us through." The voice belonged

to a guy wearing an EMT uniform, followed by a younger guy. Both of them carried duffel bags as they pushed a gurney between them down the aisle. One crouched beside Kenna, and she lifted her hands. He took a look at the wound and started barking orders to his partner.

Jax grasped Kenna's upper arm and helped her to her feet. "We need to get you somewhere you can clean up."

She looked at her hands. Wet with blood, slick and damp.

The room started to spin around her.

Jax caught her in his arms. "Whoa, easy there." He got her to start walking, holding most of her weight as they moved down the row between chairs. "Don't look at your hands. Look in front of you."

Kenna sniffed as tears rolled down her face.

Jax pushed through a door into a side hallway, where she had to ignore people standing around. He walked her down the hall.

Lights flashed at the edges of her vision, making her head spin. The pain on the back of her skull at having her head slammed into a wall thrummed. Bile rose in her throat.

Jax walked her into the bathroom. She broke away from his hold, shoved the stall door open, and managed to contain the mess. A minute or so later, he reached past her and flushed the toilet. "Come on." He held her elbows and led her to a sink. "Don't look at yourself."

But that just left her looking at her blood-slicked hands.

He held them under the warm running water, then used soap to build up a lather. The water tinged red as it swirled down the drain. Kenna got most of the blood off before splashing water on her face. He got her paper towels, and she dried off.

Kenna switched the water to cold, then cupped her clean hands and drank.

"Okay, easy." He cut her off before she felt like she was finished. "You'll just make yourself sick again."

Kenna didn't know what to say. If she apologized for her reaction to having blood on her hands, he'd tell her she didn't need to be sorry. The last thing she wanted to hear was that she'd had a normal reaction for someone with her history. That it was okay to not be okay, or that she shouldn't be mad at herself when she wasn't okay. At this point, it was far better to ignore the gaping issue and get back to work.

"We should go," she told him.

"Normally, that's my line." But instead of moving to the door, Jax stepped closer to her. He touched his hands to her cheeks and surveyed her face.

"Justine didn't give me any evidence for you to steal."

His gaze settled. "You're never going to let that one go, are you?"

"Nope."

He studied her, as though trying to figure out what to say.

Part of her liked that he felt the need to be on his A game with her. She didn't want to be anyone's afterthought. But then again, the last thing she needed right now was an attraction complicating everything.

Jax tucked her toward him and laid a kiss on her forehead. "Now we can go."

"As long as you don't insist on holding my hand."

"Do people even still do that?" He held the door open for her, and she realized this was the ladies' room.

Kenna stepped out and spotted the rest of their special assignment team over in the lobby at the end of the hall. "I've always thought holding hands was severely underrated."

"I'll add it to the bacon column."

"Because bacon is underrated?"

He chuckled. "Don't sound so aghast. I mean the list of things you think are important in life."

"Huh," Kenna said. "You mean like blue cheese on a steak, and the ability to share your fries with someone who didn't need a whole serving but still wants to eat a few of them?"

"What's this about fries?" Special Agent Dean lifted his chin.

Kenna shook her head. "Nothing." If any of them asked her if she was okay, she would start punching people. "Where's Justine?"

"Elton and Nelson went with her in the ambulance. They've got her under guard, until she can be transferred to holding."

The charges would be something close to attempted assassination of a former president. Justine probably wasn't going to see the outside of a prison in a very long time, regardless of whether her intended target had been Rushman, or another person standing on the stage. For all she knew, Justine could have been targeting Governor Pacer. Or the FBI director. Or any number of other people.

Jax nodded. "Good. Anything else new?"

At least Justine was still alive for them to question her. Kenna for one wanted to know everything Justine had to say, considering she'd admitted she had no idea where Maizie was. It was past time to get out on the streets and look for the missing girl. All the while, praying she hadn't been recaptured.

Special Agent Dean said, "We're still working to verify the video on that flash drive you brought in." His gaze shifted to Kenna. "It was good work, getting that from Santino. Do you have anything else from him?"

Apart from an entire car? "Nope."

"Well, get on it before the director starts asking why you haven't pitched Santino making an official statement."

Because this entire case hinged on what Kenna could do? Considering she had split priorities right now, that was a bad judgment call on the part of the FBI. Even if it had been her bargain in the first place, Dean was acting like the whole investigation counted on Santino's testimony. Which made her wonder what they knew about Santino's role that she didn't?

Maybe Larry from Intellectus could fill her in on that.

After she found Maizie, of course.

Dean continued, "Once we get that statement, and this crazy woman's manifesto, we can wrap the whole thing up. We'll have more leads than we can handle, and the evidence won't be far behind."

"Because you think she sat around typing up her thoughts before she came here?" Kenna folded her arms, her stomach roiling. She needed coffee to settle her. "She's been at the hospital with her son."

"Right. Jax did say that you found who you were looking for." Dean lifted his chin. "So it's time to go to work with us."

Kenna twisted around.

Jax lifted both hands. That whole *don't blame me* stance was becoming irritating.

Special Agent Dean continued, "He said the girl called you, and if the boy's been found in the hospital, then it's all done. Right?"

Kenna fought with the need for composure. "No, it isn't done. The girl is still very much in danger. So I should get out and go find her. Good luck with Santino."

She didn't even glance at Jax, just headed for the exit.

Chapter Twenty Four

"Maybe." The gas station attendant frowned. "Should I remember her?"

Kenna didn't lower the phone. With Maizie in the condition she was in, injured and on the run, it was entirely possible she would be memorable. Though, if Maizie knew that, then she would take extra steps to lay low. "She was seen in this area recently. I'm trying to find her."

"Huh." The young guy paused. "Do you want a receipt?"

Kenna shook her head. She took the cold diet soda and the snack pack of ham and cheese and headed outside, then sat on the hood of the Impala, even though it was warm. She watched a guy with a little tiny dog pace around the grass beside the gas station, remembering the last tiny dog she'd met. Dixie Cabrera had been a bounty hunter, and her dog Tilly went with her wherever she traveled.

Kenna pulled out her phone and dialed Stairs' number.

He answered, "Anything?"

She didn't want to say no—and have to admit that the last three hours had been unfruitful. "I'm not giving up finding her."

"Good."

"Do you have anything?"

"I've been digging into Rushman, but there's not much about him other than what the press release says," he said. "I have to admit, I've admired the guy for a long time."

Kenna could have said the same thing, even though it wasn't like leaders in science and technology were on her radar. She was mostly just trying not to be mad that Special Agent Dean had mentioned in passing how Jax had supposedly said she'd found both Austin and Maizie.

As if the hunt was over.

They must have gotten their wires crossed. After all, Jax had showed her the video of Maizie in this exact area.

Those old doubts crept back in. As if the FBI was simply playing her to get what they wanted from her, which was, of course, precisely what they were doing. That was how they solved cases—by flipping some unsuspecting person who'd been caught up in a situation. Getting them to work as an informant and record their associate—the person responsible. Letting them incriminate themselves.

But with Jax in the middle of it.

The rest of the FBI? She didn't trust them one bit. He, however, was a totally different story. Probably against her better judgment, Kenna actually trusted an FBI agent.

"You think the FBI will let you talk to Justine?" Stairs said. "I mean, you're the one that has a rapport with her. And this is all under the purview of the FBI director."

Kenna frowned, heading for her driver's seat so she could turn the engine on and get the AC running. Beat back some of this stifling heat. "What do you mean?"

"Totally off book. Far as I can tell, no one at the FBI even knows what's going on except the director. He's officially on vacation, not even at a conference in Vegas. He's just gone and out of contact according to his assistant."

"So they wanted to keep it quiet." She should ask Jax about that. "But it stands to reason, if this is such a high-profile case, then the minute Rushman gets wind of the fact they're investigating him, he's going to batten down the hatches and make sure they don't have anything."

"Like shredding every document in his office?"

"You're so old-school." Kenna angled the vents so air blew out her face. "It's more like dumping hard drives and erasing servers these days."

Stairns chuckled.

"Something funny?"

"I'd like to say I'm laughing at your attempt to bring me in to this century, but Cabot is rolling around on the floor with her teddy bear, looking at it like no one else exists in the universe."

Kenna frowned. "Good to know she's forgotten all about me."

Stairns chuckled louder.

"How about we focus." As soon as the case was over, Kenna planned to drive to their house and spend some time with her favorite dog. But she would work the case until she was free to do that without painting a target on anyone.

She wanted to know why Maizie hadn't contacted her again. If she had heard Kenna's motel and room number over the phone, maybe she felt like she couldn't go there. Especially if she believed someone could have listened to their conversation on the phone. Kenna's part in this had always been to solve the cold case. She had to trust that Maizie knew where to find her.

Kenna needed to get info, get some answers, and start solving this.

"What about that guy, Deacon?" he asked.

She thought about Austin's father in the hospital. "He didn't know anything about a girl baby. But was that ignorance, or untruth? I don't even know if the kid is older or younger than Austin, though I would guess older and gone before he was born if Austin hasn't met her. He's just heard stories." She remembered the look in Justine's eyes as the woman lay on the ground, bleeding. Asking for her baby. "No wonder she's twisted up mentally. If someone took her child from her, it stands to reason she would lose her mind."

"Enough to try and kill someone?"

"How would *you* react if someone had taken one of your girls?" Probably similarly to the way her dad would have reacted.

A thought that gave her pause.

The man outside her trailer in her dream. Her dad and their mad dash from Vegas. Was that why they had left so suddenly? A couple of days later, the trailer had been in storage, and they'd been on their way to London. Her dad had told her that a case came up out of the blue and he was requested. What if it was his attempt to safeguard her from the person they'd been trying to take down?

She needed to look more at those journals. Find out for sure.

Her phone chimed. Kenna looked at the screen. "Larry, that Las Vegas police detective who's with Intellectus now, is calling me back."

"Good." Stairs' voice had thickened. "Find out what's going on."

"I will." Kenna would do it so he never had to get choked up at the idea of his girls being targeted again. They were grown women now, but probably he didn't feel any different about them than if they were younger and vulnerable.

She switched over to the other call. "What's up?"

"Four messages? Seriously?"

"Because I need to talk to you."

"Then meet me at Santino's," Larry said. "If I'm going to talk, then so is he."

Kenna drove over, pulling into the driveway right behind a red compact. Larry hefted his body out of the driver's seat. Kenna locked the Impala and held on to the keys as she walked over to him. "Is the front door open?"

Larry drew a gun from the holster at the small of his back. "Looks like it." He eased the door the rest of the way open and went ahead of her.

Kenna kept her gun angled down. The hallway opened into the living area, everything askew. Books and magazines tossed on the floor. Even the couch was on its back, cushions everywhere. "Hello?"

No one answered.

Larry kept moving. "So the whole place is empty?"

Kenna looked around. "Santino doesn't have the staff he used to."

"Got him." Larry holstered his gun and strode through the kitchen, where Santino sat in a chair at the dining table, holding a bag of frozen peas to his head. "What happened?" He pulled back the peas and took a look. "Yeesh."

Santino made a face. "That girl is crazy is what happened."

Kenna got him a glass of water, wondering how long he had been sitting here. The bag of peas looked a little melted. "Justine...or Maizie? Who did this?"

Santino blinked, a slight shake of his head.

Kenna pulled out her phone and flipped to her pictures. "This woman?" She showed him Justine first. When he shook his head, she showed him Maizie. "Her?"

Santino reacted. "One of my guys tried to grab her. Big mistake. I sent them all away so I could talk to her by myself. Didn't know if she'd clock me, so I couldn't follow her."

"How long ago was she here?"

Larry glanced at her with a frown. He turned back to Santino. "What happened?"

Santino tossed the peas on the table. "She wanted to know where the evidence is. The stuff we collected to take down Rushman." He took a sip of the water Kenna had found in the fridge. "I had to tell her I destroyed it."

Larry groaned.

But Jax had found the flash drive in the car. So Santino wasn't telling the truth—because Larry was here? Why would he need to keep from Larry the fact he still had it?

She had a feeling her dad had taken her away so that she wasn't in danger. But the rest of them had just given up, hidden the evidence? Now they were lying to each other.

Santino paled. "Rushman gave me pictures of my daughter. Sick stuff. Messed-up things you don't ever want to see." Tears spilled from the gruff man's eyes. "Things that made my wife medicate herself to death." He broke down and began to sob. "My child."

Kenna hung her head. Larry cleared his throat. Neither of them bothered Santino while he grieved for what he had lost.

After a couple of minutes, he regained enough composure to continue. "Rushman told me if I destroyed what we'd gathered or gave it to him, he would give her back to me."

Larry seemed unsurprised by this, so they probably talked about it at some point.

Kenna wasn't sure the daughter had died, though. Not all the victims were killed. "Did you get her back?"

"I had to put her in an institution." Santino stared off to the side. "She won't ever recover from what he did."

"You could have gone after him. Retaliated...and tried to take him out." She would have. Kenna knew that much about herself. After all, she was cut from the same cloth as Stairs. Someone who put it all on the line to get justice.

"When I tried," Santino said, "he ordered Dmitri Alekhin to be killed."

That had been a couple of years after Kenna and her father were in Vegas. So his answer fit the timeline. "But why him?"

"Dmitri was the only family I had left, my best friend. Everyone else was gone or dead." Santino scrubbed his hands down his face. "The family had cut me loose. We met the day our daughters were born. Same ward, in the same hospital, when Dmitri's wife died. We were staring through the glass into the nursery and got talking. I couldn't help it. The guy was a mess." He sighed. "We became friends, and Rushman used it against me."

Larry pulled out a chair on the other side of the table. "That's what Rushman does in this town. How he keeps everyone in line."

"Targeting their families?" Kenna said.

Santino nodded. "He threatened to expose Dmitri's vices to the Russian government. Hand over proof he was betraying his country to America."

"So he could have Dmitri's child? Or yours?" Kenna asked.

Santino nodded. "What Rushman wants, he takes. No one can do anything to him."

Larry told Kenna, "That's why your father ran."

She nodded. "He left a case unfinished."

"Rushman would have come after you," Santino said. "Your dad did what was necessary to keep you safe."

Even making her believe he was a coward?

That meant instead of explaining and allowing her to feel the same fear he felt in his bones, he'd told her a lie. All to keep her from having to understand the depth of depravity with its eye on her. The man in the window. A sick person with countless victims.

But Kenna hadn't been one of them. Because her father had kept her safe.

She studied Santino and Larry, two broken men in a trail of broken people left behind by one person. Not a whole organization. Just one person. "Are you going to continue to let him destroy others, or are you going to end this?"

Larry huffed. "You think you can go after Rushman? That's nothing but suicide."

Kenna unlocked her phone and showed him the picture of Maizie. "She's already doing it." Which was exactly why she came here—to get the evidence from Santino. Because Maizie believed there were others like her, determined to fight this man.

No way was Kenna about to let her down. Or leave her alone to do this by herself.

Santino said, "Rushman only got more powerful over the years. He's connected now and has been for decades. He's unstoppable."

Kenna laid the phone facedown on the table. "That just means it has to be done right. And that girl is the key."

Santino covered his face with his hands again. Larry stared at the table.

"What do you both know about the baby that was taken from Justine?" The others Rushman had were older—young women he could exploit or use and discard. But it seemed as though Maizie had been his captive for her entire life.

"They told her she was dead." Larry pushed out a breath. "I knew her. Used her as a confidential informant some. She was a druggie, and after she had the baby, she was in no condition to argue. She went back to the drugs right away, and within a few weeks social services got involved. She wouldn't stop screaming about the baby's father."

Santino said, "I was told it was a deal. He didn't want anyone knowing he'd fathered a child outside of his marriage, so he gave her"—he swallowed—"*sold* her to Rushman. Like she was payment for a debt, all so Rushman wouldn't expose what the father had done."

Larry frowned. "Where did you hear that?"

"From Deacon. Now I know he heard it because he worked for Rushman. He probably fed me that information because Rushman told him to. I don't know if he's aware it was Justine. A couple of years later, she was clean and showed back up. I knew who she was right away, so I told her I knew nothing." He sighed and shook his head. "She and Deacon ended up with Austin, but I'm pretty sure it was all so she could try and find her baby." He winced. "Justine left with Austin, and I found a way to get rid of Deacon. But not before Rushman took Dmitri as well."

Kenna wasn't sure if that meant Deacon had been lying to her, or if he was simply ignorant. But given everything, it was likely a mix of the two. At least he seemed determined to take care of Austin now.

After all these years, it didn't appear as though Rushman still had Deacon under his thumb. But with a man out there who had slammed her against a wall. A guy no doubt hunting Maizie. Kenna had to be on the lookout for an assailant.

At least she could honestly say it wasn't either of these men who had attacked her in that lobby. Santino was too thin, and Larry wasn't nearly tall enough.

"Justine knows exactly what her child has been through," Larry said. "No wonder she's messed up."

"You're right when you said that kid has been in this her entire life." Santino stared at her with a dark expression. "A bargaining chip, and who knows what Rushman subjected her to. I'm surprised she's still alive. But I could tell she hates him as much as we do."

"So where is she now?" Kenna asked. "Because it's high time Maizie knows she's not in this alone." She stood, pressing both palms to the table. "Rushman is going down."

Chapter Twenty-Five

Kenna had to wonder if she hadn't just painted a target on their backs, trying to convince Larry and Santino to take up the fight against Rushman again. After all, going after such an "untouchable" person would mean backlash. The exact reason the FBI had kept it quiet.

She'd tried to tell them the best course of action was for them to give statements to the FBI as part of the case. To tell the Bureau everything they knew about Rushman's activities —his history. There would be birth records for Santino's and Dmitri's daughters that would corroborate their stories. A death certificate for Santino's wife.

Justine was under arrest. She needed to give her statement, too.

Even if she was facing jail time, she had to explain it all. Not only so the prosecutor could take into account the circumstances, but to aid in the evidence against Rushman.

Kenna could hardly believe the ins and outs of this case, and how it seemed to relate. Reaching back to the past, to connect to her father somehow. Not leaving one piece of this puzzle untouched. Bishopsville—where the sheriff had been her father's friend. Even that connected. Which made her wonder if Sheriff Joe Don Hunter might've looked into the case that her father hadn't been able to solve, and his town was targeted as part of the fallout.

Since he was dead, there was no way to know.

Kenna gripped the wheel as she pulled out of the driveway. She called Stairs, just for the sake of not talking to herself out loud. When he answered, she said, "I don't know how much I trust either of those guys." She then explained the whole conversation with Santino and Larry.

"Wow. This is..."

"Yeah. Pretty unbelievable he's gotten away with it for this long. Weaving a web of deals, blackmail, and coercion to keep secret some sick need to have power over young women."

"The fact they're the children of his associates adds another layer of power," Stairs pointed out. "He's got a captive girl, and on top of that he knows exactly how much pain he's causing the parent."

"It's sick," Kenna said. "He gets satisfaction out of destroying people. He needs to be stopped."

"Will Larry and Santino help?"

"I don't even know if I trust what Larry says." She pulled out of Santino's neighborhood. "He's like an odd side piece that fits but doesn't." She had to think for a second to figure it out. "He has little skin in the game, yet Rushman cost him his job. Maybe he got leaned on to make cases disappear and keep the victims quiet."

"Which makes me want to know why he doesn't kill the women and make the bodies disappear."

She'd had the same question in Bishopsville when the young women were let go—left to live their lives with the memories. He'd done that in Vegas, and then had one girl for years since then. The business model repeated in Bishopsville and who knew where else, creating digital content that could be sold over and over again.

"He knows what he does," Kenna said. "The way he breaks them. They have to live with that, and his satisfaction continues. I'd be surprised he doesn't keep tabs on them for the rest of their lives."

Stairns muttered a choice word.

"Pretty much." Kenna nodded. "Maybe there are more who are dead, and they're the kind of girls no one would ever know are missing."

"On top of the ones we know about that were cut loose?"

"Those are like you said, children of his associates."

"Bad way of doing business." Stairns grunted. "Hi, Cabot. You like sitting on my couch by me...yes, you do."

Kenna smiled to herself, unsurprised when she felt the burn of tears. "You better be taking good care of her."

"It's not me who's sneaking her those bacon treats."

"Bacon, or bacon *flavor*? Because there's a difference."

Stairns chuckled. "Don't worry about her. Worry about Maizie."

"I'm trying not to get sick just thinking about her being under his thumb her entire life."

"If that's where she was."

"Because the father didn't want it to get out that he'd had a love child?" Kenna tapped the steering wheel with her thumb. "What kind of sick person gives a man like that a baby?"

"Someone with a huge debt to pay. Or he wants a favor that big."

Her stomach flipped over. But the thought she had would be nearly impossible to corroborate. It could be completely fictitious—or exactly what'd happened. "He has surveillance. Evidence on everyone."

"What's that?"

She didn't want to say it out loud, it was that fantastical. "Former president Masonridge."

"You think he's the baby's father?"

Kenna had met Avery Masonridge just a few months ago. Did she have a sister? If she did, it was highly likely she had no idea. "Would you give a baby to a man like that, knowing he could make sure that child never saw the light of day, and in return he gets you in the White House?"

"You think Masonridge bought the presidency with a baby?"

"I know." Kenna sighed. "It's a leap, but it would explain a lot."

Stairns said, "And for the record, I would not do that. Not even to be president. But you know that about me—and most people in the world. So who does that?"

"People with no conscience." Was that the kind of man Masonridge was below the surface of public opinion?

She drove to the medical center where Jax had told her in a text they'd taken Justine. She hadn't replied. Now she wanted to at least attempt to talk to the woman. "No one has tried to take him down. Rushman has been doing whatever he wants for decades."

"It's possible someone has tried, and he had them killed. He could make it so no one ever finds out."

"I really don't want to believe the worst about a former president, but somehow it wouldn't surprise me if it's true. If he's got Rushman covering up every indiscretion in a way that makes him look squeaky-clean."

And the down payment? The life of an innocent girl.

Where are you, Maizie?

Stairns said, "I need to phone an old friend."

He ended the call.

Kenna couldn't help respecting the girl's determination to take down Rushman, but first she had to be free of him. Kenna wanted to sit Maizie down and tell her that her safety—her freedom—was more important than anything else. Even Rushman going free.

No way was Kenna going to let that happen, anyway. He would pay. But as it had become with this case, Maizie's safety was more important to her than anything.

It wasn't lost on her that being like that made Kenna more like her father than she cared to be. But like the rest of the things Kenna didn't want to process, she pushed it from her mind and got back to work.

Two FBI agents stood outside the medical office when she pulled up in front. She locked the Impala and strode over.

"Nice ride." Special Agent Elton lifted his chin. The other guy stood beside him with that FBI smirk she knew well.

"Thanks, I probably stole it." She passed them and pushed open the door.

Jax stood in the empty waiting area with Special Agent Dean.

Kenna asked, "Where's the director?" Because she couldn't help considering the possibility that if this touched former president Masonridge, then it could also touch the man in charge of the FBI. At least the Utah governor hadn't been at the ceremony because of Rushman, who'd missed it anyway.

There was no love lost between Pacer and Rushman, at least according to Pacer. Something Kenna was exceedingly glad for. She wouldn't hesitate to go after Bradley's father if he were connected, but it would still make some people wonder if Kenna hadn't targeted him on purpose. Some people in the world would think, even after all this time, that she still had it in for the Pacer family.

That she wanted revenge.

What she wanted was justice.

"Let me talk to her," she said.

Dean folded his arms. "And why would we do that?"

"Is she willing to talk to you guys?"

He pressed his lips together and glanced at Jax.

"She'll talk to me. You know that."

"Far as I can tell," Dean said, "your friend in there went after the former president because of you."

Kenna lifted her brows. "What if she was going after someone else, like Director Billings? Did that occur to you?"

Jax sighed. "I'll go ask if she'll talk to you."

While he wandered off, she said to Dean, "How was it because of me?"

"Putting all that stuff in her head about her missing kid. Getting her hopes up and dragging all this out. We were supposed to keep our focus on Rushman. Get the evidence from Santino to take Rushman down."

"Wouldn't it make more sense to investigate everyone connected to Rushman, not just try to flip one guy? Go talk to people who know the kind of man he is, but they've never said." She paused, measuring her words. "They allowed him to continue, unchecked, for *decades*. Playing sick games. Victimizing young women. Driving others to kill themselves. Destroying families and businesses. All because he *can*."

"Take him down, and the whole house of cards crumbles."

"Like cutting off the head of the snake?"

He nodded. "That's exactly what the director said."

"That typically just makes another one grow in its place. And why let that happen?" Kenna shrugged. "Unless the director has something to lose if we start looking into Rushman's associates."

"Okay." Jax strode back down the hall. "Kenna, let's go. Dean, head outside."

She trailed after him, not glancing back at the special agent. "Was it something I said?"

"Do you intend to make a habit of pointing fingers at people in a way that could jeopardize the entire Justice Department?" Jax asked.

"Everyone should be able to withstand some scrutiny," she replied. "Especially if they have such a high-profile position."

"I don't disagree with you. But now isn't the time to get into a discussion on government and big business transparency." He winced. "Also, you do realize saying stuff like that only makes people wonder why you're so solitary." He lifted his brows. "Because you have something to hide, perhaps?"

"You know I don't." As if. And out of anyone in the world, as one of her close friends, he should know she had nothing to hide. If he—of all people—wanted to know anything, he only had to ask.

"No one else knows that. Because you don't let them in."

"Why would I?" Kenna frowned. "Three's a crowd." Did he want her to let other people in?

"Ryson, Stairs, and you?"

"No, although maybe you have a point." But she didn't share everything with Stairs, and he wasn't here. And she'd had to put distance between her and the Rysons. And she would keep it that way until Rushman was behind bars—stripped of all his power. Otherwise she'd be putting baby Luci in danger. And that was the last thing Kenna wanted.

She shook her head. "Anyway, I was talking about you and me."

"Can I have that in writing? I may need it later to refer back to when I have to convince you there *is* a 'you and me.'" Jax stopped at a closed door and switched to a high-pitched voice. "I don't have anything to steal, Jax. I have a case to work."

She fought to keep her face impassive because that was actually pretty funny. Especially after the day she'd had and the topics of conversation she'd been privy to. But was she going to let him know he'd actually told a joke?

No way.

She lifted her chin. "I think I need to throw up again... before I go back to doing your job for you."

Jax grinned. "You know, you're surprisingly well-adjusted for someone who has a mile-deep moat of denial around every single part of them."

"You should do some yoga and meditate on it all some more." She spread her hands. "The great mysteries of life."

He honestly looked like he was thinking about kissing her again. "Tried that. It didn't help, and I ended up on an undercover mission where I bumped into you."

"I'm pretty sure *I* bumped into *you*," she countered. "On purpose, to save your life. You're welcome by the way. It cost me—"

"Your camper van. Your *home*. Believe me, I know."

She caught the edge of something in his gaze. "What?"

"After." He twisted the door handle.

Justine lay on the bed in a gown, hooked to an IV.

Special Agent Torrow stood to the side, arms folded across that expansive chest. Of all of them, he reminded her of Ryson. Though, considering how Torrow had saved Cabot's life outside Hatchet in that huge traffic collision, maybe he should be her best friend rather than the police lieutenant she'd left behind in Salt Lake City. So what if Ryson had an adorable baby who...oh, who was she kidding. Kenna even liked helping with the dishes and laundry while she was there.

Maybe Jax was onto something about that moat of denial.

"The two of you bicker like an old married couple." Torrow didn't move one inch. He didn't even look like he was breathing.

"The doctor said I didn't need the stress." Justine glanced aside to stare at the wall.

"You have had a busy day." Kenna hoped one thing would get through. "I know where Maizie was earlier today."

Justine flinched.

"I've almost found her," Kenna said.

"So you *haven't* found her."

"I'm getting closer with every step I take."

"Then why are you here? Go take steps or whatever." Justine huffed. "I don't need you here, rubbing my face in the fact you were right. I'm a screwup."

Kenna thought about everything she now knew Justine had been through. Being victimized. Having to work through addiction and how that had affected her. Having a baby who was taken from her. Not knowing where Austin had been for days—worrying if it was her fault.

Justine had done what it took to survive, and not always the right way. She'd manipulated people when she had no power to do anything else and saw no way out of her predicament. She hadn't done the right thing with Deacon.

No one ever made all the right decisions. Kenna knew that, but she tried to do the right thing as much as she could. Like being here, knowing Justine and her daughter suffered at Rushman's hands while Kenna's father had saved her. Kenna had no right to be a survivor—she just hoped she could use that life wisely.

Helping others heal. Finding innocents. Shining light in the dark places.

"If you tell the FBI everything Rushman did to you, they can make sure he goes to jail."

Justine burst out laughing, the sound shrill and void of humor. There was nothing light about this woman.

"I know he victimized you." Kenna strode to the bed. "I'm going to stop him so he never hurts anyone like Maizie ever again."

Justine gripped her arm, whispering as though she'd worn out her voice, "He isn't the one who gets hurt. That's not how he likes it."

Kenna ignored the punishing grip of Justine's fingers. "Talk to me."

Chapter Twenty Six

Kenna pocketed her phone and stepped out of the room. It didn't take much effort to pull back the emotion. Justine had told her plenty, and Torrow had agreed to get on board with the rest.

She swiped at her cheeks and sniffed.

Jax pushed off the wall, Special Agent Dean close by as well so when Jax said, "How'd it go?" she had to give him the canned answer.

"I know how we're gonna get Rushman." Kenna gave them both a relieved smile. "I got a voice recording of the whole statement, and Torrow can write up his report. Get Justine's words in writing for the case file."

Meanwhile, Kenna was going to see who followed her from this medical center in order to take the phone from her.

She had no doubt in her mind Rushman had attempted to coerce someone on the special assignment into doing his dirty work and keeping his secret. Though, part of her had to wonder if it was actually the FBI director who was the weakest link here.

She intended to find out.

"Heading out?" When she nodded Jax motioned with a wave. "I'll walk you."

"Sure." They'd bantered on the way in, but the fact was Dean had told her the special assignment had quit looking for Austin and Maizie. That Jax had told them both were found. Misunderstanding or not, she wanted an explanation.

Austin had been found, sure.

But Maizie?

Kenna pushed out the front door, ignoring the people in the urgent care waiting room who watched her leave with one of the FBI agents in the building. An entertaining shake up to what they'd expected going to a doctor's appointment today.

Nelson headed up the stairs. "Elton went to the hospital to see if he can talk to Deacon Frost. Convince him it's in his best interests to testify against Rushman."

Kenna nodded. "Good idea. If he's in the frame of mind to make reparations all the way around, he could be willing to do the right thing."

Nelson continued inside. Kenna walked to the Impala in the parking lot, aware of Jax beside her.

But that wasn't what had her attention.

A shiny blue Ford compact had been parked a couple of rows over. Hadn't she seen that car before? Her head pounded so bad she couldn't remember but had a few guesses.

Kenna winced. "I need some pain meds."

"And you need to tell me the plan."

Kenna unlocked her car and turned the engine on so the air-conditioning could get going. Then she grabbed her sunglasses, shut the door, and turned to him, sliding them on. "Who says I have a plan?"

"You could've had Torrow step out and let me stay."

As if that meant she trusted Torrow more than she trusted

Jax? "It would've been obvious we wanted to keep what Justine said quiet."

"We do, don't we?"

"It's not my special assignment." For her, it was locating Maizie before something bad happened and solving the cold case.

"So you're shutting me out?"

"Did you tell the others that Austin and Maizie had been found?"

"Austin, yes." Jax didn't flinch or let anything slip in his expression. "They might've got the wrong impression about Maizie when I told them about the phone call. I've been looking for her. I don't know about the rest of the guys."

He'd searched the building where the surveillance video spotted a young girl. Even if it wasn't Maizie but someone else there, he'd at least looked for her or, he said he had.

Kenna blew out a long breath.

"What now?"

"I'd love to bait a trap. Keep trying to reel in a fish." Namely whoever had hit her over the head. She was ready to turn the tables and get this all figured out. "But I also need to talk to President Masonridge. He said he wanted to talk to me after the ceremony, and then when they rushed him out we didn't get the chance."

Plus, she'd been busy in the bathroom throwing up.

"Right." Jax stuck his hands in his pocket. "What did Justine tell you?"

"She wasn't trying to kill Rushman. She was purely focused on Masonridge—the father of her baby."

"If we can get him to testify..."

Kenna nodded. "Exactly. It'll hold a lot more weight than Justine, whose recollection is foggy at best. When Rushman had her she was on drugs and barely lucid. She's got flashes of memories and a whole lot of mental and physical scarring to show for it. She's not going to be a good witness in court. Her testimony will get torn apart. Unless she's talking about Masonridge. She remembers a whole lot about how Rushman handed her to him."

"Like a trade?"

"She's been a commodity most of her life." Kenna swallowed. "I'd like to believe she hasn't suffered some kind of mental breakdown, but that might be her best defense regarding the attempted assassination of a former president."

Jax reached up and squeezed the back of his neck.

"I need Masonridge to do the right thing."

"Pretty sure that's an FBI special assignment task."

"You don't want my help?"

He frowned. "Why don't you focus on Maizie, and I'll work the Rushman case? We can share information and help each other out."

"Why didn't you just say that in the first place?"

Jax chuckled. "I kind of figured it was a given. Guess not." He squeezed her elbow, then took a step back. "Be careful."

Kenna climbed in her car thinking over everything she knew about Dmitiri's death. She still had no idea who killed him but did know it was because Santino refused to back down. When her father had cut and run Santino had found himself with no help and no family. He'd safeguarded his daughter from the world—and the world from her—in the way no one ever did for Justine.

Would Kenna have to do the same thing with Maizie?

After focusing so hard on finding her, Kenna hadn't really considered what would happen when she did. She had no idea what condition the teen was in—physically or mentally. She might be a danger to both herself and others, even if only in her desperation.

Just like when she'd trashed Santino's house, she might hurt someone else and possibly even worse next time.

Where would she go looking for evidence against Rushman?

Kenna hit a gas station, hoping whoever worked for the guy would follow her there and try to take her phone to get the recording of Justine's statement. Whoever it was hadn't been able to keep her from talking. Torrow hadn't allowed her to get hurt after she was arrested, and Kenna didn't allow her to be killed before.

She partially wondered if the FBI director was intentionally running interference with Rushman, not allowing him to know the special assignment agents were working to take him down, but also had to consider if this was all to keep Rushman from being arrested.

Even if he was arrested, how long would he even serve out what would probably be a cushy sentence? And would the people he blackmailed allow him to live to see sentencing?

She looked around for the shiny blue Ford but didn't see it close in on the gas station.

Kenna washed up in the bathroom and bought herself some lunch—along with several ice-cold bottles of water. Lingering long enough she got a few odd looks from the cashiers and other patrons.

As she went back to the car, her phone started to ring.

She didn't recognize the number, but it was the new Washington, DC, area code. "Kenna Banbury." She turned up the air and pointed it at her face, blowing strands of her hair back so that they fluttered in the breeze.

"It's Masonridge." He sounded disgruntled. "Your colleague said you wanted to speak to me still?"

"Yes, I do." *Because you're the one who wanted to speak to me.* "Can we meet somewhere?"

"I'm on a plane." Now that he said that she did hear that dull drone of an airplane engine in the background. "I won't be back to Vegas for a long time, I'm afraid. Business in Baltimore, and my people advised me against remaining in Vegas considering what happened after the ceremony."

"I can confirm her intention was to assassinate you, but she's been arrested. Justine Greene poses no threat to you now."

"Hmm." Masonridge paused. "That's good to know. Thank you."

"You didn't believe she wanted to kill Rushman?"

"Would she have reason to attempt to murder him?"

Kenna leaned the knot on the back of her head on the headrest and hissed.

"That bad?"

"I'd love to talk to you about Rushman." Kenna gripped the phone. "And how you fathered a child with Justine Greene. But mostly about Rushman."

"So you're not interested in blackmailing me with that knowledge to get me to talk about him?" He sounded surprised.

"You think I'd hold that over your head to get what I want?"

Masonridge stayed quiet for a second. Then she heard, "Huh."

"There's far too much of that going around. If this is going to happen, it'll be because of integrity and truth. Not more of precisely what Rushman does to the people who work for him."

"Maybe he just pays well."

Kenna frowned. "Did he pay you?"

"Nice try."

"Have you had any contact with the child recently?"

"Why would I have? Trying to entrap me, Kenna?"

She could tear his world wide open, and he knew it. With one phone call to Avery she could put his reputation in question. Then tell the world what she had on Masonridge. Not just the baby, but everything that occurred after the affair and all his dealings with Rushman would be dragged out into the light.

"Rushman has to be shut down. He cannot be allowed to victimize people anymore." She hissed out a breath. "And how could you allow him to do that to your *child*?" She wanted to see him in person so she could shake him. Except, would that also be seen as an assassination attempt? "What kind of person trades a baby like a commodity, knowing full well they're handing an innocent life over to a sick monster like that?"

The line went dead.

Kenna lowered the phone, sighing. The former president intended to distance himself from anything to do with Rushman and simply ignore what was happening. She could imagine why he might not want the child of a drug addict. But handing Maizie over to someone like Rushman was nothing short of unconscionable.

It was easy to take that stand when she didn't know all the ins and outs of why. The bargain would be wrong no matter how it had gone down. But the fact was, Masonridge could have a million reasons she would never be privy to.

He'd played a dangerous game.

Instead of owning up, or even allowing the consequences to land on him, he'd allowed Maizie to continue to suffer. Not to mention Justine. Or the others Rushman victimized.

She couldn't hope to understand his reasoning unless he talked to her.

As much as Kenna wanted to send him a text that said, "This isn't over." That could possibly be construed as a threat.

She headed for the hospital, as Special Agent Elton had gone there to talk with Deacon and it didn't look like anyone intended to follow her, but first she went to the building where that video had spotted someone who looked like Maizie. Maybe. Possibly.

Kenna slammed the creaky doorway too hard.

Walking around alone in out-of-the-way places was a recipe for getting jumped. Still, that was kind of the point, right? Flush out whoever might not want Justine's statement to get out.

She surveyed the building as she walked. Some defunct office complex up for lease, four stories. Was she going to walk through the whole thing?

"Where are you, Maizie?" Kenna whispered the question to herself.

Unsurprisingly, no one answered.

She rounded a corner into a shaded alley considerably cooler than the sun-bleached side. Two steps and someone shoved her. Kenna stumbled and whirled around, drawing her weapon as she moved.

Special Agent Dean was right behind her, a second assailant coming around the corner behind him. Or so she thought, until Jax slammed him against the side of the building.

Kenna held her gun up, aimed on the FBI agent. "Both of you were following me?"

"I was following him." Jax strained the words out, his effort focused on holding Dean against the wall. "Where's Maizie?"

Kenna started, the flinch rolling pain through her head.

Maizie. Not the first thing she'd have thought would come out of his mouth.

"How should I know?" Dean struggled to be released from the wall. "Get off me, Jaxton."

"Not until you tell me where the kid is."

Kenna glanced around, confirming no one watched as well as searching all the spots someone could observe them for the blonde she'd been looking for the past few months. *Where are you?* Was Maizie watching?

Dean said, "Fine. She got away from me."

"So you are the one who hit me over the head." Kenna shook her head. "Nice. Thanks."

"He wants her. I had no choice."

"So why tell us now?" Unless he wanted to be exposed.

Dean huffed out a breath. "I had no choice!"

Jax said, "Aren't you supposed to keep quiet the fact you work for Rushman?"

"Rushman? This is about the director's orders. He wants the girl brought in, as soon as she's found. I tried to catch her in that condemned building but she ran off. When Kenna came in I figured she was one of Rushman's people. That's why I knocked her out."

Jax said, "You actually expect us to believe that?"

Kenna frowned. "It's far more likely you're on Rushman's payroll. Tell us how he got to you."

"That's not what this is." He shoved off the wall. "Let me go, Jaxton."

Jax backed up a fraction. "Stay where you are."

Special Agent Dean turned around, brushing off his clothes. He glanced between Jax and Kenna.

She lowered her gun but didn't put it away. "You were saying this was an order from the director himself?"

"He wants everyone we can get our hands on," Dean said. "That means the girl you're looking for."

"So why work on the basis that she's been found?"

Dean said, "Because I didn't want whoever *is* working for Rushman to get to her before I could find her."

Jax glanced at her. Kenna didn't give him any indication she believed what Dean said.

"You're going to flip a victim, traumatized for years, so she'll hand you what you need for your case?" Kenna didn't like saying it aloud any more than contemplating it might be the truth. "She doesn't need that. She needs help."

"She's looking for evidence on Rushman," Dean said. "That means she's on our side!"

"How do you know that?"

He frowned. "I talked to Larry Nelson. He told me she showed up at Santino's."

Jax glanced at Kenna, a look on his face that meant he wasn't happy learning that information this way.

Kenna said, "So where is she now? Do you have any idea?"

"Larry is gonna call if she shows up at Intellectus next."

"Funny." Kenna set one hand on her hip. "Larry told me the same thing."

"Sounds like he's playing you." Jax shook his head. "Kind of like everyone related to this case."

"Except Masonridge," Kenna said. "Since he just cut and run instead of facing it."

"I don't work for Rushman." Dean lifted his chin. "Let's just get it straight that I hate the guy with every fiber of my being and leave it at that."

Thus the reason he was on this special assignment. Something the director knew and was leveraging in order to get a result.

Without telling anyone else the plan.

What else had been hidden so that even the special assignment agents didn't know what each other were doing?

"Question is," Jax said. "Do we figure the agent going to talk to Deacon is dirty and go to the hospital, or do we go back for Justine, assuming either Torrow or Nelson is working for Rushman and she's the target?"

Kenna said, "What if it's both?"

And all of it was designed to allow someone else to find Maizie before her.

Chapter Twenty-Seven

After Austin got out of surgery, hospital staff moved him to a quiet floor where he could be observed. They hadn't given Kenna any more information than that, but Jax had passed it on to Special Agent Torrow so he could tell Justine.

Kenna glanced over at Jax as they headed to the room. "Thanks for going with me."

"Sticking together is always a better plan." He didn't look at her, though. Which was probably a good thing—they had to avoid any distractions in order to stay focused on the case.

"This isn't convincing me..."

Was she actually going to tell him she had feelings for him, even if it was because they were irritating her? She could guess he liked her, but were they supposed to talk about it?

Her and Bradley...

She didn't need to keep comparing them, but that was her frame of reference. Every step she took was a journey away from a life where the past eclipsed everything she was. One step at a time got her further and further from that life with

Bradley. What she should've had, and the happiness she'd experienced mixed with all that grief.

"I know. I'm getting a suspicious vibe as well." He sighed. "Are we really supposed to believe that Dean is just on orders from the director?"

Ah, so he hadn't thought they were talking about feelings. More that she wasn't convinced about Dean, maybe.

Kenna said, "Depends on whether you believe Billings is honorable in his intentions bringing this sketchy 'special assignment' group here with no paperwork. It's highly irregular and everyone knows it, but no one is saying that."

"The only thing that makes sense to me is you being here." He glanced over. "That's how I know there's someone to save, and justice to be found in all this complicated mess." He knocked on the door.

He banked all his forward movement on the fact she was involved? Probably he didn't want to talk about how he was losing faith in the Bureau right now. Or at least the director and the veracity of this special assignment.

It might not be a false alarm, but something sketchy was definitely going on.

When there was no answer to his knock, Jax eased the door open. "Oh."

She stepped around him into the room. Someone lay on the bed, which was lowered to be flat, with a sheet over their head. "*Austin.*"

He hadn't pulled through.

Deacon sat beside the bed, elbows on his knees. Looking haggard. He lifted his face. "They said there was a blood clot on his brain."

Kenna's head pounded in response.

"It happened just a bit ago." Deacon pulled in a shuddering breath. "There was nothing they could do."

She didn't want to ask, but... "Did an FBI agent come by to talk to you?"

"Told him to get lost. It wasn't the time."

Kenna nodded.

Deacon stood. "It's time now." He stepped with them into the hall, lumbering slowly. "You got a car? We need to go to my place."

Kenna nodded.

"I'll drive." Jax held out his hand for the keys.

"Isn't it better if you have your own car?"

He might need it later if they had different things to do. Or had he decided that he'd stick with her and see what happened? He probably figured if anything was going to kick off, that it would be around her.

To be fair, that was likely correct.

"Fine. I'll follow." He lowered his hand.

"You just want to drive the Impala."

Jax shot her a look. Then his focus moved to Deacon, and his expression changed. "I'll be right behind you."

Deacon slumped next to her in the passenger seat. Kenna followed her phone directions to his condo. Every once in a while, she'd glance over and see him staring out the window.

She needed to draw him out, get him talking. "I'm so sorry about Austin." Kenna pulled up to a stoplight. "It probably feels like you just got him back and now he's gone."

"I didn't even get to talk to him." Deacon's voice sounded like the grind of an old broken-down machine. He cleared his throat. Leaned his head back and shut his eyes.

She pulled into a visitor's space outside his condo, as the only open one she could find was around the corner away from the front entrance. "We're here."

Deacon shoved the door open.

Jax approached them as they climbed out and Kenna locked up.

She didn't like leaving the journals in the Impala, but it was better than leaving them even farther out of sight in the motel room. Since someone had torched her vehicle not too long ago, she didn't like risking being away from her stuff. But sticking close by it meant buying an inconspicuous house on wheels. Which would be difficult, even just another camper van. Next time, maybe she would drive an RV and tow a car behind it. Or haul her father's trailer—if she could find out who had it.

"Is there a reason we came here?" Jax kept his body tight. Wary in a way she knew was about both the case and her. His protective streak wasn't overblown, thankfully. He didn't act irrationally any time she was in danger, but let her do what she needed to do.

Then he just grabbed a bag, invaded her room at the motel like it was nothing, and slept on the other bed. Because he'd been exhausted and still wanted to make sure she was safe.

Focus. She didn't need to get distracted still trying to figure out why Jax was acting like this.

"I need to show you guys something." Deacon took them upstairs to his condo. Even before they reached the front door, both Kenna and Jax had their weapons drawn. "My front door is open." Deacon surged forward.

Jax halted him with a hand. "Easy. I go first."

She stuck by Deacon even though she'd rather have been backup for Jax. Maybe there was a middle ground. "Let's step inside."

Deacon entered right behind her and immediately hissed. "It's a mess."

"Someone broke in and ransacked the place." Kenna

winced. "What did you want to show us?" Hopefully it hadn't been stolen.

Jax reappeared. "Whoever did this is gone. But it doesn't look good in here."

Did Maizie do this? The same way she'd broken into Santino's house, looking for something?

"Depends if they found it." Deacon headed for the living room. He stepped onto the couch in his boots, reached up for the ceiling fan, and twisted the mechanism so the housing for the motor dropped onto the fan. Then he reached in and pulled out a flash drive.

"What is it?" Kenna asked.

He hopped off the couch and handed it to her. The thing looked like an old flash drive, from back when they barely had any storage capacity. "It's a story."

Jax holstered his gun. "Start talking."

"I guess it's time." Deacon slumped onto the couch. "Austin is gone. I don't have anything left to safeguard, and I don't care anymore anyway."

Kenna holstered her gun, too, even though she didn't feel like putting it away. Something about having it in her hand made her feel better, even if she didn't think it was Deacon or Jax she'd need to protect herself from. "Justine is in jail."

Deacon sort of rolled his eyes, making a face that clearly communicated how little he cared about her. "She was messed up, but she hid it well. Played the part."

"She was in a relationship with you because she was told to be?" Kenna wasn't sure why that would be when Deacon had been low level. It wouldn't help Rushman to order Justine into a relationship with Deacon. Unless it was only about keeping an eye on him and reporting back. Was that the kind of thing Rushman had people do?

"She was jaded, that much slipped through. I think she

came back here this time just trying to get to Rushman so she could find the baby. I didn't know about it when we were together." Deacon lifted his hands. "I didn't lie about that. She never mentioned it, but I could tell she wanted something. Every time I called her on why we had to talk about Rushman, she flipped out. Then other times she went almost catatonic. She'd disappear for three days, then show back up with new needle marks."

"I'd like to say she did what she had to do in order to survive, but I don't think it's as simple as that." Kenna didn't know exactly how much Justine had suffered. The woman hadn't done what some might in order to at least attempt to heal. She worked on the basis of whatever judgment she'd made in her own mind. Whether that decision proved sound, or not.

Kenna looked around at the carnage. Someone looking for something had tossed everything Deacon owned all over the condo—but they hadn't found it.

Who had done this? Rushman's people, the FBI after Deacon refused to talk to them, or someone else? Right now she didn't have enough information to figure it out. Deacon didn't have a doorbell camera, or internal cameras like some people used.

Maybe the condo had a lobby camera, and they could get the footage? Jax could flash his badge and get access.

Deacon pushed out a long breath. "She got pregnant with Austin. I think something flipped in her, and she suddenly had this...focus."

"Someone to take care of." Justine believed she'd been given a second chance. After the impossibility of getting her first child back, she suddenly had Austin to take care of.

Deacon nodded. "She took off." Probably so no one could steal the baby from her.

"And you were working for Rushman, embedded in Santino's crew?" For years after Larry, Santino and her father had tried to take down Rushman, and then Justine and their relationship. He'd kept the secret all that time.

"Dmitri Alekhin."

Kenna blinked.

Jax shifted his stance. "You killed him?"

Deacon stared at the coffee table.

"Or you're the one who put the body in that room." Far as she was concerned, it was one or the other.

Deacon nodded.

"So you know who killed him?" She wondered about the flash drive. "Is the drive proof who did it?"

"Just the connection between him and Rushman."

Jax shifted his weight from one foot to the other in a way that seemed like fighting off a rush of adrenaline. "Who is he, the person in the video?"

"I don't know his name. I never did."

"Who gave you that flash drive?" she asked.

"I took it off Dmitri."

"When you dumped his body so it would be found in a room registered to Anthony Santino."

Deacon nodded.

Kenna continued, "So who killed him?"

"The guy on that video."

"Whose name you don't know."

Deacon shrugged. "Maybe I don't wanna know."

"Did ignorance work?" Kenna wanted to shake the guy. "Did it save your life, and get you free of Rushman?"

"He left me alone, hasn't he?"

"So he knows you have this drive." She waved it, wanting to know who was on it. "And he just let you be? If you're the one that can bring his whole construct crashing down, then why aren't you dead? I'd kill you and burn the whole condo complex along with it."

Jax glanced at her, but she ignored it.

"Sure, it's a *little* homicidal," she added, "but one could argue it's effective."

"The flash drive is insurance to make sure that doesn't happen." Deacon's jaw flexed.

"So now you just hand it over?"

"Like you said, I've got nothing left." Deacon shrugged. "Santino can deal with the fallout on his own. He didn't care when I tried to talk to him. He just cut me loose. So I could 'hang myself by my actions.' Can you believe that?"

"A man with mob connections?" Kenna paused. "I can't believe he didn't shoot you himself."

"He had no fight in him by then. Now he's just a shadow of what he was." Deacon sniffed. "The family cut him off. He had no one except that girl he keeps in the psych ward. I probably should've put Justine there as well."

At least one person in the world would argue that about Kenna. Even if it was only someone like Angeline Pacer, who'd wanted her to suffer for what happened to Bradley. Except being locked up was her worst nightmare. All her freedom and the ability to choose for herself...stripped away? She shivered just thinking about being trapped like that. She'd be like a wild animal caged.

Jax paced to the kitchen and looked out the window.

Kenna turned back to Deacon. "Tell me about this man who killed Dmitri, and why?"

"Dmitri had that video. Near as I could tell, that was why he was killed, but Rushman never got his hands on it." Deacon's grin contained no humor. "That guy is the one under his thumb. Probably thinks he has it, not me."

"Why did Dmitri need to die?"

"Some plot to expose Rushman." Deacon shrugged, looking every bit of his fifty years. "That cop, and Santino. Your father as well, I guess, when they came up with that plan to expose me. I heard them talking."

"You knew they were going to fake Larry's death?"

"Pretty good ruse, I'll tell you. Nearly fooled me when it happened in front of you. But Rushman already knew your dad was in town. What else was he supposed to do when Max Banbury is talking to Santino?"

"Because he knew Santino wanted revenge?" And her father had been targeted, which meant Kenna also had been. In a way that meant they'd spent almost a year in Europe before they came home.

"When Santino met with him in the restaurant, Rushman already knew. That's what is in the video."

"I saw that video already. Santino gave it to me." The flash drive stowed under the carpet in the Impala.

"This one is different," Deacon said. "They cut the video into four files. One for Santino, Larry, Dmitri, and your father. I don't know where the others are."

Jax turned from the window. "You've watched the one you took from Dmitri?"

"It's the end of their conversation, where he walks in. The guy who killed the Russian. That bigshot waltzes in and starts ordering people around like he's in charge. Rushman put him in his place."

The biggest bigshot Kenna knew was former president Masonridge, but they needed to watch the video to confirm.

"The bigshot told me he'd skin me alive if I didn't help him." Deacon huffed.

She looked at Jax. "We need to watch this."

"Tuck that away," Jax said. "We need to get out of here."

Deacon stood, faster than she'd have thought he could move. "What's going—"

The kitchen window exploded in a volley of gunfire, blowing glass and debris across the room. Deacon's body jerked, and he fell back to the couch.

Blood all over his chest.

Chapter Twenty-Eight

"Door!" Jax tugged Kenna with him while he hurried to the front door. "We're going out the back exit."

"Assuming they don't have that covered."

He looked out into the hallway. "Let's pray that was a lone shooter and now that the job is done, they're hightailing it out of here."

"That's a tall order." Smacked a little too much of wishful thinking for her taste, to be honest. Her father had been what she now called a "stone-cold realist." Which was rare in the world, and occasionally so stubborn it was irritating. That unmovable force she had to apply pressure to, even though it wouldn't move.

Once he decided, there was no changing his mind.

Why she'd thought of that right now, Kenna had no idea.

She followed Jax down the hallway, glancing behind to ensure no one intended to pick them off from the rear, and pushed away thoughts of her father. Another frame of reference to a man in her life.

She didn't need to puzzle this out now.

She could just be thankful it wasn't Rushman who had

influenced her, and work to help those who had suffered because of him. What more could anyone ask of her?

Jax took her to a fire exit at the end. He pushed the door open and let a swath of hundred-degree sunlight in. Waited. When no gunshots slammed the open doorway, he headed out and she followed right behind.

Their footsteps echoed on the metal, each pounding footfall radiating down to the ground floor and making the whole staircase vibrate.

Kenna grabbed the handrail and hissed. "Hot."

He looked back at her, barely sparing her a glance. "Come on."

"Yeah, yeah." Fine if he needed to reassure himself that he had some semblance of control. "Right behind you."

"My car."

"Nope." She tugged out her keys. "But you can drive."

Jax shot her another look.

"Pay attention so we don't get killed." But it seemed to be that the coast remained clear. Even with their vigilance, he might be right that whoever shot Deacon had made a run for it.

He got the engine running, and she turned the vents to her that she'd turned to the driver seat since the journals didn't need cooling. He kept scanning, instead of driving away.

He tapped a finger on the wheel. "I need to call it in." He got his phone from the inside pocket of his jacket.

She adjusted the vent upward so it blew on his face—not where hers would be if she were in the driver's seat.

He held the phone to his ear. "Yeah, I'd like to report a dead guy in a condo." He sounded like a surfer from California. He gave the address, then hung up, probably right around when they asked for his name.

Kenna looked around, but there was little movement, even though someone tore up Deacon's condo from across the complex. Apparently, no one cared. Or everyone who lived here was gone during the day? Or asleep?

Tears gathered in her eyes. "He gave his life for this."

"It was taken, not given. You know that."

"He had nothing left. You think he wouldn't have made that trade to get out from under the limelight of it all and start fresh?" That was what death was, right? The chance to move on, like walking through a doorway.

Kenna liked the idea of heaven but didn't plan to go there anytime soon if she could help it. The other place? Hell was more than a curse word. It grated her just thinking about the trade-off a person made that landed them there. No one liked that, even if it was reality and most folks avoided thinking about it.

"You okay?"

Kenna rolled her eyes. "My brain wants to contemplate everything but what just happened."

"You seem so cool in the middle of it all. I'm surprised."

She shrugged a shoulder. It wasn't that hard to project something other than what was going on beneath the surface.

"Have you ever been so low that you contemplated suicide?" he asked, his voice gentle.

Did he really want to know the answer to that? He knew her history and how it would feel to even think about that. Kenna settled on saying, "I'm here, aren't I?" And before he could drag all that up, she added, "Let's go."

"Where?"

Kenna looked at her phone. "Whoa."

"What is it?"

"Fifteen texts, six missed calls." She thumbed down the thread, her heart sinking to her stomach as she processed what was happening. "Drive." She gave him the address of that old church. "Maizie was at Intellectus. Or she's still there. I can't figure out what happened, but looks like she showed up. Throwing things and making demands."

Last time Maizie had done that, she'd hurt Santino, even if only inadvertently.

He hit the gas and used the Impala's muscle to get them to the church. As soon as he pulled up outside, she flung the door and jumped out, running for the front entrance.

Kenna slammed into it at full speed. "Maizie!"

She didn't care what happened, or what the teen had done. She just wanted to find her.

"Kenna!" Elaine appeared at the end of the hall.

She heard Jax in backup mode, bringing up the rear, but hurried to Elaine. "What happened?"

"She came in here screaming. At first I didn't know who she was, with that hood up. Yelling about the video. She pulled books off the shelves. Nearly toppled a whole bookshelf." Elaine waved at the discarded books across the floor. "Stan about had a heart attack, woken up from his nap with all the yelling." She touched a hand to her front and sucked in a couple of breaths.

"Is she still here?"

Elaine shook her head. She pushed open the door to the hallway and headed through. Toward the break room. "She didn't want to listen about how I didn't know *what* video she was talking about—specifically. She just kept screaming. And then..." Elaine slowed at the door to the break room.

"What happened?"

"You'll want to ask Larry what happened when he put his *hands* on a scared-out-of-her-mind young woman." Elaine glared into the room.

Something smashed. Larry cursed loudly.

Jax moved between Kenna and Elaine into the break room. "Calm down."

Kenna stayed with Elaine, touching her elbow. "What happened?"

"She *freaked* like you'd think he'd tried to...you know...*touch her*."

"Good." Kenna glanced at Larry. "Not that it's good she was completely traumatized. Just good she didn't freeze up. She let you know there was a problem."

"And she did it *loudly*." Elaine glared at Larry again. "But then she ran off." The librarian's eyes filled with tears. "She was so scared."

Kenna squeezed her shoulder. "Thank you for calling. I've been looking for her, so I can help her."

Elaine nodded.

Kenna didn't explain they'd been shot at and ran for their lives—she just went into the break room and got a look at Larry. Sweat dampened his undershirt, between the open sides of his white button-down that he'd untucked from his belt. "I need to find that girl."

"So go find her." He paced to the sink and back to the tiny TV. "Don't know why you came here. Other than to tell me I'm a horrible person."

Kenna folded her arms. "Are you? Because it's never really sat right, your part in this. Santino lost his child. Dmitri was his best friend. My dad liked taking down bad guys. Deacon played his role. What about you?"

"I lost my career over this!"

"Over what?" Kenna said. "Rushman leaned on you to fail to solve the case? Dmitri Alekhin didn't need to be a cold case. Just point the finger at someone else and they go to jail." She lifted her hands. "What's the problem?"

Jax stiffened and glanced at her.

She shot him a look. Obviously, sending an innocent person to jail would be problematic. "Find someone guilty of something else, and you can't prove it, but you know the world is better with them off the streets. So what's the problem?"

"I did what I was told!"

"Oh, yeah? What was that?" Kenna wanted to get out and find Maizie. But this wasn't a waste of time. "Feeding information back to Rushman?"

Larry shot her a look.

"Too close to the truth?"

"I hate that guy. I would never work for him." Larry ran his hands through his hair. "He never found enough to leverage my help, but he tried." The former detective let out a dark laugh. "Boy, he tried. Leaned on my ex. Even threatened the kids. She tore Rushman's guys up one side and down the other. They didn't bother her after that."

"She probably saved their lives."

"Yeah, by getting them away from me." He moved to the couch and sank into it.

"Do you know the young woman who came in here a short time ago?"

He shook his head. "Probably works for Rushman, though. If she's looking for the video."

Jax pulled over a chair and sat facing Larry. "What video would that be?" He didn't pull out his badge, and Larry didn't ask who he was. Maybe the former detective knew—or didn't want to know.

Kenna leaned against the wall by the door, trying to figure out where Maizie might go from here. They could get the FBI to pull camera footage from traffic cams or other surveillance around her. But right now she wasn't sure she exactly trusted the FBI—apart from the agent in this room.

"I was supposed to find it." Larry scrubbed both hands

down his face. "After the Dmitri Alekhin case landed on my desk, I was supposed to find the video he had, the footage that is part of the evidence against Rushman."

"What you were gathering with my father and Santino?" Kenna asked.

Larry nodded. "Rushman took mine. The way he takes everything. I never found the one Dmitri had—what Santino gave him for insurance. A way to ensure we didn't double-cross each other."

Kenna had that one in her pocket, courtesy of Deacon, who had given his life for this. She wasn't going to let it go to waste, regardless of whether anyone in the world would mourn his death. Some people went unnoticed to the afterlife. Kenna remembered those she could and tried to honor them in her own way.

He might have had it purely for insurance, but she was going to finish what her father and Santino started.

"But it all fell apart, right?" Jax held Larry's attention with that FBI intensity. "Rushman is still doing whatever he wants. Hurting whoever he wants. You all failed."

Larry's face scrunched up. "I tried! I looked for Dmitri's video, but without it, we didn't have much. No one would've believed us." He looked at Kenna. "Even your father thought the risk was too great."

"You make him sound like he was a coward, when in fact he did what he did to keep me safe." Now she would pay that forward, and safeguard anyone Rushman might target in the future. Give the past victims some semblance of justice. Make it right.

Her way.

"All this has been about some kind of *conspiracy*?" Elaine strode past Kenna—who wanted to stop her, but also wanted to watch her next move—and stomped her foot. "This is unbelievable! You hurt that little girl's feelings. I can't believe you."

"I didn't know she'd freak," Larry said. "I told her to talk to me."

"Why would anyone do that when every word out of your mouth is nothing but a pack of lies!" Elaine stopped, breathing hard.

"Better than being a joke." Larry geared up to keep going.

Jax cut him off. Kenna couldn't even see him with Elaine in the way. "That's enough."

"Yeah, Larry," Elaine said, "that's—"

The gunshot cracked in the room, eclipsing everything. Larry's body jerked. Blood blossomed in the center of his forehead, and he slumped back on the couch.

Dead.

Pain thrummed through Kenna's head. She winced, already turning to the shooter.

Anthony Santino stood at the door beside her. There one second, and then he was gone before Jax could even stand to draw his weapon. Kenna didn't even reach for hers.

"FBI!" Jax darted around Elaine, past her, to the hallway.

Kenna strode to Elaine and reached out. "Let's go somewhere else."

Elaine gasped. "I can't believe... He just..."

"Give yourself a minute." Kenna walked her down the hall to the library area. Jax strode through the door just as Elaine sank into a seat.

He shook his head. "Jumped in a car—yours actually. The beater you were driving. I need the license plate so I can call it in."

Kenna could give that to him. "Elaine, where are the old guy, and that other guy?"

"Stan had a gash on his head from saving the bookshelf before it fell over. I think Ben took him to the hospital."

Kenna recalled the younger guy from her first visit here, and the old man who looked ex-military. "Okay."

Jax said, "Kenna, that license plate? I need to call this in."

Elaine reached for a cell phone plugged into a port in the center of the table. "I've trained my whole life for this." She held the phone so face ID could unlock her device. "*I'm reporting this murder.*"

"Elaine, I'm an FBI—"

"I know!" Her eyes gleamed. "Hello? 911?"

Kenna wandered away from the librarian, trying to wrap her head around this. Maybe proximity was a factor, and now that Elaine didn't have to see a dead man's body—or recall the moment the shot went off—she'd rallied.

Kenna pulled out her phone.

"You, too?" Jax said.

She shot him a look. "Maybe I can get Santino to turn himself in." Yeah, that sounded like solid reasoning. "Or find out where he's going next."

He answered after the first ring. "I did what I had to do."

"There's a lot of that going around." Kenna stepped away from Jax's disapproving stare. Didn't he have a dead body to deal with? "Did you kill Deacon?" Rifle to a handgun—it wasn't impossible.

"Like I said." Santino paused. "I did what I had to do."

"You could've killed me or an FBI agent in the process. Do you really need that kind of heat on you?" She gripped the phone and paced a couple of steps.

"Doesn't matter. I'm ending this."

Kenna went cold at his tone. "What are you doing?"

"Finishing it. The way it's supposed to be."

"Santino—"

"Goodbye, Kenna."

The line went dead.

"I need to go." She turned to Jax. "Give me my keys."

"I have to stay with this murder scene." He frowned. "I can't leave."

"We can catch up later." Kenna waved her hand, and he handed over the keys. "I need to at least try and find Santino."

"I think I locked the driver's door, but that might've been it. Anyway—" He gave her a tight nod. "Please be careful."

She didn't know if she should hug him...or kiss his cheek...or...

Kenna nodded back. "You, too."

Her face flamed in the Vegas heat as she descended the front steps and headed for her car. She blew out a breath. Two men had died today, and she'd been there for both.

Rushman's destruction of people's lives continued.

Maybe Santino was right and everyone involved needed to be stopped no matter what. Only what was he going to do? She presumed it was him who'd killed Deacon, the way he killed Larry. No attempt at hiding his actions from anyone. He hadn't even waited until the room was clear of other people and the target would be alone.

The fact he didn't care who saw him wasn't good.

She looked in the back seat as she approached the car, because she was a single woman in the world who traveled alone and that wouldn't change for a while—if it ever did.

Kenna paused before sticking the key in the lock on the door handle. She hung her head for a second.

Thank you.

She didn't even know who she was talking to—or acknowledge who they were. Not when this was finally happening.

All because Jax had left the passenger door unlocked.

Kenna slid in and drove without a look back to see. She

barely cared where she would end up, except when she saw a sign for the freeway. North. She pulled out the phone and called Stairns on the road, put it on speaker, and slid it in the cupholder.

She held the wheel with both hands, and when there was no one else around for a hundred feet in front or behind, she glanced back.

Dark clothes, the hood of the sweater still pulled up over her hair. Huge brown eyes stared at her.

In the second Kenna looked back, which was all she could safely do, she clocked a whole lot. Maizie had taken a risk getting in the car. She was trusting Kenna to do the right thing —and the fear and doubt glistened in her eyes.

Stairns answered. "Yeah, what's up?"

Kenna focused on the freeway in front. Was the car bugged, or her phone? She had to risk it to get Maizie out of here. "I need a pickup. I've got precious cargo." Aside from being the truth, it was also a code they'd come up with.

"Copy that. Just me, or Elizabeth also?"

"Both of you." She heard Maizie moving in the back seat. "Thanks, Stairns. You're the only ones I trust."

He stayed quiet for a second, then said, "Cabot needs a friend anyway. That dog of yours is lonely, and when she's restless, she tries to eat the pillows from the couch. Just because I tossed one on the floor. And who needs those things —they're just uncomfortable when you're relaxing try'na talk to the kids on video chat."

"How are they?" Kenna wanted to smile to herself. He was doing a great job showing Maizie exactly who he was, even if he sounded like a rough former Marine.

"Oh, good. My Nancy she just got a promotion at her job. She's the head nurse now, still on the pediatric oncology ward. Those kids are so amazing. Breaks my heart." Stairns paused.

"Leah called because her husband bought her an air fryer for her birthday. I do *not* know what that boy was thinking."

Kenna chuckled as much as she could. "Did she forgive him?"

"She'll get there." Stairns eased into, "You want that pickup in Vegas?"

"How about St. George? I have a need to be nowhere near that place right now. I feel a road trip comin' on."

"We land at six. See you soon," Stairns said. "And if anyone tries to hurt either of you? Kill them."

The line went dead.

Kenna spotted a rest stop up ahead. She pulled off the road but didn't go into the main entrance. Instead, she drove around the corner and headed to a quieter area behind the chain fast-food restaurant attached to the gas station and away from long-haul truck parking. She put the car in park, unbuckled her seat belt, and turned around.

Now they could start this new chapter. In both of their lives.

Mazie shoved the door open and ran.

Chapter Twenty-Nine

Kenna climbed out of the car. Maizie had made it across the blacktop, after nearly getting hit by a pickup truck rolling along the edge of the lot. She kept going, toward the dry brown grass that stretched out to that side. The expanse of flatland in this part of Nevada had mountains to the left, just as dry and brown as the rest of this area, where sprinklers were a waste of time.

Maizie's grueling pace slowed. A semitruck passed between them, so Kenna lost sight of her for a second.

In every fiber of her being, Kenna wanted to run. But she leaned against the side of the car, close to the passenger door.

Maizie glanced back, her expression changing the moment she realized no one was chasing her. That she could go wherever she wanted. Get lost, hitch a ride.

Kenna watched over her from about five hundred feet away. Anything could happen before she ran over there to try to intervene, but with no one around, Maizie didn't have to worry about it. She would see the threat coming.

Maizie turned back to the field. She walked a little

farther, then kind of flopped down on the grass. Like she'd been exhausted—or living in terror—every day of her life.

Kenna pushed off the car, still trying to decide if she needed to help.

Maizie bent her arms and rested her head on her hands, elbows beside her ears. Lying there in the sun, looking up at the sky. Probably as safe as she'd ever been except from heat exhaustion—and whatever injury she'd had during that phone call.

Kenna went in the gas station, got a bag full of ice-cold drinks and a couple of other items, and crossed the asphalt.

Maizie had her eyes closed.

As Kenna grew near, she slowed down her pace.

Maizie still stiffened. Her eyes flew open, a second of wariness registering there.

Kenna sat down on the ground. "Here." She tugged the tag off a pair of sunglasses.

Maizie slid them over her eyes, her expression now inscrutable. In a lot of ways, sunglasses were a defense. A way to shield yourself.

"And here." Kenna held out a pint of ice cream, another one in the bag. "I got spoons. Do you want chocolate...or vanilla with chunks of strawberry?"

Maizie slowly eased up to sitting.

Kenna held both pints, one in each hand. "Your choice."

No matter it was a full minute before Maizie reached out and took one. All the while, Kenna wondered if she should offer Maizie the chance to try both. The girl was thin, but that didn't mean she'd never had ice cream in her life. Kenna could make a whole lot of assumptions about how she'd lived but wouldn't know the truth until Maizie told her.

Would she ever tell the whole story?

If she did, Kenna would probably turn into Santino, on a

rampage with a gun and no one there to stop him. It would be Kenna's obligation if she was still in Vegas and not doing something far more important.

Kenna focused on her ice cream, giving Maizie a break from the attention. As she ate, she people watched at the gas station. More for security than as a study of human behavior.

Maizie wore all dark apparel. Distressed skinny jeans with holes all down the front. Black boots laced halfway. A dark-gray hoodie still pulled up over her hair. She had to be sweating under all that material soaking up the sun.

A million things crossed the tip of Kenna's tongue. She swallowed them back with the ice cream, not wanting to disturb the détente.

Halfway down the pint, which she seemed to be enjoying, Maizie shoved back the hood. Sweat had plastered strands to the sides of her face, roughly chopped hunks of blond hair that barely hung to her jawline. It looked like she'd taken a pair of dull scissors to the long blond curls Kenna had seen in the photo. That picture had been bait.

This was the real Maizie.

Kenna knew exactly why she'd chopped it off. Because she *could*. Because she chose to do it, rather than have long hair that could be pulled. The same reason if Kenna headed into a fight, she braided her hair or tied it back so some unscrupulous person with no honor—which was basically everyone she faced—couldn't drag her around.

She'd put Maizie's age at nineteen, but in person the girl looked more like sixteen, even though she was older than Austin. Kenna wasn't sure if she should tell her that her brother had died in the hospital. That her mom had been arrested for trying to kill the former president. Maybe she knew—or she didn't care.

Maizie held the pint up so the last drops could drip onto her tongue. She made an endeavor of licking the spoon.

"So you like strawberries." Kenna smiled.

Maizie stiffened. She threw the empty pint and the spoon away from her onto the grass, her shoulders taut. Her breath coming heavy in a way that would make her sick.

Kenna, sitting cross-legged, turned slowly to the bag and lifted it across her. Then set it between them. "Here. Choose whatever you want. We'll get heatstroke if we sit out here too long." She slid out a water, twisted the cap, and downed the whole thing before she crushed it and replaced the lid. She levered forward far enough to grab the ice cream trash, refusing to think about Jax's insistence that she should be able to get up off the ground without using her hands. Something about "functional strength" or whatnot.

She should call him.

Kenna let it ring on speaker, the phone on the ground. It went to voicemail. "This is Special Agent Oliver Jaxton. If you'd like to leave a message, I'll return your call as soon as I'm able." *Beep.*

"I'm...running an errand right now."

Maizie didn't let go of her tension.

"But I still want an update." Kenna hung up.

Maizie let out a breath.

Kenna turned to her. "No one is going to hurt you. Not anyone, ever again." Wasn't that why she'd reached out to Kenna? Even if it was about taking down Rushman, it had to also be—at least in part—about Kenna's ability to keep her safe. That shouldn't be a surprise.

She wanted Maizie to believe down to every broken place inside her that Kenna could take care of her. That no matter what happened, she would be all right. But regardless of what Kenna said to her, it was up to Maizie to believe it.

She'd walked that journey, spending two years alone. Working cases. Taking those tiny steps every day that it took to believe she would be okay. That she was free. She could make herself safe. Fight back the fear, find strength even when she was all alone.

Maizie's gaze roamed the field. She didn't once turn back to look behind her, not even when they could hear people talking—calling loudly to each other.

She trusted Kenna to have her back while she sat here drinking a cold soda. Watching the view, and the way the earth rose and fell but remained so still. Like paper crumpled and tossed aside. Bent and broken in some places. Whether a person believed it happened quickly or over millions of years, the result was the same.

As Kenna looked at the land now, that stillness settled in her. A kind of peace she didn't get looking at the motion of ocean waves.

Had Maizie ever seen the beach?

Again, a hundred questions crossed her mind. She pressed her lips together for a while as they sat in silence. Then she drank another full bottle of water, not so cold as the first one. Maizie chose orange juice and took two sips. She handed it to Kenna and grabbed a soda instead.

Strawberries, yes—maybe. Orange, definitely no.

Kenna's shirt clung to her, heavy with sweat. They both needed a shower, but no way would she opt for using the truck stop one. Maizie needed a controlled environment, and being around strange men, even in a hallway, wasn't going to help.

Kenna said, "I'm gonna go bring the car over so the air-conditioning can start running. That way it won't be an oven when we get back in." She uncrossed her legs and planted her feet, rocking a couple of times before she stood.

Maizie got up as well.

Kenna didn't react, or look over, as they walked to the Impala. No one around. Thankfully, no one noticed them. There didn't seem to be anyone on their tail, but still Kenna didn't plan on letting down her guard.

"Wanna sit up front?" Kenna kept her tone as casual as she could. She opened the passenger door and held it for Maizie.

The teen ducked her head and got in. Kenna left her to close it herself and headed for the driver's side.

It wasn't far to St. George. Barely two hours from Vegas, the subdivision town was more like a small city. And the amount of Indian restaurants made Kenna a fan, even though the place was like a California city in Utah, but with no personality.

Maizie stared out the window as they headed north and skirted the populated area for the airport, in an out-of-the-way part of the red desert. They still had a few hours until six, when Stairs would be there, so Kenna found a thrift store, and they both bought an outfit since that was easier than doing laundry and having nothing to wear in the meantime.

Since Kenna paid, she helped fold the clothes and got the chance to slip a tiny tracker in the pocket of the pants Maizie had picked out. Just in case the girl ran farther next time.

After she'd asked Maizie to tell her if she needed medical attention, and the girl had explained how she'd taken care of herself, Kenna checked them into a chain three-star hotel with gleaming plastic features and clean rooms, then carried the duffel from her trunk into the room. Two queen beds, even though they weren't staying overnight unless it was necessary.

"Wanna shower first?" Kenna dumped the sack of thrift store clothes on the bed and kicked off her shoes. She did exactly what Jax had done and stretched out in her clothes on top of the bed, closing her eyes as she eased her head back onto the pillow.

That was when she realized exactly why Jax had done that. For someone like Kenna—and maybe Maizie too, for different reasons—who needed to get used to being safe even while another person was in the room, that other person had to present themselves as entirely unthreatening. Maybe even vulnerable.

Kenna heard the bag rustle. The bathroom door closed.

She waited so long for the shower to turn on, she fell asleep. Even as gritty and sweaty as she was, Kenna drifted into a broken slumber. Half aware that she needed to protect Maizie if anyone kicked the door open.

Images flashed behind her eyes, dark figures. Shadows that lashed out. Pain whipped like hot lightning that slammed into her forearms.

She came awake moving, sitting up, reaching for her gun. Maizie stood at the end of the bed in a rock band T-shirt and light-blue jeans, her hair wet and unbrushed so that it hung in a tangled mess around her face.

"My turn for the shower?" Kenna turned to the side and set her feet on the floor, unbuttoning the sleeves of her shirt. She pulled up both to her elbows so she could rub her palms down the scars on her forearms. She was fine. Okay, only relatively speaking. "Fine" wasn't quantifiable, and everyone had their own measurement.

"Uh, yes." The teen cleared her throat. "The shower is free." Her voice rasped with the husky tone of someone who had permanently damaged their vocal cords from screaming.

"Great." Kenna shot her a smile, then grabbed the sack of clothes and her duffel of weapons and headed for the bathroom.

Like this was a normal day on a normal vacation. Like

they hadn't met earlier the same day and had never spoken more than a few words to each other.

At the bathroom door, Kenna glanced back. "Wanna get cheeseburgers after I'm done?"

Maizie just stared at her.

"Or whatever. I'm hungry." Kenna left off on a chuckle.

She closed the bathroom door, partly wondering if Maizie would still be in the room when she came back out. Her phone rang, but it wasn't Jax. She stuck it between her shoulder and ear. "Yep?"

"I'm going to explain this to you simply, and you're going to listen."

"Special Agent Dean?"

"Quiet!" he snapped.

There was a rustle on the line, then a groan. "Kenna?"

She gripped the edge of the counter. "Jax?"

Another rustle. "Now you know how this is. So you give me that girl, and I let your boyfriend live. A simple trade. No fuss. No games."

"I'll have to find her first."

Dean didn't need to know she knew *exactly* where Maizie was, or that she had no intention of ever taking her back to Vegas. Let alone trading her to a guy who didn't need to keep his word, and probably had no intention of leaving any of them alive.

Kenna stared at the mirror. "If I find her, I can let you know—"

"Six a.m. we trade. Her life for his. I'll call with where you can bring her."

Kenna said nothing.

Special Agent Dean hung up.

She sent Stairs a text he'd get when his plane landed and he took it off airplane mode.

We've got a problem.

Chapter Thirty

Stairns and Elizabeth ended up on the ground at the St. George airport for barely two hours before they were back in the air with Maizie.

Kenna didn't tell the teen anything about the call she'd received, relying instead on text messages. She'd debriefed with Stairns while Elizabeth chatted with Maizie in the departures area of check-in.

The last thing Maizie needed was to worry about Jax, who she probably didn't know and definitely didn't care about.

Still, Stairns had given the teen a burner phone, and she and Kenna had exchanged numbers. Kenna had sent a few texts so far, and Maizie let her know when they were about to board the plane.

She had no idea if Maizie had even been in the air before.

Kenna drove back into Vegas just after ten in the evening, thoroughly exhausted but with no plan to sleep that night. She avoided the motel room and headed for someone who might be able to help. If she was still alive.

Three voicemails and Santino wasn't calling back.

Whatever he was up to, and wherever he'd gone, he wasn't interested in her inserting herself into his business.

He was going to do what he thought he should—or had to —regardless.

Which meant she only had a limited amount of time to find him. Stop him. Convince him to help her, rather than jeopardizing taking down Rushman's empire. Since Kenna figured the goal was to kill the guy the way he'd killed Deacon and Larry.

Or had the cops caught up to him yet?

No one had any reason to kill Elaine, the librarian from Intellectus. There was a good chance she was okay when Kenna pulled up to the tiny white house on the outskirts of Vegas, in an older neighborhood with smaller lots.

She knocked on the door, then rang the bell just in case.

Elaine eased the door open a couple of inches, the chain taut between the door and the frame. "Kenna?"

"Hey, can I speak with you?"

Elaine was the last person Kenna knew likely wasn't connected to Rushman who'd seen Jax. The librarian closed the door and unhooked the chain. She held it wide.

Kenna entered, turning so her back was never to the other woman. "Have you seen that FBI agent, Jax?"

"Let's get out of the hallway and go in the kitchen." Elaine went first, so Kenna followed.

The light above the oven was on, but Elaine turned on the kitchen light, which was harsh until she dimmed it all the way. The fixtures matched the exterior feel of original to when the house was built, except the refrigerator looked like a newer model. An old landline phone hung on the wall, probably defunct now.

"Tea?" Elain asked. "I find it settles me, usually. But seeing Larry get shot today?" She touched a hand to a necklace hanging over her theme park pajama shirt. "I'll confess I'm still on edge from it."

Kenna hung back by the door, hands in her jeans pockets. The T-shirt she wore covered the gun holstered at the small of her back. "That's understandable." She'd seen so many people get killed, more than anyone should probably. Not to mention the rapport of a gunshot. Mostly she was mad at Santino for firing it right beside her. She would lose her hearing earlier than most, but still. That would exacerbate the problem considerably.

"Did you find that girl?" Elaine said. "Is she okay?"

"I'm sure, wherever she is, she's doing all right." Kenna didn't want to get into a conversation about Maizie, even if Elaine was honest. "But have you seen my friend?"

"He spoke with the police and helped direct them in processing the scene. One of the officers was very young. I told them about a murder I helped solve a few years ago, but they only wanted to know what happened to Larry." Elaine tipped her head to the side while the kettle boiled. "Maybe to see if my story matched your friend's?"

Kenna figured that was true. An FBI agent's statement would count for a lot, but if it could be corroborated by another witness with no stake in the case that would be different. "And after that?"

"He got picked up by another agent, I think."

"What time was it?"

Elaine frowned. "Did something happen?"

"I think it might have," Kenna said. "What about Anthony Santino?"

"That man." Elaine shuddered. "He's gorgeous, all Italian and mysterious."

"You saw him shoot someone today."

Elaine flushed. "After I got over the shock, you know what I realized? He looked good doing it."

Oh-kay. "Do you have any idea where to find him?"

Elaine shrugged. "He met with Larry sometimes. I think they were friends, but it didn't seem amicable...if you know what I mean?"

"They argued?"

"More like tension. There was a vibe." Elaine worked her mouth back and forth. "Are you trying to find him before the police do?"

"I would if I had a clue where to look."

Santino was her only ally right now. Another person she could count on to not be working for Rushman. The FBI were *all* suspect as far as she was concerned—except Jax, of course. And *especially* the FBI director. He was probably the dirtiest one of them all. Which she didn't know for sure, of course, but he hadn't been trained like the rest. Drilled about loyalty and integrity. If he worked for Rushman, it was more like Masonridge's agreement—if the former president had one—a mutual back scratching, quid pro quo thing.

If she could team up with Santino, that would mean she stopped him from doing whatever he had planned *and* she had someone to help take down Rushman. After she got Jax back from Special Agent Dean.

Kenna clenched her teeth.

...give me that girl, and I'll let your boyfriend live.

As if she would hand a traumatized teen to the FBI, or Rushman's guys, when Maizie had been through more than enough in her life. Even if she'd spent some time doing computer work for Rushman's company—the only way Kenna could see her having access to a computer. Who could contemplate the horrors she'd been through in her life?

Elaine grabbed her phone from the kitchen table. "So I'm in this Facebook group for local single women...of a certain age. We post pictures of men we'd like to meet"—she cleared her throat—"and discuss how to make our approach or happen to cross paths with said men. Santino is a legend because of how long he's been single, so I'll ask if anyone has seen him out tonight."

Kenna frowned. "That could work."

"Assuming an army of menopausal women don't try and beat us to him, if anyone has seen him, we should be able to..." Elaine trailed off. "Okay, apparently he caused a stir at a gentlemen's club one of the ladies works at. About an hour ago, he was yelling for security...and something about the FBI director. They tossed him out onto the sidewalk."

At least he hadn't shot anyone.

"Do they know where he went?" Kenna asked.

Elaine lifted her head from her phone. "Someone thinks they saw him down the street at the Bergamot."

"If he's there, the FBI is going to take him out." They wouldn't let him walk, or go to jail. They would simply kill him.

Unless they were elsewhere with Jax, keeping him guarded at an alternate location.

Either way, her dad would've wanted her to save his life. Santino might know where to find the FBI. Or they'd found him, and she could follow them back to wherever they had Jax.

"I need to go there," Kenna said.

"Dressed like that?" Elaine wrinkled her nose. "You'll stick out like a sore thumb."

Kenna looked down at her outfit. "What's wrong with this?" There wasn't much time. Like she could afford to quibble about fashion?

"Huh."

"Thanks for your help, Elaine." Kenna jogged to her car as the librarian stood watching from the porch.

Not far from the Bergamot, her phone rang. It was Stairns.

She swiped the screen and put it on speaker. "I'm about to go into an underground parking lot, so make it fast."

"Our mutual friend would like to express her displeasure at being shuffled out of the picture but is willing to admit she doesn't want to experience the risks inherent in being present where you are."

Translation: Maizie wanted to be with Kenna, but also didn't want to get turned back over to Rushman if the worst happened? "Give her your speech about playing it smart and keeping yourself safe. How that comes first before taking down the bad guy."

"Because you always listen to that?"

"They're going to kill Jax."

"Don't let them." Stairns' tone darkened. "But what do you think I'm gonna say in the event it comes down to him or you?"

"I don't trade lives like that."

"You saved mine," he said. "You saved her because she felt safe enough to trust you. Now we're all trusting that you get through this without giving *your* life. Even if that means someone else who is valuable in this world doesn't make it out."

She didn't want Maizie to hear that bringing down Rushman would take a back seat to rescuing Jax, but she also wanted to do both of those things still. "I'll get him. Then I'll get Rushman. Don't worry about that."

"Try not to burn down the *entire* city in the process. People might get mad."

"I'm about to lose you."

"One more thing," Stairns said. "I might've told our mutual friend about my role in your business. She'd like to help if you need it."

"Of course I do. As soon as you both can get in front of a computer, I'd love all the intel you can give me." She still even had the flash drive Deacon had given them, and had no clue what was on it. Her laptop was at the motel. "I should've given you guys that flash drive from my other pants."

"When we get to the house, we'll call."

"Copy that." Kenna pulled into the parking structure attached to the Bergamot. "Drive safe."

She should approach security and get them to tell her where Santino was. That would've been easier with a wardrobe change—if Elaine had a roommate Kenna's size who happened to be an entertainer or had a tiny dress in her closet. Still, wearing jeans and a T-shirt in Vegas wasn't that astounding. She had no desire to attract attention to herself.

Kenna walked the carpeted path through the casino, scanning for Santino. She called his phone just in case she was close enough she'd hear it ring, even though she was pretty sure he had no intention of answering. If he even still had it on him.

Halfway through the casino, she spotted Special Agent Elton, and Nelson from Miami. The two of them walked together along one side of the room. They were tracking someone. Doing surveillance.

Not Kenna...but...

Up ahead, Santino leaned against the wall, as though trying to be inconspicuous. Except one of Elaine's Facebook group friends had already seen him.

Kenna picked up her pace. She grabbed his arm as she passed and slipped a tracker in his pocket. "Walk with me."

Santino stiffened but came with her.

She maintained her grip on his arm. "Two FBI agents, my ten o'clock. We need a way out of here."

"You think I didn't see them? I was waiting for them to go to an out-of-the-way spot so I could pick off one and get the other to call the director."

"Then you'll kill him."

"He knows what he deserves is far worse than that."

Kenna bit her lip. "So first it was Deacon. Then Larry. Now it's the director. Or did you kill anyone else today?"

He didn't respond to that.

"After the director, who's next on the list?"

"Who do you think?"

Kenna sighed. "Rushman?"

"They'll kill me before I even get in the door. It's a suicide mission, but I just need a way to get close enough to put a bullet in him before they put one in me."

"You're right."

"I am?" Santino glanced at her.

"It's a suicide mission."

Kenna's phone buzzed. She read the text from Elaine.

> You've been spotted. Head to Olivette's Café.

She found it to their right, in the corner, and pointed. "That way." She didn't glance behind her. "So how are you going to get to Rushman?"

"The director will tell me how to get through the gate," Santino said. "It's keycard access."

"Connected to the same network his house is on?"

"I don't—why?"

Kenna shrugged one shoulder. "I know someone."

Maizie had proven she could do a whole lot with computers, hacking the back end of the Utah True Crime website.

And she'd managed to escape from Rushman, or his men. So could she help them break *into* the same place she'd broken out of?

Worth asking.

"I might be able to get you in." She smiled.

Santino glanced at her, then said, "Incoming," as though something behind them had caught his eye.

Kenna sped up, almost to a jog.

Someone pushed through the doors that went outside. Olivette's Café was to their right.

The woman who rushed in wore a sparkly red dress, her hair teased out to twice its size, and stage makeup. "Hey, girl!" She held a tall glass—two feet tall and slender with a straw that went to the bottom—and waved with the other hand while she took a sip. "Hey, hey, girl!" She practically screamed the words like she was trying to communicate with a friend on the complete opposite side of the casino.

It took her a split second, but Kenna realized who the woman was.

"Yeah, girl!" Elaine had to be wearing sneakers, the way she moved across the carpet angled right toward them. She sidestepped right behind Kenna. Followed by, "Oof. Watch where you're goin', bucko! You made me spill my *drank*. Now I gotsta go back and get another one. No thanks to..."

Santino got the door to the café open.

Kenna glanced back to see Elaine had collided with both FBI agents, knocked them over, and spilled her drink on them. Now she stood over them in a teacher stance, one finger pointed while she continued her lecture.

"Go." Kenna shoved Santino forward. "Run."

The two FBI agents would be right behind them.

Santino raced down a straight hall. The worst place they could be, giving whoever was behind them line of sight to shoot them. He turned at the end into a closed-off section. Kenna skidded after him around the corner.

"FBI! STOP!" Elton raced after them.

Santino found a door that led to the patio. He shoved at the handle. It didn't budge.

"Don't move!" Elton rounded the corner, followed by Nelson, both of them red-faced and damp, weapons raised. "Hands up. Both of you."

Chapter Thirty One

Kenna slowly raised her hands. They'd probably figure she and Santino were armed. What she didn't know was which side they were on. The last thing she needed was to get shot because Santino decided to go down in a blaze of glory in a café.

Hopefully his intention to finish the mission would end up more important than not being arrested right now.

She started to say, "Okay," when someone rounded the corner behind them.

Elaine hefted a chair up, stronger than Kenna would've guessed. She swung it before the two agents could react and clipped Nelson on the back of the head. She caught Elton's shoulder.

A gun went off. The bullet went wide to the right into the dining area of empty tables. Nelson slumped to the floor, out cold. Santino pulled his gun and shot Elton in the chest. The agent's body jerked, and he hit the floor as well.

Elaine lowered the chair and screamed, "Stop shooting people right in front of me!"

Santino strode to Nelson and hefted the guy up, paying no mind to the gun on the floor.

"Should I get that?" Elaine pointed to the agent's duty weapon.

"Leave it." Kenna needed a plan. "You want to call this in as well?"

"She's coming with us." Santino's tone didn't invite argument. He shifted Nelson on his shoulder. "Let's get going."

Elaine jimmied the exit open.

They stepped onto the sidewalk, and Kenna had to admit that one man carrying another over his shoulder wasn't the strangest thing that could be seen in Vegas.

Whoever was in charge of that café probably found the body already. They had to have heard the shot. It wouldn't be long before cops were right behind them. So when Santino headed into a crowded convenience store, she ducked her head to keep from being noticed by the security camera.

"Where are we going?" Kenna asked.

Elaine scurried ahead. "Bathroom, right? It's back there." She led them to the restroom, which turned out to be single occupancy and smelled like vomit.

Kenna's stomach roiled, and she swallowed back the nausea.

Santino laid the agent, who was still out, on the floor. Nelson's head lolled to the side. "Shut the door."

Kenna grabbed it before Elaine had a chance to enter, considering too many people were already in there, then told her, "Keep watch."

"Oh, okay. Good idea." Elaine beamed.

Kenna clicked the door shut and locked it. She didn't need a mystery addict wannabe detective, someone she liked, to get caught up in even more charges than she'd racked up in the last half hour. She then rounded on Santino. "What are you doing?"

He crouched and started going through the agent's pockets. "No one will think twice about a guy passed out in a bathroom like this. When they find him later."

"And before that?" He pulled out a phone, so she said, "Gimme that."

Santino handed it over. "We'll be long gone. They're at the scene right now."

"Your third murder. In one day." The phone was locked. "That's a spree. I should subdue and secure you until the police can find *you*."

"But then you'd never take down Rushman, because he'd be alive." Santino straightened, Nelson's wallet in one hand. "You think this will be over with him in jail? If he's not out within twenty-four hours because the evidence conveniently disappeared, he'll be sent to some cushy facility and get whatever he wants."

"There was a guy in New Mexico, a killer. They had him in prison but let him out so he could kill whoever they wanted dead and he'd have an alibi."

"Exactly!" He looked a little confused.

"I could've explained that better, but there's not much time for serial killer stories." Kenna crouched and used Nelson's thumb to unlock his phone. "See if there's a room key card in that wallet. I need to know where they're keeping my friend."

"They have someone?"

"They're going to kill him. But I'm not going to give them what they want, so I need to find him." She blew out a breath, willing to be honest. "You have a lot of people looking for you, but I could use your help."

Santino shook his head. "Busy. I need to kill Rushman.

After I kill the FBI director." Nelson started to come around. Santino grabbed a handful of his hair and cracked his head on the toilet bowl.

Kenna winced. "Don't give him brain damage."

"Do you honestly think any of them deserve to live after what Rushman has done, unchecked, for *years*?"

"I'm not going to let you kill yourself."

"Who will care?"

"You know." Kenna held his gaze with a steady one of her own. "You know she'll miss when you don't visit."

"She doesn't even know who I am."

"Yes, she does." Kenna eased a little bit closer. "She needs you to take care of her. Like you've been doing. Now we're almost at the finish line and you're going to give up?"

"I'm going to finish this." Tears shined in his eyes. "My way."

Kenna pressed her lips together. "And I'm supposed to just let you do whatever you want, kill whoever you want, and stand back? Let you take people's lives?"

There was a fine line between justice and murder in this case. Usually it was not so fine.

She continued, "If I know a murder is about to take place, then I'm legally obligated to report it. Right now? I'm harboring a fugitive in a convenience store bathroom. It'll be easy for them to argue I'm complicit, maybe even an accessory. Elaine's life is destroyed. My career and my integrity are *done*. You'll be dead, so what do you care?"

Santino lifted his chin. "Rushman will be dead."

"You get your revenge, consequences be damned?"

"Yes."

"No more of my dad's friends are dying." Kenna didn't realize she felt that way until after the words came out.

Santino flinched like she'd slapped him. In a way, maybe she had.

"I lost him. I lost Joe Don Hunter, who I barely knew." She looked at the phone, mostly because it was too hard to talk about. "I need to find Jax. Do whatever you want. Who cares if anyone else has a better idea."

"Do you?"

"I'll tell you after I find Jax." Her phone started to ring. Kenna tugged the door open. "Leave this one alive, Santino. Or it's premediated."

Elaine stared at her, wide-eyed.

Santino said, "Kenna!"

She turned back.

"Your father was here looking into your mother's death."

She stared for a second, then shook her head. "Too late." She stepped out past Elaine. "Don't go anywhere near that guy. He's not for you."

She hoped Elaine would heed that advice.

Kenna found the special assignment group text thread in Nelson's phone.

Who actually names their group threads?

She wasn't in any, but rather than question it, maybe she should be grateful.

Fine.

Okay, so she was talking to herself. But once she got Jax back, she could talk to him, so no big deal.

Kenna sent a text to the thread.

> Santino killed Elton. I barely got away.
> Where you guys at?

She had no idea if this would work. The priest would've told her to pray, but maybe she was a little too like Santino to expect an answer. It was easy to believe she was on the path of right actions, and honorable work. But when she'd let Rushman go free to save Jax? Kenna wouldn't think twice.

She had Maizie.

If that evil man had to keep operating in order for her to save Jax—if there was no other way—she could honestly say she'd let him. It made her sick to the stomach just thinking about it. Whether Jax made it through this or he didn't, the very next thing she planned to do was take down Rushman.

If he was still alive by then, and Santino hadn't enacted his plan.

Kenna blew a strand of hair off her face. The phone buzzed in her hand.

> W/J in conf rm

Did that mean he was with Jax in the conference room? Her mind wanted to believe that. She sent a reply.

> And dir?

The response came back.

> Laying low until it's done

Kenna headed into the Bergamot, using an entrance as far from Olivette's Café as she could find. That corner was so full of cops and bystanders, she couldn't even get near, and they were directing people to back up. She skirted the edge of the crowd.

Her phone rang.

Stairs. "Hey."

"What happened?"

Kenna frowned. "I'm going to get Jax."

"You found him?"

"I think so." That was the truth.

"It's a trap."

"Of course it is. And they want Maizie, but is that the point? She's states away now, and that's precisely where she's supposed to be. Free of *all* of this." Maybe she was nearer to Santino than she'd even thought before, because she said, "And if I have a say, it's never going to touch her again."

Stairns stayed silent.

Kenna entered a bright walkway that intersected another, dodging water puddles. From the pool to the casino, some people didn't even bother drying off. "What?"

The phone rustled. "Kenna?"

She grabbed the rail, even though there were barely three steps. "Yeah, Maze?"

"I could help you."

"From there?"

"I can work for you, like Stairns said he does. But I type faster."

Kenna already knew what kind of kid this girl was. The kind who tried to take down the man who'd held her forever, even though she'd escaped him and she could flee. Maizie knew it would never be over.

If she didn't end it herself.

Kenna spoke softly. "Do you know who I am, and what I went through? Like from news reports."

"I know."

"So then you know I'm telling the truth when I say you need time. Take some time, please. Be safe for a while. Do your thing from a computer, because you can help, but there's no way I'm gonna let him touch you. Not *ever* again. That's why I put you on that plane with Stairns and Elizabeth."

"Dr. Stairns is really nice." Maizie sniffed. "So is Cabot. She let me feed her cheese."

"Oof. Watch for the farts later."

Maizie let out a laugh, and it was the sweetest thing Kenna had ever heard.

"You're in the best place you can be. Don't feel obligated to do anything."

"But..."

"You caught that, huh?" Kenna said. "I could use eyes here."

"Hotels have closed systems. Some of the best in the world. How soon do you need me in there? Because it might take some time to get into their system. Is it the Bergamot?"

"Yes. And when you say *some time*, do you mean like an hour...or three days?"

"Somewhere in between. I don't know until I try. And Stairs is looking at me like maybe I shouldn't be talking about hacking a hotel network."

"Tell him it'll save lives." Still, Kenna didn't need her openly breaking the law. It could get them all in trouble, and there was enough of that going around right now. "If you can, find out where the FBI director is, or have Stairs call his office. Tell them there's a threat to his life—which is totally the truth—and he needs to seek out law enforcement protection."

Santino might get there, but if Billings was surrounded by cops or agents—hopefully legit ones—it could save their lives.

"Done." Maizie paused. "And Kenna..."

"Yeah, Maze?" Kenna hit the button at the elevator banks.

"Find your friend."

"I plan to." She hung up and stowed her phone, looking again at Nelson's. The screen was locked, and she'd forgotten to remove the security protections or program her thumbprint. The time in the corner glared at her. Each minute that ticked past meant another second Jax's life could be taken.

She wanted to call Special Agent Torrow. Find out if Justine was still alive. Doing that might tip off whoever held

Jax to the fact there was an agent in their ranks who wasn't loyal to the director—and Rushman. Dean had said the director ordered him around. Deacon had mentioned a man on the video she hadn't watched.

Masonridge? Maybe.

Billings? More likely.

This whole thing was nothing but a tangled mess either way. She just hoped Elaine stayed free—the way Maizie was free—instead of getting caught up in it.

She's free. Because she'd trusted Kenna to take care of her. The way she'd trusted her father, even when she hadn't been sure of his motives. She'd railed at him for quitting, but he'd put her above solving a case.

The way she was now willing at least to put Jax's life before this one.

As much as she might not like it, she wasn't so dissimilar to her father at times. He'd taught her a lot. And most of it was very good.

Kenna stepped off the elevator.

She tugged her gun from the holster at the small of her back, cataloguing the other weapons she had on her. If someone searched her they'd probably find a good few. Maybe she needed something a little more nonlethal.

She stowed the second phone and pulled out pepper spray. She could push that down with her off hand, which she had a hard time using to fire her weapon still. Kenna held the pepper spray up and set her gun hand over it, like she was holding a flashlight but ready with both weapons.

No matter what.

She approached the conference room. Banged on the door with the side of her fist.

Footsteps tromped to it, and the door opened to—

"Special Agent Torrow." Instinct had her hit the pepper spray.

He turned away with a roar, coughing. He grabbed her arm and dragged her through the cloud. She held her breath and shut her eyes. Then stumbled two steps, opened her eyes, and spun back to him.

They held their weapons pointed at each other.

On the far side of the room, opposite corner, Jax sat on the floor with his hands cuffed in front of him. She couldn't see below his hands because of the table, but he had sweat on his shirt. Disheveled, his collar open. Blood from his nose on his shoulder like he'd wiped it away.

The corner on her side? A man lay on the floor, blood pooled on the carpet around him. Special Agent Dean.

"Did you kill him, or did Jax?"

Torrow shut the door, both of them still holding weapons on each other. His eyes were bright red, and tears streamed down his cheeks. "Does it matter? I didn't need him anymore. You're seven hours early, and no Maizie."

Kenna shook her head. She turned to Jax. "I don't think dogs are good judges of character *at all*."

Chapter Thirty Two

Torrow stared at her. "Lower your weapon." He swung his gun around and aimed it at Jax. "Or I'll—"

She fired.

The shot hit his shoulder and slammed him back against the door. His gun fell from his fingers—probably the only reason he didn't make good on his word to kill Jax. Assuming that was what he'd been about to say.

She strode toward him.

He leaned over to reach for the gun with his good hand, unaware that the hole in his shoulder had left a smear of blood on the door behind him.

"You know, I'm getting pretty sick of guys working for Rushman." She kicked the gun hard, sending it along the carpet toward Jax, who was out of sight. "You'd better not be dead."

Torrow grunted, shifting to lean back against the door. "I'm not unless you plan on killing me now."

"I wasn't talking to you." Jax hadn't been shot, had he? She wanted to go check, but that would mean taking her gaze off Torrow. "Blah-blah, Rushman has you in a corner. You've got no choice but—"

His leg swung out, and he twisted his hips, knocking her off her feet.

Kenna hit a chair on the way down and fell with her gun between the carpet and her body, her trigger finger at an odd angle.

Torrow jumped on her back.

Breath expelled from her lungs, crushed under the force of two hundred plus pounds. She let out a cry with all the air in her. But then she couldn't breathe. Couldn't push him off.

He grunted, felt around, and ran his hands up to her throat.

Bile collected in her mouth.

Kenna gritted her teeth and tried to use her legs. His arm snaked around her throat.

Torrow's head slammed into hers, and he slumped onto her, deadweight. Someone rolled him off her.

Kenna rolled the other way and stared up at Jax. "Why didn't you shoot him?"

"Why didn't you?" He held out his hands, still cuffed.

She grasped his hand and tried to get up. Pain roiled through her forearms and her trigger finger. She sank back onto the floor.

"Okay." He crouched, wound his arm over her head. She had to thread hers through his to grab the shirt on the back of his neck. He wound his arm around her back. "Ready?"

She wanted to say no. Honestly, she wouldn't mind staying like this with his chest right in front of her face. All that warmth and strength. Then she saw the blood on his shoulder. She managed to get out, "Mm-hmm."

Despite the handcuffs, Jax stood, hauling all her weight up to standing with his.

Then they were close, nearly face-to-face. His cuffed hands were behind her back, his arms around her. "I should find a key for those cuffs." He tugged her close so they were flush against each other.

Kenna tilted her head in Torrow's direction. "He's gonna wake up and come at us again."

"Not this soon." Jax leaned down, his warm face close to hers.

After all that time complaining to herself about the heat, she liked it right now. When she couldn't do anything but shudder out the fear of being trapped.

His nose touched the side of hers. Then his lips, on her lips. "Thank you for saving me." His breath caressed her face.

"You think I want to face down Rushman by myself?"

He frowned.

"I need my backup." Kenna turned and ducked out from his arms. She checked Torrow's pockets and found a set of keys, which thankfully had a handcuff key on them. She went back to Jax and handed him her gun, ignoring the pain in her finger. She'd already had enough physical issues.

"Right, your *backup*." His expression took on a new note. "Stairns is busy?"

"Yep." She tossed the cuffs on the table, then set her hands on his shoulders. "He took Maizie back to Colorado. She's safe."

"And you?"

"Can we get out of here?" Surely he didn't want to stay when two bodies were in the room. "Are you gonna go all FBI agent on me again? Last time I left you at a scene, you got kidnapped." She palpated the sides of his face, assessing his nose. "Yep, you got hit."

He chuckled. "It's not broken. Mostly because I can touch it without almost passing out."

"Who do we trust in this town? Or are we on our own?"

Jax settled on the edge of the table. "We need a phone."

After she handed him the one that belonged to Nelson, she said, "I figure if we tell the hotel about this, it'll get back to Rushman. He'll know his plan of killing you and getting Maizie back is blown." She glanced at Torrow, still unconscious on the floor. "You know, that really ticks me off."

"Because you were all friendly with the guy."

"He saved Cabot!"

"Maybe it's just people he doesn't care about."

Kenna sighed.

"I need a phone I can use. Unless you want me to call 911?"

She frowned, trying to figure it out. Her mind stayed traitorously blank. "Santino..." How to start explaining that mess? "Maybe you should call LVPD. I mean, they can't *all* be under Rushman's thumb."

His chest expanded in a breathy way that made her think he'd been kicked and his ribs were bruised—if not broken. "I would hope so. But who knows. And in a hotel he owns?" He shook his head.

"Where's the director? It's been days." In fact, Kenna hadn't seen him since that ceremony. "And Justine?"

"They were making plans to have her killed in lockup." Jax eased open his jaw, then touched the side. "Another call to make." He looked at her phone. "I have an idea. If Stairns is out."

"What?"

"We call people we know we can trust."

Kenna frowned.

He put the phone to his ear, reached out, and snagged her hand. The gun beside him on the table. She turned with her pepper spray, shifting her broken finger so her middle finger could spray the mechanism if she had to.

"Yeah, it's Special Agent Jaxton." He paused. "That's right, and I could use your help. The special assignment here in Vegas could use a few extra agents as backup. The situation is serious, and we need help." He paused. "Kenna needs help."

She winced.

"Got it." He hung up the phone.

She groaned. "Why did you mention me?"

"Miller said he would be here personally with a contingent of agents."

That was the worst idea she'd ever heard. "He hates me. And all his friends."

"Actually, after everything, they tell stories about you and Bradley in the office. All the cases you solved. People you saved."

"That might be worse."

He squeezed her hand. "They want to help. Not because of me, but because of *you*."

"We need to go back to the bathroom."

Jax used Nelson's phone to make an emergency call 911 without having to unlock it and left it on the table. They used the cuffs to secure Torrow to the table but took the gun. Then they headed out.

As they made their way out of the hotel, looking like two bedraggled people who had a bad experience in Vegas but drew nearly no notice, he squeezed her hand. "What bathroom?"

She didn't realize he'd taken her hand again. Instead of thinking on that and looking like she'd hit her head, she told him about Elton and Nelson, and the convenience store bathroom. Elaine. Santino.

"Elaine did all that?"

"She was pretty amazing." Kenna pushed open the door with her shoulder. Cop cars—flashing lights and sirens going—streamed past on the street. She had no idea which incident, or something else completely, they were responding to. "She did great."

"And you saved Maizie?"

"She trusted me. And she saved herself."

"That's what happens when you're strong." He tugged her closer as they walked down the sidewalk, so the outside of their arms touched.

"I might have you tell Maizie that yourself. She'll need to hear that over and over again."

He glanced down at her.

The two of them strolled down the Strip, heading for the convenience store. Getting lost in the crowd of people. Entertainers on the street they sidestepped, while others stopped to watch. An overpass walkway over the street, stairs on both ends.

She noted another injury in the way he walked. "Do you need a doctor?"

"Do you?"

Sure, she'd checked herself out of the hospital, but that didn't mean he couldn't get checked out. "It's not a contest."

"Because you aren't sure you'd win?"

"You think being still, and doing handstands, means you have more strength of mind than me?"

He chuckled for a second, then blew out a breath that sounded like it hurt. "No, I do not. You're the strongest person I know."

If she told him she thought he was pretty great, would he quit his job for another "lateral move"? The fact was, he'd go home to Salt Lake City when the case was over—the place he should be. Working on his career.

She would go back on the road. First to Maizie and Cabot, and then on to the next case. At worst, she had two employees now. She might actually have to pay Maizie.

They worked well together. She could confidently say they liked each other.

Did that mean they would end up in a relationship?

Maybe rather than asking that question, she should just enjoy the fact he was next to her and the feel of his fingers wound in hers, and work the case.

The rest of it would take care of itself.

Kenna let go of his hand, and the doors to the convenience store swished open. She stepped inside to a crowd and a couple of police officers. She ducked sideways and went down another aisle.

Jax followed. "Why are we hiding?"

She focused on the shelf, trying to look interested in...oh, these were laxatives. "Maybe because I was there when Elton was shot. If Nelson is alive, and awake, the first thing he'll do is call for my arrest."

"He was with Torrow in the conference room."

She glanced over at him. "They jumped you?"

He nodded. "After I woke up, 'cause Dean stun-gunned me in the car, on the way from Intellectus back to the hotel."

"Where is the director?" She realized he hadn't answered her question, just the one about Justine. "Santino intends to kill him."

"Clear a path!" EMTs pushed a gurney through the store. Nelson appeared in the corner.

Both of them ducked out of sight.

Kenna went to the end of the aisle and peered around.

The gurney had a body on it, covered with a sheet. "Who..." Her voice came out barely a whisper.

Nelson followed the gurney, talking with a police officer. "She gave me no choice. It saddens me to say that, but I had to kill her." He shook his head as if he really were sad. The agent and the uniformed officer with him stepped outside.

Kenna twisted around. "We need to find Santino."

"I need to stop Nelson. He's the last remaining agent except me before you get to the director. If we follow him, he might lead us right there." Jax winced. "But without him seeing us?"

Kenna pulled out her phone and called Maizie.

When the girl answered, she sounded tired.

"If you're resting, I don't want to bother you," Kenna said. "I can call Stairns."

"I don't want to sleep."

Kenna ducked her head and looked at the cough drops. "Nightmares?"

"Please give me something to do."

"I need to follow someone on traffic cameras." Kenna explained about the special agent who'd just walked out of the store and gave Maizie the cross streets so she could grab the address. She could look up the GPS tracker on Santino from her laptop.

"How long ago?" Sounded like Maizie was moving. "No, Cabot, I'm okay. Go back to sleep."

Kenna smiled, aware of Jax watching her. "A couple of minutes."

"Perfect," Maizie said. "After it's live, it's shifted to where it's stored on a server. Easier to hack than the live feed."

Kenna watched another police officer take up post at the mouth of the hall to the restroom. "You're pretty good at this stuff."

Jax grabbed her hand, tugged on it, and led her out.

"It's like..." Maizie paused. "I understand it. Like seeing a foreign language for the first time, and you already know how to speak it."

"That's amazing."

"But I didn't learn it. It's just something I know how to *do*."

Kenna and Jax trotted down the store front steps onto the sidewalk and slipped back into the crowd away from the cops. "Sounds amazing anyway. Like a gift."

Jax squeezed her hand.

Kenna remembered the flash drive. She shifted the phone away from her ear. "We need to get back to the car. I still have that flash drive from Deacon."

Maizie gasped. "You got one?"

"What's with them, Maze? Santino had one. So did Deacon. And Larry said Rushman took his."

Maizie made a noise, hearing that name.

"He isn't going to touch you."

Maizie was quiet for a second, then said, "Don't let him touch *you*."

"I have backup," Kenna said. Her turn to squeeze Jax's hand. "I'm not doing this alone."

"I'm still scared."

Probably the only reason she'd agreed to run to Colorado with Stairs and his wife, where she would be safe. "What's with the flash drives?"

"I looked everywhere, trying to find them on hard drives and online servers."

"Santino's was in the carpet in his car."

"That's your father's car." Maizie paused. "He lost it to Santino in a bet. After you and your dad went to England,

Santino had to get it out of storage." It was like she knew more about Kenna's life than Kenna did.

"How do you know all that?"

"Credit card receipts. Travel bookings. The title on the car changed from your father to Santino after you guys left the country."

"When did you start looking into me?" Kenna asked.

"A couple of years ago. I read all about that killer, and how your partner died. And the FBI files. I even emailed that doctor lady at the Bureau and told her she shouldn't have said that about you." Maizie huffed out a breath. "Anyway, I'm in the traffic cam server. I'm at the right time, so I'll send you a picture and you can confirm it's him before I stalk his traitorous be-hind across Vegas."

Jax stopped at a crosswalk. He glanced at Kenna, and she grinned back, about to ask Maizie if she wanted a job, when someone pulled up in front of them.

The dark sedan slowed to a stop right in the crosswalk.

A window at the back rolled down, then a gun appeared.

Jax yelled, "Run!"

Chapter Thirty Three

Kenna didn't slow quite in time. She slammed into the car door.

"This one?" Jax asked.

She clicked the key fob on the rental and unlocked the doors. "Less conspicuous than the Impala. Plus, it's in the name of one of Stairns' fake IDs. I rented it in Utah."

"These things are GPS tracked. You know that, right?" He wedged himself between her and the car when she opened the driver's door. "And I'm driving."

"Speaking of GPS..." Kenna needed to call Maizie back, since she'd hung up right when that driver started shooting at them. Not Nelson—it had to have been some lackey of Rushman's. Didn't matter, because they were alive, and it was going to stay that way if either of them had anything to say about it.

While he got the engine running, she grabbed her laptop from the duffel and another GPS tracker, which she stuck in her own pocket. So far she was two for two on these, so why not? It was going to come in handy in a second when she got Santino's location.

She logged into the system. She clicked on the icon for each tracker until she found one not in this car or in Colorado with Maizie. "Santino is on the freeway, heading south out of the city."

"You think he's making a run for it?" Jax pulled out of the space.

She shook her head. "Who knows. Maybe this is where the FBI director is."

"Put the laptop on the dash so I can see where he's going," Jax said. "You need to close your eyes for a while. You've had a long day."

Kenna turned her laptop back, because the hinge folded both ways so the keyboard faced down and the screen faced them like a stand.

"I'm serious." He looked both ways and bumped up onto the street. "Get some rest."

"Because you ordered me to?" She knew it was a good idea, but why let that slide without arguing?

Jax said nothing.

She stared at the line of his jaw, the knot on the back of her head radiating pain in a way she might need to take pain meds.

She didn't like that Nelson had killed Elaine. The librarian had been so excited to help out, and Kenna should've known it wouldn't end well. Whichever way it shook out, she'd lost her life as the cost of her participation.

Kenna's eyes drifted closed, and she wound up picturing Elaine in her kitchen. The glow of excitement on her face. The way she'd called 911 at Intellectus after Larry was killed. *I was born for this.*

Now she was dead because of it.

Sadness weighed down her body. Her mind floated from thoughts of Elaine to Jax. To her father. That rushed escape to the UK. His trailer, the one she hadn't been able to find. Kenna wasn't even sure if she could handle the memories of going inside it. Maybe it would hurt too much to see it, whether it was the same or if it had changed so much she no longer recognized it.

Kenna woke up in the passenger seat of the rental, one of her father's journals in her lap. Jax sat in the driver's seat after insisting he drive.

"What time is it?" She rubbed her eyes.

The dash was dark, the interior of the car dark like the outside world. He'd parked on the side of the road off in some trees that had been specifically planted here, because they were all evenly spaced out and midsize rather than mature, and everything else had been configured around it.

To the left there was nothing but open darkness.

"And where are we?" Kenna asked.

"Just before two." Jax took a sip from a paper cup. "And we're outside a mental health residential facility about thirty minutes south of Vegas, trying to hide even though this desert has no cover."

"Seems like you did okay."

"Anyone who drives by will see us. But I guess with Santino in there. That's the point."

Kenna shifted to sit up in the seat, adjusting her position to get some fresh blood flowing.

"I did some research. This is where his daughter lives."

Kenna scrubbed her hands down her face, then ran them through her hair. She should find a brush or get a ponytail going so she didn't look so haggard. Though, doing that might not help much. "He's saying goodbye."

She reiterated her conversation in the bathroom with Santino to Jax, giving him a clue into his mindset. The fact Santino was working on the assumption he wouldn't live through this, but he was still determined to get close enough to take out Rushman.

"We need to find out where Rushman is, and not wait until Santino shows up guns blazing."

"But he's going to find the FBI director first." She texted Maizie.

> You still up?

Then she turned to Jax. "So where is he? And how is Santino going to find him? We could warn both of them that there's a hit out on them and they should take precautions to ensure their safety."

"But that only stops Santino from doing something stupid. It doesn't shut down Rushman and his entire operation."

Kenna nodded, watching her thread with Maizie, waiting for a reply—if she was awake.

Her phone started to ring, and Maizie's name flashed on the screen. She answered it, turning the brightness down. "Hey, you okay?"

"It's Stairns."

Kenna frowned. She put the call on speaker. "What's going on?"

"The kid will be okay. But...she found the FBI director. You were right that Nelson headed for him. She tracked his car across Vegas to a house on the outskirts. She got into a neighbor's doorbell camera that faces the entry gates on the mansion."

Kenna glanced at Jax. "Okay."

"She flipped out." Stairns sighed. "She recognized the house and threw the laptop, shattered the thing. Cabot started barking. Elizabeth got her away from the debris, and the three of them are in the sitting room, drinking tea."

"Okay. That's good, but I need the address." And a way to do this without utilizing Maizie's skills. The girl didn't need to be constantly traumatized every time Kenna needed information.

"I think she's more worried she let you down reacting like that." Stairns groaned like he was easing into a chair. "Like you won't want her help because you think she's damaged."

"We're all damaged in our own way." She just needed the chance to tell Maizie that herself.

"That's true," Stairns said.

Jax looked back from the window. "Yes, it is."

"Do you have the address?" Kenna tugged the laptop from the dash and hit the power button. Jax had it on battery-saving mode, but she could use the power port in the car's center console to charge it. She had 38 percent, which was enough. "That's probably where Santino is heading after he says goodbye."

How he knew where to find the director, she wasn't sure.

And for all she knew, Santino didn't have a clue. What she didn't need was to end up leading him to the director herself.

As tempting as that might be.

The threat of death could loosen his lips enough he might admit what he'd done.

"Someone's coming." Jax shifted in his chair.

Stairns said, "I'm texting you that address."

"We're gonna follow Santino," Jax said. "If this is him."

Kenna pulled up the GPS tracking program and confirmed. "It's him on the move. We can hang back far enough he doesn't see us."

"Stairns?" Jax said. "Were you able to contact the director to warn him his life might be in danger?"

"I got as far as his assistant, but she told me he'd call back tomorrow. What with it being important that I speak to him and all." Stairns' voice rang with a sardonic tone.

"At least you tried," Kenna said.

"I just don't get why he's still in Vegas." Stairns paused. "Why not run like Masonridge did after that assassination attempt?"

"Maybe Maizie knows."

Stairns groaned in a way that sounded like pure sadness. "She said that house is locked up like a fortress. No way out. It's why she couldn't escape from there, she had to do it elsewhere. Also no way in without being spotted."

"Could she turn it all off, all the surveillance if we needed her to?" She didn't want to cause the teen more distress. She wanted Maizie, or Stairns, to say no to her so Kenna had to find a different way in. Maybe with Jax going first, drawing the director to let them in so they could talk to him. Get him to confess to his involvement with Rushman.

"I'll ask Elizabeth if she thinks that's a good idea. But Maizie did say that one of the videos shows *Billings* at that dinner with Santino and Rushman. Long time ago, back when he was a captain in the air force and used to visit Vegas when he had leave. Every time he had leave."

Jax pulled out and flipped on the car's headlights as he headed after Santino, who wasn't even in sight.

She laid it all out. "US Air Force to the Senate to this appointment as FBI director. There's a clean intersection between Masonridge, Billings, and Rushman. And it involves getting Rushman those military contracts he has."

"Yeah," Stairns said. "Because of Maizie."

"How's that?" Kenna frowned. Jax glanced over at her, but she realized he was actually looking at the computer screen and the GPS to track Santino.

"She told us a little more of her story on the plane. I think she was scared no one would ever hear it, so she needed to tell someone before she was recaptured or killed."

Kenna balled her hand into a fist on her leg. "That's not gonna happen."

Jax covered her hand with his.

"I know, and you know," Stairns said. "Because we aren't going to let it."

Jax moved his hand back to the steering wheel, as though laser focusing on Santino. Which was good because Kenna was all over the place right now. "Tell me what she said."

"Rushman figured out pretty early on how special she is. Got her tutors, and people to show her science and math. Computers. She's been working for his company since she was eleven. Basically everything new they've come up with since then was Maizie." Stairns paused. "I checked. It tracks with the timing of when they started making serious money. Coming up with new tech, getting more and more government contracts. She's smart enough she negotiated with him. An agreement regarding...what she was willing to do and what he would get in return."

Kenna winced. "Did he keep his word?"

"What do you think?"

"I think maybe I don't care so much if Santino kills Rushman."

Jax spoke up. "There's an FBI team from Salt Lake on their way down, remember? We're going to tear this guy's business and his life apart. First the director, then Rushman."

Stairns responded, "Just tell me when it's over so I can tell Maizie she doesn't have to worry anymore."

"Copy that," Kenna said.

Stairns hung up.

"You want him to get killed?"

She glanced at Jax, wondering at the tone he'd just used.

"If the alternative is Maizie never being free of that monster, wondering every day what he's going to do to get her back? Even knowing he could be thinking about her is nothing short of torture."

Jax gripped the wheel.

"The trade-off is he's dead? You better believe I want that. I want her free of him. For good. Or who knows when she turns up like Santino, determined to end it the way he wants to. And there's no chance of persuading him otherwise."

"Tell me how he knows where he's going."

"He's been living this for years." Kenna shrugged one shoulder, even though it was dark and he wasn't looking at her. "Maybe his daughter told him where she was held. Or someone else gave him the information. We have no idea how far he and my father, and *Larry* got"—she uttered that name with not a small amount of disdain—"before Rushman hit back at them and took all their options."

Jax let out a long sigh. "We have to at least try to do this right. Otherwise, in a way, we're no better than any of them. Taking the law into our own hands, doing what we want whether we think it's right or not, for our own ends."

"I don't want to hand over my integrity," Kenna said. "Not even to take out the biggest evil in the world. I don't want to become what I'm fighting." And that was the crux of the issue with the movies that'd been made of her father's life. They showed him in a lot of ways acting no different than the people he took down. Where was the honor in being no better than the bad guys of the world?

"Santino is definitely headed to that house."

"Then let's intercept before he gets there."

Jax hit the gas. "I thought you'd never ask." He changed lanes and sped up until she saw the taillights of a car in front. Santino had pulled into the neighborhood.

Kenna pointed. "There he is."

Jax flashed his headlights and pulled up close behind Santino. The other car sped up. Jax let out a low chuckle.

"Um...is there something you want to tell me about high-speed chases?"

"Yeah. You know there are places where they're illegal? Where a city is too dense to make it safe to pursue a suspect."

"Okay..."

He jerked the wheel and got past Santino, jerking it again to cut off the Italian in a way that forced him to stop, or they would crash. He put the car in park. "I don't ever want to live in one of those places."

Kenna pushed out of the car with her hand close to the gun holstered on her hip. The Italian had his hands on the wheel.

Jax strode to the driver's side of Santino's car and knocked on the window. "Get out. We need to talk."

Kenna pulled her gun and held it aimed at the front windshield.

Jax knocked on the window. "Hands where I can see them. All the way out." He cracked the door and stepped back. "Nice and easy."

"You're ruining it." Santino eased out of the car like a man with twenty additional years, then sniffed. He'd been crying.

Kenna holstered her weapon. "We're saving your life."

"We are?"

She was glad Jax asked that question because she could say, "Santino, we know why you're here. But you need a plan before going in."

Chapter Thirty-Four

Kenna blew out a breath, her body up against Santino's in the trunk of the car. Only because they didn't have a couple of blankets to hide under on the back seat.

The car slowed, pulling up to the gate. She lay silent on the carpet, careful not to roll into the Italian. The screen of her phone illuminated the space between them, with a call to Jax connected and the volume turned down on his end—just in case.

She could hear enough to know when to get out.

"You knew where I was." His low voice rumbled to her, not far from her face.

"How is she?" Maybe that was the wrong question to ask, considering. "Did you get to see her?"

The car started forward. She pushed back the elation at their gaining access to the mansion grounds. The whole neighborhood consisted of huge houses, and the one Nelson had traveled to after the convenience store was no exception. Owned by Rushman's corporation. The same company that owned the Bergamot Hotel.

Santino said, "There's an orderly who hates Rushman as

much as I do. They've all heard what he put her through, even though the sessions with the therapist are supposed to be confidential. She talks sometimes when she doesn't mean to."

Kenna's stomach clenched. "I'm sorry."

"He's the one that will be sorry. I'm going to make sure of it."

The car rolled to a stop.

"The orderly admits me after hours and keeps it off book. Rushman can never find out. If he cares enough to check on her, which he says he does."

Kenna heard the driver's door open through the phone line.

This model of car had a release button to pop the trunk from the inside, but she'd wait. At least until Jax had entry into the house—so they didn't get stuck outside with no way in while Director Billings hid from the consequences of his association with Rushman.

She managed to ask, "Have you tried to kill him before?"

Santino replied, "He may suspect, but doesn't know for sure, it was me that attempted to kill him with that poison. He stopped before he ingested enough to do more than put him in the hospital. They pumped his stomach. Twelve years ago."

She stared at him through the dark.

"I haven't always made the right choice. That's part of being human, I guess." Santino let out a breath. "God knows that about me. I've made my peace with it. Like I made my peace about how much time I have left."

Kenna heard a note in his tone. "How much time?"

"God knows I can't leave this earth without repaying this debt."

"And I'm supposed to let you?"

The doorbell rang across the open phone line.

"Showtime," Santino whispered. "I've made my peace, Kenna."

She pressed her lips together. It was up to Jax to talk his way through the door. They had no idea if there were staff guards, or how many might be present. Whether Billings was still alone, or if Nelson had stuck around after he showed up.

Billings could be dead for all they knew.

"Special Agent Jaxton?" The FBI director's voice echoed through the phone line.

"Sir," Jax said. "Thank you so much for seeing me. As you can see from my injuries, it's been a long day. Can I come in?"

"I suppose it's time for an explanation."

Jax nodded. "I appreciate it."

That was the signal.

Kenna hit the button under her index finger, and the trunk lid started to rise.

She rolled, sitting up simultaneously to lever herself out of the trunk. One arm gave way, but she climbed out—before Santino managed to drag her back and hop free first. She nearly slammed the trunk shut over him before he could. Probably he'd hit his head on the inside and get knocked out.

Another option was to shut him out of the front door, and not even let him in the house.

Instead, she held him back with one hand so he didn't rush in too fast. Kenna drew her weapon and strode to the door. Jax had left it ajar. She pushed in behind him, seeing the surprise on Billings' face right away.

He backed up, down the hallway.

Santino slammed the door behind her.

Billings' face paled. "*You.*"

Jax said, "Is there anyone else in the house, Director Billings?"

His boss stumbled back a couple more steps. "You're all here to kill me."

"Answer the question." Kenna could control Santino, but allowing him to be here got Billings talking more than just her and Jax. "Is anyone else here?"

Billings gaped at them. "You can't be here! There's audio and video surveillance."

"So shut it off." By now Rushman knew full well what was happening. So maybe he would be listening in, but only to protect his own assets. Not because he cared about Billings. Kenna didn't think he cared about anything but getting what he wanted.

Jax let out a breath, a quick exhale reaction. "Don't look in the living room," he said.

Which made Kenna want to do the exact opposite. "Jax."

"It's framed above the fireplace." He pointed. "A photo. It's Maizie, and that alone gives me enough to arrest Director Billings on suspicion of child solicitation." He turned to Billings. "You knew we were coming, and you didn't destroy the evidence?"

Kenna nearly threw up. Everything else in the house that implicated anyone had likely been destroyed. Only the holding company tied it to Rushman, and she figured he had a way out of that. She still wanted the FBI to get a warrant and see what they could find.

Once they were done cataloging everything in the house, she was going to get some C4 and blow it to pieces.

Then she would hire the best hacker in the world and get every single image and piece of footage of Maizie from the internet and have it destroyed.

Yet, even that wouldn't stop the industry.

She'd have to rely on people who fought that tide of evil every day. Those who took a stand against exploitation.

Santino shoved Kenna and Jax apart with a roar and went for Billings' throat, pushing the man over the side of an armchair. "You took her from me! You take all of them, and you destroy them!" He slammed his fist into Billings' face over and over.

Jax looked at her. "We need to stop him."

"Sure." Kenna didn't move. "In a sec, maybe." Right now, while it might be seen as vindictive, she just didn't have it in her to keep justice from finding Kenneth Billings' face.

Jax gave it a few more seconds, then went over and pulled Santino off. "Enough. We need to ask him questions, and he needs to be able to answer them. Before he goes to jail for the rest of his life."

Santino swung around, red-faced with bloody knuckles. "I'm going to search the rest of the house to make sure he doesn't have another victim here."

Billings swallowed. "There isn't..."

Santino was already down the hall.

"Rushman won't allow me to get arrested." Billings spoke around bloody teeth. "I'll be dead before the trial. He won't allow anyone to take him down."

"We're going to." Kenna folded her arms, still holding her gun. "So Rushman can consider himself on notice." If he was listening. "We are going to take his personal and professional lives apart piece by piece. No matter what he has in place to stop us"—she shook her head—"it's not going to work."

Jax carried on where she left off. "So if you want to avoid being swept up in Michael Rushman's arrest and the fall of his empire, you're going to start talking. Because if you don't tell us *right now* what's going on, then we don't know how entrenched you are in this. For all we know *you* could be the mastermind."

Rushman probably got a kick out of being referred to as

that. If Jax kept going, he'd be the kind of man Maizie's captor wanted to best just on the principle of it.

Which took the focus off her.

Personally, she wanted this to be over before the agents from Salt Lake showed up.

Billings righted himself on the chair, turning so he could lower his feet to the floor. His breaths came fast, a reaction to being smacked around by Santino.

"You're a participant in the destruction of lives."

He turned to glare at Kenna. "Well, when you put it like that it sounds bad!"

She strode to the wet bar in the corner, lifted a whiskey bottle by the neck, and threw it above the fireplace mantle without looking at the huge three-by-two printed image. "You destroy lives!" She screamed the words. "It's *over*."

"Sir," Jax said, "if there's a time to tell us the truth, it's now."

She halfway wanted to go after Santino but didn't want a quality secondhand account of everything. She needed it right from Billings' mouth. "What does he have on you?"

She faced off with him from across the coffee table, sick to her stomach about what happened in this house that made Maizie react the way she had just looking at the front of it. Kenna decided then that the teen wasn't getting anywhere near anything dangerous.

Not ever.

She was going to live the rest of her life safe. Peaceful. The recipient of only compassion and kindness from other people. If anything else happened, Kenna would put it right. She'd have a hard conversation with anyone who even looked at Maizie funny.

"It can't get out."

"That you're in a video of a restaurant conversation with

Rushman and Santino?" Kenna shrugged. "Are you guys talking about planning an assassination or something?" Maybe they wanted the current guy dead, and Masonridge back in. Or it had been before Masonridge was even elected. She hadn't watched it yet. "Or does he have far more...sensitive information that will expose you?"

They waited while Billings stared at the coffee table, his eyes wide. The guy was going to pop a blood vessel if he wasn't careful. And then where would they be?

Finally, he grimaced. "I was in the military for years. Then a senator. I did things I wasn't proud of, set down on a path I didn't think would lead me too far off course at the time. But each one he had evidence. Documents. Things I threw in the trash or shredded. Documents deleted from servers he should never have been able to access. He knew everything."

"And the special assignment team?" Jax asked. "All those agents except for me also work for Rushman, except maybe Dean. So why invite me?"

"It needs to be *over*. He needs to be taken down, but he made me pad the assignment team with his guys." Billings' eyes filled with tears. "I can't do this anymore. You have to help me. I can't...be here." He waved behind Kenna.

"The truth offends your sensibilities?" Kenna folded her arms. "Because it *should*."

"He has to rub it in my face. What he...does." He motioned to the photo behind her again. "So I don't forget he can do whatever he wants and there's no way to stop him."

Rushman wanted the thrill of power. She was surprised he hadn't run for president yet, but maybe that was his new plan—once he had killed or recaptured Maizie, and killed everyone involved in this.

The way he had with the church bombing in Bishopsville.

"We need to get out of here." Kenna strode to the hall, then the front door. She grabbed the handle. It didn't budge. "Jax!"

When he appeared, she said, "See if you can get the door open," and let him by.

He said, "Locked."

"I'll find Santino." She whirled around. "Don't let Billings out of your sight."

"Copy that. Try and get a callout. We might need the local fire department to get us out."

Kenna pulled out her phone. No signal. She tried to call 911 anyway but heard only angry tones. "Santino!"

She cleared rooms, gun first. No staff. No bodyguards. Not even a housekeeper.

She opened every door on the ground floor but found nothing indicating a basement. A place like this probably had hidden rooms. The hotel she'd been to in Albuquerque had two whole floors that had been reconfigured as a giant maze where a serial murderer had stalked and tortured his victims—until she'd killed him in the place he tormented others.

A gunshot echoed through the house.

She raced up the wide staircase to the upper floor.

Special Agent Nelson emerged from a room, blood on his face. A gun in one hand.

"Drop it!"

He raised it at her instead, pulling the trigger just as she squeezed off a round.

The world narrowed to that one point of focus. Kenna's momentum took her across the hallway, the bullet hit somewhere behind her, but Nelson jerked and went down.

He fired two more times.

She slammed into an end table, and a huge vase toppled,

shattering on the fancy carpet. Then she crouched behind the scant coverage of the table, her gun still aimed at Nelson.

He slumped back to the floor.

"Kenna!" Jax called up from downstairs.

She yelled back, "Clear!" but still needed to see who he'd shot, so she forced her legs straight and kicked the gun away from Nelson's body. She crouched and pressed two fingers to feel for his pulse.

Nothing.

"He's gone?"

She didn't glance back at Jax. "Yes."

She went to the door where Nelson had emerged and pushed it open. Santino sat in a chair, a bullet in his forehead. Two women in housekeeping uniforms lay on the floor in the corner, piled on top of each other, close to the entrance to a bathroom. Plastic sheeting lay on the tile in there, along with bottles of chemicals.

"He was going to destroy physical evidence." She figured that meant the house wasn't about to blow up. But still, no one was supposed to leave.

Jax scratched his jaw. "We need to know who else disappeared locally over the past twenty—or forty—years. Get a feel for how many victims."

"One is too many."

He turned to her. "She'll heal. Even from this, she can come back."

"She got herself free of him." Kenna swallowed. "I just want to know what it cost her."

"Come on," Jax said. "I knocked Billings out cold, but we should get him and figure out how to get out of here."

She nodded. They headed downstairs. "I can smash out a window. They can't be bulletproof, or shatterproof or whatever, can they?"

"We'll find out."

"Hopefully before Rushman decides to blow this place to smithereens," Kenna said. "I've always liked that word. *Smithereens.*"

"Sounds like a pharmacy."

Kenna started to chuckle, then spotted that framed image, displayed prominently, above the fireplace. "I might blow up this place if he doesn't." She'd seen bad things in her life. But that photo of Maizie was one she would never ever forget.

"Sir?" Jax stopped by Billings and shook his shoulder. "Sir, can you hear me? Time to wake up, Director."

Kenna holstered her gun. She hauled that photo off the wall. It tipped and the corner smashed on the floor. "Oopsie." It was awkward, but she swung it around and hurtled it toward the wall. It shattered, and the wood splintered on an oak sideboard. "Darn, I still need to smash a window. I'll have to break something else."

"Kenna?"

She turned to Jax. "I think I need a chair to throw. But if it's too heavy, you'll have to do the honors." That was far more entertaining than simply checking if the back door was open—or a window latch.

The director moved.

"Jax, watch—"

Director Billings shoved him onto the coffee table and ran for the back of the house.

Kenna fired two shots but hit only the wall right by the hallway and air.

Chapter Thirty-Five

Kenna raced after Director Billings. Jax called out something behind her, but while her mind heard the sound, her brain couldn't process what he'd said. She was moving too fast, too determined to take down this man.

Santino was dead. Nelson as well.

Others—whether innocent or not so innocent, it didn't matter. Their lives had been taken inside a house where unspeakable horrors had happened.

The fact Nelson might've been the one who hit her over the head the other day didn't even factor. Dean had said it was him, but as far as she was concerned it could've been any of them.

Kenna skidded across the gleaming kitchen floor. The counters and appliances sparkled, not a single speck of anything to indicate the area was used to prepare food or eat.

He'd run out the back door. Now it stood wide open, a key card inserted in the handle. Her momentum slammed her into the open door, and it rocked back, absorbing the impact. When she passed through, it started angry beeping. Kenna's

Converse slammed the patio, and she caught herself before she rolled her ankle.

Billings was across the lawn, headed for the fence on the right.

She figured he'd grasp the top and launch himself over. She would have a hard time following if he did that. There just wasn't enough strength in her forearms, and they already ached from the tension and firing her gun not so long ago—plus throwing that photo frame.

She focused. Gripped her gun so she didn't lose it. Ran after him as fast as she could, trying to keep all the errant thoughts from her mind.

A dog barked.

Billings slowed at the fence. He hit something—a latch—and a gate swung open. He disappeared through it.

She bit back the urge to yell at him and pressed on. Skidded through the gate and into the neighbor's yard. A pool in the middle. House to the right, the back patio all lit up and music playing. Which she didn't hear until she ran into the yard—so they had to have some kind of sound system that pushed the noise in a single direction.

"Billings!"

He ran toward the pool and around the edge. A couple of people in the pool turned to look at him.

"Billings, stop!" Kenna pumped her arms and legs. Maybe they shouldn't have a showdown in this yard, in front of people, but in the next one. She kept her mouth shut and ran.

A woman screamed, "She's got a gun!"

Someone yelled.

Kenna just wanted to get past these people before—

Billings grabbed a young woman in a swimsuit over by the gazebo at the far end. He swung her around in front of him, a gun pointed at Kenna. "Don't come any closer!"

Kenna slowed her sprint to a run. She didn't lower her weapon.

"I'll kill her!"

Someone gasped. A kid started to cry. It was like three in the morning, but these people were going strong all night with a backyard party apparently. They couldn't have been tucked into bed safely? This was why Kenna tried to go to bed before midnight when she wasn't working. Nothing good happened in the middle of the night.

"No one is dying!" Kenna stalked toward him, about twenty-five feet of this expansive yard between them. Soft grass compressed like luxury carpet under her shoes. She had no badge and no authority to arrest this man.

And where was Jax?

She didn't glance back—she couldn't. She looked down the length of her gun at the FBI director. "Let that girl go. Now."

The young woman sniveled, then muttered something, as though she might be drunk.

Kenna pushed out all the peripheral input of people by the house to her right, where she was pretty sure more than one person had their phone out. And whoever was in the pool to her left—behind her—and took another couple of steps. "Let her go. Put the gun down. It's over."

He moved the gun to the girl's throat. "What if I don't?"

Because he wanted to die? "Don't kill her. Don't destroy more lives."

"That blood isn't on *my* hands."

"I know." Kenna took another step on the soft grass. "But no one else does. And what do you think Rushman will do if you die? You think he won't blame you for *all of it*?" He had to understand that staying alive meant he could own his story rather than leaving someone else to tell it.

"It's too late."

"Bill—"

He shoved the girl away. She stumbled and fell on her knees in the grass, crying and sputtering. Then he turned back to her, raising the gun to fire it at the girl.

Kenna squeezed off a shot that hit the FBI director square in the chest. Another one, and her gun clicked empty. His body jerked, and he fell back onto the grass.

Someone touched the back of her gun hand.

Kenna flinched, realizing she was breathing hard. Sound coalesced in her ears until she heard kids screaming and someone crying. *Jax.*

He was the one right next to her. Speaking low in her ear. "Give me the weapon, Kenna."

She blinked and sucked in a breath.

"Surrender your weapon."

She let go of the gun so Jax could take it from her.

Now it was evidence. Not in a crime, but a justified shooting, even if she was no longer a federal agent.

She turned to him.

"Cops will be here in a second," he said.

She nodded. Her gaze started to drift to the people over his shoulder.

"Nope." His fingers slid into her hair, his hand warm on the side of her neck. She felt the grime and sweat on her skin under his palm. "Look at me."

She lifted her gaze to his eyes.

"Stay right here."

She closed her eyes, reached up, and touched the back of his wrist by her shoulder. He leaned his chin on her forehead, and she took a few cleansing breaths. Let the moments slip by while she stood there, still and quiet. And just breathed.

"Ma'am?"

She opened her eyes. Jax's hand dropped, and she saw the police officer beside them.

"I'm FBI Special Agent Oliver Jaxton. This is Kenna Banbury. She's a private investigator."

The cop blinked.

"And you are?" Jax's voice rumbled.

Neither of them had moved.

"Officer Outray."

"Nice to meet you." Jax nodded. "The man on the ground is the FBI director, Kenneth Billings. I need to call the local FBI office and my Supervisory Special Agent, as well as my Special Agent in Charge."

Kenna squeezed her eyes shut again and took another long breath.

"Ma'am, I need you to come with me." The officer waved her over. "I'm going to have to ask you to accompany me to the station so we can get this figured out."

That was how Kenna found herself at the police department in a tiny suburb of Vegas. Unfortunately, a suburb where Rushman had a house he used for… *Don't think about that photo of Maizie.* She leaned back in the uncomfortable metal chair, facing a one-way window.

Darkness stared back at her.

The room echoed with silence.

How long she'd been sitting here, she had no idea at this point. Her eyes were now as gritty as the rest of her. She wanted to close them, but that would lead to her falling asleep in this chair.

The door swung open, and a suited male detective strode in.

"I don't think so, Allenson." A female voice.

The detective turned back.

A woman entered, wearing a white skirt and blazer paired

with a pale-blue silk shirt and a gold necklace. Her hair was short and curly, with tones of brown, gold, and light blond. "I'll be speaking with Ms. Banbury alone."

"Are you my lawyer?" Maybe Jax had called someone on Kenna's behalf since he hadn't been able to speak to her. At this point, she didn't even know why he'd taken so long to chase after her and Billings.

"I'm not your lawyer." The woman set a big leather briefcase on the chair across the table. "Would you like one?"

"Not at this time, no." Just so she'd know Kenna might ask for one at any moment.

"Of course, that's absolutely your right."

Kenna just looked at her. *I know.*

Did this woman work for Rushman? She couldn't help thinking it, even if a sense of feminine solidarity didn't like the idea of a woman taking his side. More blackmail that led to duress?

As far as Kenna was concerned, a small police department so close to Rushman's second home was suspect. Every single person who worked here.

"My name is Rebecca Rodriguez. I'm an Assistant District Attorney for Clark County."

Kenna frowned.

"And you're the woman who's going to help me *bury* Michael Rushman."

Kenna bounced one knee under the table, an exercise in control so she could let go of some of the adrenaline and the tension building. She counted a beat with each bounce, making the motion a sequence that amounted to a rhythm. "Why don't you tell me everything you know about him, and then I'll tell you what I know."

The ADA tugged a file folder from her briefcase. "What I know is that he needs to be stopped. Preferably before the District Attorney, my boss, gets back to work on Monday."

"And you think I can help you?"

"I saw the footage." Rodriguez laid a hand on top of the file, her manicured fingers splayed. "You saved people's lives in that backyard. You gave Director Billings the chance to surrender his weapon, and instead he moved to take lives. You had no choice but to take him out so an innocent didn't die."

"Are you trying to reassure me...or practicing for the press conference?"

Rodriguez studied her. "You have no idea how connected Michael Rushman is. If what we do in the next thirty-six hours doesn't work, you and I will either be dead...or his next victims."

Kenna wrinkled her nose. "So why take the risk?" There was a team of FBI agents she and Jax actually trusted on their way, but maybe Ms. Rodriguez didn't know that. "It's not like we have the evidence." All she had were a couple of videos that may not amount to much.

"This is why I'm taking the risk." Rodriguez flipped the file open and spread a stack of photos across the table.

Autopsy pictures.

All young women. Different races, ages, and hair colors.

Kenna thought back to Bishopsville. "Looks like a smorgasbord."

"A menu." Rodriguez nodded. "Delivered to order. Some go unnoticed, others show up. I've got addicts. Psychiatric patients. Deceased victims. Multiple killers. Multiple manners of death."

"Sounds like an impossible task." Pull on one thread, and it led somewhere different than the others. Maybe the cops, or the FBI, could put a few cases together and tie them to one person—but it would only ever be a customer. One of many.

Rushman had been at this for years.

Operating as the head of the snake, with his own proclivities. Providing the same to others. All making Kenna want to get another piece of furniture and start throwing.

"Unless we can prove Rushman is the one thing that ties them all together."

Did she know about Maizie?

Nothing—at least yet—made Kenna want to call a teenage girl and ask her to testify. They were going to finish this without a witness. That was a nightmare in the best of situations, rather than ones where the victim was grilled like a suspect on the stand and made to relive everything. She wasn't going to put that on Maizie.

She'd rather make sure Rushman was done. Permanently. But as with Billings, she would have to do it right.

Otherwise, the ordeal might be over, but this would be the case that cost her integrity.

"I know that Director Billings is a close associate of Michael Rushman." Rodriguez folded her arms. "The same way I know my boss is also an associate. He's got the District Attorney and the FBI director in his pocket."

"And a lot of other people," Kenna added.

"So you understand my dilemma." Rodriguez motioned to the photos. "And why I will *never* let this go."

"You're willing to burn your entire career on this?" That's what would likely happen to this ADA. It was possible she had nothing Rushman could leverage. Maybe she was squeaky-clean with no vulnerabilities.

"This will cost me everything I've built." Rodriguez paused. "But there's a miniscule chance I end up the DA after it."

"So it's a power play."

The other woman's lips thinned into a line. "I haven't

always done the right thing. I've made...choices t
am. But this is the right thing. And if I can do som...
make a career out of continuing to do that, then I'll be able
look myself in the eye, at least."

Kenna nodded. "So what do we do about evidence? Because as far as I've been able to tell, Rushman has a hundred layers of anonymity between him and everyone else involved in this—customers and victims."

Director Billings had pointed to Rushman out of the blue as their lead suspect. Which made her wonder whether the entire special assignment had been a ruse. All just to get her and Jax here so Rushman could...what? Bury them in a scandal or have them killed—Jax in the line of duty.

She didn't know why he hadn't ended her in some accident like Thomas. But maybe she'd done an adequate job of hiding.

Plus, Maizie had escaped.

And Rushman had to want to know *what* they knew.

The last thing she wanted was to get tangled up in a confrontation. ADA Rodriguez needed enough for a search warrant, which the FBI could execute. Whatever it took to get inside Rushman's house.

Rodriquez didn't respond.

Kenna said, "The FBI director might be dead, but only Jax and I know exactly how dirty he was. Even if we can't prove it."

"Your point?"

She shifted in the chair. "He testified before he died. Gave us enough to implicate Rushman in suspicion. Whatever you need to get a warrant."

"So you'll manufacture the probable cause to get us inside his house?" Rodriguez tapped a finger on her elbow. "But what if there's nothing in there? Maybe he destroyed everything. He wants to come out of this squeaky-clean."

"I think he wants his toy back." Kenna swallowed back the bile of calling Maizie that. "That's why he hasn't disappeared to a nonextradition country. Plus, he thinks he's untouchable."

"This is a power thing. We aren't going to trick him or trap him."

Kenna nodded. "He wants me to play the game." And in order to figure it out, she had to think like her dad. "Where's the flash drive that was in my pocket when I got here?"

"Special Agent Jaxton took possession, so it didn't get *lost.*"

The door opened, and Jax appeared. "You think it's worth watching now?" So he'd been in the viewing room the whole time.

Kenna shrugged one shoulder. "Worth a try."

The last thing she wanted to do was drag Maizie back into this and ask her to give them what they needed.

Between the file packet cold case and everything else, Kenna wondered if the teen already had.

Chapter Thirty-Six

Jax straightened. "Well."

Kenna had settled on the edge of a neighboring desk in the bull pen of this police department—after they'd cleared out most of the officers. She sipped from a paper cup. "Michael Rushman just laid out every piece of the murder of Russian diplomat Dmitri Alekhin. Precisely how it was done. Days *before* it happened."

She glanced at the clock but still couldn't believe it was after seven in the morning. The FBI team from Salt Lake City was an hour out. Their chartered airplane had already landed at the Vegas airport.

It wouldn't be long now.

The ADA sucked in a breath through her teeth. "Even if this matches how he died, it's still not proof he committed the murder."

"He didn't do it," Kenna said. "But he ordered it."

Rodriguez turned on her fancy pumps. "Who did?"

"Director Billings killed him. A guy name Deacon, who worked for Santino at the time, moved the body to where it was found." She was almost breathless, a function of how tired she was. But this was nearly over.

"Still circumstantial." Rodriguez shrugged. "Billings could have done it that way purely to implicate Rushman."

Jax reached up and squeezed the back of his neck. "We need a way into that house."

"I don't need probable cause." Kenna raised her hand. "I'm not a cop."

"But what will you do when you get in there?" He shot her a look. "A citizen's arrest?"

"As satisfying as that would be..."

Rodriguez set her hands on her hips. "We need something. Tax evasion. Accounts fraud. A housekeeper that will tell us he's got kiddie porn in a drawer." She was closer to the mark than she knew—and she'd find out soon enough.

Kenna winced.

The ADA continued, "Maybe there's an employee who knows he's been embezzling from his company. A disgruntled yard guy he smacked around. *Something.*"

Jax glanced at Kenna.

"No." Kenna shook her head.

Rodriguez turned to her. "What do you have?"

"A child who needs to remain where she is."

Rodriguez strode over. "A child with *evidence?*"

"She already sent that to me. That's how we know Rushman ordered the hit on Dmitri Alekhin." And if the Russians actually cared anymore about getting vengeance for that guy's death, she'd have called them first. Rushman would be their problem.

Kenna sighed. "Why can't there be secret CIA facilities where they hide prisoners with no name and we can just put him in one of those? But he probably owns them already."

"If he doesn't know where they are," Jax said, "he at least designed their security systems."

"I need to speak with this child."

Kenna turned to the ADA. "No disrespect, but you and I met like *five minutes* ago. So I don't know you. I don't trust anyone except Special Agent Jaxton."

"So you'll sit on the answer, because you don't trust people."

"They have to give me a reason to first." Kenna shrugged.

Jax said, "She might be able to give us a way in."

Kenna glared at him. "She's a child! She's safe, and it's going to stay that way now. Especially if I have something to say about it."

His expression softened. "You didn't know she'd react like that to the house Billings was holed up in. You couldn't have known." He shook his head. "She has to heal."

Kenna gritted her teeth. They both knew that she had lived something at least similar, so she already knew it was true. Healing was a strange creature. Some days it snuggled up next to you, and others it launched out of the dark to take a bite.

"It might not hurt to ask." He spoke softly, holding out his phone.

She kind of hated that tone of his. "It'll hurt *me*." But she took the phone. Stairs answered, so Kenna said, "How is she?"

"Good morning to you, too." He chuckled. "Our mutual friend is currently drinking coffee with one hand—pretty sure it's more cream and sugar than actual coffee—spraying the flowers with the other and giving Cabot a drink from the hose." He paused. "The sunrise was a good one. She liked it."

Kenna's eyes burned with tears. "Thank you."

"As if you have to say that." He chuckled, a rough sound

like rocks. "Don't get soft on me. She isn't. This is one tough cookie. You have no idea."

"As if I'd get soft." Kenna cleared her throat, pretty sure she knew exactly how tough Maizie was. But the façade and the person she was underneath might mean she had good days and bad. Times when she conversed, and others when she slipped into near catatonia. This would be a long road to something even resembling a normal life. "I need to ask Maizie something. If she has a minute." *Tell me no.*

Stairs let out a sigh. "She told me that's not her real name. Or not what he called her, anyway. I don't think she knows who she is."

Kenna frowned. "I thought that Maizie is who she was?" The student intake form the girl had sent to the high school in Bishopsville had the name Maizie Smith on it. Kenna had never been sure it was a real name, or a made-up one.

Who was this girl?

Stairs replied, "She said it's who she wanted to be. The person she wanted you to meet." He paused. "Maizie Morrow is listed as an employee of Hammerton Dickerson. Maybe she was planning on whistleblowing, and she needed an official contract she planted and hid in their database, or she was getting paid and stocking up money on the side where no one knew. Kept it from everyone for years, planning to get out." He sounded proud. "Pretty sure she wants to be your crime-fighting sidekick, but she didn't actually say that."

"Yet." Kenna felt like she imagined parents do. Wanting to give kids what made them happy but terrified of the danger. "Tell her to rest first. She's had a lifetime of—" Her throat closed. "She needs time."

"She'll get there." Stairs sounded like he was moving. "I'll ask her."

Kenna heard muffled talking.

Then Maizie said, "You need my help?"

Kenna squeezed her eyes shut, aware of the ADA and Jax's attention. Then the door opened, and a stream of familiar agents strode in. "Yeah." She got up and walked to a corner, by the empty captain's office. "I don't want to, but it looks like we do need your help."

Being honest was the only way to build this relationship. Maizie had been lied to and manipulated her entire life. The fact she was a genius might've saved her. She should be mentally and physically broken, used up by a sick man's sadistic enjoyment. Instead, she'd fought her way free. She was like a phoenix rising from ashes.

"You're pretty amazing, you know that?"

Maizie said nothing.

"There aren't many people who could go through what you have and survive it with enough sanity to keep going."

"You did."

A tear rolled from Kenna's eye. She swiped it away.

"What do you need? Is it going to...destroy him?" Maizie's voice quavered.

"I'll make sure of it." Kenna sniffed. "I need a way onto his property."

Maizie moaned. A tiny sound, but it echoed louder than a single bird crying out in the desert. "I can give you the gate code. But he probably changed it. Maybe I should hack his network. But I can't figure out how to do it without him turning the hack back on me and finding *me*."

"Don't do that," Kenna said, not meaning to sound so harsh. "Sorry. But I don't want you in danger. I need a legal reason the FBI can search his house."

"They'll never find evidence. He hides it too well."

"Then tell me all his hiding places and what's there,"

Kenna said. "Or this will never be over." She heard Cabot bark in the background.

Maizie said, "I'm okay." Then louder, "What if I know where a body is buried?"

Kenna turned to the room. "I need to put you on speaker. There are agents and a prosecutor here who need to hear this."

The ADA's eyes gleamed with hatred for Rushman—or so Kenna hoped.

Jax nodded. "Go ahead." He had his phone raised and the voice recorder app open.

Kenna tapped the screen. "Can you tell me what you know about a body buried on Michael Rushman's land?"

Rodriguez came close, an almost greedy look on her face. She held a pen and notebook.

"I don't know her name," Maizie said. "She was my nanny." Her voice broke. "He strangled her. His men dug the hole, and he threw me in there with her."

Rodriguez let out a noise and paled.

A couple of the SLC agents glanced at each other. Kenna didn't want to acknowledge that agents she'd worked with alongside Bradley—before he died—were here. She trusted them, and that was enough. This wasn't about that.

It was about taking down Rushman.

"What happened?" Kenna nearly called Maizie by her name but caught herself.

"I couldn't breathe. I thought I was going to die. Until they dragged me out and put me back in the cage."

Kenna squeezed her eyes shut. "Honey..." She didn't care how many people were listening.

"I don't know how long it lasted. But the next time I got to go outside, there was grass over it. It looked like nothing had happened."

"Where on the property was this?" she asked.

"Under the plum tree," Maizie replied.

"Was this woman ever mentioned? Did he ever say anything about her?"

"He said if I displeased him, he would put me back under the earth with her. And the worms. And—"

"We're done." Stairns' voice rang from the phone.

"Yep." Kenna took the call off speaker. "Tell her I said thanks." It was a ridiculous sentiment for what had just happened, but she had to say something.

"I got it," he said. "You get him."

"Count on it." Kenna hung up, wanting to rage. To flip tables—in the figurative sense if her arms weren't strong enough to do it physically. Screaming was also a solid plan.

Anything that could release the pain and anger in her.

If she confronted Rushman like this, and lost it, he would have the advantage of a cool head. Then she would lose twice. And after that, Maizie would lose her shot at freedom.

Everything that amazing teen, a survivor, had done would be for nothing.

Because Kenna reacted emotionally.

Supervisory Special Agent Miller stared at her from the middle of the group. "Was that Stairns?" Of course he'd recognized the voice of his former boss.

"I need a minute." Kenna stowed her phone. Then she passed Jax close enough to touch the outside of his arm with hers—a tiny gesture of solidarity that wasn't about giving but what she needed to receive.

A small bit of connection before she did what she was about to do.

Kenna swiped the keys from the desk behind him and headed for the back hallway. They would all assume she would be using the restroom...the one she'd just walked past.

At the end of the hall she turned, found a fire exit down the next hall, and practically sprinted to it.

In front of the building, she clicked the key fob until headlights lit up on the rental across the lot. She'd been brought here in a detective's car, but Jax had driven hers. There were enough supplies in her duffel to get her through this.

She slipped behind the wheel and texted Stairns.

> I need his address.

Kenna could barely see the road. She made it around a corner onto a side street and parked crookedly part way up on the curb.

She gripped the wheel and screamed out all the pain and frustration she felt over what this child had suffered.

And no one had ever bothered to save her.

Kenna sat back in the seat and swiped her face with the hem of the thrift store T-shirt.

Her phone rang.

She figured it was Jax wondering where she'd gone, but the screen said, *Stairns*, so she slid her finger across to answer it. "Yeah?"

"It's me." Maizie sounded like she was crying.

"Are you okay?"

"Are you?"

Kenna let out a breath that would've been a laugh at any other time. "Touché?"

"I don't know what that means." Before Kenna could explain, Maizie said, "I have something for you."

"What do you mean?" Kenna asked, looking in the rearview to check there was no one around. She half expected cop cars to pull in—or Jax and the other agents. But they were working on the search warrant, and then they would be raiding Rushman's house.

Maizie replied, "I can take down his whole company, dissolve the whole thing, but it has to happen from inside the house. From the computer at the desk in his office." She choked over a couple of the words but continued, "In the file packet there was a worm. If you copy what you downloaded onto a flash drive, you can upload it onto his computer even if he's logged off, and bypass his password."

"From the computer in his office." Kenna winced.

"Yes."

"I downloaded the file packet to my phone." The printout. "*That's* why the copy place machine only spit out pages of gibberish code."

"Do you have it on your laptop?"

"Yeah, but I gave the only flash drive I had to the ADA." And it had evidence on it. Plus, it was super old, so the video file was the only thing that fit on it and now the thing would be out of storage.

"You'll have to find a store and buy a flash drive," Maizie explained, "One of those tiny ones that's like a stick of gum."

Kenna twisted around and tugged her laptop from the duffel in the footwell behind the passenger seat. "Okay. Just copy the whole file to the flash drive, find Rushman's office computer, and stick it in the USB port?"

"Mm-hmm. The program will do the rest."

"Would it have destroyed my life if I'd put the file packet on a flash drive and plugged it into my laptop?"

Maizie practically squealed. "You didn't, did you?"

"No."

The teen let out a sigh. "Thank goodness."

"Thank you." Kenna wanted to say more, but that would

only delay what needed to be done. "I'll be there when this is over."

"Stairns said you'd better be. I think I agree with him."

"Yeah, yeah. I just wanna see my dog."

Maizie made a rough sound, a lot like a laugh. Had she ever really laughed? Kenna wasn't sure she needed another one, but that would be worth it.

The pure joy of a free person, with no fear. She wanted to hear that sound from Maizie, even if it took their whole lives.

They would both be free.

Chapter Thirty-Seven

Kenna pulled the car to the side of the road behind a swarm of SUVs, police cars, and unmarked vehicles with flashing lights. Whoever Rebecca Rodriguez trusted to participate in exercising this search warrant, Kenna hoped that trust was warranted.

She climbed out, wearing her clean black suit and white shirt. Looking the part of an agent would get her farther in the house than the jeans, T-shirt, and Converse. She'd needed to wait until after the warrant was served so she could walk in, but that meant going to the motel. She'd grabbed all her things and changed into official-looking clothes, then checked out.

Now the tiny flash drive—with a USB-C port on one end and the bare middle of a flash drive end on the other—was tucked in her pocket. Kenna hadn't even known they made them that small.

She was ready to do this.

Maizie had said doing this would take down Rushman's company. She believed the girl had the juice to do it, with her knowledge and the fact she'd been behind Hammerton Dickerson's technological advances for years.

If Maizie wanted this payback, Kenna would give it to her.

Kenna wove between the crowd of agents and ducked under the tape. She gave her real name to the officer.

"Special Agent Jaxton said you might show up." The guy reached for his radio.

"I'll find him." She headed for the circular driveway.

The house was lit up, inside and out. A multimillion-dollar mansion that looked gorgeous with its Greco-Roman columns, but hid untold horror beneath. Like anyone who did what Rushman forced them to do.

She'd turned to one of those Bible-teaching radio channels on the way over. Her father had done the same thing to settle himself and focus on something else, and she wanted to do it more regularly again.

The pastor had been teaching from Matthew. Something about white-washed tombs.

That's what this house was.

Beautiful on the outside, but the interior was decay and death.

She spotted an agent from Salt Lake City exiting the open front doors. Kenna ducked right and rounded the outside of the house. Around back, on the expansive lawn, agents with ground-penetrating radar stood by that plum tree in full pink bloom.

It wasn't that she *wanted* them to find a body—but it would help nail shut Rushman's coffin.

Figuratively, of course.

Kenna passed an outdoor dining area and entered through the French doors into a kitchen that gleamed like the one in the other house. Just a pretense, rather than somewhere food would be prepared.

She needed to teach Maizie how to cook a hot dog over a fire.

They needed to do all those things kids should do but which she probably hadn't. Then again, the way Kenna was raised, she didn't exactly know what normal was like. They could figure it out, though. While she also figured out how to tell Maizie she was *not* going to be Kenna's sidekick.

A girl who'd been in danger that much?

She wasn't going up against anyone ever again. Maizie's life was going to be comfy pillows and unicorns for the rest of her life. Or whatever she wanted to choose for herself. Except danger.

Kenna lifted her chin to a cop and kept going. She turned into the hall, and someone grabbed her arm.

"Not so fast."

Jax. "I could've shot you."

He patted the vest over his chest. "How about you? Did you bring a weapon?"

She lifted her chin. "I don't have a gun on me currently. I wasn't sure I needed one with so many strapping law enforcement agents and officers all over every inch of this house."

"So why are you here?"

"Just making sure it's over." She didn't want to lie. "I need to see for myself."

"You can't be in here." He winced. "And you're not going downstairs."

"What's downstairs?"

"As far as we can tell, the basement was Maizie's...living quarters." He glanced aside at the wainscoting on the wall. Dark wood, in this dark house where dark things happened.

She wanted to see the basement, so she would know what the girl had been through, but also didn't have any desire at all to go down there. Not when it would likely just make her sick. "Any sign of Rushman?"

"We've arrested six men so far. And two women we think are housekeeping."

Kenna glanced around, then lowered her voice. "I need in his office."

Jax's jaw flexed.

"For Maizie."

"So you can take something from this crime scene?"

Kenna held up both hands. "I promise on my honor I'm not *taking* anything. Or planting evidence, so don't worry about that either."

"But you aren't going to tell me what this is?"

"You get that it might be better if you don't know, right?" She took a step back and turned to the hall Maizie had indicated. Following texted directions like,

> Left at that awful painting of the freaky guy.
> Right at the ugly Chinese vase.

She wanted to believe Maizie would be able to move on from her past, but it was equally as possible her history would eat away at any hope she had for a future.

Kenna had given her a decent shot, getting her out of Vegas and seeing a licensed counselor. Open space. Time to heal.

The rest of it might be up to Maizie—or it could be a matter of time before that bomb went off. Before they all realized she could never have a healthy relationship.

Since Kenna had believed the same about herself before she'd met and become friends with Jax, she would have to talk it through with Maizie. Everything that'd happened with Jax the past few days at least gave her the idea it might be possible.

Even if she never reached out and took hold of it.

If the timing wasn't right.

Or geographic distance kept them apart.

She had the hope of what *could* be. Even if it never was.

Kenna turned into the room and stopped. Books lined the walls, floor to ceiling. "He's probably never read any of these, and he just keeps them here so he can pretend he's someone who reads." She sighed. "I really hate this guy, but I'm trying to do this anyway. Quickly, so I don't lose it."

Before he could comment on that, she said, "Did the FBI get schematics for the house so you guys can search *every* inch of it?"

"There are areas of the basement we can access which aren't on the blueprints." Jax looked around. "You think Rushman is somewhere in the house?"

"Not for me to find. That's your job." She strode to the desk and flung the chair back. The computer tower had the lights on, like it was just asleep. She pulled the keyboard tray out, shook the mouse to wake it up, then crouched and inserted the flash drive from her pocket.

Then she sent Maizie a text that it was done.

She looked at Jax, who stood watching with his arms folded. "Don't you have FBI things to do?"

"And let you disappear again?" He huffed. "You shot Billings last time."

She wasn't going to remind him she hadn't brought a gun with her. Though, that didn't mean she was unarmed. She would never, ever, go into another situation unable to protect herself. She even took a shower with a ceramic knife on the soap dish.

Kenna said, "Why did it take you so long to catch up?"

"The door clicked shut. Once I took the card out, it was a couple of seconds before I could insert it again and get it to let me out." His brows rose. "Though, I'm not sure that stands up against you taking the car keys—"

"My rental."

"—and running off in the middle of a planning meeting."

Kenna's phone buzzed.

> That must not be the right computer.

She removed the flash drive, wondering where Rushman would keep his "main" computer if not here.

"What is it?" Jax asked.

Before she could answer his question, Rebecca Rodriguez strode in wearing heels. Along with a bulletproof vest. Which didn't match the skirt and blouse. "Ms. Banbury, so nice of you to join us."

Kenna paced over to a shelf. "We need to take this house apart."

"We are. And it doesn't—" Rodriguez made a strangled sound.

Kenna felt a shift in the air, and someone grabbed her, hard and tight.

Jax yelled, "Kenna!"

A door clicked shut, and everything went black. She was still awake, and those concrete arms were still around her.

She blinked but couldn't see anything. He dragged her back, hot breath on her ear, grunting as he kept going, then turned and let go. Shoving her away from him.

Kenna hit a wall, and stars exploded, but she settled into a fighting stance with her weight to the left so she could kick with her right if she had to. She slowed her breathing.

A yellow light clicked on, flickered a couple of times, and hummed to life.

The room was barely six by six. A panic room, or some

kind of closet. One wall had a bank of computer monitors. A security office? The screens showed the basement rooms, and FBI agents moving in and out.

But Kenna had no time to study the footage.

Michael Rushman walked toward her. One eye stared at her with pure evil. The other oozed something pale. His suit and shoes were perfectly unrumpled.

He pulled out a handkerchief and dabbed at the moisture trickling from his eye. It gooped on the fabric.

Behind him, someone slammed on the door.

His eyeball on that side swam with something cloudy. An infection?

"Did she do that to you?" Kenna asked. Maybe that was how Maizie got away.

No way was Kenna telling him her name now.

"Where is she?" Rushman's voice was low and lethal. He looked like a fancy cult leader—the head of a major corporation. Someone who had destroyed numerous lives and had so many others keeping his disgusting secrets.

Kenna lifted her chin. The backup pepper spray was farther than the blade under her shirt. "She's somewhere you'll never touch her again."

"Then she must be dead." His voice echoed in the small room. "And I will die as well, and we will continue our marriage in the afterlife. As it is written."

He walked far too close to her. But close enough she could reach under the back of her shirt without him noticing. Her arm hurt bent so she could reach the strap in the center of her back.

"Perhaps I will take you with me." He reached up and caressed her. "For when I'm in the mood for something different."

Kenna whipped her arm out.

He grabbed her wrist and looked at the tiny ceramic blade in her hand.

"Don't tempt me to make your life miserable for eternity," Kenna said, "because I would be the one enjoying myself."

He started to turn his head toward her.

Kenna grasped his shoulder with her other hand and brought up her knee. He cried out. Then he grabbed her waist while he still held her right arm up with that punishing grasp on her wrist.

She took the knife with her left and brought it down on the back of his neck.

His body jerked.

The door flew open just as Michael Rushman fell to the floor, her blade in his spinal column. White liquid eased from his eye.

Jax lowered his gun. "Are you okay?"

Kenna took a stumbling step to the right, planted a hand on the desk, and slid the flash drive into the port on the computer. Her arm gave out.

Jax caught her. "Come on."

She let him lead her to the door but grabbed the frame. "One sec." She turned back and lifted her phone. It buzzed.

> That's it. I'm dumping the company server to the internet, and piecing out his intellectual property for whoever wants it. He's done.

Kenna opened the camera and took a photo of Rushman, dead on the floor. She replied with the image and Maizie's two words.

> He's done.

Chapter Thirty-Eight

Two days later

The TV in the bedroom of the vacation rental Kenna had booked, after refusing to go to a hotel, flickered to life. Jax had moved his stuff to the other bedroom without even asking her, saying he didn't want to stay at the Bergamot.

Who knew who owned it now.

"In Colorado news, local county sheriff Elliot Preston gave a statement to reporters this morning detailing what he calls an assassination attempt after his nephew, Brian Preston —a local rancher—was murdered at his home just a week ago. Two other nephews were also shot. One died from inflicted wounds, and the other has been hospitalized in critical condition."

Sheriff Preston flashed up on the screen, surrounded by cell phones and mics. "Whoever targeted my family will regret what they have done."

The screen flicked back to the anchor. "Strong, and understandable, words from that sheriff." The brunette took a breath. "In local news, the death of Michael Rushman, long-time Las Vegas resident and leading national businessman, was killed during the FBI's execution of a search warrant at his main home. Some viewers may find the following scenes disturbing."

Kenna grabbed the remote off the bed and hit the power button.

She smoothed down the front of the dress. She'd told Maizie it looked ridiculous, but Elizabeth had insisted it looked *perfect*. As if it wouldn't be just fine if she turned up in jeans and boots, and a shirt that covered her scars. But it didn't matter what it looked like.

The sleeves of this dress tickled the scars on her forearms.

Rushman's board of directors at Hammerton Dickerson were currently arguing over who was responsible for dumping all his intellectual property on the internet. Even the sensitive stuff. The government had deleted a portion of the weapons research, and other things were still being argued over.

It would take months, and probably a congressional hearing, to figure it all out. In the meantime, the media had latched onto Rushman's secret life like a giant squid. Or a cobra trying to squeeze the life out of their prey.

Either way, no one even knew Maizie's name, so the girl who'd shown up at a tiny Colorado farm belonging to a retired couple—though the wife still took some therapy clients—had nothing to do with any of it.

"Ready?" Jax appeared in the bedroom door. "Oh...wow."

"I look ridiculous." She turned to her jeans, crumpled in a heap on the floor. Then she saw the display on the alarm clock. "We don't have time!"

"We are gonna be late." Jax nodded, straight-faced. "You'll have to wear that, even though it's awful."

"You look horrible too, by the way. Like you're late for a meeting with your Supervisory Special Agent, or the Special

Agent in Charge, or who cares which is which and who you report to now. Since your *lateral move*."

"I'm driving." He turned and disappeared down the hall.

Kenna grabbed her purse and her shoes. She walked barefoot to the rental on the drive and slid into the passenger seat.

"Miller said they landed back in Salt Lake."

She nodded and checked her phone, ready to get on a plane herself. She didn't want to talk about Miller. That would lead to the last thing her former colleague had said to her before he left.

Special Agent Jaxton is going to lose his career over his friendship with you.

As if she didn't know that could happen? And it wasn't like she controlled his actions. *He's a big boy. It's not like I bewitched him.*

Miller had tipped his head to the side, genuinely confused. *You don't think you do that?*

Kenna had no idea what to think about it.

Jax continued talking. "Of course they just wrote up reports and then left me to debrief everyone." He glanced over. "Even the Nevada governor showed up. Though Masonridge has been suspiciously absent, and I didn't see Governor Pacer anywhere. The state attorney general has some uncomfortable questions to answer."

"What about Rebecca Rodriguez?"

"The DA was taken into custody by Nevada State Police." He pulled into the chapel parking lot. "Everyone is coming in looking for a piece of this. But I'm guessing ADA Rodriguez will run for his job soon."

"Good." It was over for Maizie, and Rushman's other victims.

"The phone line the FBI set up at Quantico has been buzzing with people calling in to talk about how Rushman blackmailed or victimized them. I'm pretty sure they'll divide up his assets and make reparations. It won't nearly cover it, but it's not nothing." He parked the car and turned to her. "Everyone wants to know who the person was that lived in the basement. Since there was a body in the yard, they think that was Rushman's victim."

"Good."

"Are you—"

"Let's go, or we'll be late." She shoved her door open, unwilling to answer yet again the question of whether she was "okay." It wasn't a yes or no answer. Who knew how long it would take her to find some equilibrium?

Settle back into a routine.

Get a home again.

Find a new case.

After she finished the last one by walking into this Vegas wedding chapel, which she did with Jax beside her.

"I think I'm gonna ask for a transfer."

She stopped dead while he held the door open. "To where?"

Jax shrugged a shoulder. "Somewhere new. Maybe somewhere warm. That sounds good."

She made a face and he laughed. "I wanna go somewhere windy where it's chilly in the morning." She stepped inside and saw the young Hispanic couple waiting. The man wore a pair of clean jeans and a blue shirt with pearl buttons, a Stetson on his head. His arm was around a slender woman with a tiny baby bump and a wide smile. Her red dress was simple but gorgeous and she had flip-flops on, which made Kenna immediately jealous.

She smiled. "Luca."

He came over and hugged her. "Thank you for coming, Kenna." He turned to the woman. "This is Camilla."

The girl gave her a gentle hug.

Jax and Kenna stood up as witnesses as the young couple married, exchanging glances but refusing to comment on the officiant's handlebar mustache. At least he wasn't in costume.

As they kissed to seal their commitment, Kenna slipped out.

She found the office door unlocked and slid open the file cabinet first drawer. Nope. She tried the second, leafing through last names until she found what she was looking for.

She slid out a credit card receipt stapled to a piece of paper, a booking for two years ago. Paid for but never used. Her name. His. The date they were supposed to have been here. At the bottom, he'd signed it. The printout wasn't even his real signature, just a copy.

She stared at the swirls and strikes.

Bradley Pacer.

She folded the paper and tucked it into the only redeeming part of this dress—the fact it had pockets.

Jax stood in the doorway. "They want a picture with us."

"Right. Let's do that." She smoothed down the skirt and moved toward him.

After all the photo taking awkwardness, where Jax ended up far too close to her, and she actually had his arm around her waist at one point, Luca and Camilla said goodbye and got into their car. Jax and Kenna stood on the chapel's front steps and waved them off.

She glanced over, about to ask if he wanted lunch.

The look on his face halted her. His intense gaze that saw far too much, focused on her.

"What?" She had to swallow.

"I bought your father's trailer. It was for sale."

She sucked in a breath.

"You just need to come and get it. I used my friend's truck, so you'll need something to pull it with."

Kenna frowned. "Where is it?"

"On the side of my house in Salt Lake."

"I don't..." She didn't even know. "It's really his?"

What was she supposed to do with it? Maizie was the one who had found it for her and sent her the information. When someone snatched it out from under her, she hadn't known what to think.

If she even wanted to see it.

Then she'd half convinced herself to give it to Maizie if she ever got it.

Jax nodded. "It's really his."

"I think Stairs should come get it." Kenna stepped back. "I need to go see Maizie, and he's got a truck so he'll be able to haul it back to Colorado."

"I thought you might want to come visit."

"If you're getting a transfer, you don't know where you'll be." She took a step toward the car, desperate to get this moving rather than stand here at a stalemate. "Maybe you should settle, and *then* I'll come visit."

She pulled open the door and climbed in, not ever meeting his gaze.

"So, nowhere hot?" Jax said. "How about Maine?"

She bit back a laugh. "I think you'd love North Dakota, actually."

"The Chicago office would probably be good for some action."

"No doubt."

Jax pulled out of the space. "Let's get a pizza and we can look at options. See what I want to ask for."

"Then they'll send you wherever there's an open spot."

He reached over and squeezed her hand. "But you agreed to come visit, so it won't be all bad."

Kenna rolled her eyes. Now that they'd kissed, things would be different. Would they settle into a similar friendship of phone calls and texts, with hints of something more? Or would it be completely new. She just hoped it didn't turn awkward. That was the last thing she wanted.

Maybe she should talk to Elizabeth when she went to see Maizie.

Just like the teen, Kenna was free of the pain and the past.

Now she just needed to figure out how to live.

Brand of Justice continues in *Skin and Bone*, the 5th book in the series, releasing July 2023! Find out more on the series webpage:
https://authorlisaphillips.com/brand-of-justice.

I hope you enjoyed *Over the Limit,* would you please consider leaving a review? It really helps others find their next read!

Also by Lisa Phillips

Find out more about Brand of Justice at my website:
https://authorlisaphillips.com/brand-of-justice

Book 1: Cold Dead Night (Aug 2022)
Book 2: Burn the Dawn (Nov 2022)
Book 3: Quick and Dead (Feb 2023)
Book 4: Over the Limit (June 2023)
Book 5: Skin and Bone (August 2023)

―――――

For Lovers of Romantic Suspense check out
-Benson First Responders-

―――――

Other series by Lisa:
Last Chance Downrange
Chevalier Protection Specialists
Last Chance County
Northwest Counter-Terrorism Taskforce
Double Down
WITSEC Town (Sanctuary)

Numerous other titles including several with *Love Inspired Suspense*, find the complete list here:

https://authorlisaphillips.com/full-book-list

About the Author

Find out more about Lisa Phillips, and other books she has written, by visiting her website:
https://authorlisaphillips.com

Lisa's Website

Follow Lisa on Facebook and Instagram, and subscribe to her newsletter to stay up to date and be the first to find out about raffles and giveaways!
https://authorlisaphillips.com/subscribe

Made in United States
Troutdale, OR
09/12/2025

34475881R00215